SILVER SERIES

SUPERB WRITING
TO FIRE THE IMAGINATION

Robin Jarvis writes: 'Whenever I am asked where I get my ideas for books and characters, I always wish I could come up with some weird and wonderful answer. "I dream them," for example, or, "I get inspired whenever there is a full moon." But, unfortunately, neither of these is true. Like many writers, I sometimes base my characters on real people (or parts of real people) and sometimes they are the complete product of my imagination. But they generally all start as a sketch or drawing and then take shape as a character is developed around them.

'I started making sketches of mice because they were the smallest things I could think of to draw. When I sent them to a publisher, I was asked if there was a story to go with the drawings. At the time there wasn't, but I sat down and thought of a project visually and drew a story board as though I were making a film. I had envisaged it as a picture book, but it became a 70,000 word manuscript and I've been writing ever since.

'I can't think of a better way to earn a living!'

D1428302

THE DEPTFORD HISTORIES

BOOK THREE
Thomas

ROBIN JARVIS

Hodder
Children's
Books

a division of Hodder Headline Limited

First published in Great Britain in 1995
by Macdonald & Company (Publishers) Ltd

This edition published in Great Britain in 2000
by Hodder Children's Books

A Catalogue record for this book is available from
the British Library

ISBN 0340 78867 4

Typeset by Avon Dataset Ltd, Bidford-on-Avon, Warks

The paper and board used in this paperback by
Hodder Children's Books are natural recyclable products
made from wood grown in sustainable forests.
The manufacturing processes conform to the environmental
regulations of the country of origin.

Printed and bound in Great Britain by
Clays Ltd, St Ives plc

Hodder Children's Books
A Division of Hodder Headline Limited
338 Euston Road
London NW1 3BH

CONTENTS

OLD WOUNDS

Gwen Triton put down the little square of cotton which she was attempting to embroider and passed a weary paw over her tired eyes. At her side a stubby candle flickered, painting the small snug space with rich, golden hues. Sighing, the mouse tidied away her reels of coloured thread and gazed wistfully around as she waited for her husband to return.

Situated within a hollow figurehead on board the Cutty Sark, the midshipmouse's quarters were certainly a great deal more homely than when she had first moved into them. A curtain of lace had been draped across the entrance and with the few odds and ends she had rescued from the wreck of the Skirtings she had virtually transformed the place.

Flowers now garlanded her husband's model ship and his rough blankets were replaced by a quilt of patchwork; his lead anchor charm hung alongside Albert Brown's mousebrass and next to all the maps and charts of exotic places, Gwen had put up a few pictures that her children had drawn when they were very young.

She thought of them now with a mixture of sorrow and pride – how grown up they both were!

Her daughter, Audrey, had occupied the august office of the Starwife for some time and ruled the squirrel colony of Greenwich with as much tenacity as her predecessor ever did, and thinking of this, Gwen could not help but smile. She saw Audrey quite often, when official duties allowed, and it was comforting to be so close to her realm. Arthur, however, was another matter.

Gwen's son, Arthur Brown, had quickly grown impatient with life on board the Cutty Sark. From the start it was obvious that there was not enough room upon the sailing ship for all those who had fled the old empty house. The lack of space got on everyone's nerves and tempers had smouldered with the shortest of fuses. Generally it was the younger mice who resented the new life, for they had seen a tiny glimpse of the world outside and were aching to view more.

Finally it had all come to a head one day when Arthur got into a bloody fight with one of the old Landings boys. That was enough for the plump Master Brown; the very next day he bade his mother and stepfather farewell and left the Cutty Sark for good.

Arthur did not go alone however, for the large group of discontented youngsters decided to accompany him and elected him as their leader.

For the first three weeks after his sad depature, or 'the great abandonment' as it eventually came to be called, Gwen Triton had very little sleep and spent many troubled nights worrying about her son. Then, one evening a water vole crept aboard the ship with a message for her. Arthur was now the new Thane of the city. He had led the others through the sewers to the old mouse tunnels of Holeborn that his late friend Piccadilly once spoke of with so much affection.

Suddenly Gwen snapped out of her thoughts.

The lace curtain was roughly pushed aside and into the cosy, candlelit room strode her husband. The fragrant coolness of the midsummer night airs flowed after him and, with a shudder, Gwen recognised the foul humour that had overwhelmed him.

'Plague take it!' Thomas roared, stomping over to the shelf that housed his pipe and tobacco. 'A body can't get a minute's peace – not nowhere any more. Always some danged fool a-yammerin' or a-cluckin' somewhere.'

The midshipmouse slipped the end of the wooden pipe into his mouth but made no attempt to light it. Instead he began to pace about the room, his white, wiry eyebrows twitching and tangling together as a sombre frown settled over his face.

'Thomas,' his wife began in a gentle voice, 'come and sit down, please, dear.'

'Your Arthur was right!' he bellowed. 'This place is too crowded. Each way you turn there's some blasted fool getting in the way. There are times when I almost wish . . .'

He glowered at the mouse sitting forlornly upon the bunk but could not meet her sympathetic gaze for long. Spinning on his heel he lunged for a leather flask and poured its contents into a bowl.

Watching him, Gwen shook her head. 'You said you weren't going to touch that any more,' she reminded him gently.

Thomas raised the bowl to his lips but paused before drinking the rum it contained. 'What else am I to do?' he cried. 'It's my only release – the only way to dull the bite of that old wound.'

'It seems to have been gnawing you rather a lot of late,' she observed a trifle wearily. 'Thomas my love –

you're drinking far too much.'

The midshipmouse glared at her for a moment then in one rebellious tilt of his whiskery head, drained the bowl of its heady contents.

'Let me be,' he uttered huskily after wiping his mouth upon the back of his paw. 'There's nowt I can do.'

'It might help if you talked about it instead,' she answered, 'instead of drinking yourself into a stupor every night. After all this time together you still won't let me help you. Why do you continually keep that part of yourself closed to me?'

Thomas dragged the blue woollen hat from his head and hurled it to the floor in exasperation. 'ENOUGH!' he yelled. 'Belay that badgering – can't you see how it is? I can't tell you – I can't tell no one!'

Gwen rose from the bunk and put her arms around him. 'You must do something, my darling,' she comforted. 'You're destroying yourself and building a wall between us.'

The midshipmouse hugged her desperately, scrunching up his eyes and bitterly repenting of his harsh words. 'Oh Gwennie,' he murmured, 'forgive me. When this mood takes a hold there ain't nothing I can do. Why do you put up with this scurvy old rogue?'

'You know why,' she told him, 'but I was thinking, dear, if you can't tell me – why don't you write it down? I know we've spoken of it before but perhaps if you began your memoirs and put to paper all that torments you, the pain might ease. You never know, it could exorcise your demons for good.'

Thomas looked into her soft brown eyes and the anguish that burned his soul eased a little.

'Aye,' he mumbled, 'maybe you're right. There ain't no harm in tryin' – though I don't want no one to read it when I've done.'

Gwen gave his paw a gentle squeeze to reassure him. 'They shan't,' she said, moving across the small room and taking a sheaf of papers from the shelf. 'I promise.'

Thomas sat himself down and gingerly took up a quill which he dipped into a pot of black ink.

Quietly, Gwen tiptoed away so as not to disturb him and threw a shawl over her shoulders before stepping from the figurehead to visit the Chitters – leaving the midshipmouse alone with his troubled memories.

With the candlelight playing over his frowning face and flaring in his fine white hair, Thomas Triton began to scratch his firm, well-ordered script over the first page.

For the first time in many grim years he summoned to the fore those thoughts which he had so desperately attempted to forget.

It was long ago, when he was a young mouse eager to see the world, that it first began. How easily he remembered walking down that country path, the narrow stony road that wound down to the harbour where his adventures were sure to start and the humdrum life of the landlubber would be left behind forever.

Yet Thomas had made the mistake of setting out upon his journey just before one of the worst winters was about to seize hold of the country, and even as his light footsteps carried him ever nearer to the coast the first flakes of snow had started to fall.

A far-off look settled over Thomas' face when he recalled how he scampered for the nearest shelter and found it in a quaint and ramshackle farmhouse where a community of fieldmice took him in and made him welcome.

The quill trembled in the midshipmouse's fingers as the images and feelings which he had locked away and sealed in the rum-drowned bilges of his mind bubbled to the surface. Faces swarmed before his vacant eyes. Visions of those friendly mice all beckoning him into their winter quarters and offering him hot food from their tables.

And then, one grinning face appeared before him as he knew it would and the sturdy seafarer's heart quailed within his breast.

Try as he might he could not bring himself to look upon that small, trusting face for long and he threw his paws in front of his eyes in an effort to dispel it.

Wailing, Thomas pushed himself away from the small desk, knocking over the ink and flinging the papers to the floor as he reeled away from his own guilt.

'I can't do it!' he called. 'There's no going back fer me. I can't dwell on what I did – I can't never bring myself to relive it.'

Wretchedly, the midshipmouse lurched for the leather flask and great tears rolled down his hoary whiskers as he gulped the warming, numbing liquid down.

When the flask was empty, Thomas cast his eyes

about the room and stared at the pool of ink that oozed over the floor. Its glimmering surface was like a mirror of black glass and he peered down at his reflection in an agony of turmoil.

Then his liquor-stained lips parted and, in his distress, a name formed upon them.

'Woodget,' he whispered softly, 'forgive me.'

1

A Bowl of Berrybrew

Before the sun had edged over the blossom-laden trees which massed on the horizon like a dense bank of snowy clouds, the preparations for this special day were already complete.

It was the morning of the Great Spring Celebration and the fieldmice who had taken refuge within the farmhouse over the harsh winter months were at last ready to move out.

In those half-remembered days, Betony Bank Farm was small, having only one large barley field and a meadow in which four fat dairy cows grazed contentedly. Across the yard were two outbuildings: the stable where a shire horse resided, snug in his straw-filled stall, and next to that a shabby-looking barn.

As the first weak rays of the climbing sun flickered

over the distant trees, a group of yawning but excited figures emerged from the farmhouse.

Across the dusty yard the fieldmice scurried, each laden with carefully prepared decorations. The Hawthorn Girl and Oak Leaf Boy were carried proudly into the meadow and set down in the centre of a small clearing where two mousewives immediately began to sew the special favour ribbons upon them. The foraging parties were dispatched to find sprays of fragrant blossom whilst the others toiled within the nearby hedgerow to construct the Chambers of Winter and Summer.

When two hours had passed and the sun was higher in the sky, the clearing was filled with the heady sweetness of hawthorn and a delicious feast had been spread upon the ground. All was now ready and those youngsters who were to come of age were marched with great solemnity up to a leafy entrance fashioned in the dense and gloomy hedge.

Everyone loved this time of year and though their stomachs were growling, they waited patiently until the ceremony of the mousebrass giving was over before they tucked into the food.

Standing a little apart from the main group, a lovely young mouse maiden with curling tresses of chestnut-coloured hair closed her soft brown eyes and lifted her face to the warm sunshine.

Bess Sandibrook was a kindly creature, whose sweet nature had made her a favourite amongst those who dwelt on the farm. With a smile traced upon her comely features she idly fingered her own mousebrass which she had been given the previous year. It was the sign of the fieldmouse, as good and as worthy a symbol as any, and she followed the shape of the gleaming metal with her fingertips. Tilting her head to one side, she listened to the squeals of joy and gasps of mock horror that floated out from the hedgerow and smiled happily.

Few events in a mouse's life were as important as today's festivities and everyone threw themselves into the merrymaking. A ghostly moan issued out over the meadow and the assembly giggled, knowing that it was only someone in the Chamber of Winter trying to scare the youngster passing through.

Bess grinned and sat herself down upon a heap of soft, sun-warmed moss. She recognised that hollow voice – it belonged to her lifelong friend, Woodget Pipple – and she laughed softly, thinking of her small companion's delight at the prospect of taking part in the ceremony this year.

So eager had Woodget been to participate that he had spent several evenings making a ghost costume, chuckling incessantly at the fun he would have leaping out at those unsuspecting youngsters or appearing suddenly above them – emitting ghastly and woeful shrieks.

Bess was very fond of Woodget but she forgot about him for an instant when a second voice, deeper this time, came echoing from the hedge.

Undoubtedly that was Thomas and the mouse maid hugged her knees and nibbled a length of grass as she took time to consider this handsome outsider.

Thomas Stubbs had been with them for nearly five months now. He had first stumbled upon their little community on the night of that terrible blizzard. Were it not for Woodget's large and sensitive ears his pitiful cries would have been lost forever on the gale, but the little fieldmouse had bravely faced the storm and found Thomas in the yard, close to death.

With the aid of the others Master Pipple brought Thomas indoors and placed him near the fire. The stranger had been an alarming sight for he was covered in snow and the frost had made his whiskers so brittle that most of them had snapped off. With tender concern, the fieldmice saw to his needs and it was Bess who gave the freezing newcomer a bowl of hot soup to thaw him.

A few days of recuperation followed in which Bess and Woodget became Thomas' closest friends and now the trio were inseparable.

Bess liked Thomas enormously. Not being a fieldmouse, he was taller and stockier than the others and had already proven how brave he was. Once he had courageously ventured into the haunted barn in the dead of night and returned with a chilling and ghostly tale of what had happened there.

Suddenly a jaunty tune was struck upon a whisker fiddle and a reed pipe and the mouse maid stirred from her thoughts. The ceremony was over; all the youngsters had received their brasses and the proud families were eagerly pressing around them to see what symbols they had been given.

Then a giggling cry was heard as, from the entrance, stumbled two outlandish figures and a ripple of mirth spread through the fieldmice as they roared and pointed.

First came a small, black, flapping spectre, whose billowing body was a mass of carefully sewn cloth. The face of this apparition consisted of a large mouth painted into a toothy grimace and two round holes which served as eyes.

Unfortunately, the outfit was rather too long and the ghost came tripping into the clearing uttering little squeaks and grunts of annoyance when the ample skirt was stepped upon from within.

Behind this clown-like phantom appeared an even more startling creature. Out of the entrance lumbered a completely white and deathly-looking mouse whose dark eyes seemed sunken and empty by contrast.

In the crowd a tiny mousechild let out a doubtful whimper as the two horrors staggered and reeled around in a wobbly circle until the black-shrouded one lost its footing and flew headlong into his pale comrade. On to the grass the gruesome pair collapsed and writhed in a confused tangle as swathes of the thrashing material became utterly twisted and snarled around them both.

'Ooer!' chirped a high gurgling voice from behind the painted cloth face. 'I got me frock in a muddle! I can't get up – I'm all in a knot, where's me feet got to? Now the hood's shifted – the peepholes have moved round – I can't see nowt!'

Beside this wriggling spectre, Thomas Stubbs finally managed to extricate himself from the ensnaring costume but was powerless to help his friend – for every time he caught a glimpse of him squirming in that ridiculous outfit he burst into fresh laughter.

Most of the flour that Thomas had covered himself in before the festivities had started was now gone, either brushed off on the grass, rubbed on to the black cloth or washed away by the tears that streamed down his chuckling cheeks.

He was a fine young mouse, with a proud and defiant air about him that demanded respect, and in the brief time he had been at Betony Bank had made many friends. None however were as close to him as the one presently endeavouring to disengage himself from the ghost costume and with a hearty laugh, Thomas reached across and tore the hood away.

Blinking, and with a wide grin that split his little face in two, Woodget Pipple let out a grateful sigh.

'Thank 'ee, Tom,' he cried. 'I did think I were lost fer good in there.'

With his russet-gold head poking out of his ghost outfit and his paws lost inside the voluminous sleeves, Woodget was a comical sight.

Master Pipple, eldest son of Herbert and Marigold and brother to Burdock, Cudweed and little Throgfittle, was small even for a fieldmouse. His ears were larger than his head and his long whiskers were continually trembling, for his senses were extremely acute and it was said amongst the others that he could smell the weather changing and always knew at what hour the rain would come.

'We really put the frightners on them younguns, din't we, Tom?' he cried, staring up at his friend with wide, glittering eyes. 'Our Cudweed din't half yowl when I popped out from them leaves and did that horrid moanin'. Did you see how she went a-scamperin' out o' there into the other chamber? She'm plain daft!'

Thomas smiled and offered a paw to help him up.

'Well, I'd be careful if I were you,' he said. 'Here's your sister now and she don't look well pleased with us at all.'

'Green save us!' Woodget yelped as he turned to behold a plump mouse girl with straggly pigtails and a grim expression fixed upon her round face come barging through the crowd towards them. 'Let's scarper, Tom! She's got that same look as when I pushed her into the brook. Awful hard paws has our Cudweed.'

'You come back here, Woodget Pipple!' the girl's outraged voice shrieked when she saw her brother making a dash for it. 'I'll teach you to scare me. You too, Master Thomas – I'll learn you both.'

Out of the clearing ran Thomas, laughing all the way until he realised that Woodget was not following him and he knew that his friend had fallen victim to the treacherous costume once more.

Chortling, he made his way back and heard Cudweed's scolding voice berating her brother.

'You're a wicked pair,' said another by his side.

Thomas turned and there was Bess.

'Scaring them half to death! Don't you have nothin' better to do?'

'Was only Cudweed who didn't like it,' he protested. 'Mind you, Woodget did go a bit far with her. Chased her right out of the chamber, he did.'

'Well, he's paying for it now,' Bess observed. 'Listen to that girl; just imagine what she'll be like in a few years.'

'I pity the one she marries,' Thomas added. 'His ears won't never stop ringing.'

Bess flicked her hair over her shoulders and gazed

mischievously at him. 'I heard that she likes you,' she said. 'Set her sights, she has.'

'I'd feed myself to an owl before I'd let that happen,' he shuddered. 'That Cudweed really is summat to be scared of and no mistake.'

'Maybe, but once a mousemaid has made up her mind who she wants, it's as good as settled.'

Thomas gazed at her and saw in her eyes a strange light that he had not noticed before and wondered what it could mean. But he could not discover the answer, for at that moment Woodget ambled towards them, with his outfit now bundled under his arm and his left ear glowing a bright crimson.

'Oaks and ivy!' the fieldmouse exclaimed. 'That were lucky! Only cuffed me lughole that time. I reckon Cuddy's got soft now she's growed up.'

For the rest of that day the three friends laughed and chatted lightly with one another. When they had tucked into the food and stuffed themselves until their stomachs ached, they found a cool shady spot and watched the games and entertainments unfold in the clearing. Eventually the afternoon stretched by and a group of five musicians prepared for the long night of dancing that lay ahead.

'Come on Bess, lass!' Woodget squeaked, jumping to his feet as *The Green Revels* commenced. 'Let's you and me go show Tom how we country folk can frolic.'

Propped upon his elbows, Thomas watched them skip into the midst of the other gathering dancers, but a furrow creased his young brow as a strange and unexpected idea occurred to him. Although he loved both of those happy mice dearly, he almost resented them being together and enjoying themselves without him.

Surprised and mildly alarmed by these dreadful stirrings of jealousy, Thomas shook himself to dispel them and drew a paw over his eyes.

'You're tired, Tom lad,' he told himself, 'that's all. No wonder, you were up early and have eaten more in one sitting than most folk do the entire week.'

Yet he could not take his eyes off his two friends whirling in time to the sprightly music and, more often than not, his gaze was fixed upon Bess.

Two more tunes and dances passed before the others returned, hot and breathless but bearing a jug of berrybrew from the feast which was now spread with dainty biscuits and little cakes.

'Here y'are, Tom,' Woodget said, passing him a bowl, 'right good stuff this is. Old Vetch makes it hisself and only brings it out for the Spring ceremonies. In the autumn we all go a-brambling for him – daresay I picked some of this 'ere brew meself, two year back.'

Thomas took the bowl and sniffed the dark purple liquid his friend poured into it. 'Smells like over-ripe fruit,' he commented. 'Daresay it's good for wasps but I don't want any. We didn't have none o' this where I come from.'

'Why, Tommy Stubbs!' Bess chided, sipping at her own bowl and shivering slightly at the drink's potency. 'I do believe you're afraid. See, it's perfectly delicious. Go on – you must try it at least.'

Stung by her gentle teasing, Thomas lifted the bowl to his lips once more and took a great swig.

Woodget and Bess stared at him expectantly as the

mouse held the liquid in his mouth for several moments and swilled it around his tongue, wondering whether to spit it out or not.

' 'Tain't poison, Tom,' Woodget chuckled. 'Old Vetch makes the best brew hereabouts.'

Thomas gulped it down then opened his mouth and gasped loudly as the powerful drink tingled on his tongue and his eyes began to water.

'Poor Tommy!' Bess cried, throwing her arms about him. 'It's a strong brew to sup as your first. P'raps we should put some water in it for you next time.'

Spluttering, Thomas shook his head then clicked his tongue a few times before a stupid grin appeared on his face.

'It weren't that bad after all,' he announced. 'Tasted quite nice really. Is there any more?'

'Not for the moment, Tommy Stubbs,' Bess laughed, taking the bowl from him. 'I'll have this next dance if you don't mind – a couple more of them and you won't be able to stand up straight.'

With Woodget waving them into the clearing, the two mice took hold of each other's paws but the music changed before they could begin and when the musicians struck up the next tune it was a slow, romantic waltz.

With his berrybrew in his little pink paws, Woodget regarded them contentedly. They were the two friends he loved more than anything in the world and it was strange to reflect that before the winter he had never known Thomas.

'Don't know what I'll do when he decides the time's come for him to pack up and set off on that voyage he's always speaking of,' the fieldmouse mused into his bowl. 'Me an' Bess'll miss him real bad.'

Into the evening the music played and the two mice continued to take it in turns to dance with the comely maiden. The first jug of berrybrew was emptied and when the second was only half full and Masters Stubbs and Pipple were momentarily alone under the leaves of the hawthorn tree, Thomas began the conversation which was to alter their lives forever-more.

The scent of the blossom laced the darkling air as strongly as Old Vetch's intoxicating beverage and, staring up at the first pale stars which glimmered in the dusky heavens, Thomas said, 'I like that Bess girl.'

Twirling a spray of flowers under his twitching nose, Woodget nodded drunkenly. 'Bessh's a goodun,' he slurred. 'I knowed her all my life you know, Tom. Did . . . did you know that? All my lickle life I knowed her. She . . . she'sh a goodun, I tell 'ee.'

' 'At's true enough,' his friend agreed. 'I never did think to find a mousemaid like her, not ever. You know, Woodj – she just might be the sort a body might give up his dreams for.'

Woodget planted the spray in the ground and kissed it benignly. 'Now you grow into a luvverly big tree,' he said with all the seriousness he could muster. 'Can't have too much hawthorn – oh no, that we can't. Green'sh own tree it ish, ain't that right, Tom?'

Thomas rubbed his chin thoughtfully and the resolve mounted in his heart. 'I think I've decided, Woodj,' he said finally. 'It's the right thing for us both. I see that now.'

'That'sh nice,' the fieldmouse tittered, his blurred interest now taken with a beautiful silver moth which was fluttering close. 'I agree – oh mosht defin . . . deff . . . oh yesh!'

'Then that's what I'll do,' Thomas muttered. 'Forgo those idiotic dreams of seeing far-off lands. Why go all the way to find summat that ain't there? This is where my heart'll be the whole time – I know that now.'

'You shtayin' then, Tom?' Woodget sighed happily. 'That'sh wunnerful.'

His friend nodded and stared at the other mice gathered in the clearing. Small glass jars containing candle stumps were twinkling in the thickening gloom; paper lanterns were strung across the hedgerow and standing in the light of them, with her hair catching the glints and flickers of the flames, was the object of his devotion.

'I love her, Woodj,' Thomas muttered. 'She's the loveliest maid on the good Green's earth.'

The moth spiralled directly over Woodget's head but the fieldmouse was suddenly blind to it and gazed across at his friend with a look of disbelief and sorrow written upon his face.

'What . . . what was that, Tom?' he whispered, sobering quickly.

Thomas drained the rest of his bowl and took a deep, determined breath. 'Tonight,' he said firmly, 'I'll ask for her paw in marriage.'

Woodget's eyes opened wide and his large ears drooped mournfully. 'You . . . you sure, Tom?' he stammered. 'What if'n she says no?'

'Oh, she'll not do that,' came the awful reply. 'I

know what's in her heart same as I do what's in mine. That maid's right for me and me for her – we were meant. Why else was I brought to this place if not for that? I always reckoned it was fate what drove me out last winter; it weren't to set forth on no voyage, but to find her.'

Woodget said nothing, but his world had crashed in around him and his spirit grieved bitterly. He had never said anything but he too had thought that one day he and Bess might wed – it seemed the most natural thing in the world – yet now that dream was shattered.

Oblivious to his friend's despair, Thomas scrambled to his feet and straightened the red kerchief he wore about his neck. 'Right,' he said flatly, 'this is it, now or never – I'm going to ask her.'

In a moment he was gone and the small fieldmouse was left alone feeling wretched while dismal tears welled up in his eyes. How could he bear to remain here? How could he stay and watch them begin their life together? Woodget's despairing heart fluttered in his breast and he sniffed desolately. There was only one thing he could do and bleakly he stumbled away into the night.

'Hello, Master Thomas,' Cudweed cooed as the mouse strode determinedly by. 'I've forgiven you for frighting me this mornin'. Won't you dance with me? Thomas?'

Not hearing the plump girl's call he pushed on to where Bess was chatting to a group of her friends. Hearing the cries of Woodget's frightful sister they turned and saw him approaching.

'Ahem,' Thomas began, clearing his throat to ensure

14

his voice came out level and did not betray the nerves which were jiggling inside him.

'What is it, Tommy?' Bess asked. 'No more dancing for a while – I swear you and Woody are trying to wear my feet out between the pair of you.'

Thomas caught hold of her arm. 'It isn't about the dancing,' he said with urgency in his voice.

Bess stared at him puzzled for a moment then gripped his paw tightly. 'Nothing's happened to him, has it?' she cried. 'Where is he?'

'Woodget's fine,' Thomas hissed back. 'Look, can we walk a little? Just over there out of this crowd. I got me something to say.'

Bess raised her eyebrows questioningly but allowed him to lead her away from the main gathering and they strolled through the wild grasses, each wondering what the other was thinking.

'What is it, Tommy?' she asked eventually. 'You can tell me now, there bain't no one here to mark what you say.'

Thomas stared at the ground, and fumbled with his kerchief before answering – then it all tumbled out in a great rush of words.

'It's like this, see,' he spluttered, 'there ain't nowt for it but to tell you and mebbe it's Vetch's brew made my tongue loose or mebbe it's give me the pluck to ask you what's been on my mind but I didn't have the nous to recognise. One fact I do know is that what I feel is true and ain't no giddiness caused by that stuff so don't you go a-thinking it is.'

Bess stared at him, taken aback by his outburst and wondering what he could be talking about.

'Let me finish,' he declared, seeing that she was

about to interrupt. 'It's like this, Bess, and I can't say it no plainer, though I'll wager others might be able to say it prettier and p'raps choose better moments but I ain't them and so this is it.'

He paused to catch a breath before continuing and Bess was even more perplexed although a shadow of doubt was forming at the back of her mind.

'What I say is this then,' he jabbered. 'I likes you and I thinks you like me so what you say we get hitched, us two?'

Bess merely stared at him in bewilderment.

'I said, will you be my wife?' he cried, squeezing her paws desperately.

'Thomas,' she finally managed to utter, 'I had no idea – I never reckoned.'

'I'll be a good husband,' he promised. 'The sea won't never tempt me – that were just a boyish fancy. You're the strongest anchor a mouse could have – I never want to see another place if it means being away from you.'

Bess's expression changed from confusion to sorrow and she bit her lip anxiously. 'Oh Thomas,' she wept, 'I'm so sorry, I never meant to give you the wrong notion. I thought we were just having a good time, we three. I'm so very sorry, but I don't love you – I likes you but that's all there is. My heart belongs to another.'

The mouse pulled away from her and a horrible cold feeling washed over him. 'A ... another?' he mumbled, turning aside so that she could not see the pain upon his face.

'Did you not see?' she asked softly. 'Could you not guess? I love Woodget, we have always been together and always will. That is the way of it.'

'He . . . he never mentioned it,' Thomas said thickly.

'Well, he wouldn't, would he? I've been waitin' and a-waitin' but still no word – I know what he feels better'n him but he's shy when it comes to matters like that. If he don't speak soon I'll have to do the asking myself – don't know why I haven't already.'

There was an awkward silence broken only by a miserable sniff from Thomas' nose and he wiped it on the back of his paw.

'Don't take it so hard, Tommy,' Bess said. 'We can still be friends, can't we?'

The mouse shuffled uncomfortably and when he next looked up at her she could see how she had hurt him. 'Course,' he muttered, 'but I won't be stoppin' round here for much longer. I've done decided now – there's nowt to keep me, so come tomorrow I'll be settin' off on that voyage.'

'I'll miss you,' she said honestly, 'and so will Woodget.'

Thomas glanced back at the dancers, across to the hawthorn tree where he had left the little fieldmouse. 'He's mighty lucky to have you, Bess,' he managed to say. 'I . . . I think you'd best get back to him. I got to get my bits an' pieces ready if'n I'm to leave first light.'

Bess nodded and began walking back the way they had come, then turned and said softly, 'You don't have to leave, Tommy.'

'Yes, I do,' came his regretful reply.

The mousemaid gave a sad, understanding smile and left him standing alone in the tall grasses.

Thomas's head was swimming, partly from the

effects of the berrybrew but mainly because of Bess's rejection. How could he have been so wrong? Morosely, he stared up at the stars and wondered what his future held – what would become of him now? The sea journeys he had once yearned to embark upon now seemed uninteresting and contained no hope of joy.

'A right Tomfool you are,' he rebuked himself aloud. 'What did you have to go and open your big stupid mouth for?'

At that moment his wallowing thoughts were interrupted by a heartfelt cry which rang out over the glimmering meadow, and at once the music ceased.

'Bess!' he shouted.

In a trice, Thomas bounded back to the clearing. The assembled mice were already scurrying back over the yard to the farmhouse to discover the source of the commotion and he jostled past them impatiently.

'Thomas!' Bess cried. 'Thomas!'

As the mice hurried to the building, Bess came racing towards them clutching a scrap of paper in her paw and searching for the tall mouse amongst the crowd.

Then he was before her and to his dismay he saw the anguish in her face.

'What is it?' he demanded. 'What's happened?'

'He's gone!' Bess replied, thrusting the paper into his grasp. 'Look!'

With trembling fingers, Thomas uncrumpled the note and his brow grew stern when he read the unhappy message.

To Tom and Bess,
This is just so as you don't think I've done owt daft, tho I doesn't blame no one for thinking I would.

My dad allus said I couldn't see wat was under my nose and it looks as if he were right. I never reckoned you were keen on each other, now I feel as though I've been gettin in the way all this time. Must have been real narksome for you to have me tag along wheresoever you went and whatsoever you did. But as my dad also says, a body can't trip over a thing and not know it's there.

I know how things are twixt you now. Oaks and ivy – I sure does feel right gormless for not twigging sooner but there you are – I didn't and so I don't fancy staying in Betony Bank no more. That's as plain as I can make it. I ain't much good at my letters so I'll say goodbye here and have done.

Woodget

PS
Tell our Cudweed to look after our folks and tell them I wish them nowt but the bestest cos they were real good to me and I'll think of them allus.

Thomas raised his eyes from the paper and his face was set and grave.

'This is my fault,' he cursed himself. 'That poor lad's head is stuffed with the nonsense I was spouting.'

Around him the fieldmice shook their heads and Woodget's parents held on to each other for support.

'We must find him,' Bess said. 'He can't have gone far.'

'But he could be anywhere!' came the flustered

replies. 'There aren't enough of us to search – he's sure to be lost forever.'

'Well, he can't have gone through the meadow,' she told them, 'we'd have seen him. We must split into groups and try the other ways.'

'Hold!' shouted Thomas unexpectedly. 'I know where he's bound. There's only one place he'd go.'

Bess gazed at him fearfully as the truth dawned on her. 'The harbour!' she gasped. 'He's gone to catch a ship!'

'That's how I read it,' Thomas nodded. 'He thinks I've taken his place so he's gone and took mine – the moon-kissed ninny.'

'Then we must hurry!' she urged. 'He might be half-way there by now and if he should find a ship before we get to him—'

'Wait!' Thomas said. 'This is all my doing and mine alone. I'll go after him and bring him safe home. No need for anyone else, this is my task.'

Bess gazed at him imploringly. 'Bring him back to me, Tommy,' she whispered. 'Bring him safe home.'

The mouse took her paws in his and looked steadily into her tearful eyes. 'I swear, Bess,' he told her, 'I swear he'll be in your arms before long, as the Green is my witness. I'll atone for the mess I've made.'

And with that, Thomas ran from the yard, darted under the hedge and out on to the narrow stony path beyond where the wild darkness claimed him.

In the long despairing years that followed, he never once set eyes on Bess Sandibrook again, and in those after-times the generosity of the Betony Bankers was diminished and they never again trusted outsiders nor welcomed them into their homes.

2

Mulligan

A peaceful calm lay over the small harbour and with a contented, graceful motion the fishing boats rose and fell upon the gently lapping waves. Mooring ropes were softly creaking, sloshing abstractly in the sluggish seawater and trailing up to the quayside where they were lost amidst the creels and lobster pots which were stacked into mountainous and unsteady wicker steeples.

The buildings that rose, stark and threatening, beyond the old harbour road were silent and those who dwelt there at rest. No one marked the goings-on upon the quayside; no one was witness to the steady traffic of small creatures who frequented that place in the dark, moonless hours.

Shadowy shapes, intent on their own pressing business and paying no heed to any other, were flitting

21

over the wide, salt-scrubbed stones. It was an unusual and unsettling location to be for one unaccustomed to the bustle of harbour life and there were always some who endeavoured to exploit the gullible traveller as best they could.

As the night deepened and the gulls sleepily rode the waves, a small and solitary figure wended his sorry way down the path from the grassy hills and stood stock-still when the vast expanse of the great midnight sea ranged into view.

With a blue woollen hat that Bess had knitted for him last winter pulled down just above his ears and a cloth bag containing his personal treasures slung over his shoulder, Woodget gazed at the limitless waters and held his breath. Straining his bright eyes, he tried to see the edge of the briny realm, but it merged with the night and the only indication of its immeasurable size was when the shimmering reflection of the starlight was caught in the foaming waves far from shore.

Never had he imagined anything could be so immense and unbounded. The sky didn't count because you could never touch that, whereas the water was actually there – you could feel it; and as he breathed once more, the little fieldmouse's sensitive nose thrilled at the rich salty reek that spoke of waving weeds and cold fathomless depths.

'Oaks and ivy!' he murmured. 'I did think the barley field were big – but that was as an acorn is to a forest. 'Twould take a lifetime and more to cross that and no mistake. Ain't no ship ever built could sail from here to yonder.'

Amazed at this wonderful spectacle and doubting

if Thomas's stories about sea-going vessels were not just a fanciful make-believe, Woodget ambled down the path and made for the harbour.

Presently the steep road became a gentle slope which gradually levelled out. The gravel was replaced by smooth flat stones and the fieldmouse found himself upon the quayside.

Timidly, he looked about him and swallowed nervously. To his left and rearing high above him was the shape of a fishing boat. To Woodget the craft was huge and he stared warily up at the mast and the rigging that radiated from it like the web of a gigantic spider.

'I doesn't know if'n I likes this 'ere place,' his whimpering voice murmured. 'Just look at that there girt contraption – and see, there's more and bigger too!'

After some minutes of doubt and indecision, wondering if he ought to retrace his steps and go anywhere else but here, the fieldmouse finally concluded that to have a quick scout about would bring him to no harm.

Cautiously, he picked his way over the quay and soon forgot his fear of the ships, marvelling instead at their shapely beauty. It was as if the strong smell of the sea had affected him more potently than any batch of Old Vetch's berrybrew, for he found himself trying to imagine what it might be like to sail upon one of these lovely vessels.

As his tiny feet pattered over coiling ropes which smelled of pitch and tar, he suddenly became aware that he was not alone.

Scampering around the screening crates and barrel

towers, to his surprise Woodget discovered a number of stalls set out in the middle of the thoroughfare as if it were a kind of market.

The proprietors were mainly mice, but here and there he noticed other creatures fussing over the carefully laid-out trestles and vying for the attention of the passers-by.

As far as Woodget could see and from the information assailing his nostrils, they sold everything – from simple maps of the surrounding country to hot shrimps toasted over a candle flame. There were stands full of souvenirs for the outgoing traveller to remind him of home, and gifts for the returning wanderer to purchase as last-minute presents he may have forgotten to buy for the family whilst abroad. There were painted shells, dried starfish tied on strings, useful items like small bottles and leather flasks, all manner of hats and scarves to keep out the cold ocean breezes, packets of dried orange and lemon rind to keep away scurvy, and decoctions of herbs guaranteed to ward off the dreaded sea-sickness.

With his eyes growing rounder every moment he drew closer, Woodget drank in the lively scene.

Many of the stalls were covered with colourful canopies, and within each of these swung a lantern that shone through the fabric and illuminated the market with a cosy, cheery glow of countless warm and friendly hues.

Tentatively, the fieldmouse approached the first of the stalls and at once every vendor was aware of him.

'Hoy there!' cried a blousy shrew with a pronounced squint who beckoned him madly with her stunted arms. 'If you're setting off tonight, you can't afford to miss these, my lovely. I'll bet you're doing some worrying right now – am I right, sir? My, but he's a handsome fellow – such ears he has! Worrying about all that plaguey water out there and what happens – stars forbid! – if the boat is wrecked and in you tip.'

'Oh dear,' Woodget muttered, 'I hadn't thought 'bout that.'

'And neither you should, my brave little captain,' she tutted, smiling beneath her prodigious nose and fanning her paws over her wares for his inspection. 'Can you swim? I thought not. Well, fear no more! Just one of these around your neck will keep your head above water – three and you can sail home all on your ownsome.'

Woodget looked at the objects laid out on her stall and considered them dubiously. They seemed to consist of a loop of string on to which had been threaded a lump of cork no bigger than his own tiny fist.

'What ... what are they?' he asked, a little embarrassed to convey his ignorance.

The shrew clasped her paws to her breast and sucked the air through her teeth in mock horror. 'And there was you all ready to board ship and not know that these here little miracles existed. Why, you're not safe to be let out on your own, are you, my delicious duck egg? These charming and, if I might say so, fashionable items are invaluable to the mariner. Why, I don't know no one who sets sail without one round his neck. Must've saved hundreds of lives in their time, these beauties, and here's you without one. Why, you're just not prepared properly, are you – the poor unfortunate.'

Woodget felt very foolish, especially when he caught her giving the vole in the next stall a knowing wink. He really must appear to be untutored in the ways of the sea and privately thanked the Green that he had been shown his error before it was too late.

'I'd better have one then,' he told the shrew. 'How much are they?'

'A piece of silver for one – three pieces for two.'

The fieldmouse furrowed his brow and fumbled inside his bag. 'Oh,' he mumbled, 'I don't believe I've got no silver. Fact I'm certain sure I bain't never had any.'

'Hortichuke Sciatica!' the shrew scolded herself with a gleaming crossed eye fixed upon the tantalising contents of her victim's bag. 'You always were a soft touch and that's the honest to allblimey truth of the matter. See here, young master, I can't let you go a-roaming on no ship without the protection of one of these.'

'But I don't have no coin,' Woodget informed her.

The stallholder gave a gracious and understanding nod then reached out her stubby, grasping paw. 'I know that, my dewy cowslip, but there might be another way. You just hand over that there bag of yourn and we'll see if there ain't something worth trading.'

Woodget wavered, but she really was so very kind and putting herself to so much trouble. 'Here y'are,' he said, passing it over. 'Is there owt worth a piece of silver in there?'

Hortichuke fell on the bag as though it were a worm and she a starving crow. With greedy fingers she tore at the opening and delved inside.

'A little knife,' she trilled to herself, flourishing the blade and hunting for more trinkets, 'a brass buckle, a waistcoat, nothing in the pockets except a loose button – hmm, not bad quality – a small wooden figure, poorly carved . . .'

'That's Bess,' the fieldmouse piped up. 'I never did get round to finishing it.'

'A pewter bowl, a tin pot – you *are* a collector aren't you? A few more worthless bits and pieces and what's this – a brooch?'

'My mum's, that is.'

The shrew held the ornament up to the candlelight and tried to hide the delight she felt on seeing the coloured glass wink and flash in her fingers.

'Well . . .' she began with a half-hearted drawl, 'I don't know if it's worth my trouble after all. There isn't much here, is there? I'd turn back and go home if I were you.'

Woodget shook his head. 'I can't do that,' he said. 'I got to get me one of these here danglers. Is there nowt you'd take fer one?'

The shrew's black eyes glittered almost as much as the brooch she still held in her paw. 'I suppose I could trade you one for this,' she shrugged.

'Oh, I dunno,' he breathed, 'I did so want summat to remind me of my dear old mum. I didn't tell her I was takin' it neither.'

'If it's stolen then I won't touch the wretched bauble!' Hortichuke snapped, still clutching the brooch tightly and showing no sign of letting go. 'Mind you, if you were to throw in the buttons off that waistcoat as well, I might consider it this once.'

'Done!' Woodget cried before she could change her

mind, and quickly defaced his Greenday best.

With a triumphant smirk upon her face, the shrew received her booty and handed him one of her worthless pendants.

'Oh, thank 'ee!' Woodget declared, feeling ever so pleased with himself and displaying the lump of cork with the utmost pride.

'Excuse me!' smarmed a treacly voice as the neighbouring stallholder, who was a fat vole, saw that Hortichuke had finished with the fieldmouse. 'I couldn't help but noticing that you don't appear to be wearing any lucky shells in your hat; perhaps you would care to peruse my humble stock . . .'

By the time Woodget came through the far side of the market he had lost not only his mother's brooch and his waistcoat buttons but also his knife, the brass buckle, a handkerchief, the pewter bowl and tin pot as well as the waistcoat itself. In their place he had obtained the ridiculous cork pendant, a sprig of dried but immensely (so the vole told him) magical seaweed, two crudely painted shells which would keep storms at bay, a piece of sea-polished glass that everyone knew ensured a safe return home and a bag of orange and lemon rind.

The last item had been given to Woodget free of charge by a couple of kindly mice who took pity on him and managed to prevent him trading his bag for a fishbone which always pointed north, but only once it was out on the open sea.

With his purchases either around his neck, worn upon his hat or tucked safely into his bag, the fieldmouse sauntered further along the quayside to take a look at the other vessels moored there.

Away from the cheerfully lit stalls, this part of the harbour was lost in gloom, and presently Woodget began to grow nervous again as lakes of shadow spread out before him and he gave his sprig of seaweed a hasty pat.

Then his keen ears heard a peculiar tapping noise coming from directly in front of him and he hesitated as the sound grew steadily louder.

'What in the barley can that be?' he whispered.

Tap, tap, tap.

With unswerving purpose the steady rhythm came ringing from the darkness, chiming off the flagstones and getting closer with every second.

Woodget peered into the gloom, but whoever it was remained invisible in the murk and the fieldmouse took an apprehensive step backwards. Even in the secluded haven of the farm he had heard rumours of cruel and hideous creatures which existed in the wide world. What if this was one of those monstrous beasts? Perhaps it was a nightmare of horn and shell that had crawled out from the muddy deeps in search of prey; perhaps even now it was hunting him and its crab-like pincers were wide open, ready to snap shut about his little body. Woodget pressed his paws to his mouth as his panic increased and he hopped about wondering what to do.

Then the muttering began.

Amid the clamour of the staccato drumming a harsh, gruff voice was mumbling to itself, but not even Woodget's sharp ears could make out all that was said. His trembling nostrils could not tell him anything either, for the breeze was against him, and he suddenly felt incredibly vulnerable and alone upon the quayside. All the fieldmouse wanted to do was find somewhere to hide and let the unseen mutterer and maker of mysterious noises clatter past.

Hastily, he scurried to the side, where a mass of fishing nets was draped across two tall iron posts, and he dived smartly into the deepest depths, burying himself beneath the loosely woven mesh.

'Over half the journey done,' rasped the burbling voice which came floating on the salty airs, 'over half an' yet it ain't right. To be sure, there's a bad feelin' out tonight, so there is . . .'

The stranger lapsed into a more subdued and unintelligible babble which the fieldmouse could not catch and still the tapping advanced.

Cautiously, Woodget raised his nose from the netting; the sound was very close now and he was anxious to see who would emerge from the gloom . . .

'Spies everywhere,' he heard the voice grumble. 'It shouldn't be like this, so it shouldn't. None were to know, not a one – so keep it close and peel them gogglers.'

From his hiding place the fieldmouse held his breath and shrank back a little further as, from the concealing darkness, came the source of the unsettling sounds.

To his surprise, out of the shadows there hobbled a large and solid-looking mouse. His fur was a deep slate grey, the colour of an angry sea and brindled around the jowls like foam-crested waves. Faded tattoos adorned his brawny features and in one of his strong, calloused paws he grasped a gnarled stout stick.

In fearful silence Woodget stared as the stranger

laboured tetchily along, leaning heavily upon the stick and cursing continually under his breath. A large leather bag was fastened securely about his broad shoulders, and with his free paw he clutched at the straps, almost as if he expected to be waylaid at every turn. The mouse's eyes roved from side to side, mistrusting the concealing shadows, and one corner of his mouth was drawn into a challenging snarl – fierce enough to scare away the most heinous of footpads.

'Just let 'em try,' he growled. 'I know they're here. I can smell out one o' them weasly, venom-hearted snake scum at a hundred leagues, that I can.'

As the figure lumbered further along the quay, Woodget dared to raise his head a little more from the netting, greatly intrigued.

Then he noticed for the first time that in place of the mouse's left leg there was a thick stump of wood, and it was this that thumped and tapped its way over the flagstones. A stifled chirp of understanding issued from Woodget's mouth before he was able to stop himself, and at once the peg-legged mouse whirled around and glared harshly at the swathe of netting.

'Come out!' the imposing figure bawled, yet in his voice there was a deadly and overwhelming sense of dread. 'Crawl out of there, you scaly heathen!'

Woodget froze, not knowing what to do.

'I'll flush you out if I have to!' thundered the other, brandishing the stick like a cudgel and taking a menacing step closer. 'Won't grieve me none to dash out your sly cunning and feed your giblets to the fish. I've done it afore now and sure enough I'd do it a thousand-fold more without turning a whisker!'

The mouse's face was twisted with fury, yet as he went pounding towards Woodget's hiding place there was also a wild glimmer of terror dancing in his eyes and he thrashed the stick before him, bellowing for all he was worth.

'You'll not strike me down with your foul venom, you fork-tailed slime! I'll not be seeing Fiddler's Green this night! By the Holy One, I swear I won't!'

The sight of this enraged creature so horrified the petrified fieldmouse that he leapt up and gave a shrill squeal of fright, then hid his face and waited for the violence to reach him.

Rampaging into the nets, the attacker threw back his powerful arm to strike, but the blow never came, for just in time he beheld Woodget's stricken and trembling form and he cast his aim wide.

'By the Green's beard!' he barked, huffing from his exertions, 'What have I here?' and he gave the terrified Woodget an inquisitive prod with the end of the stick.

'Ho, ho! A fieldmouse, so it is – and a minnow of a one at that! What brings him to this brigand-crowded shore? Think yourself lucky, me lad – you nearly ended up as a gull's supper.'

Woodget peered up at the figure from between his fingers and gave a thankful but shuddering nod.

The mouse scowled at him. 'To be sure I didn't lay into you, but I'm still wanting to know what you was doing spying on me. Did someone put you up to it? For it's plain you're not one of them foul pagan crew – though ever artful in disguises and deceit they are. Stop dithering, for glory's sake! Did a cat get your tongue?'

'P-p-please, sir!' Woodget finally managed to stammer. 'I weren't a-sp . . . spying on you – honestly, I truly weren't. I don't know nobody roundabouts. I got meself all afeared out here on me ownsome, and what with the peculiar noise an' all I plum darted for cover, not meaning no harm nor offence.'

'Peculiar noise?' the stranger repeated, but his tone was warmer now for he found himself liking the fieldmouse and was greatly relieved that it was not who he had been expecting.

'Your leg, sir,' Woodget replied, 'beggin' your pardon like. I didn't know what it were a-stompin' and a-tappin'.'

When he heard this, the mouse threw back his head and gave a hearty roar of laughter. 'Here's fretful!' he cried. 'To flinch at the sound of the timber toe – ain't you never come across one afore, lad?'

'Not ever, sir.'

'Then you've had a sheltered life and that's the truth, so it is. But stow all that "sir" calling – Mulligan's the name and that's how all folk hail me, plain and simple like.'

'How do, Mister Mulligan,' the fieldmouse said, feeling a little braver and holding out his paw in greeting. 'I be Woodget Pipple, from Betony Bank.'

'Glad to know you, matey,' Mulligan replied, shaking the paw and grinning widely. 'Tell me of yourself. I been traipsing round this country too long with no company 'cept mine own, and mighty weary I've grown of the sound of my voice. Now let us away from this troublesome netting and jaw awhile till I reach my ship.'

'Where you headed?' Woodget asked, clambering

out of his cover and making certain his lucky seaweed was still in place on his hat.

'To the Greek Isles, lad. A lovelier necklace of gems you won't never clap eyes on. Too long have I been in this chill clime – it's water clear as diamonds I'm hankerin' for and a sun that burns your ears to a crisp in the noon hour. Don't sit well on this one to stay ashore for long – too much brine in my veins. No, the open waters for me it is; them were the days when I could roam where I wished, with no obligations nor yokes imposed.'

With a faint smile upon his grizzled face Mulligan gazed out across the harbour to where the dark sea stretched into the dim night and he gave vent to a sigh of longing. 'Soon it'll be over,' he breathed, 'aye, soon it'll be done and you can rest, Mulligan.'

Woodget looked up at the old seamouse and wondered if he dared to make the request which had hatched within him. Finally he could stand it no more and cried urgently, 'Would it ... could it ... might I ... ? Please, Mister Mulligan, can I come with you? I got to get me away from this place and I doesn't know what to do nor what boat to take. I won't be no trouble, I swears.'

Disturbed from his thoughts, Mulligan looked at his new friend, and although he had been forbidden to take anyone with him on the journey in case they proved false, he was sore at heart and needed companionship. The burden he had been entrusted with was too great to bear alone and the buoyant enthusiasm of the little fieldmouse touched him deeply.

'I'd be honoured, matey,' he said at length. 'Let's

you an' me go find our ship an' clamber aboard; she'll be setting sail before long. Ho, ho! Did you see them cut-purse stallholders yonder? What limp kippers do they take folk for? Why, last time I was 'ere one of them scoundrels had the gall to try and sell me some magic seaweed! Whoever heard of such witless tripe?'

The fieldmouse said nothing but pattered happily beside him. His eyes were glittering with excitement and it was impossible to guess what new adventures lay ahead. His old life was over now, and although his feelings for Bess pained him still, he tried to think only of the future.

As they made their way along the quayside, skulking in the dismal shadows behind them a pair of watchful eyes narrowed and a low hiss escaped into the darkness.

Wrapped in a long cloak of deep green with a great cowl obscuring its face, a single figure stole along the path as silently as a melting shred of grey mist. About the concealing garment's heavy folds the chill night seemed to gather and collect, clinging to the dank fabric like a thick cloud of flies swarming about something dead and decaying. So complete and concealing was the shrouding raiment that no clue as to the nature of the creature beneath could even be guessed at, but deep in the hood's blank void the eyes blazed with hatred and a vile curse issued from invisible lips.

'Greater allies than that shall you need, seafarer,' the dry, evil voice needled, 'for now your wandering is complete, you are far from help and guidance. The charm that has saved you till now has ended, for the plots and contriving schemes of the Green Council are laid bare unto me.'

Turning, the cloaked figure raised an arm and in the gloom two bitter points glinted coldly. Fixed upon the creature's claws were a pair of curved talons wrought in burnished gold and they flashed through the night like razors through a dark curtain.

The instant this signal was given there came a cackling and a slobbering as a pack of five young rats bounded up. Their eyes shone a burning crimson, for the sinister figure had introduced the bloodlust into their craven hearts and inspired them to murder.

Pigsniff, Clunker, Mouldtoes and Licemagnet were all brown rats, but their sprightly and eager leader, Spots – who got his nickname from his piebald colouring – had been nurtured in malice for longer by the cloaked creature and into him more than the others had been instilled the love of slaughter.

'Is it time, master?' the rat begged. 'We been awful good like what you said, keepin' a safe distance and not making too much din – all 'cept Clunker; I had to crack him one.'

'You filthy tell-all!' snapped Clunker.

His piebald leader ignored him and stared fawningly up at the deep cowl. 'Is you sure now?' he implored. 'Is it the one yer after?'

'I am certain,' came the hissing voice and the rats shivered at the sound of it.

'What's the plan then? Does we creep up an' slit his mizribble throat?'

'I bags first guzzle!' piped up one of the others.

'You snick yer own gash, Mouldtoes!' Spots rapped back. 'Tell us, master – what is your wish?'

The hooded one glanced back at the two mice ambling along, chatting lightly to one another.

37

'Your prey has found a companion,' hissed the voice. 'Hear now my decree and obey me to the full.'

The rats sniggered and their tongues lolled from their dribbling jaws.

'You may do what you will to the fieldmouse,' came the hideous instruction, 'he is of no matter, yet before you slay the other, bring him to me and all that he bears.'

'Cwoorrr!' gurgled Clunker, smacking his lips. 'That littl'un looks a tasty tidbit – be the work of an instant to peel that squirt!'

'Make haste,' their master commanded, 'lest they draw too near those stalls and aid. Be swift and deadly, let no hint of your attack warn them. Twice has that Irish fool evaded me, but no more. Now – begone!'

With a slap of their tails, the rats leapt away, their murderous eyes fixed upon the unsuspecting mice a little distance ahead, and their throats burned to taste their succulent life blood.

'That be our goodly ship,' Mulligan told Woodget, pointing his stick at a large cargo vessel.

The fieldmouse stared up at the beautiful curving lines of the craft. A light shone out from one of the portholes and he wondered where on board they would be staying.

'It's the hold for the likes of you an' me, matey,' Mulligan said, 'providing the bosun lets us aboard. You can't be too careful these days – a lot of weird and roguish characters about. I've heard some right rum tales of late, so I have. A ship is no place to find yourself if there's a villain on the loose – out on the open ocean there ain't nowhere you can hide nor escape to, save the hungry deeps.'

'How does we get aboard?' Woodget asked, thrilled at the prospect of this new life and all it had to offer.

'See that mooring rope there? Well, it's up that we'll be climbing, and even with old Peggy here I'll warrant I'll do it in double-quick time afore you.'

But even as they headed for the edge of the harbour wall, from out of nowhere, or so it appeared to the two astounded mice, there came a crow of delight and the gang of rats was upon them.

Clunker's claws came sweeping around Woodget's neck and the fieldmouse let out a horrified scream until the powerful talons squeezed about his throat and his voice was choked into a gasping silence.

'This way, my little mouthful,' Clunker spat. 'There's a peeling blade I'd like you to see,' and he hauled the struggling Woodget back into the shadows.

Mulligan, however, was not so easily overcome. Like a wild beast, cornered and beset by scavenging jackals, he bellowed at the top of his lungs and struck out with his stick.

Crack!

The weapon smashed into Pigsniff's snout and a shattered fang went clattering over the flags, leaving the rat howling and clasping his bleeding jaws. But Mouldtoes took his place and, with his fist, dealt the seafarer a dreadful blow across the head, sending him reeling backwards – straight into the clutches of the piebald, who wrenched him completely off balance and threw him to the ground.

At once the others leapt on top of Mulligan and

scrabbled at his throat, each trying to lunge down and snap at the exposed fur.

'Oi!' Spots screeched at them. 'No killin' – not yet. You heard what the master said. Take his bag, then drag him back there to account.'

'Accursed filth!' Mulligan raged as they tore the pack from his shoulders, biting the straps with their teeth. 'Scum of the Scale! You cannot have that! No! Never!'

The mouse lashed out as the bag was wrenched from him and his protests were answered by a savage kick in the ribs.

'Give it back!' he cried, gritting his teeth against the pain. 'You don't know what you're doing!'

'On yer feet,' Spots ordered. 'Shift yerself, there's a personage back there wants a word with you.'

But Mulligan was not cowed yet; he was made of doughtier stuff than they had realised. In a final, desperate act, he jerked back on to his feet then charged head-down at the rat stealing his belongings. A startled yowl blasted across the harbour as the mouse rammed Licemagnet right in the stomach. Doubling over in shock and battling for breath, the villain let go of the broken straps and Mulligan snatched at them frantically.

Incensed at the mouse's stubbornness, Spots hurtled forward and sank his teeth into Mulligan's shoulder.

The weight of the piebald rat, combined with the searing agony of his bitten flesh, proved too much for the seafarer. At last his strength and courage failed. With a whine, he felt his legs buckle and he collapsed, helpless, on top of his bag.

'Get him to the hooded one!' Spots snapped,

sucking his filthy whiskers clean of the mouse's blood. 'Mouldtoes, you take his arms, Pigsniff the legs.'

'Pigger's run off,' Mouldtoes answered. 'Lost a fang he did, and Licey ain't in no fit state – I'm not luggin' this fat beggar on me own.'

'Where's Clunker got to?'

'He carted that midge off, leavin' us all the hard work.'

The piebald rat bared his teeth. 'Did he now?' he rumbled. 'Well, I'll not be standin' fer that.'

Behind a row of packing crates, the squirming Woodget had been pulled and dragged. Clunker had no intention of sharing this dainty; the flesh was tender on the bone and already his belly was growling fiercely. Cackling softly to himself, he listened to the others struggle with Mulligan, making sure they were thoroughly occupied before focusing his full and deadly attention upon the morsel in his grasp.

'It's a rare treat this is,' the rat grinned unpleasantly. 'I usually have to make do with their left-overs but not this time, oh no; you're gonna be mine and taste the sweeter fer it.'

Woodget stared up at the hideous rat's face and screwed up his own as the grip tightened about his throat and the dribbling lips of his captor curled back to reveal sharp and yellow fangs.

Rejoicing in his excellent fortune, Clunker gave the fieldmouse a customary sniff to savour the shivering portion's terror, then bore down for the kill.

Yet the lethal snap of his jaws never came. Suddenly Clunker was yanked backwards and the harsh voice of Spots rang in Woodget's trembling ears.

'You thieving lump of dirt!' he snarled. 'Keep him

fer yerself, would yer? The lads won't like that; them'll be right displeasured, in fact.'

Clunker glared at him for a smouldering instant until he thought better of it and hastily tried to explain.

'Spots!' he exclaimed with injured innocence. 'I would never do that. This little gobbit slipped by me. I'd only just caught him and was about to bring his stinkin' hide back to you – honest I was.'

'Get you gone and help Mouldtoes,' the piebald muttered, his beady eyes twinkling in a most horrible manner in Woodget's direction. 'I'll deal with this one.'

Clunker's face fell; he knew what Spots was going to do. The little delicacy was going to be all his – Clunker and the others would be lucky to get a finger to chew. Spots always got his own way, especially recently. He had become peculiar of late, ever since they took up with that cloaked devil. Clunker didn't like that one – oh no, he did what he was told but it weren't natural and downright frightened him and the others. They had no idea what this business was about, and if truth be known they didn't want to. Let Spots bow and scrape to him, they'd just about had enough.

'Prob'ly stringy anyway,' he said sourly but, just as he was about to pass Woodget over, a malicious notion flared in his mutinous mind and he let the fieldmouse slip from his claws.

Squealing loudly, Woodget bounded away, nipping under the piebald's swiping grasp and fleeing back to the quayside.

'HELP! HELP!' he shrieked, but for all his fear he did not run to the safety of the little market. Upon

the ground he saw Mulligan's stricken form and
Mouldtoes poring over him, dabbing a sampling claw
into the scarlet wound and lifting the dripping talon
to his impatient lips.

Wretchedly, Woodget knew that he was too small
to be of much use to the fallen mouse but he had to
do something.

'Get away from him!' he yelled at the rat, taking a
flying leap at Mouldtoes and beating him with
his tiny fists.

The fieldmouse's efforts merely made Mouldtoes
laugh and he threw him off with a casual flick of his
claw.

'Mulligan!' Woodget cried. 'Get up – get help.'

Groggily, Mulligan tried to stand but it was too late,
for Spots was already tearing on to the path with
Clunker close behind.

'Licey,' the rat yelled, 'don't just sit there – stop the
grey one! You two – help me catch the runt.'

The entire operation was going horribly wrong and
the piebald was aware that some of the stallholders
were already staring in their direction, alerted by the
fieldmouse's cries. His master would not be pleased
with him at all.

In a moment Woodget was caught and Spots drew
out a glittering knife.

'That's enough trouble from you,' he said, pressing
the blade against the fieldmouse's chest.

'Mouldtoes, Clunker, Licey, take that one to his
lordship. I'll gut this 'un here an' now.'

'Stop!' Mulligan called, as the others lifted him to
his feet. 'Let him go – he's nothing to do with this. He
knows nothing.'

'I don't care if he does or not,' Spots snapped. 'He's less bother dead.'

Suddenly there came a ferocious roar and before the rats knew what was happening, a vicious and brutish maniac came barging into them.

All they saw was a blur of soft brown fur, a flash of red about the nightmare's neck and a long wooden staff clasped in its paws. Shouting terrible challenges, the horrendous fiend immediately set about the gang like a vengeful whirlwind.

The first blow fell upon Spots' claw and the knife went spinning through the air. The piebald howled but clung on to Woodget, who cheered the attacker gleefully – chirruping with delight to see him.

Held firmly between Mouldtoes and Clunker, Mulligan realised with amazement that their saviour was in fact another mouse, and he tensed his aching muscles preparing himself for the struggle ahead.

Then the strange mouse's second blow was dealt. This time it smashed across Mouldtoes' back and the rat staggered sideways, teetering perilously close to the edge of the harbour wall. With a determined shove, Mulligan sent him flying down into the dark water where the rat landed with a loud splash and a high-pitched wail.

While the unknown but courageous mouse dealt with Licemagnet, Mulligan threw off Clunker's faltering grasp and punched him on the chin. That was enough for Clunker; squawking in fear he raced off – leaving Spots and Licey to cope on their own.

Wrathfully the piebald spun around. Woodget remained trapped in his claws and the rat's talons dug into his skin until the fieldmouse whimpered piteously.

'Leave it!' Licey snapped, 'We've been worsted!' and he hurried after Clunker, disappearing into the surrounding gloom.

Deserted by his comrades and alone with the three mice, Spots snarled and gnashed his teeth. He wouldn't go down without a fight; besides, he still held Woodget.

'One move and the puny radish gets squeezed till his eyes pop out,' he threatened. 'Drop the pole, me boy, and I'll set him loose.'

Before him, the mouse with the staff looked at Woodget's scared face and knew he dared not risk it. Reluctantly, he threw the weapon out of reach and waited.

But Mulligan had no faith in the words of a rat; he knew that Spots would murder his little friend just out of spite and he took a sidling step to the left, stooping in one quick movement to snatch something from the floor.

'You maggot-brained fool!' Spots chuckled at the newcomer and he gripped Woodget's head in his claws ready to tear it from his body.

'No you don't!' Mulligan roared, bringing the piebald's own dagger slicing down.

A tremendous scream echoed out over the sea as the rat's tail was hacked in two. Casting Woodget away from him, Spots stared down at the truncated and bleeding stump and the agony of his wound consumed him utterly. Leaving a trail of blood behind him, he fled along the quayside, screeching vilely.

Breathless from fear, the fieldmouse stared across

at the one who had saved them and rushed forward to embrace him.

'Thomas!' he cried. 'You came after me – we'd have been dead if it weren't for you!'

'Course I came after you,' Thomas Stubbs replied, still shaking from the fierce encounter, 'but what's going on here? Rats is usually stupid and scared – what got into them?'

Woodget shrugged but could not reply, for he was so happy to see a familiar face after all the horror that he burst into tears.

'The poor lad's had a sore time of it, so he has,' Mulligan declared, holding out his paw for Thomas to shake. 'There's bad folk in these parts – get some nasty pieces a-coming in from outside. A good job you saw us when you did – my thanks.'

Thomas looked around for the staff he had used as a weapon. 'I ought to take that back,' he said. 'It was holding up the canopy of one of those stalls. You all right now, Woodj?'

The fieldmouse wagged his head and wiped his eyes.

'I'm glad you came, Tom,' he sniffed, 'but I won't go back to Betony Bank.'

'You got it all wrong,' Thomas told him, 'it was all my fault. Listen Woodj, it isn't me she loves – it's you.'

The fieldmouse looked at him in disbelief.

'Honest,' Thomas assured him, 'you're the one. Turned me down flat she did.'

All the recent traumas were forgotten and a smile of the purest joy widened in the fieldmouse's face.

'Is it true?' he gasped. 'Oh, is it really? Oh Tom, you don't know how unhappy I was. Mister Mulligan, did you hear? She loves me, Bess loves *me*.'

The fieldmouse turned to his newest friend and blinked, then he stared back at Thomas, but neither of them could guess what the seafarer was up to.

Kneeling upon the flags, the one-legged mouse was examining the severed length of the piebald's tail.

Gingerly he prodded the gruesome object and muttered under his breath. Obviously whatever he was looking for was not there and a look of concern crossed his face.

'Then he was just local riff-raff after all,' he breathed. 'So the adept is still out there, watching me right now, no doubt. Well, you managed this time Mulligan, old lad, but only by a whisker – who knows about the next?'

Abruptly he became aware that the others were staring at him and Mulligan rose stiffly.

'A grisly trophy of tonight's trouble,' he said, grimacing at the bloody tail and trying to sound cheerful.

'What were you doing?' Thomas asked.

'Doing? Why, nothing – just taking a gander at it, as I said. Make a rare proof of this yarn when it's told.'

Thomas eyed him doubtfully. It was plain that the mouse was not telling the complete truth but he was in no mood to enquire further.

'Well,' he said, clapping Woodget on the shoulder, 'I promised her I'd get you home so we'd best set off.'

The fieldmouse nodded and pattered over to Mulligan to make his farewells.

'Don't look like I'll be voyaging with 'ee after all,' he said. 'I reckons that I'll miss out on more excitin' times but it's by Bess's side where I belong. Goodbye, Mister Mulligan – it were nice to know you even if it were just a short while.'

Mulligan looked at Woodget keenly then glanced over to where Thomas was standing and an anxious idea born of doubt and necessity formed in his mind.

'Oh aye!' he agreed quickly. 'To be sure it's missing your company I'll be doing, but before you trot along homeward could you and your friend there not see your way to helping me one last time? I wouldn't ask but that scurvy knave done took a bite out of my shoulder and I doesn't think I can clamber aboard my ship without assistance.'

Woodget took a look at the wound. It certainly looked vicious and he marvelled that Mulligan had not fainted from the pain and distress it must be causing him.

'We don't mind, do we, Tom?' he answered. 'Come on, you lay your arm on me and Tom'll take the other.'

'Wait,' Mulligan insisted. 'I must have my bag.'

'I'll fetch it after we've put you on board,' Thomas told him.

But Mulligan would not hear of it. 'No,' he demanded, 'I'll take it with me now . . . I wouldn't leave anything for them scoundrels to find if they come back.'

Woodget thought this very sensible and paused to go hunting for his own bag which he had lost in the initial struggle with Clunker. Then, with himself and Thomas supporting the wounded seafarer, they made their way to the ship and began to help him up the rope.

A little distance away the cloaked figure uttered a

repugnant hiss and gazed down at the piebald rat who had fallen in a swoon before him.

'Mistaken was I to put my trust in one so unworthy,' his cruel voice spiked in the dark. 'The fool was yours and yet you allowed a mouse to rout you.'

Upon the creature's claws the two golden blades winked and flashed as it crouched down and drew them menacingly across Spots' throat.

The red-rimmed eyes rolled in Spots' sockets as he slipped out of the dark sleep that had engulfed him. Yet the first sight he saw when his vision cleared was the sinister shadow-filled hood, and with a quiver he felt the chill gold touch his skin.

'Master?' he whined. 'I tried, but it were them others – they skedaddled and left me. Oh my tail – it hurts so bad. Don't kill me, My Lord, I begs you. I know what them blades can do.'

Spots shivered uncontrollably and hot tears streamed down his hatchet face.

Stooping over him a repellent chuckle floated from the dark cowl.

'Thrice now have you failed me,' came the accusing hiss. 'All I have to do is break your rancid flesh and you shall be condemned to a hundred agonies before Death takes you.'

'Noooo,' implored the rat.

The glittering blades pressed a fraction closer to the piebald's neck then, with a dismissive snarl, the cloaked figure rose.

'Begone!' it hissed. 'Death shall find you in his own way. Yet slink away under the restraint of these ruinous words and may they torment you until the end. For failing me, you shall never find rest; always and forever will your mottled skin be in the service of another, and grant that he is less merciful than I. Go now to that pitless destiny, loathsome stump-tail! It will pursue you down the years until you despair of your very existence; then alone shall you wish I had dispatched you now.'

Spots wiped the sweat and tears from his face, and although blood was still pouring from his severed tail and his soul was screaming inside him, he somehow managed to scrabble to his feet and, without glancing back at his former master, sped from the harbour.

'You're well out of that,' he moaned. 'If you can heal this nasty mess then you've really gotta get out of this stinking hold. Go to some big and crowded city where the scum and slime are ripe for the picking. Who knows, there might even be some mousies to peel, if I'm lucky.'

So it was that Spots, or Morgan as was his real name, vanished from that place and the curse laid upon him was roused – its unswerving malevolence bearing down and hounding him for the rest of his miserable days.

Yet upon the gloom-laden quayside, the hooded figure staring at the Greek ship in the distance came to a solemn conclusion. It was useless entrusting such urgent and vital matters to witless and profane underlings. No, to ensure he accomplished his mission he would have to execute it personally.

Carefully, the two golden blades were slipped from the creature's claws and stowed securely within a small travelling bag, then the hood was thrown back and the dark green cloak cast aside. Once this too was safely put away, the figure stole towards the ship and quietly climbed aboard.

3

Aboard the
Calliope

'Not much further mates,' Mulligan told the two mice who were helping him clamber up the mooring rope, 'then you can leave me. Real grateful I am for this kindness, aiding a poor old wretch to his bunk. Princes, the pair of you.'

When they finally stepped aboard the *Calliope*, the trio were met by a burly mouse with dark brown fur, whose chin was covered by a neatly clipped and pointed beard. This was the bosun – one of the few mouse crew. His main duty for this watch was to ensure that no undesirables boarded the vessel and, to aid him in this, a short but lethal-looking sword was fastened at his waist.

All ships, whether their official crews know it or not, are utilised by other creatures. Since the first galleon was launched into the uncharted waters there has been a secondary crew. Their task it was to oversee all who journeyed below decks, ensuring that they were kept in order and that the true cargo remained untouched.

Throughout long nautical history the ranks of this secret, ancillary navy were in the main, and by vigorous tradition, made up of stout-hearted mice. Of all creatures they had proven the most loyal and trustworthy, for although rats voyaged often, their craven, ever-greedy spirits were unsuited for such duties.

The size of each vessel dictated the number of the crew; small fishing boats were generally left unmoused for there was nowhere for any unauthorised passengers to hide and the craft never travelled to another port anyway. A ship the size of the *Calliope*, however, required a captain and three officers to make sure that the goods stored in the hold were not tampered with, and one of these redoubtable characters was the bosun who now stood before Thomas and his friends.

The armed mouse's name was Able Ruddaway and it had been a long, tiresome night. He had grunted and growled audibly when he had first seen the three figures labouring up the rope and flexed his fingers near the hilt of his sword in readiness. Through long years of experience the bosun had learned not to trust anyone and lately his mettle had been tested by the increasingly rough folk who wished to traverse the seas.

'Name yourselves!' he had called out as the struggling trio wobbled and toiled towards him and he uncovered a lantern to get a sharper glimpse of these indistinct arrivals.

A look of recognition gleamed in the bosun's eyes when he saw Mulligan and he muttered under his breath before consulting a much-thumbed notebook and adding the Irish mouse's name to a long list.

'Cutting it fine, Mulligan,' he sniffed once all three were safely on board and he eyed Thomas and Woodget suspiciously.

'These two are friends of mine,' the one-legged mouse answered. 'Master Woodget Pipple and Thomas . . . I didn't catch your last name, lad.'

'Stubbs,' Thomas replied.

'Aye, Stubbs. As I said, mates of mine they are so don't you go askin' them none of your infernal questions, Mr Ruddaway. Is it a full hold you'll be having on this voyage?'

Still scrutinising Mulligan's companions, the bosun nodded. 'Aye,' he said, 'the *Calliope*'s not carried so many for a fair while – seems everyone's a-travelling. It's the time of year, I suppose; always busy in the spring but we can't be too cautious, lot of scum swilling about.'

'You don't have to tell us that,' Thomas broke in. 'We've already met some real nasty villains.'

Mr Ruddaway glanced at him but did not respond; instead he pointed at Mulligan's shoulder and jerked his head to one side.

'You'd best get that seen to,' he said. 'There's a physician down below – go seek him out. He'll be by the cotton bales with the better sort.'

'It's obliged I am to you,' Mulligan replied. 'When you can spare a moment or five, come find me and we'll share a sup of my own special medicine.'

The bosun chuckled and returned his attention to

the notebook, adding Thomas and Woodget's names to his list.

'Here we go, lads,' Mulligan told them. 'Just get me to the hold and I'll manage from there.'

As they ventured down into the ship descending a steep and narrow passage, Woodget turned back and peered behind them.

'Why for was he puttin' our names down?' he asked.

Mulligan coughed and raised his eyebrows as though he hadn't noticed. 'Did he?' he muttered with feigned innocence. 'Well, always been one for order and setting things down proper has that Ruddaway. Likes to know exactly who's who and where they are – a real stickler for them bits of paper he is and that's the truth sure enough.'

'Not as if we'll be on this 'ere ship for long though,' Woodget added thoughtfully, 'I mean, I got Bess a-waitin' on me back home.'

At that moment Mulligan winced and uttered a cry of pain as if his wound had grown abruptly worse.

The fieldmouse forgot his doubts immediately. 'Don't you worry now,' he told his ailing friend, 'we'll see you to where you want to go and make sure you can manage afore we leave – won't we, Tom?'

A grim smile twitched over Mulligan's face, but in the dim gloom of the passage neither of his companions noticed it. Besides, Woodget's whiskers were already trembling, for a slight draught was issuing up the cramped way and with it the slightly stuffy air brought other, more fascinating insights as to what lay ahead.

A myriad of opposing scents laced the fusty atmosphere. Beneath the pungency of the by now familiar pitch, Woodget could smell a score of suppers being cooked over small and carefully tended fires. There were vegetable stews, delicious mouth-watering soups, roasted parsnips and, from some remote corner, his delicate senses caught the sweet aroma of fried elderflowers.

Presently the narrow way came to an end and, with the feel of rough timber boards under their feet, the three mice found themselves in the hold of the *Calliope*.

Thomas and Woodget came to a halt and they stared around them in wonder.

The hold was enormous; to their right, the curved hull of the ship reared into the high darkness above, whilst the far, port side could not be seen at all. Filling the great space, enormous crates towered over them like square and wooden mountains and in the murky distance they could just make out the vague outline of other cargo peaks. Yet at the foot of these lofty ranges, in the valleys and within the cramped channels and canyons, was a multitude of varied creatures all preparing bunks for themselves and trying to make their allotted berths as comfortable as possible.

Many of those closest to the new arrivals were rats. These idle, dirty specimens had made no attempt to find a cosy corner to curl up in and were simply sprawled across one another. Evidently they had just enjoyed a late meal of raw and, to Woodget's shrinking nose, rather putrid fish.

Most of them were belching and licking their dirty snouts free of grease and salty, dribbling ooze. In lazy contentment they perched upon every available space, stupidly sucking their teeth and swinging their great, bunion-covered and scaly feet in a childish fashion as they ruminated and rocked slowly back and forward.

Upon the crowded deck the remains of the supper that they had enjoyed was being picked at in a disinterested and bored way by several of the older rats. Humming ridiculous and mindless ditties to themselves, they played with the left-overs, flicking a fish scale at one of their lolling neighbours or fanning themselves with a half-chewed fin.

Mingled amongst them were other slovenly vagrants. A group of four weasels and two sour-faced shrews were playing dice in a rare clearing, a drunken hedgehog who had celebrated the coming of spring with too much enthusiasm was hiccuping uncontrollably and, sitting all alone in the middle of an alley-way formed by the gap between the crates, a glum-looking mole shook his head as he heaved a regretful sigh – remembering the folk he had left behind.

But Woodget's attention was fixed solely upon the rats; the sight of them and the stink of their grimy, unwashed fur brought an immediate fear to his heart and he drew back instinctively.

'Don't you fret none,' Mulligan reassured him. 'These motley cringers ain't gonna harm you. Look at their ugly faces; they've more to dread from us than we of them.'

As if to prove the point, he took a hobbling step forward and glared at a group of dishevelled and woeful-looking rats who were picking their brown and yellow teeth with old fishbones. When they saw Mulligan raise his stick and shake it at them they threw their claws before their snouts and their bottom lips quivered as they flinched, expecting him to strike their bony heads.

'That's the normal way of things,' Mulligan grunted with satisfaction as he lowered the stick and chuckled at the whingeing rats. 'A more skittish and yellow-spined breed I ain't never chanced upon.'

'Then what made those outside so wicked?' the fieldmouse asked, recalling the hatred that had burned in Spots' red-rimmed eyes.

But the seafarer did not seem to hear him and touched his wounded shoulder gingerly.

'Let's away from this place,' Mulligan muttered hastily; 'the dregs are always to be found on the outskirts. A little further in and we'll meet fairer company than this mixed jumble and sorry-looking crew.'

And so Thomas and Woodget helped him to limp his way deeper into the hold. As they progressed, the rats who lounged in their path crawled swiftly aside, with many a grovelling apology for causing any inconvenience. But the fieldmouse remained wary and his flesh crawled if he accidentally brushed against them.

Passing into a wide space that separated the two halves of the packed cargo, they found themselves in what was obviously the main thoroughfare of this strange community; the numbers of snivelling rat folk grew fewer and this part of the hold possessed a more wholesome air.

Genial mouse faces were to be seen sitting in snug berths with small lanterns glimmering above their bunks and, in the narrow alleys that radiated from this central road, other habitations could be glimpsed, for the glowing and sporadic trail of candlelight stretched in all directions.

'This is more like it,' Mulligan announced with a wave of his stick. 'Here's where the decent ones are quartered. 'Tis a strange life aboard ship, lads; like a village in miniature it is and when we're afloat there ain't nothing you can do to change the neighbours. Like it or lump it.'

Woodget was mildly astonished to find that there were numerous families aboard the *Calliope*. Here and there groups of mouse children who were too excited to sleep could be heard giggling as they listened to their father's amusing stories. Other youngsters were dozing peacefully but at least one was determined not to go to bed and almost ran straight into Thomas on his scampering flight from an irate and scolding mother.

'You'll have plenty of folk to speak to, Mulligan,' Woodget said. 'I never did see such a gathering. I reckons you could talk to someone new every day of this voyage and still not know all of them by the time it's done.'

A peculiar glint shone in Mulligan's eyes but he said nothing and hobbled on in pensive silence.

Thomas gazed around them and nodded smilingly at the sleepy faces who glanced in his direction. But a heaviness was stealing over his heart and he was beginning to worry about the time. 'Where do you think the physician will be?' he asked.

'Oh, he'll not be far,' the seafarer replied, stirring from his thoughts. 'Look yonder; those bales will make a fine soft bunk for me if there's any room left and that's where the bosun said I should find him. Let us head over there and I can get settled.'

The cotton bales were great square bags of bulging sacking, stuffed to near-bursting with countless soft and fluffy wads. Although most of them had been stacked so high as to make any attempt at sleeping upon them a momentous and dangerous climb, four spare bales were ranged in a line at the base of this unwieldy peak and it was these that a host of mice had claimed and made their own.

A number of smaller wooden boxes and sawn-off blocks had been hauled to one end of the row and organised into an irregular stairway leading to the top of the four bales, and when Mulligan and the others arrived they found that all the space was fully occupied.

Countless disdainful faces stared imperiously down at them. Apparently this was where those who considered themselves to be above the rest of the common sort had congregated in a select gathering, and Woodget nearly surrendered to the powerful urge to blow a raspberry at them.

Thomas also disliked the arrogant scorn that flowed down from above, but his mind was too preoccupied to care. All he wanted to do was return to the quayside and he wished Mulligan would settle somewhere soon.

Whether Mulligan himself was aware of the hostile contempt their presence was causing to the finer sensibilities of the uppish and supercilious residents, neither Thomas or Woodget could guess. Apparently deaf to the huffs of marked intolerance and blind to the pursed lips of displeasure, he began to clamber up the steps.

'Make way there,' he said gruffly when he reached the top. 'Must be a space where I can plant my weary hindquarters.'

This base remark caused all the prim females to gasp and fan themselves as if they were going to faint. Then they saw the blood oozing from Mulligan's shoulder and two of them really did wilt into their dithering husbands' arms.

'If you want the physician,' a bony-faced mouse with a long thin nose began, 'he isn't here.'

'Thank you, matey!' Mulligan replied jovially. 'Then I'll just wait till he returns.' To the chagrin of his fellow snobbish travellers he manoeuvred himself down, sighing with pleasure as his bottom sank into the yielding hessian of the bale.

'There's uncommon comfort,' he grinned, pummelling the soft bunk with his fists. 'I could get used to this. It's like an emperor I'll be feeling when this is over.'

Thomas and Woodget were standing at his side and he looked up at them gratefully. 'However can an old salt like me begin to thank you two fine fellows?' he asked.

'Just you get well,' Woodget told him, 'and next time you find yourself in these parts, come visit me.'

'Who knows,' Thomas added, fidgeting with his red kerchief and impatiently shifting the weight from foot to foot, 'you and Bess might be wed by then, if you ever get round to asking her.'

The fieldmouse chortled shyly and Thomas held out his paw to bid Mulligan farewell.

' 'Fraid we can't tarry,' he told him. 'Already we've been longer than we ought.'

But the grey mouse was strangely anxious that they should not leave him just yet and became most insistent. 'I can't let you pair disappear without sharing a sup of rum with me,' he declared. 'I've a flask put away someplace; I'll just take it out.'

'We really ought to be heading home,' Woodget began.

'What nonsense are you talking?' Mulligan muttered, carefully unbuckling his pack and rummaging inside. 'A fine lad like you wouldn't decline a drink with a mate.'

Thomas glanced at Woodget and gave him a look that told him they had no time for this.

'It's already very late,' he said, 'and there's still a tidy walk we've got in front of us.'

'All the more reason you should take a tot to set you on your road,' Mulligan answered, blithely disregarding their polite refusals and removing a large leather flask from his bag which he carefully fastened again and kept close by him.

'Not for me, thanks,' Thomas said as the seafarer pulled out the cork with his teeth. 'I had my first taste of something similar this night and I've no wish to try any more. We really have to go!'

With the flask in his outstretched paws, Mulligan stared from Thomas to Woodget and a hurt expression crossed his whiskered face.

'It's real offended I'll be if you don't accept what's offered,' he breathed. 'Is that your intent – to give me a second wound this night? To be sure this pains me more sorely than any rat bite could.'

Confronted by this, Thomas and Woodget had no choice but to accept the mouse's invitation.

'There's my fine young mateys,' Mulligan cheered and he could not disguise the relief in his voice. 'I knew you wouldn't fail me and be so harsh.'

Thomas took the flask from him and lifted it to his lips. He had the uneasy feeling that Mulligan was deliberately trying to prolong their stay, but he was determined that as soon as they had taken one drink then he and Woodget would most certainly depart. As he tilted back his head, a rich exotic smell rose up from the flask – filling and burning his nostrils – then Thomas drank.

Almost immediately he was coughing and spluttering. The rum was nothing like Old Vetch's brew; it was far stronger and he leaned against the bale wheezing and gasping.

'I'll bet that warmed your innards,' Mulligan laughed, 'and set a fire raging in your veins.'

By this time Thomas had given the flask to Woodget and now it was the fieldmouse's turn to squeak and choke.

Mulligan regarded them happily as he took his turn at the rum and gulped down a great swig.

'What I still don't understand', Thomas began when the breath returned to his lungs and he found his voice once more, 'is why those villains out there were after you in the first place – I mean, what did they want?'

Mulligan paused in wiping his mouth and he wavered for a moment before answering. 'Isn't that the strangest occurrence?' he replied. 'For here's me with only my few worthless bits an' pieces, and look how those bloodthirsty devils were set on cutting my throat. I tell you, lad, the world is growing stranger every day. Mind you – no one can fathom the workings of a rat's worm-eaten brains. Like as not it was with someone else they'd muddled me.'

Thomas was still not convinced but he let it pass and declared that now they really had to leave.

'What?' Mulligan asked. 'Not stay for just one more tot?'

'It's very kind,' Thomas answered, but his anxiety to return to the quayside had mounted to near panic, 'but no, this time we really must go. Come on, Woodj.'

Mulligan looked at them squarely and he cocked his head as if he was listening for something, then a broad grin lit his face. 'Well, go with my blessings on you,' he told them. 'You've made a true friend this night, so you have.'

Woodget held out his paw in farewell but at that moment, without warning, the deck lurched under him and he stared wildly at Thomas.

'Oaks and ivy!' he cried. 'What is it?'

Thomas scowled as the ship tilted again and in horror he realised that what he had feared had indeed come to pass.

'She's set sail!' he yelled. 'Quick, Woodj – before it's too late!'

Frantically, the two mice pelted from the cotton bales, too filled with anguish and urgency to take their leave of Mulligan.

Sitting upon the soft hessian, the seafarer chuckled mildly to himself as they scurried down the steps, and gave his belongings a thoughtful pat.

'Weren't nothing else I could do,' he murmured severely to himself. 'There's more at stake here than some paltry romance, so there is. The poor young lad'll get over it – if he comes through this perilous business.'

Recorking the flask, the grey mouse was at last able to consider all that had happened that night and his face grew extremely grave and stern.

"The road ahead will be hard and deadly,' he breathed. 'All that matters is to keep the fragment from the enemy's grasp.'

Over the slumbering bodies of mice – young and old – Thomas and Woodget leapt until they were in the central road once more. Blundering past those creatures foolish enough to get in their way, they knocked them to the deck – heedless of the yelps and angry cries which rang out in their wake.

'Hurry!' Thomas bawled over his shoulder when the fieldmouse began to lag behind.

Woodget was running as fast as he could and when they reached the edge of the cargo crates where the rats were gathered, their sprawled filthy figures no longer held any fear for him. Even when he accidently stomped on one of the tails which snaked over the dusty boards and the rat let out a deafening yowl, he did not pause in his flight.

The thought of Bess was filling his mind – nothing else mattered. He had to see her. Yet even as he followed Thomas up the narrow sloping passage which led to the upper decks his spirits were sinking. The gentle rocking movements of the ship and Thomas' ominous words struck a miserable chord in his heart and a chill dread was creeping over him.

'Hoy there!' roared the bosun when they stormed

by him as he trotted down. 'Where do you think you're going?'

Desperately, Thomas scrambled on to the upper deck where he darted to the side of the ship and stumbled to a halt.

In a few moments Woodget joined him and they both stared out across the dark water in utter dismay.

The *Calliope* had left the harbour and was already sailing over the open ocean. To the mice's distress, the little Cornish town was now only a glittering hoard of amber jewels shining in the distance and Woodget shivered violently.

'Bess,' he whimpered. 'Tom, what'll we do? I can't stay here – I got to get back. This is terrible!'

Thomas hung his head. 'Even if you could swim,' he began sorrowfully, 'it's too late. You'd never reach the shore – we're too far out.'

'Then, what will become of us?' the fieldmouse breathed in a small and defeated voice. 'Won't we never get home?'

Thomas gazed at him and knew how crushed his little friend was. 'Course we will,' he answered, rousing a little. 'Ships don't go sailing round and never stop. As soon as this vessel puts into a port we'll hop off and find another to ferry us back.'

'Really?' Woodget asked, putting his paw to his eyes to check the brimming tears. 'Is you telling the truth, Tom?'

'I wouldn't lie to you, Woodj,' came the sincere reply. 'You just remember this – it was me who got you into this fix so I'll not be easy till I deliver you safe and sound to your Bess. Rely on Thomas Stubbs, Master Pipple, he'll never let you down – ever.'

The fieldmouse smiled faintly then rested his chin on his paws as he stared bleakly out at the dwindling lights in the distance.

'Hope it don't take long,' he muttered. 'She'll get so worried – not a good worrier, Bess ain't.'

Thomas put his arm about his friend and let his eyes drift upwards, up to where the stars blazed with a cold, white fire.

He had never seen them burn so brilliantly before and despite the predicament he was in, found himself dazzled and rendered speechless by their beauty.

At his side Woodget remained unmoved, for his thoughts were elsewhere. The enveloping darkness was but a mirror of his own feelings and he wondered how many days or weeks would pass before he found himself treading familiar paths with the mouse maiden at his side.

Under the great awning of night the *Calliope* journeyed, further from the coast until the craft was lost from sight altogether and a complete blackness closed about it. Only the silver-flamed splendour of the springtime stars punctuated the devouring dark and to Thomas it seemed as if the sea fell away beneath them and the ship rose silently, with a noble and dignified grace, up into the heavens – to sail amid the celestial and everlasting lamps.

Thomas' first voyage had begun.

Yet in the hold of the *Calliope*, amidst the weary travellers and masquerading as one of their number, something evil was stalking. With watchful eyes and a black soul consumed with malice, the figure passed between bunks and berths, seeking out the one who had thwarted his followers upon the quayside.

A lust for death and slaughter boiled behind those unwavering eyes. Somewhere in that labyrinth of wood and bale, the object of his hatred was resting, no doubt congratulating himself on his escape. But from the nightmare which prowled stealthily through that meandering, unsuspecting warren there could be no deliverance. An end was coming, the final throe in the unrelenting agonies of the world was close at hand and no one, certainly not an ageing mariner, could prevent that. The time of the usurping Green was nearly over and the ancient shadows were already lying heavy over eastern shores. The terror of the Dark Time was rising; that which had been cast out in ages past was nigh.

The night deepened and unaware of the black fate which lay ahead, the *Calliope* journeyed on – towards the awaiting doom.

4

Steeped in Venom

In the days that followed, Thomas saw little more of the watery world outside, for that first night when his wonder at the beauty surrounding him had waned, he had begun to feel queasy.

With an almost green pallor, he had spent three days down in the hold, groaning at the slightest movement of the ship and feeling thoroughly miserable.

'It's the sea-sickness all right,' a hearty Mulligan had told Woodget. 'Nowt for it but to let him squirm and suffer with it; seen the condition a hundred times afore – the malady'll right itself as soon as he finds his sea legs. Mind you, some folk never do. A fine mariner he's proving to be.'

The fieldmouse had stayed by his friend's side for all of the first day but by the evening he had grown restless and, when Thomas had fallen into an uncomfortable slumber, he decided to investigate the hold a little more.

There was no more room by the cotton bales so he and Thomas had been forced to take what quarters they could find and eventually discovered a warm berth amongst a veritable hill of large wooden barrels bound about with hoops of iron.

From the midst of these, Woodget crept and stretched his arms wide. Before him wound an alleyway walled by great oaken chests, intersected by many tapering ravines that were too narrow and cramped to sleep in but which served as handy back routes to other parts of the hold.

Woodget did not dare attempt to explore any of those just yet for he was certain he would get lost in the connecting canyons; they were still like one gigantic maze to him. So, keeping to the familiar path, he set off and his heart was light.

Gone was the misery of the previous night. The fieldmouse was not one to wallow in self-pity and, since there was nothing he could do to speed up his return home, he had resolved to learn as much as he could about his fellow travellers – looking forward to the day when he could recount their tales and histories for Bess's delight.

'First off I'll have another word with Mulligan,' he told himself, 'see if'n that physician who tended his shoulder hasn't got summat to ease poor Tom's tum.'

Wandering through the alley, Woodget headed for the hold's central trackway. Passing beneath a wide pillar that reached all the way to the dark heights of the ceiling, he was astonished to discover that a family of dormice had built a neat nest around a series of pipes that ran the length of the towering column.

Three timid faces were poking out of the twiggy entrance and regarded him meekly. Woodget tried to remember the correct way to greet these distant cousins and nodded his head three times.

'How do up there!' he called. 'That looks like a cosy home – a bit like the ones we make in my field. Did you lug them sticks an' straw all this . . .' but the dormice had already disappeared inside and the nest trembled as they shivered within.

On the timbers below, the fieldmouse chuckled and shrugged. No doubt he would get acquainted before the journey was over. There were still many hundreds of other folk to meet.

'Wouldn't bother with them if I was you, Titch,' came a croaking voice. The sound was so unexpected that Woodget jumped and looked about him.

'Dormice ain't good fer anythin',' the voice continued. 'All they ever talks about is the state of their sweaty old nests and if you're real unlucky they'll recite the roll of their ancestors at you. Bore the prickles off a hedgepig, that would.'

Woodget squinted into the darkness that obscured the entrance to one of the narrow ravines and, amongst the shadows a little distance away, he thought he could just make out the tall silhouette of a rat.

Woodget's throat dried and he caught his breath as he began to edge away. From somewhere inside of him he knew that here was another of that foul race who would not be cowed by mere angry words and shaking fists.

'And where might you be a-going?' the cracked

voice flowed from the darkness. 'Off to see that peg-leg chum o' yourn? I'd be careful if I were you, Titch. I done heard odd tales about that one. More to him than meets the eye or I'm no judge, and what do you suppose he keeps in that bag of his, the one he guards and binds so close to him the whole time?'

With that the rat shape stirred and took several steps closer to the opening but still remained hidden in the dim gloom, immersed in the concealing shade.

Woodget glanced back nervously, wondering if the creature would suddenly rush out at him, and he bit his lips as he tensed himself, preparing to run.

'Don't you be afeared of old Jophet now,' the voice drawled at him. 'He never does no one no harm, not unless they threaten him first, o' course.'

'Why are you lurkin', an a-hidin' – creepin' up on folk?' Woodget demanded in a frail voice. 'Why aren't you with the rest of your kind? Go . . . go pick at the slime and stink of your wormy fish gruel.'

'Happen I got tired of their company,' came the hissed reply. 'That's not to be amazed at, for they don't have an ounce of sense betwixt 'em. Jophet wanders where he will and won't be quartered nor shown no boundary. 'Tweren't my intent to scare you though, my tiny friend.'

'I ain't scared!' Woodget rallied, not very convincingly. 'And I ain't your friend!'

'Then you ought to be,' the dark shape uttered softly. 'A green-eared fellow like you don't have the first notion about the wild world. There's terrors out there to wither your tail and staunch the blood in your veins. Were I to tell you half the yarns I heard or the foes I seen, you'd jump straight into the gurgling deep and drown yourself stone dead rather than face them. Be warned, Titch, and put your faith in no one – 'specially not that soused old peg-leg. Lead you in a deadly dance, the halt-footed one would.'

Even as he spoke, there came the sound of footsteps and the lamplight in the alleyway where the fieldmouse stood flickered. The croaking voice was silenced and Woodget turned from the dark ravine to see who was approaching. With a smack of his tail against the crates, the shadowy rat turned about in the cramped passage and scooted off into the distance – vanishing into the dark.

Woodget rubbed his eyes, unsettled by the things the unpleasant creature had said, but he did not dwell on them for long.

'Broken biscuits!' cried a much lighter voice which, compared to the croaking tones of the rat, seemed to Woodget like the sound of clean spring water trickling through a parched and stony ditch.

'You'd best find them what knows, Dimmy,' it went on. 'Find 'em quick an' tell 'em like. How come they aren't a-doing summink about it? Oh deary dear! We'll never be getting nowhere if it goes on. Aunty was right – as sure as birds got beaks and slugs is stickier 'n lickrish.'

Shuffling down the alleyway, with his sloping shoulders bowed and his slightly flat-shaped head slowly shaking from side to side as he stared with solemn intensity at something held in his paws, came the figure of a young mouse.

His fur was a pale grey colour, but as he shambled past the lanterns their radiance scintillated around his slight form, bestowing upon him a halo of gold.

Woodget watched the newcomer cautiously before making a move, for as yet the mouse was unaware of him. A satchel with a letter 'D' painted large and red upon the front flap was slung over one of the drooping shoulders and his heavy-lidded but wide brown eyes were still fixed upon the mysterious object dangling in his paws.

'Thistles and nettles!' the grey mouse continued woefully. 'Round and round we're goin', round and round without a stop. I don't think I feel so good, spinnin' like a sycamore key. It's giddy I'll be.'

The stranger was quite close to Woodget now and at last the fieldmouse was able to see the baffling object twirling from the other's fingers.

It was a fishbone attached to a piece of string and Woodget let out a gurgle of laughter when he recognised the ludicrous compass he had almost bought from the quayside market. Then he saw that around the newcomer's neck there was not one cork talisman but three.

At once the stranger looked up and his large eyes blinked in surprise. 'Who's that?' he gasped, his large head bobbing upon his thin neck. 'What's so far-fangled funny?'

'Beggin' your pardon,' Woodget declared, 'I was just so relieved you weren't another o' them awful rats. There was one here a moment ago, down that snicket there.'

The grey mouse regarded him for a moment then grinned stupidly. 'I done seed nothin' and I aren't no rattybigfootsnottynosescabtail!' he affirmed, running the words together so that he had to take a great gulp of air before continuing. 'Them's no family of mine,

least my Aunty Lily never said so, but one of my cussins was a mucky scamp, she always said.'

Woodget smiled and introduced himself, but the mouse shook his head sadly, causing his ears to flap as he did so.

'Isn't no use a-telling you my name's Dimlon, nor that Aunty always calls me Dimmy, for what's the good in that if we're all a' squirlin' around and around? Come a cropper we will and what's the use of gettin' hintroducted and parlourmanneredbestcrocksout then?'

Taking another deep breath, he held up the suspended fishbone and pointed to it glumly while his eyes rolled in their sockets as they followed its slowly spinning progress.

'There now,' he breathed emphatically, 'see how we're all fixed and lumbered. Always to the north this here hamulot points, but you just mark how it turns and twists, never stopping still. Can only mean one thing. In a circle, that's where this big daft boat's goin'. I reckon I ought to have words with someone, an' I will too if I knew who to tell.'

Woodget chortled and found himself wondering if he would have been taken in by the absurd compass if he had gone ahead and purchased one.

'I'm sure we ain't going round in circles,' he told Dimlon tactfully. 'P'raps you haven't got the hang of that gadget yet. Maybe you ain't holdin' it proper.'

Dimmy's face clouded as his dull wits struggled with this new thought, then he brightened and he tucked the fishbone into a pocket of his satchel.

'Pickle me!' he groaned, tutting at his previous fears. 'Aunty said I weren't no good at anythin',

"Dimmylackwitdunderhead" – she was right there. Course, she didn't think I'd ever find the harbour, let alone get on a boaty. Just wait till I sees her face when I come back with summink rare an' forrin to put on her table, poshdustcollectin'whatnot. A statyoo of an effylump I'm hopin' for – she'd fair flip for that, she would. Always told me tales of far shores, she has, tales she'd heard from when she was little. Scary some of them were, some nights I never slept a wink, but I'd dearly like to see a munkie and hear a lie-on. Not the other way round o' course – 'case it saw me too and ett me for a snack then be pickin' bits of me out of his teeth all week.'

Woodget laughed at his idiotic talk. 'Well, I'm pleased to have met you anyways,' he said. 'I was just off to find my friend Mister Mulligan. I'd be glad of the company and I'm sure he'd be glad to meet you if you're willin' to join me.'

Dimlon consented and trudged happily alongside the fieldmouse, telling him of his former life with his aunt. This embittered old spinster had taken him in as an infant when his parents had died, and from that day to this had crushed and ridiculed him at every opportunity until he was the butt of every joke where they lived and she treated him like an unpaid servant.

The more Woodget learned about this formidable-sounding old battleaxe the more he felt sorry for his companion, yet Dimlon would not hear a word against her.

'A real grand lady she is,' he said in her defence. 'Not nobody with nicer knick-knacks than what she has. So patient too, always watches me when I does the dustin', givin' me careful advice on how to do it proper and reminds me when I do it wrong or miss a bit. That's why I told her, "Aunty," I said, "you got all these lovely trinkets an' you're so kind to let me clean them every day after I done my chores, 'tain't fair that I done gave you none of them." Oh, how she laughed at that – always laughing at my funny ways, she was; did my heart good to hear her 'cos I knew how much she cared for me, see.'

By now they had reached the main thoroughfare but the grey mouse continued to chatter as they strolled along. The evening meal had taken its toll on the rest of the passengers for the wider way was almost deserted. In their berths the families were either dozing or trying to keep the youngsters from raiding the rest of the precious provisions. Two of the more rebellious infants were chasing one another in and out of the narrow alleyways and their fraught parents had given up any hope of keeping them under control.

Woodget eyed them with a measure of concern, remembering that the rat who called himself Jophet might be lurking down one of those dimly-lit channels. But the screams of the youngsters were cries of giggling mischief, and under the bewildering spell of Dimlon's inane blather he gave the croaking creature no further thought.

'The look on Aunty's face,' Dimlon babbled, childishly avoiding the cracks between the timbers as he ambled along, the three cork pendants swinging like clumsy pendulums. 'Didn't reckon I'd akshually do it, she never. Just wait till I bring her a gloryorse treasure. Make the others sit up, that will.'

Suddenly the two mouse children came running

back on to the main thoroughfare, their faces drawn and their merry voices changed to whimpers of dread.

Woodget stared at them in dismay as they tore back to their parents and he shifted his gaze to a dark opening between the huge packing crates.

'Mother! Mother!' the youngsters cried. 'It's following us, look – look!'

A furious scowl appeared on Woodget's face. How dare that rat pick on children and frighten them?

But then the object of the youngsters' fear stepped into the lantern light. It was not Jophet, but a creature far more outlandish and the fieldmouse gaped in astonishment.

'A wizard! A wizard!' the children sang, pointing at the bizarre stranger with a mixture of awe and excitement.

Woodget had never seen anything so peculiar before. The 'wizard' was almost as short as himself, but what manner of creature he was he could not tell. The enigma was swathed in a cloak of blood-red velvet, richly embroidered with golden images of suns and moons and weird, plainly magical symbols. A large hood edged with a silken fringe concealed the unknown's face but from the deep shade sprouted many pale whiskers and for a brief moment two dim points glittered out in Woodget and Dimlon's direction.

In one of the stranger's small, gloved paws was a slender staff painted with a spiral of silver and black, topped by a carving of three rayed stars. With his free paw he traced a curious snaking pattern in the air.

A thrilled, expectant murmur rippled through the gathered families.

'A travelling magician!' they whispered. 'Will he perform for us, do you think? That'll keep the young ones entertained. They think of everything on these trips, don't they?'

All eyes were trained on the hooded figure and their whiskers trembled with glee as he raised the staff and waited for quiet to descend.

Suddenly from the fringed hood a sonorous, clear voice called out and all marvelled that such a booming sound could have its origins in such a diminutive creature.

'Hearken to me, voyagers all!' the mysterious stranger cried. 'Know now that Simoon – wanderer of the ancient pathways, obeah pilgrim, far seer, chanter of spellcraft, mage and prophet, diviner of fortunes, treader of the forgotten track and guardian of the old rituals – is amongst you.'

A murmur of approval swept through the onlookers; so far this was just what they anticipated and some even cheered, only to be hushed by their neighbours who were eager to hear what else the magician had to say.

'Many days shall we journey together,' Simoon called, 'and in that time thy hearts will grow weary. When you tire of this airless place and the dull company of those colourless folk about you, come seek me out and you shall learn all that you are able to bear.'

A sense of disappointment welled up in everyone, as well as a twinge of resentment for being pronounced 'dull'.

'He's only touting for business,' grumbled a disillusioned mousewife. 'Well, that prophet won't profit from me. Agnes, Pip, come away – there'll be no free show from that one.'

Feeling cheated, the mice slowly went back to their bunks until only Woodget and Dimlon were left looking at the hooded creature.

Within the cloak the one called Simoon shrugged his shoulders then, with a parting glance at the two who were still watching him, fished inside a pocket of the red velvet and cast a pinch of grey powder to the ground.

At once there was a bang and a flash of yellow flame which instantly turned into a cloud of thick blue smoke shot through with fizzing orange sparks.

When the swirling, glittering mist cleared the magician was nowhere to be seen and Dimlon let out a whoop of delight.

'Plop me in a jam pot!' he declared. 'That's a gogglin' good trick and no mistake! Real mighty witcherypocus that is – wouldn't like him to aim his spells and curses on me. Purplebelliedpinkspottednatterjacker, that's what he'd turn me into.'

Woodget did not like to tell him that Simoon had simply ducked back into the dark opening under cover of the smoke screen. 'Come on,' he said, 'Mulligan ain't far off now.'

Leaving the central road, they ventured through the crate canyons to where the cotton bales reared high and bulging into the towering darkness, and made for the stairway.

Past the pompous faces and snooty upturned noses of those who dwelt there they went until they heard a loud, raucous voice raised in lusty laughter.

'Then we trussed him up and locked him in a creel

for the rest of the night,' Mulligan's unashamed tones seared through the refined berths, 'so drunk he couldn't remember his name that stoat was, and sang such a lewd ballad that the beadle came bowling over and washed out his mouth with carbolic.'

Dimlon's eyes shone as he listened and he quickened his pace in his urgency to meet the owner of this brash voice.

When they reached him, Mulligan was sitting with his wooden leg resting upon his pack. The wounded shoulder was bandaged and his whiskered cheeks buckled with mirth as he waved the leather flask beneath his nose.

But the seafarer was not alone, for sitting beside him, dangling his toes over the bale's edge was Able Ruddaway, the bosun, and it was obvious that he too had been drinking. The crew member's head was lolling to one side, his eyes were strangely glazed and his usually neat beard glistened with spilt rum.

'Ahoy there!' Mulligan boomed when he noticed the two mice approaching. 'And how's young Pipple? Making friends by the looks of things.'

Woodget grinned and introduced him to Dimlon.

'Sure, I'm pleased to meet you,' Mulligan declared with a nod.

'You got a leg missing!' Dimlon exclaimed.

Mulligan peered down at his peg-leg and affected a look of horror. 'Keelhaul me if that ain't so!' he bawled. 'To be sure the real one was there a minute ago! Oh Master Dimlon, help me find it! The wilful wretch is always hopping off on its own, so it is.'

Dimlon stared at him incredulously, until the mariner winked back impishly. 'Why, you were a-

83

pullin' *my* leg,' he guffawed. 'Legs don't go off on their own. But you must call me Dimmy, Mister Mulligan – my Aunty Lily does an' everyone else too.'

'It's not a bit surprised I am to hear it,' Mulligan chuckled. 'Well, Dimmy, let me present an old mate of mine to you. This sorry swab is the bosun of this fine ship.' He jabbed Mr Ruddaway in the ribs with his elbow and the mouse jerked his head up, startled.

'All's safe below decks, Captain, sir!' he yelped drunkenly. 'No scum allowed, throw 'em in the brig or overboard, we runs a smart ship on the *Calliope*.'

'Now then,' Mulligan began, turning back to Woodget, 'tell me, how's that chum of yours? Has the sickness passed?'

The fieldmouse shook his head.

'That it hasn't,' he replied. 'Poor Tom is still bad. I was hopin' you could ask the physician for somethin' to help him. I'd have come sooner but I met a rat on the way. He weren't no cringer, more like them what attacked us.'

Mulligan's face changed immediately. Every trace of humour melted and his twinkling eyes dimmed to two flinty points that were both anxious and severe.

'You sure of that now?' he snapped, recorking the flask and laying it by his side.

'As I'm standing here,' the fieldmouse asserted. 'Said you were a-pretendin' to be something you aren't – I didn't like him at all.'

'What did he look like?'

'I . . . I couldn't tell,' Woodget stuttered, taken aback by the unnerving transformation. 'He kept in the shadows . . . but he said his name was Jophet.'

Mulligan repeated the name under his breath but it

was clear that it meant nothing to him. Turning from Woodget, he lifted his stick and pointed it accusingly at Dimlon.

'Did you see this rogue?' he barked. 'What of his tail? Did you notice any disfigurement?'

The pale grey mouse shook his head, shaken by the severity of the question. 'I didn't see him, no!' he said hastily. 'Nor his flyflickermuddragger-scabwiggler. All I saw was the magicwitchyspell-throwertoadymaker, but he made a crash and a bang and was gone.'

'He means the magician,' Woodget explained, seeing Mulligan's confusion.

'A magician?' the Irish mouse breathed gravely. 'Tell me of him.'

'Well, we didn't see much of him either,' Woodget explained. 'All swaddled up in a cloak he was, with a big hood an' all.'

'Then it could well be,' Mulligan whispered to himself. 'Either of those two sound right, unless they're working together of course.'

Shifting around, he shook the bosun by the shoulders and the bearded mouse spluttered indignantly.

'Able!' Mulligan demanded. 'Do you remember what happened after I came aboard with my two young mates – did ought else follow us? How many other passengers joined before the ship left harbour?'

Mr Ruddaway rubbed his eyes and peered hard at his old friend as he struggled to remember.

'Yes . . .' he said eventually, 'there were some later than you, can't remember how many . . . but let me see . . . was it one or two? Might have been five – busy night that was. No, hang on . . . no, I can't recall who they were. That medicine of yours is a real brain-wiper.'

Mulligan grasped him tighter than ever. 'Your book!' he demanded. 'You'll have entered all their names in there. Where is it?'

The bosun groped at his belt where he normally stowed the well-thumbed notebook, then gave a silly titter. 'I left it in my quarters up on deck,' he laughed.

'I have to know!' the Irish mouse insisted forcefully. 'Get on your feet, you stupid oaf! We'll both go see!'

Woodget was alarmed and almost afraid by Mulligan's behaviour and he recalled the panic he had first heard in his voice upon the quayside. Perhaps there was some truth in what the unseen Jophet had told him after all, and this unwelcome thought sent a shiver down the fieldmouse's tail.

Around them the other passengers stared at the scene with distaste on their haughty faces. In spite of the fact that they considered Mulligan coarse and vulgar and that he ought not to be permitted to remain with them, they were all listening with interest to what was said.

'No, no,' the bosun blurted, 'you stay here and see to your company, I'll go fetch my register and bring it down. Though by rights you oughtn't to clap eyes on it, old mate, crew use only – but just this once, eh? Can't do no harm. If you don't tell the skipper then I won't.'

Staggering to his unsteady feet, the bosun saluted them with his sword, then tottered down the steps and out of sight.

An awkward silence followed his departure, broken only by the disapproving tuts of the disdainful onlookers.

Woodget felt uncomfortable and Dimlon looked scared. Mulligan's face was terrible to see; a tempest of emotions was ravaging his features and his paws reached for his pack which he dragged from under his stump and clutched tightly to his chest as though he expected it to be torn from him.

'I . . . I better go see how Tom's gettin' on then,' Woodget mumbled as he watched him. 'Happen that physician wouldn't be no use nohow. See you later, Mister Mulligan.'

No reply came and Woodget beckoned Dimlon to follow him as he picked his way between the sniffing, snooty spectators.

Alone with his bag, Mulligan stared into space, ignoring the pert mutterings that rustled about him. From the beginning he had known that his was a dangerous road, beset by perils. But unexpected hazards had waylaid his quest far too early. The trust the council had put in him was proving to be unfounded and his spirits ebbed to their lowest point thus far.

Lowering his gaze, he was suddenly acutely aware of the many curious eyes turned in his direction and he flinched from their unwanted attention. Any of those seemingly innocent passengers could be the one, he thought. Behind their fair masks, what horrors lay hidden? Kindly words poured easily off sharpened tongues. Even the youngest were to be suspected, for his enemies were born into their hellish cause and dedicated to that foulness with their first breath.

Coldly he reflected that even the weakest paw could hold a poisoned knife.

Mulligan trembled and he snapped his eyes tight shut. In his troubled mind he had turned all the merry faces into a mob of snarling fiends with lidless eyes and he felt utterly besieged – helpless and without any hope of aid.

In his heart he knew he could no longer go on alone; he would have to share the terrible burden or be driven insane. What manner of mouse was he becoming, when he was forced to question even the motives of children?

'A poor choice I was,' he murmured. 'Aye, it's well I've done what I have.'

His face settled into an expression of stone, like an image hewn by chisel and hammer from solid rock. In his pack, hidden and wound about with yards of cloth, resided the most fearful secret entrusted to any living creature – and its very presence terrified the mouse to the core of his being. It was a perilous charge, ever it gnawed at him and he yearned to be rid of it. But he had sworn many solemn oaths and vowed to surrender his very life before yielding up the ninth and most precious fragment.

Bowing his head, he prayed that his courage would not falter; though the vile forces of his foe's legions march against him, he begged that he might remain true. The fate of the world was in his keeping and if he stumbled, then endless night would fall.

Able Ruddaway stumbled to the upper deck and reeled backwards as the keen salt air gusted into his lungs. It was already dark but that night no stars glimmered above, for the heavens were hidden by a suffocating expanse of black rolling cloud.

Only the lights of the *Calliope* shone over the open sea and from where he stood, leaning against a rail, the bosun was lit by the bright yellow rays which streamed from the small bridge of the official crew.

For many minutes he stayed there, waiting for his head to clear, listening to the water washing against the ship as it ploughed unnerringly on and, thoughtfully, he groomed the rum from his beard.

It had been pleasant sharing a tot with Mulligan, and to speak of old times. Strange, he reflected, that of late his mind often lingered in the past, treasuring dusty memories with more fondness than the present, or the future that was left to him.

For all of his adult life, Able had been at sea – having left home on the very day he had come of age. Many trials he had been through, but as he stood there, breathing deeply of the sea air and savouring the beloved briny tang which formed upon his tongue, he longed for those youthful, reckless days.

'The world's changing,' he sighed regretfully. 'Who'd have thought I'd end up stuck on a cargo ship ferrying passengers to an' fro? What happened to that early madness? Where has the ocean-haunted youngster gone – that lad enamoured of the shifting tides? Lost forever he is now and there's no reclaiming him; he began to perish the very day you wrote in the first of those accursed logs. When you accepted this post your joy of the deep was ended. How long has it been since you caroused like tonight or gazed down at the waves and set your mind free to watch them and wonder what marvels lay beneath?'

A corner of the bosun's face twitched and he gave a wry smile. 'Wouldn't be doing to tell that scoundrel Mulligan how much I envy him, now would it?' he mused. 'But he's a strange one for all his bluff talk; never says much about where he goes when he's ashore. And the travels he's made in recent months! Like a gull without a roost he's been. Not like him, that isn't. Still, we all got to steer our own course.'

Able shuddered, for the night was chill, and he moved away from the rail, briskly rubbing his goose-pimpling arms with his paws.

'Better get that passenger list for the rogue,' he said, striding a little more surely now that the rum-induced haze about his brain was lifting.

Over the deserted deck he went, crossing to the bow where he entered the livid green glow radiating from the starboard lantern, and ducked beneath a low wooden shelf.

Under this, great coils of rope were stored alongside huge rolls of coarse tarpaulin, and the bosun deftly hurried past them to where a triangular hole lay open in the timbers.

In a trice he disappeared within – down to a well-ordered though humble space which served as his quarters.

Once inside, Mr Ruddaway fumbled in the darkness, reaching out for the tinder box he always left just below the entrance. When he found it a spark crackled and flared and the ember of a candlewick kindled into flame.

The modest room contained everything that he owned and that was not much, for a wanderer such as he had been put down few roots and needed little in the way of belongings.

Most of the small space was filled by a hammock that was stretched clean across two opposing corners. Upon the walls such meagre mementoes that he did possess were regimently displayed; two pictures, one of his mother, the other of his father, hung side by side as souvenirs from his former, landlubbing youth. Under them, a tobacco pouch was suspended by a silken cord and finally, on the adjoining wall, there was an oilskin coat and hat.

Beneath the hammock and classified into ascending years was a prodigious row of books. Every passenger that had ever journeyed or even boarded the *Calliope* during Mr Ruddaway's time was entered in their correct and balanced pages and it comforted him at times to peruse some of the older volumes and remember those early voyages. Most of the faces that leapt from those yellowing pages were no longer to be seen roaming the wide world. Many had been regular travellers but now only a few die-hard rovers were left. Mulligan was one and, remembering his request, the bosun took up the most recent notebook and turned the pages.

'Mulligan, Mulligan,' he muttered, searching the final entries. 'Ah, *Mulligan and two comrades boarded, being a Master Woodget Pipple and Master Thomas Stubbs.*'

Holding the book a little closer to the candle flame he peered at the names entered beneath and fingered his beard.

'There *were* three more then,' he mused. 'Seems he was nosing the right scent for a change – though that last one's a surprise! How could I have forgotten him?

91

Well, let's hope this'll ease the old rogue's mind when he sees it.'

Tucking the book into his belt, he snuffed out the light and clambered through the opening once more.

Upon the deck, bathed in the green glow of the lantern, someone was waiting for him. Two eyes watched the bosun's burly form emerge from the shadows and a low hiss issued into the cold sea breeze.

Leaving the low shelf behind, Mr Ruddaway straightened then, with a jolt, saw that he was not alone.

'Hoy!' he said sternly. 'You shouldn't be up here. Early evening and at dawn – that's when passengers are allowed on deck – no other times.'

The eyes that watched him narrowed and a soft, sibilant whisper flowed from tight lips.

'I was seeking you,' it said.

'Aye, well you've found me now,' the bosun said. 'You can go back down and speak to me there if you must.'

'Verily I shall return to that place,' came the answering hiss, 'yet those words I must share with you now, there cannot be any delaying of them.'

Mr Ruddaway stared at the glowing green figure and tapped the notebook with his paw.

'Just been reminded when you joined us,' he said, but his voice faltered when he looked on that face whose fur was shining like sun-drenched grass. Was it an illusion caused by the lurid light or were those eyes truly changing? Golden they appeared now and their pupils shrivelled into dark slits.

'Your . . . your eyes,' Able stammered, 'you . . . you look . . . unwell . . .'

'I am indeed most hale,' the figure replied, 'more so now, for my task is drawing to its conclusion.'

The bosun shivered, for the voice had become dreadful to hear and his paw strayed to the hilt of his sword.

Before him, the sinister shape gave a flick of its tail and Mr Ruddaway choked back a cry when he beheld the hideous sight before his eyes.

'Green save us!' he gasped. 'Then it's true – the stories from the East.'

'Assuredly so,' the watcher laughed hollowly. 'The Scale do exist, but too late have you learned the truth, woebegotten and forsaken mariner. That knowledge shall die with you.'

With that the creature leaped forward and upon his claws two golden blades glittered like slivers of emerald in the ghastly light.

Mr Ruddaway drew out his sword and sprang back, slicing at the air and hacking wildly. Expertly, his attacker dodged aside and whipped smartly around – the gleaming razors raking twin lines across the bosun's cheek.

The mouse howled with pain and the blood streamed into his beard but he parried the next blow and with a fierce shove pushed his assailant back.

Snarling, the figure fell against the deck rail but his cruel eyes blazed with fury and, with his bared fangs snapping, he lunged a second time.

Valiantly the bosun fought, yet the wounds in his face burned and the blood which now poured from the ribboned flesh was black and frothed – giving off a putrid stink of mouldering decay.

'Why spend your last strength?' the figure mocked him as his golden blades clashed against the sword and the hideous notes of their desperate striking rang over the deck, chiming like the toneless bells of Death.

'Already you have lost!' he crowed. 'Did you not know that our claws are dipped in venom? Can you not feel the dark fires raging in your veins? They are eating you alive, Master Bosun – an agonising torment now awaits you! It would be better for you if I were to dispatch you swiftly!'

Mr Ruddaway balked at these words, for he could feel a blistering heat scorch his cheek and his teeth ground together as every nerve began to scream.

'If I die – then I'll take you with me!' he bawled through the pain.

Only hissing laughter was his reply, for the bosun's strokes were losing their might and the sword no longer flashed with a blur of steel.

Cackling, the enemy drew away from him, waving the golden knives before his face, taunting the dying seamouse and revelling in the racking agony that consumed him.

Able stumbled after him, but a black mist was closing over his eyes and his sword thrusts became ever weaker.

'Much would I enjoy to view your death,' that evil voice needled, as finally Mr Ruddaway's vision faded and he was plunged into a gulf of absolute dark. 'Yet no time have I for that amusing diversion. I must not be missed below.'

The sword fell from the bosun's paw, for now he

was too weak to grasp it and with a wail he fell to his knees.

'HELP!' he yelled. 'HELP!'

But he had thought to cry too late. His voice was thin and strangled by pain – in his throat black blood was boiling and the venom burned down into his rasping lungs.

With a callous leer, his attacker came forward and Mr Ruddaway felt the notebook wrenched from his belt.

'Too soon is it for the peg-leg to suspect me,' the bosun heard above the screeching of his own blood in his ears.

Fiercely, the book was hurled over the side of the ship and was at once lost amid the churning waters far below.

Scornfully, the creature turned back to his victim and a contemptuous sneer split his face.

'Of you there shall be no trace,' he spat and with a high, frightful laugh he hoisted the mouse to his feet and dragged him to the side.

But Mr Ruddaway was too consumed with despair and torment to know what was happening. The vicious black froth had welled around his eyes and was already devouring them.

Shaking with pleasure, the foul creature perched him upon the rail and allowed him to teeter there for a moment.

'To the fish you go,' he sang, 'but to show how merciful the Scale can be, I shall speed your end and draw those cold breathless mouths all the more readily to you.'

Sniggering, he placed the glittering knives at the

bosun's throat and plunged them deep into his bubbling flesh.

With a triumphant shriek, the monster sliced the mouse in two and a steaming fount of poisonous blood gushed into the sea beneath.

Able Ruddaway's torment was over and with a violent shove his killer cast the gored and butchered body out over the side.

Malignantly, the creature stared as the limp corpse tumbled down, plummeting into the lathering waves.

'Yet no fish shall venture near,' the fiend spoke. 'None shall come within a league of him; the bitter juice of the Serpent now claims those fathoms. All hail him, all abase themselves before him – for he will come amongst us once more. The exile is nearly over.'

And so the evil creature left that place and carefully removed the knives from his claws before returning to the hold where his true victim sat and waited in vain for Mr Ruddaway's return.

5

Simoon

'He'll be nursing his head someplace no doubt,' the skipper had said when Mr Ruddaway failed to turn up for his next watch duty. 'Well I'll not be treating him too tender when he finally shows his bilious face. Go rout him out of his quarters and bring him here at the double.'

Captain Gabriel Hewer, a tall, stern-looking mouse with many furrows creasing his forehead, sent the first officer to fetch the errant bosun but even when he returned without him the skipper was not unduly alarmed. There had been several other occasions when Able had not surfaced promptly from whatever hole he had collapsed into after drinking bouts with old friends.

'There's work to be done and I won't have my crew carousing if it affects their duties,' he bawled. 'Get you below and scour every dark corner till you unearth the old sot!'

Yet the search yielded no clue as to the bosun's whereabouts and, when the day crept into the afternoon, the hunt became more serious and the captain was compelled to ask the passengers for their assistance.

Leaving Thomas to suffer with the seasickness alone for a while, Woodget found Dimlon and together they helped in the great endeavour to locate the missing bosun. At first the mouse families who took part did so in an amused fashion, not understanding the grave implications of the mystery and viewing the entire affair as a type of entertainment. Yet when evening came and there was still no sign, their seeking became more frantic and spurred by grim desperation.

Never had the ship been so thoroughly searched; every possible niche was pried and poked into, but eventually after much exhaustive labouring, the disturbing conclusion had to be drawn – Able Ruddaway was no longer on board.

Speculation crackled through the hold like a fever; the troubled imaginations of the passengers invented a hundred different reasons for the bosun's disappearance and each of them was darker and more frightening than the last. Finally the captain was forced to quell the rising panic by declaring his own opinion of what had happened. He had arrived at the regrettable conclusion that whilst in a stupefied state, Able Ruddaway had no doubt stumbled and fallen into the sea. A tragic and ignominious end to a worthy and much respected member of his crew – but to suspect treachery and murder was absurd.

As the captain addressed them with this version of events, Mulligan muttered to himself and knew that the skipper could not be more wrong. He had suspected at once that some wicked cruelty or act of malice had befallen his friend, knowing that the search was in vain and making no attempt to assist in it.

'They can turn the ship upside down and back again,' he mumbled darkly to himself, 'but Able won't never be found – not alive anyway.'

Mulligan's fears doubled, for now he was certain that his enemies had followed him. No doubt the demise of the bosun was to ensure that the identity of those who boarded the *Calliope* after Woodget, Thomas and himself would remain unknown – but there was possibly another reason.

' 'Twas a signal to myself – old Able's death. Sure, the black-souled devil who committed the hellish deed is gloating now. Somewhere here, possibly helping in the hunt himself, he's laughing at me, knowing that I'm aware of what he's done. And I must do nothing, I cannot go to the skipper and open my mind to him, for the fewer who know my business the safer it is. Alas for Able, I ought to have gone with him as first I offered.'

The failure to find the bosun had a marked effect upon the mood of the other travellers. Once the initial shock at his unaccountable loss had faded, a disquieting sense of forboding settled to burden everyone's hearts. The former, expectant atmosphere of those voyaging in the hold curdled and soured into an unpleasant feeling of dread that no song or story could lift.

When the children snuggled into their bunks that

night they went without protest and, although sleep was slow in gathering them into its soft deep pockets, their small plaintive whimperings could be heard throughout the hold.

Here and there, by the corner of a large crate or at the intersection of a narrow way, dismal gatherings of unnerved passengers collected. In subdued voices they murmured their anxieties and whispered their fears. Whatever pleasure the journey once held for them was now crushed beyond recall and many began to doubt the innocence of their all too near neighbours, the rats, in this chilling matter.

But even those unwholesome chewers of slime and gnawers of gristle were ill at ease, for they knew that if any dirty work was suspected then they would be prime candidates for the fingers of doubt and distrust. Tetchily they argued with one another and became sullen and withdrawn, unwilling to talk with their scabby-nosed fellows, preferring instead to watch the comings and goings of the remaining crew and listen for any new developments. Not a sign was seen of Jophet. The owner of the croaking voice in the shadows kept well out of sight, forever dodging the searchers and keeping his own thoughts to himself.

The air in the hold became charged with a bristling tension and when Thomas finally crawled out from his bunk, the discord almost took his breath away.

With his back against one of the barrels, he propped himself up and rubbed life into his stiff, aching legs. He felt as though he had been asleep for a fortnight, but it had been a disturbed slumber and one that brought no rest. During his unpleasant ordeal, Thomas had eaten very little. Woodget had tried to make certain that his friend ate something, but whatever Master Stubbs managed to swallow it did not stay down for very long.

Now his limbs were weak and he patted his shrunken, growling stomach ruefully.

' 'Tis a woeful time, Tom,' Woodget said, emerging from the gap between the barrels behind him. 'You won't know the place now, it's changed so much. Folk are all on edge – I doesn't like it.'

'Even here I can sense the tension,' Thomas murmured. 'Why, it might be an entirely different ship we're on. What did happen to the bosun? Do you think it was an accident?'

Woodget shook his head. 'If the captain says it was then it must've been,' was all he could utter, 'but it's a bad end whichever way. I wouldn't fancy gettin' drowned – an 'orrible finish that is.'

Thomas breathed deeply, but the air was stuffy and stale. 'Wish we could go up on deck,' he muttered. 'I've had enough of this dank place already.'

'We're only allowed up at dawn and dusk,' Woodget told him, 'and then only in small groups for a few measly minutes. Well, we done missed the first go. Let's find Dimmy while we wait for the next and see what we can do in the meantimes. I haven't been up myself yet, what with one thing and another, mind you – poor Dimmy's afraid to try, in case the wind whisks him over the side or a wave washes across and does the same. You'll like him, Tom – he's dafter than me. Kept me company the whole time you was sick he has and popped in to see you once, but you was fast in a doze and we didn't like to wake you.'

The glimmer of a smile appeared on Thomas' face.

'You like this new friend of yours don't you?'

'He makes me laugh,' Woodget nodded, 'and that's not been easy of late.'

'So how's Mulligan? What's he been up to?'

Woodget shrugged but said nothing.

'What's the matter?' Thomas asked.

The fieldmouse twisted his mouth to the side and Thomas recognised that expression as the sign which meant his friend was troubled and thinking deeply.

Patiently he waited until Woodget was ready to answer.

'I haven't seen much of Mister Mulligan,' he said. 'Not since that night when the bosun upped and vanished. Fact, I been avoidin' him. There's summat not right there, Tom. I dunno what it is but I ain't easy no more in his company. He's so edgy and glaring, I doesn't know which way his mood'll swing from one moment to another.

'Not once, to my reckoning at any rate, has he left them cotton bales the whole time he's been aboard. And always he keeps his bag with him – must be precious whatever's in there but I wonders how he came by it. He's not actin' like an honest mouse should. P'raps it's treasure an' jewels. That's what I'm thinking, though Dimmy thought it might be a stash of "choklittybiskitts". Whatever it is I don't want to know, nor have nowt to do with it.'

Thomas grimaced. 'I'll wager it's three more flasks of rum,' he said, 'but if you like we'll steer clear of the cotton bales today. Come on – you can take me to meet this Dimmy.'

With his friend at his side once more, Woodget felt

happier than he had done since leaving the harbour and chattered freely of the characters he and Dimlon had met in the past few days.

Thomas listened in mild amusement and was glad that Woodget had found such a good friend so quickly, although at times he did suffer the slightest twinges of jealousy whilst hearing of their rambling explorations of the ship and wished that he had been there.

'There's still a mighty pile of stuff we haven't seen yet,' the fieldmouse added hastily, perceiving his friend's feelings. 'There's a travelling magician on board – a sort of wizard who can look into the future from what I heard him say. We'll have to go find him, he might do a trick or two fer us if we're lucky. Looked a real tail tingler he did – bet he could make your whiskers pop out if'n he really tried.'

'I wonder if anyone's tried asking him if he knows what happened to that bosun,' Thomas said gravely. 'Surely if he's as good as you think he is he must have some idea.'

Through the alleys they went, passing beneath the nest of the dormice, but that morning no inquisitive, timid heads appeared – yet still the nest trembled.

Out to the main thoroughfare their steps took them and again Thomas was astonished to view the change that had stricken the other passengers.

The families were huddled in groups, and the eyes that turned to him were no longer friendly but seemed to fix upon him with suspicion. When he and Woodget drew near, the infants who were mournfully playing in the sawdust were briskly pulled away and scolded for venturing in the paths of strangers.

'No telling who they are,' they overheard the terse tones of one mother's reprimand.

Turning to stare at her, Thomas was dismayed to see that the poor mousewife was shaking and she wrapped her protective arms tight about her children – kissing them anxiously.

'They're all terrified,' he said to Woodget.

'Take a long while for these folk to settle again,' the fieldmouse replied. 'They got doubts a-nagging at them. There's not much cheer roundabouts.'

In silence they pressed on, and Woodget quickened his pace when they came near to the cotton bales, slowing only when they were left far behind.

'This is where Dimmy lives,' he chirped when they finally reached a dingy, neglected corner at the rear of the hold where heaps of wool sacks rose to form a ragged and shadowy mass. Situated this close to the ship's engines, a rhythmic pulse throbbed through the air like the beating of an enormous heart.

Woodget never liked this place, for the vibrations thrummed through the floor and jarred his bones.

'I always think it's as if I've been gobbled down by a great big horror made of iron and driven by clawed wheels and spinning cogs,' he said, 'and here we are in its ginormous metal belly. I doesn't know how Dimmy can bear it here but he says it's comfortin' – I told 'ee he were daft.'

Thomas looked long at the undulating landscape of mounds which rose to the right of them. The wool sacks were not stowed as neatly or as securely as the cotton bales, nor any other of the cargo, and he guessed that they were probably not as valuable. Like great rounded hills they reared and rolled, stuffed between a towering precipice of wood on one side and the bulkhead on the other.

'If it wasn't for that racket it'd be very cosy here,' he observed. 'Maybe you could get used to the noise. Least it's nice and private, hardly anyone bunked on there at all.'

Scattered in the gentle valleys and hollow dales, he saw that only a few mice and shrews had managed to endure the ceaseless chugging of the engines, but they were rough-looking characters whose mangy and travel-weary aspect suggested that they had slept in far worse places than this.

'It pongs here too,' Woodget added, wrinkling his nose.

Thomas sniffed but could smell nothing, then he moved a little closer and quickly backed away.

A bitter reek had assaulted his nose, a stink that flowed out from the unwashed and oily wool, and as he stared more keenly at the scant, dishevelled residents he saw that they were constantly twitching and scratching themselves as though a million ants were marching through their fur.

'There's fleas in the wool,' Thomas muttered, his skin already beginning to creep and itch. 'How can your friend camp over there? What possessed him? That's not just being daft, it's downright barmy!'

At the sound of this incredulous voice, a large-eared head popped up from a shadow-filled vale and there came a delighted shout.

'Ho there!' cried the voice of Dimlon. 'Hello Woody! What we a-doin' today then?'

Clumsily, the pale grey mouse sped down the spongy sacking slopes with his arms out wide, his

satchel slung over one shoulder and a stupid grin
fixed firmly in place.

'And your friend Tommy is all better!' he trilled,
gazing at Thomas with excitement. 'I saw you when
you was asleep, friend Tom – real happy I am to see
you on your legs this merry morning.'

Thomas returned the greeting, but kept a close
watch on him to see how often he scratched, but not
once did Dimlon so much as fidget. Perhaps his blood
isn't to the fleas' liking, Thomas thought to himself.

Before setting off to visit Simoon the prophet,
Woodget shared the last of the rations he had brought
with him from the Spring Celebrations of Betony
Bank and Thomas scoffed them hungrily. Presently
all three mice were talking as if they had known
each other all their lives. Ignoring the bleak and
despondent atmosphere that hung heavily over
the hold, or perhaps obstinately challenging it, they
laughed at the slightest joke and once they were away
from that dismal wool sack hillscape, Thomas found
Dimlon's absurd notions were enough to make him
forget even the lingering queasiness of his seasickness.

Chewing on a dry crust fished from his satchel,
and with crumbs falling from his lips, Dimlon gabbled
on about his beloved Aunty Lily and the other
inhabitants of his small village.

'Down by where the stream goes a
babblin'wetan'splashy,' he spluttered with a spray
of bread, 'there's the stuck-up Old Widow Froot
with her two strapping daughters Maudy and Floss.
Them's got the biggest feet and the meanest heads of
anyone I knows. It was them who chased me down
the blackberry lane and threw me in the goosegog

bushes. I were scared half to death when they ran after me a-whoopin' and a-callin'. Right nasty them girls can be. Bashed me good an' proper they have loads of times, fatlipthickearkicked-shinsmackedbehindsmartin' awfulredcheeks I've had from them. Still, my Aunty Lily always makes me feel better. When I'm a-snivelling she won't have none of it. "Stop that snotty-nosed moping, you shiftless juggins!" she shouts to snap me out of it before giving me a little job to keep my mind off of them 'orrid pair and keep me happy.'

'Those girls sound like Woodget's sister,' laughed Thomas. 'Cudweed was frightening too.'

Woodget had to agree, but the thought of his family distressed him. His departure must have been a terrible shock to them and he heaved a regretful sigh.

Thomas could have kicked himself for mentioning it, and he desperately tried to change the subject.

'I think it's time we called on this magician of yours,' he said briskly.

'Simoon!' Dimlon exclaimed. 'Oh yes, we was waiting till you were well again, Tom. Woody thinks we should govisitseekhimout but I ain't sure. Real eyepoppin'starrycrackler he looked.'

Looking at the fieldmouse, Thomas tried to draw him from his forlorn thoughts. 'I've missed everything else you two have done,' he said. 'I'll not flinch from this. Let's see if that wizard can shed any light on the mystery of the missing crew member. Who knows what he might have to say?'

'I've a feelin' that there'll be only darkness if any shedding's to be done,' Dimlon murmured softly. 'I doesn't think there'll ever be no light at all.'

With that they ventured from the central road and passed into the twilight, twisting realm of shadow that ran between the cargo – and were soon hopelessly lost.

Down a labyrinth of narrow alley-ways and ravines, beyond the populated areas of the ship – away from the snug berths and comfortable bunks, where the crates butted against the hull – Simoon the prophet had fashioned suitable quarters for himself.

Across the cramped space, two poles were wedged into the towering wooden sides at varying angles and over them was draped a length of red cloth, faded in parts by bleaching desert suns to a soft peach. Outside this primitive, variegated tent, six tiny brass lanterns were suspended from wires that spanned the alley. The shapes of moons, stars and suns had been cut into their sides, so that their glowing images were thrown upon the walls and formed a tunnel of glimmering, golden light, whose mystical patterns flickered and danced at the slightest pitch or yaw of the ship.

A highly perfumed, cloying scent hung in the air and from the tent's gloomy entrance, a faint thread of blue smoke was curling. Yet it did not rise up to the invisible ceiling of the hold, like the heats that climbed from the small fires of the other passengers. Instead, this misty strand wound slowly from the canopy with an almost purposeful stealth and crept down the alley-way, its foggy fingers catching the lantern rays as it snaked to and fro – reaching ever further along the passage.

Carefully it steered itself this way and that, never wavering nor taking an incorrect route. Out it journeyed, to find the senses of those it sought and to lead them back – to where Simoon was waiting, like a spider in a fog-woven web.

With their hearts in their mouths, and clutching hold of one another, Thomas, Woodget and Dimlon crept forward. They had spent nearly an hour roaming the empty, meandering pathways of the hold and had begun to doubt if they would ever find their way out again. But finally they had chanced upon the peculiar incense and excitedly followed its trail.

Around a blind corner they stumbled – and immediately the three friends froze as they beheld the glorious sight which shimmered eerily before them.

The tunnel appeared to be made of fiery starlight and the magical symbols were mirrored in Woodget's wide, marvelling eyes as he groped for something to say.

'Oh my!' was all he could manage to utter.

At his side, Thomas grinned, captivated by the beauty that stretched ahead, and was glad that the others had not ventured here before without him. This was a delight to be shared together and he peered through the golden haze of shifting symbols at the shelter beyond.

Behind his new friends, for it was too narrow for three to walk abreast, Dimlon peered over the top of the fieldmouse's head, his long neck swaying from side to side as he gawped idiotically at the wondrous lamps.

'Fairygrottopiskydelving,' he murmured in a half-frightened whisper.

'Come on,' Thomas urged. 'Let's go a bit further.'

Woodget nodded breathlessly but Dimlon was not certain.

'Don't disturb him in there,' he whined, squinting doubtfully at the faded canopy and dithering so much that his ears shivered and shook. 'He mightn't like us a-trampin' up to his door. There ain't no knowing what he might do. I don't want to have to eat bluebottles all day and sit by gnat-buzzin', damp ponds for the rest of my unnatural.'

Thomas smiled at him. 'All right,' he said kindly, seeing how afraid Dimlon was. 'We won't disturb him what lives in that there tent. But I'd like to get a little bit closer, just to peek at what's inside it. I'd like to know what he's burning to give off that flowery smell at any rate.'

Dimlon stuffed his fingers into his mouth in fright as Thomas moved away, nearer to the glimmering tunnel.

'You are scared,' Woodget whispered. 'Poor Dimmy! Why don't you go back – we'll catch you up in a little while.'

'What?' Dimlon asked. 'Me go down them darksome alleys on my own! I can't do that – I'd be real lost and wobblefrittedjellyjumpy then.'

By now, Thomas had moved close to where the first lantern swung gently overhead. A field of burning, softly focused stars trembled upon the floor by his feet and fanned out, up over the narrow way's walls.

Thomas wondered what it would be like to be covered in the light of those lanterns, to have the symbols of heaven play over his fur and shine into his eyes. Gingerly, he raised a paw and reached into the glimmering beams.

'Will you dawdle out there all day?' called a sudden, deep voice.

Thomas leapt back and Dimlon let out a woeful shriek. The voice had come from inside the tent and he clutched at Woodget's paw in terror.

'He knows we're here!' he yammered. 'Let's go – let's go!'

With that, the pale grey mouse turned tail and scampered back around the corner, his present fear of the alarming voice driving out his horror of venturing down those dim, twisting alley-ways alone.

'Dimmy!' Woodget shouted. 'Wait!'

But it was too late; Dimlon would not return and the fieldmouse knew he should go after him.

'Woodget Pipple!' commanded the strange voice. 'Let the fool go. I desire no speech with him.'

Woodget stared across at Thomas. 'He . . . he knows my name,' he muttered.

'Both of you are known unto me,' the resonant voice interrupted. 'Long have I awaited this moment. Come, join me.'

The two mice hesitated for a moment then Thomas stepped into the glimmering tunnel and, not wanting to be left on his own, Woodget followed.

Over the fieldmouse's russet fur, the golden lights sparkled and flashed but as he looked nervously about him, his gaze was eventually drawn to the tent as ever-nearer it loomed, with every cautious step.

When the shining stars were behind them, their radiance and splendour now playing only over the backs of their ears and the tips of their tails, the expectant mice eyed the dusky canopy uncertainly.

A small gap at the front of the shelter where two seams could be laced together was hanging open and from its dark depths the thread of incense still streamed. But however much they strained their eyes to see what lay beyond that flimsy threshold neither Thomas or Woodget could tell, for all was dark and hidden.

'Do not loiter like beggars at the door,' they were commanded. 'I bid you enter.'

Thomas moved forward but Woodget caught his arm and shook his head fearfully.

A faint, almost pitying laugh floated out, mingling with the curling smoke.

'Does the dark so inspire you with dread, Master Pipple?' the gloom asked. 'The time of such illusionary fancies is past. There are terrors real enough to fear in this world. But I forget, you are ignorant of them – not all folk enjoy the company and solitude which the darkness may house. Allow me to illuminate my home if it will put you at your ease.'

Within the tent a flame spluttered into life and in an instant a lamp was lighted.

'There now,' the occupant stated. 'May you find this more to your liking. For myself I prefer the cloaking night and the many mysteries it conceals from the harsh glare of day. Now, enter – I insist.'

A warm glow emanated from the faded shelter's entrance and Thomas stole forward.

Beyond the unlaced opening, the floor was covered by many soft and amply padded cushions. Richly embroidered fabrics festooned the bare wooden crates on either side and ponderous, brocaded tassles of the most sumptuous purples dripped luxuriantly from above. A black and silver spiralled staff was propped against one exotic, tapestry-adorned wall and at its foot were three large bags, filled and overflowing to give tantalising glimpses of bizarre instruments to view the stars, glass bottles of all shapes and sizes, pouches stuffed with powders for potions and leather-bound books crammed with secret lore.

Upon a low block of wood a lantern that was studded with pieces of coloured glass gleamed and winked, dappling everything in rainbow hues. At its side, within a metal bowl, a cone of incense was burning and, although its scented fumes filled all of the canopy, in one corner they were gathered more thickly and had collected into a dense pall of obscuring blue smoke.

Staring at this ever-moving, writhing cloud, Thomas thought he could just discern a squat figure in its choking depths and he fidgeted with his neckerchief, not knowing what to do.

Like some phantom sentinel, wreathed about by an ethereal mist and conjured from the elemental haunted, mountain regions of the air, the dim, indistinct shape appeared – but for the moment it remained motionless.

With his eyes trying to pierce the enshrouding fogs, Thomas felt sure that whatever lurked in there was able to see him quite clearly and the fur on his neck prickled at the thought of such intense scrutiny from so mysterious a source.

Only when Woodget had entered and was standing at his friend's side did the wraith-like form stir. Remembering his manners, the fieldmouse swiftly pulled the woollen hat from his head and clasped it before him – the tent might be the abode of a wizard or magician but he was still visiting and knew what was and wasn't polite.

'How their hearts are thumping,' that same ringing voice came to them from the centre of the turgid smoke. 'What harm have I done them – or what rumour of harm do they fear it is my nature to perform?'

There was a silence, broken only by a loud self-conscious swallow from Woodget.

Again the laughter flowed out to them and the blurred figure raised what Thomas assumed were its arms.

'Forgive this fug and vapour,' it said. 'I find the profound fumes sharpen and hone the blades of my thought, though maybe it is not to your liking.'

Neither mouse said anything but the nebulous creature clapped its paws together and to their amazement the smoke began to lift.

Like a crashing wave, the mists fell away, dissipating from the shadowy corner and scudding out through the entrance, swirling around Thomas' and Woodget's legs until only a single filament of smoke remained rising from the burner.

With his long legs crossed but still just as enigmatically swaddled in a robe of ruby velvet and his face hidden by a great, silken fringed hood – was Simoon. Rings of silver and gold adorned his mitten-clothed fingers and bangles set with semi-precious stones jangled over his wrists as he raised his paw in greeting.

'You are most welcome, my guests,' the prophet said. 'Nay, do not stand. Pray sit before me.'

Woodget glanced apprehensively at Thomas, but the other mouse was mesmerised by this uncanny personage and obeyed at once, plopping himself smartly down.

Timidly, the fieldmouse did the same and within the dark recess of the hood two points of light glinted.

'At last you have sought me out,' Simoon said. 'Yet still I sense that you are troubled by doubt and distrust. Maybe if I were to cast back my cowl and you could look on my face, your misgivings would be calmed.'

The two mittened paws rose up and at once the tent was filled with the clinking of his bracelets. The long sleeves of the velvet robe fell down about his elbows and the two mice caught a glimpse of pale, sandy-coloured fur.

In anxious anticipation, they watched Simoon take hold of the fringed hood and in a slow, careful movement he pushed it back over his head.

Thomas blinked and Woodget rubbed his eyes. Neither of them had seen a face like the one that was suddenly revealed and the prophet smiled to see their bewildered expressions.

His head was small and covered in the same sandy fur as his puny arms, but the first feature which struck them about Simoon was the creature's eyes. Never had they seen any so large or dark. Like orbs of polished black glass they were, and each glittered like a lens that was trained heavenward and filled with all the wintry burning of those penetrating, celestial fires. Knowledge and wisdom founded upon long years of studious learning shone from those deep wells of night. They were at once both comforting and unsettling, having the power to either kindle hope or instil despair at the core of any they wished and, as he gazed into them, Woodget found that his fears subsided.

Above the sparkling eyes, the brows of Simoon were hoary white and spiked far over his wrinkled nose like a thicket of frost-covered briar. Great age and weariness rested upon them, yet both mice felt that the care and grief which marked that face could melt in an instant and the vigour of youth could again be his to wield if he so wished it.

Below the slightly pointed nose, a small mouth was still curled into a smile and upon the chin bristled a great many more white, wiry whiskers.

'What . . . who are you?' Woodget managed to utter when the glance of those eyes had thawed most of his trepidations.

Simoon clasped his paws together and the brambling eyebrows twitched upwards.

'My common name you already know,' he said. 'But that which I was first called in the great desert long ago I tell to none. Simoon will serve for now and I am content – for it is also the term my people give to the hot dry wind which rages over the dunes, like the fury of angry jinns. Yes, Simoon will do.'

The smile widened to a grin and the eyes shone brighter than ever.

'As to what manner of creature I am, I do not doubt you have never seen the like of me before. A jerboa am I – hopper of the parched baking wastes, burrower of the dry shifting hills – he who shuns the fiery day. But not for an age or more have I journeyed in the burning heats of my own land. My paths have led me elsewhere, to places cold and chill. Often have I walked in your green land and how my bones ache from the damp that creeps up my tail. That is why I clothe myself in vestments heavy and swaddling, and why I huddle in the darkness of smoke-filled corners.'

He paused and untwined his fingers, reaching out with his paw to point at each of his guests in turn.

'But you did not come here to learn of my histories,' he told them. 'For one reason only do the curious venture into the tent of Simoon. You have come to ask that which only I can know. Of he who is no longer aboard this vessel I can tell you little, save that his part in this world has ended. But that is not the only reason for your coming. Do not deny it. Did you not come hither to learn also what I can see of your futures? Is this not the truth?'

Thomas leaned forward. 'Can you really do that?' he breathed uncertainly. 'Do you know if I'll ever be a captain?'

'Tom!' Woodget hushed. 'We ain't got no coins.'

'The price is not always set on silver alone,' Simoon answered. 'For the wisdom I now impart, the reckoning will be accounted later. Do you still wish for foreknowledge, Master Stubbs?'

Thomas glanced at Woodget's concerned face then nodded quickly.

'Couldn't you just tell us a tale or two?' Woodget interrupted as the jerboa began searching inside one of the bags.

Thomas pouted but Simoon eyed the fieldmouse shrewdly.

'And which of the hundred score narratives that are locked within my tongue would you have me recount?' he asked. 'Many fables and legends have I heard and countless dark and deadly histories. Which of those would sound sweet to your large ears, Master Barleyclimber?'

Woodget shrugged his shoulders. 'I'm willin' to listen to anything I ain't heard afore.'

The prophet turned to stare at the incense burner and his eyes became fixed upon the constantly winding smoke.

'Of stories great and horrible I have great store,' he uttered, his voice dropping to a bewitching whisper. 'Of the great war between the messengers of the moon and the treefolk of the wood I know much. Grievous was the sorrow of that dark time, when the young Ysabelle gained the throne through misery and despair. Many grim tales stem from your green lands and still deeds both noble and evil shall yet unfold there.'

'Don't tell us something from our country,' Woodget broke in. 'I'll be heading back there soon enough. What I want to hear is something strange about places I'll never see – of foreign shores and distant lands.'

'Yes,' agreed Thomas. 'What about a yarn from out of the East? I've always wanted to travel there.'

' "From out of the East?" ' Simoon repeated and his low voice grew cold and solemn. 'In that region there are many legends, yet mightiest and most terrible of all concerns that which is not a matter of idle talk and though it stretches far back to the youth of the world, its horror does not have its roots in myth nor fancy.'

Thomas beamed and he shivered with pleasure. He loved scary stories. 'Please,' he encouraged, 'can't you tell us a bit of it?'

The jerboa stared more intently at the smoke and Woodget blinked, for the ravelling wisps took shape in the air until the ghostly outline of a rearing serpent hung above their heads.

Simoon made a peculiar sign with his paws and the shape dwindled until they saw only a strand of blue smoke again.

'Now shall I speak of Suruth Scarophion,' he muttered and at the mention of that name he closed his eyes and Thomas thought the blood drained from the prophet's lips.

'He whom others call Gorscarrigern,' he continued. 'The Coiled One. Sarpedon, others cursed him – the Dark Despoiler. All titles are just, yet none do justice.'

The expression faded from the jerboa's face and his murmuring voice was barely audible above the soft sizzling of the incense and the faint, muffled sound of the waves sluicing around the outside of the ship.

'Long, long ago when the mountains were but hills and the ungirdled oceans were pools and meres, a vast darkness lay over eastern lands. Whilst on western shores the foundations of the three thrones were still part of the living rock and the Raith Sidhe had not grown to an eighth of their later strength, in the East a foulness reigned.

'Words describe him not, nor laments bewail his cruelty. But a devil he was, spawned in the freezing dark beyond the beginning of all things and clad in the form of a serpent, the like of which had never been equalled and with the Green's grace never shall.

'The length of many leagues was his full measure and high over the tops of giant trees he towered. Black were the scales that shielded him and their strength was that of iron. Whole jungles could his venomous bile wither and kill and none could withstand him. A power as old as the earth and strong as its bones was in him and for many ages he reigned with horror and without mercy.

'Storm clouds made up his crown and those whom he had poisoned into his service with the terror of his being, worshipped him as their god. Death and despair were their creed and ever were they at war. Mightier than ever did Scarophion become, his hellish eyes revelling in the torment that ravaged the lands. Unmatched was his peerless tyranny and far did his empire reach.

'Devoted to him were his followers, but their loyalty was born of madness. All instructions they obeyed, questioning never, though it might be to cast themselves from great heights, plunge into murderous rapids or shrivel in perishing flame. Further his cruel dominion spread, his savage priests gathering more into his dark service.

'Only the newborn did they accept into the black following. The parents of those tender offspring were viciously put to death, then the evil tutelage and odious instruction began at once. So were the innocents taken to the loathsome temples and upon bloodstained altars were they committed to that most infernal of fiends.'

Simoon paused and he dragged his eyes from the smoke. 'Know now the signs of The Scale,' he told the two mice. 'For when a newborn is taken into the dark fold, its tail is butchered, slit and hewn into a mockery of their monstrous lord's forked tongue. Beware any so mutilated – shun them and fear them.

'Only an adept, or one of higher rank, may cleave the halves of its tail together to pass unmarked

121

amongst his enemies. If so then look to him whilst he sleeps, for only in waking can this deceit be accomplished and in slumber it returns to its cleft state. That is but one of their counterfeits; others there are and evil are the arts practised by the High Priests, but I shall not sully the day by naming them here.'

Thomas stared at him in surprise. 'But you said this was long ago,' he declared, disturbed by the vehemence of the jerboa's warning and the apparent fear in his voice.

Simoon gaped at him, then turned back to the trailing incense. 'And so it was,' he breathed. 'In the dim, deep, bygone past. Forgive me, the teller oft gets embroiled within his own tale. I was forgetting.'

'What happened to the serpent god?' Woodget asked. 'Was he overthrown?'

'He was indeed,' the jerboa replied, 'for the history of the world would not have unfolded as it has done. Yet the Dark Despoiler was not beaten without cost.

'The shadow of Scarophion stretched far and wide. Much had he conquered and laid waste, yet still he lusted for more. Then did the forces of his enemies band together and a host of diverse creatures was gathered to do battle. But in brute force alone there was little hope. Yet there were at that time many wise folk: those who studied the wheeling stars, dabblers in mystic rites and some who could summon the powers of the Green and turn it to their own purpose.

'Through many years of blood and pain did the wars drag them and uncounted thousands were slain on either side. Yet at the last, by the combined arts of those cunning folk, Suruth Scarophion was finally assailed upon the very steps of his greatest temple.

'Long the two opposing forces grappled. Spell upon spell, might against might. Enchantment crashed into devilry and all around the ground quaked, ripping open huge pits which boiled with liquid flame. The pillars of the temple trembled and into his shrine the black horror fled.

'Fiercely did those sorcerers pursue him and their waxing powers crumbled the gore-daubed walls, throwing them down, and the roof that was scorched by sacrificial fires was torn asunder. Then did Scarophion's strength break, and the forces of good prevailed. Under their final enchantment the Dark Despoiler fell and his mortal form was vanquished.

'But even as he expired, his writhing body consumed by the passage of his demonic spirit, the tyrant belched forth his black blood and the Green host was sprayed with its venom. So too did the wisest leave this world, yet they had achieved great glory and the land was made clean once more.'

Simoon's voice trailed off into brooding silence but before him the smoke twisted into a large oval shape and the jerboa scattered it with his paws as though it frightened him.

'That were a tale and a half,' Woodget crooned, dreamily hugging his knees.

The prophet shook himself and stared at them as if he had forgotten they were there.

'Ancient myths have no place in this present age,' he said drawing the folds of his robe close about him as though it had grown chill. 'Let us not stir the ashes and brittle bones of the long-cold dead. Our fealty lies with tomorrow, not a thousand and more yesterdays. Is there aught else you would ask of me?'

'I really would like to know what my future has in store,' Thomas ventured. 'If you don't mind, that is.'

Simoon said nothing but pulled one of the embroidered lengths of fabric from the wall and spread it over the cushions between them. Then he put his tiny paw into his robe and took from a hidden pocket a pack of colourfully illustrated cards which he held out for Thomas to touch.

'Now shall your fate be revealed,' he intoned, placing five of them face upwards on the cloth.

Thomas stared at the weird pictures arranged before him. Upon the first there was the image of a fair face but it was painted green and Simoon furrowed his branching brows.

'A maiden has driven you hither,' he said, 'or rather your envious coveting of her. You have commenced your journey poorly, Master Stubbs, may you end it better.'

Thomas shifted uncomfortably and wondered if Woodget was looking at him. He was too ashamed to raise his eyes and find out.

Simoon moved his gaze to the second card. It was an alarming drawing of a glaring mask with flaming eyes.

'Danger is close to you,' he said in a hoarse whisper. 'Your way is littered with peril, but treachery will always be the main hazard – this is its face, already it is watching. Take care not to fall under its sway, never take up that slippery mask yourself, deny the hold it will endeavour to clamp upon you and make it not welcome in your heart.'

Thomas frowned. He didn't like the sound of it so far, but the third card showed an illustration of the sun and he hoped that would signify something cheerier.

'A charmed life is yours,' Simoon grunted, but when he studied the fourth picture he shook his head gravely.

'Here is the sign of the rolling waters, yet see how they are tormented by storm and tempest. When this card follows that of the sun then it is not well. Fortune may indeed be shining upon you, Master Stubbs, yet so bright does her glory gleam that those about you are lost in shadow and she is blind to them. Though you may survive great peril it does not mean your companions shall. Almost, the charm that you bask in is the very beacon which guides them to disaster.'

There was only one card left. It depicted a broken anchor and Simoon took several minutes pondering its meaning in conjunction with the others before he spoke again.

'Your life is with the sea,' he said at length, 'but no joy shall you find in it. Yet not unnumbered will your sailing days be. A time will come when you shall return and settle upon the land, although always will your heart and mind be burdened – a great weight shall ever drag you down.'

Thomas gazed at the cards uneasily, then tried to shrug off the prophet's forbidding words. 'Had me going for a little while you did!' he said.

The large, black eyes of the jerboa gleamed at him, then the lids closed over them and the mittened paws collected up the cards. Simoon breathed deeply and the thread of smoke which rose from the incense burner was drawn towards him.

'And what of you fieldmouse?' he asked. 'Do you

desire to lift the veil and spy upon your destiny?'

Woodget shuddered. He hadn't liked any part of what the mysterious character had told Thomas and he shook his head firmly.

'That I don't!' he cried. 'I'd stick my head in a rabbit hole and not come up again if'n what you said was half as gloomy as what's ahead of poor old Tom.'

The jerboa smiled faintly. 'You are wise, Master Pipple,' he said, 'for only fools attempt to see what lies beyond their noses.'

Thomas scowled at this and decided that it was time they left, but Simoon was not finished with them.

'No more foretelling shall there be,' he said. 'That grey country of what is to come should perhaps be left in the realm of the vast unknown. But this much only I would counsel you to know – in every life there is a ruling influence. Choose now one card only and see the nature of that which governs you.'

Woodget bit his lip as his trembling paw stretched out to take one of the cards fanned out before him.

'No Woodj,' Thomas said impulsively. 'Let it be – please.'

The fieldmouse wavered but the eyes of Simoon were bent upon him and it was as if he could do nothing to stop himself. Without thinking, his paw flashed out and he tapped the back of a single card.

Deftly, Simoon flipped the pack around and took out the one that the fieldmouse had chosen.

Impassively he gazed at the card in his fingers then, with a curiously theatrical movement, flourished it for the mice to see.

'Here is a picture of a pretty damsel,' he announced. 'Love is her name and under her sovereignty does your life lie, Master Pipple. Hers is a delightful dominion, for your heart's longing shall come to you and together you shall dwell till the end of your days.'

'That's Bess!' Woodget grinned.

Thomas' scowl had not lifted – in fact it had deepened. Simoon had put him in a bad mood and he lumbered to his feet.

'Come on Woodj,' he said. 'Time we went.'

The fieldmouse rose and as he did so he thought he caught upon the jerboa's face an expression of extreme sorrow and overwhelming compassion.

But the impression was fleeting and Woodget decided he must have been mistaken.

'Thank 'ee for the sit down and the story,' he said. 'Maybe we'll come back before long.'

At this Thomas mumbled something inaudible but before they passed through the entrance, Simoon held up his paw.

'One thing more ere you depart,' his clear ringing voice called forcefully. 'No charge for this visit have I laid upon you, yet this I do so now. To you, Thomas Stubbs, whose life is charted and mapped upon the seas, for a while at least, your toll is to tell he with the limb of wood that I desire to speak with him.'

'Mulligan?' Thomas asked a little sullenly. 'He won't come here. He never leaves the cotton bales.'

'And he never shall if you do not ask him,' came the grave reply.

'What do you want me to do?' Woodget piped up.

'Of you, Master Pipple, I beg only this, trust not too soundly those you hold dear.'

Then the jerboa closed his eyes and the smoke began

127

to wreathe about him once more.

Thomas pulled the fieldmouse away and muttered under his breath.

'I don't believe a word of it,' he said emphatically. 'It's all mummery and pretence. Well, I'm not taken in.'

Trotting through the tunnel of dancing light patterns, Woodget glanced back, but within the tent he could see only a vague screen of mist.

Behind the obscuring fumes, Simoon placed the cards down upon the cloth and gazed at the picture of Love he had shown to Woodget. Then he took from the bottom of the pile the one he had hidden and shuddered. Here was the true card chosen by the fieldmouse, but skilfully the jerboa had palmed it and selected one more to his liking.

Now he regarded it warily and sadly shook his head.

'I would not burden his merry young heart,' he said. 'Not yet.'

Hastily, as though the image frightened him, Simoon threw the card down and shrank further into the mist.

Upon the cloth lay the picture of a serpent. Flames dripped from its jaws and along its twisting back were painted nine bright stars.

6

Siren Songs

A little distance from the lonely alley-way where Simoon's tent was entwined with faint blue wisps of smoke, Thomas and Woodget discovered Dimlon curled up in a corner and sniffing forlornly.

'It's creepydark down there,' he whined, pointing further along the narrow passage. 'Dimmy was too afeared to go far on his ownsome. I thought the witchyspellcaster had done summat awful to you both. You were such a time, least it seemed you were in this horrid spot. What did he do, what did he say?'

Thomas helped the pale grey mouse to his feet and brushed the dust from his fur. 'He was just some travelling conjuror,' he told him. 'Nothing for you to be afraid of. It's all show with that sort; card tricks and juggling; that's all he's capable of, I'll warrant. Don't you get too excited, Dimmy, there's no such thing as magic, there really isn't.'

Instead of looking relieved, Dimlon appeared crestfallen – as if the world had become suddenly dull and uninteresting without the threat of the mysterious supernatural to add spice to his humdrum life.

'Was Simoon really a hoodwinkingswindley-bamboozler?' he asked Woodget in disappointment.

The fieldmouse cocked his head to one side. ''Tain't for the likes of me to say,' he replied. 'That'd be like askin' a leaf what it thought of the forest. He's beyond my reckonin', even if my noggin could find the proper words. I can tell you this though – he do rattle out a good tale. You have to admit that, Tom.'

'Probably made it all up,' Thomas muttered grumpily. 'Same as that phoney future of mine.'

'I wonder what he has to say to Mulligan?' Woodget mused. 'S'pose we'll have to go tell him he's wanted.'

Thomas closed his eyes and stretched out his paws, wiggling his fingers as though he were casting a spell, then in a ridiculous imitation of Simoon's doom-laden tones groaned, 'Ohhhh Mulligan, you are in great danger. Beware . . . beware . . . beware the woodworm.'

Dimlon laughed and Woodget gave Thomas a gentle shove to silence the hollow wails that were still issuing from his gaping lips.

'Let's get a move on then,' Thomas chuckled. 'To the bales we go.'

'If we can ever find our way out of here,' Dimlon added glumly.

When the maze of passageways was finally left

behind them and at last they reached the cotton bales, to their astonishment the three mice discovered that Mulligan was not sitting in his usual place and none of his snobbish neighbours knew nor cared where he had gone.

Just as they were making their way back along the central road, debating what they should do next, a hearty voice hailed them.

'Ahoy there, my young mates! And right glad I am to see you up and well, Master Thomas!'

There, hobbling towards them, with his stick in his strong paw and his pack slung over one shoulder – was Mulligan. A great grin divided his whiskery face and he indeed seemed genuinely pleased to see the three mice. Throwing his tattooed arms open wide he limped his way forward, the wooden leg drumming upon the deck's timbers.

'Where've you been stowing yourself?' he cried, clapping Woodget on the back, nearly sending him flying. 'All yesterday I was waiting for you, so this very morn I decided to haul myself over to your quarters but you weren't there. A fine chase you've led me but I'll not grudge it, so glad am I to clap my gogglers on you again.'

Woodget was not sure what to make of Mulligan's renewed friendliness. He recalled the hunted, angry look that was on his face the last time he had seen him – the night the bosun disappeared. Why was he acting so differently now? The Irish mouse almost seemed anxious that they forget his previous ill humour and was desperate for their companionship.

'We just been to find you,' Woodget said, watching him suspiciously, 'and . . . well, yesterday me and

Dimmy were helping with the search.'

Mulligan gazed at the ground. 'Aye,' he muttered, 'poor Able. But it's on account of him that I went in quest of you.'

'What do you mean?' asked Thomas.

'Has Mister Bosun been found?' Dimlon cried jubilantly. 'Is he safe? What news! What news!'

Mulligan stared at the foolish mouse then cleared his throat. 'No,' he said, 'he's still lost, but his going won't be unmarked. So, I invite you three – my friends – aboard the *Calliope* to sup with me in his honour. A final drink to an old friend, up on deck with the sea around us and the breeze in our whiskers. What say you?'

The three friends looked at one another. Woodget didn't think it was particularly appropriate considering the drunken circumstances of Mr Ruddaway's demise and shyly said as much. It was obvious to him that Mulligan knew more about that mystery than he was letting on, but he could not understand what reasons he might have for keeping the knowledge to himself – unless of course he was somehow involved in the bosun's disappearance. There were just too many secrets and riddles surrounding him for Woodget's liking and he recalled bitterly that it was chiefly on account of Mulligan that he was here now, and not at home with Bess.

At his side, Dimlon's whiskers drooped sadly and he glumly stuck out his bottom lip. 'I doesn't want to go on deck,' he whispered miserably, 'I might fall in and be dunkdrowndeddeep.'

'That'll not happen with me to guard you,' Mulligan

assured him. 'What say you, Master Thomas?'

'Yes,' Thomas answered, much to the others' surprise. 'I will come with you. For three days I've been stuck down here and I'm beginning to feel stifled and in need of fresh air. It would do us all good, I think, to be rid of this musty and heavy atmosphere for a while. I didn't know the bosun, but I'll certainly share a drink with you in his memory.'

'There's handsome,' Mulligan beamed. 'And don't you worry, Master Pipple, old Able would think this a fitting tribute – of that I'm positive sure, so I am.'

'But first we've a message for you,' Thomas said. 'We went to see Simoon, the one who fancies himself as a prophet.'

'Oh aye?' Mulligan murmured, looking at them curiously. 'And what did he have to say for himself?'

'That he wanted to see you.'

The Irish mouse sucked his teeth and tapped his stick thoughtfully. 'If pedlars with inflated opinions of their own worth and importance wish to parade their gimcrack baubles and shoddy tricks,' he said dismissively, 'then they must seek out their own audience, not turn the custom on its head. It's impudence so it is! Let the knave come to me if that is his wish – for I'll not go to him.'

Still put out by Simoon's predictions, Thomas agreed with this sentiment but Woodget stared unhappily at Dimlon.

'Now let's to the upper deck and give old Able a fitting send off!' Mulligan declared. 'I've managed to refill the flask so there'll be no want of grog.'

With Thomas by his side, and Woodget and Dimlon

trailing after, they headed for the rat district, then out of the hold.

Alone in the cloudless sky, the late afternoon sun shone warm and gold. Its brilliance sparkled over the calm surface of the sea, turning the placid waters into an unbounded rippling surface of shimmering flame. Through this burning splendour the *Calliope* voyaged, its shapely bows slicing through a flaring mesh of leaping light and leaving a fractured trail of scattered diamonds blazing in its wake.

On to the deck, the four mice came and all filled their lungs with the keen salt air.

Officially no passengers were allowed out of the hold during the main part of the day but Mulligan had had a word with the mouse on watch and told him of their purpose. Gravely the first officer let them pass but told them that if the captain caught them then he knew nothing about it.

'We'll go astern,' Mulligan instructed the others. 'Yonder we can sit and go unnoticed by any unfriendly eyes.'

Dimlon followed him around a corner but Thomas and Woodget stood as still as stones and their faces were filled with awe.

This was the first time since the *Calliope* had left the harbour that they had ventured out of the hold and the sight of the open sea in the daylight was a miraculous, almost worshipful vision to behold.

In their most fanciful dreams they had never imagined it to be so beautiful or so gigantic. No glimpse or shadow of land could they see in any direction, though they turned in a wide, staggering circle.

For them it was like waking from some drab, ashen-shaded sleep and discovering for the first time that the world was filled with colour and light. Intense sparks of dazzling hues flashed and bounced around the ship and Woodget thought that by some cunning art Simoon had imprisoned him inside his lantern of coloured glass.

A million briny prisms broke the pure radiance of the sun, hurling its vivid, vibrant spectrum into the air, shaming the deep blue of the sky for its lack of variety.

'Lor!' Woodget mouthed when at last he found his voice. 'If only Bess were here. She thinks summer flowers is pretty, but compared to all this, them's just muddy brown splots with no life in 'em.'

'It's incredible,' agreed Thomas. 'Like a wide flat country of dancing light.'

'That can't be the same old sun as shines on Betony Bank,' doubted Woodget. 'This one's fiercer and it's much warmer, ain't it?'

'What's keeping you pair?' Mulligan called suddenly and the sound of his harsh voice broke the enchantment which had kept the two mice spellbound.

Woodget looked up at Thomas and his friend smiled sadly.

'This is what I wanted to see,' Thomas murmured. 'Different places and things unexpected. But I never guessed it would be so lovely. Now I know why I longed to roam – the sea is in my blood, Woodj. There are shores out there with folk on them stranger than jerboas, and I ache to see them. I desire to know all there is to know and view all there is to view. This is just the beginning – I should have done this long ago.'

Woodget took hold of his paw and sighed.

'I'm pleased you're happy, Tom,' he said, 'but this ain't for me. Oh real grand and showy it is here, but too rich for my eyes. I'll be content to go home to the paler tints of my field, I don't need this gaudy sun – not with Bess beside me. She'm all the light I needs.'

Thomas gave the paw a squeeze. 'Then we both know what we want,' he breathed. 'This life is the one I claim and you, well your rightful place is at Bess's side. I wish I'd had the sense to see that before opening my big mouth, then you wouldn't be stuck out here with me.'

'I ain't stuck nowhere,' the fieldmouse answered. 'I'll be back at the farm before too much longer and how her eyes'll shine when I tell what happened.'

'You do forgive me then?'

Woodget gazed at his anxious brown face and nodded.

'We best hurry up afore all that rum gets drunk,' he chirruped, but he failed to add that he didn't like the thought of leaving Dimlon all alone with Mulligan. Woodget's mistrust of the Irish mouse was growing. If he was involved in whatever horrible fate had befallen the bosun then there was no knowing what else he was capable of.

Sitting by the deck rail, Mulligan and Dimlon were already taking their third swig when Thomas and Woodget joined them.

A grin more idiotic than was usual had slid on to Dimlon's face and he was giggling gleefully.

'My but that's lickytonsilgarglingfruityjuice!' he exclaimed. 'My Aunty Lily always kept a bottle of speshul tonnik which she took to make her "feel better", so she said, but it always gave her a nastybadheadhammerbangingbonce the next day.'

Mulligan fixed a despairing eye upon the pale grey mouse then raised the flask to the surrounding sea.

'Here's to you, Able,' he called, 'May the deeps of Fiddler's Green keep you – I'll not forget, nay – I'll not forget.'

For nearly an hour they sat there, at times talking gravely but mostly the speech was merry, yet always there was rum.

Under its heady influence Mulligan mellowed from the intense, suspicious creature whom Woodget had grown to dislike and back to the jovial old salt he had at first admired and looked up to. But of this new incarnation Woodget was still wary, sensing that just below the now calm and friendly surface, tamed or merely shackled for the moment and held at bay, there constantly simmered a watchful anger fanned by an embittered mistrust of everything.

Yet the unpleasant side to Mulligan's nature remained fettered and not a trace of it strayed on to the Irish mouse's features. Many a yarn he spun them and soon the three youngsters were listening enthralled. Even the fieldmouse laid aside his doubts for a while under the relentless barrage of hair-raising stories.

Of adventures in remote climes, the peg-leg regaled their attentive ears, from the coasts of Spain to the Western Indies – proudly displaying the faded scars which lay beneath his brindled fur as testimonial of the skirmishes that had found him.

Then he told them the histories of his tattoos and

what the faint, blurring pictures meant.

'See this knife with a notched blade,' he said showing them his forearm. 'That says I was one of the sixty-five who fought on the *Tantalus* back in thirty-seven when we repelled a bloodthirsty crew of river-pirating rats. Ah, that were a good contest. Who knows how many of our lads are left now? I don't and I'll wager only the Green Mouse does.'

'What about that one, Mister Mulligan?' Woodget asked, pointing to a small tattoo that had faded to a near invisible smudge of indistinct blue ink. 'It looks like a star.'

Mulligan glanced down at the mark on his right wrist and rubbed it with his other paw. 'Aye,' he muttered, ''tis the oldest of my skin scrawls. My father bore one the same and so did his before him – stretching back to I don't know when.'

'What do it mean?' asked the fieldmouse.

'Oh, why nothing,' came the evasive answer and Mulligan covered the star with his paw then tried to steer the conversation elsewhere.

'Have any of you ever clapped eyes on the land of Greenwich?' he began. 'A haven for the weary it is but governed by the grimmest old hatchet I ever did meet. Still if you're ever heartsore then it's to that restful spot you should take yourself. Almost I forgot my cares when I was last in its borders, so I did.'

'When was that?' asked Dimlon sleepily. 'I could do with a doze right now.'

'This very winter I stood before that throne of oak and endured the Starwife's withering scorn,' Mulligan replied, then he coughed and blustered about the fine weather as if he had not meant to mention that he had been there at all.

Woodget lay on his back, with his paws behind his head and his eyes gazing up at the deepening blue sky. Warmed by the dipping sun, he too felt sleepy and for a while was perfectly content to listen to the talk drift over him. Mulligan's brash voice rumbled in the air and Dimlon's fluting giggles were becoming ever more frequent. Beside him, Thomas' normally sensible tones sounded a little slurred and, as he listened, their combined voices seemed to blend into a comforting hum that pulsed in his ears and lulled him into a delicious sleep where a fair and haunting voice sang in the far-off distance.

Suddenly Woodget snapped his heavy eyelids open, for surely that voice was no figment of his drowsy brain and for an instant it seemed that it was real and called to him.

'There is one question I'd dearly like to know the answer to,' Thomas was saying as he took the flask from Mulligan. 'How did you come to lose your leg? Was it in that fight you spoke of before?'

The Irish mouse stared at him with narrowed eyes. 'Nay,' he whispered. 'Not then, them Portugese rats were a scurvy bunch but it was scum worse than they who lamed me and I won't tell of it. I was lucky to get out with my life and the leg was a cheap bounty for that. I'd have paid an awful lot more – aye a lot more to flee from that evil place.'

In the silence that followed, Woodget sat up and turned his head this way and that, his sensitive ears filtering out the rush of the sea as it washed against the hull, desperate to hear the plaintive, soul-wrenching music once more.

Woodget scratched his forehead then tutted as he wiggled a finger in his earhole. 'Dreaming you are, Pipple,' he told himself.

Then, when he had given up all hope of ever catching that blessed sound again, there it was, drifting on the warm evening breeze.

It was painfully sweet to hear and as he hearkened to the high, lilting notes he felt that he could abandon anything to continue listening. For if there was ever an end to that ravishing melody it would be more than his spirit could endure.

With a squeak, he jumped up and dashed over to the rail, hopping on to a low shelf so that he could peer over the side.

Behind him his friends regarded the fieldmouse with amusement. 'Sure, there's something biting that one,' Mulligan commented. 'Been restless and nervy all the afternoon, so he has.'

Thomas called Woodget's name, then his jaw dropped and he too heard the heavenly voice.

Immediately he sprang to the fieldmouse's side, and when the sound finally came to Mulligan and Dimlon they hastened to join them.

'What is it?' Dimlon breathed, flapping his large ears. 'It's a delishuslugholeticklin'serenadey – coo.'

Now the divine music filled the air, and those who listened prayed that it would never cease.

Profound yet light was the refrain, being both wrung with unquenchable sorrow and inspired by limitless joy. Tears unbidden came to the eyes of the four mice as they held their breaths and the sound unfolded, but none of them knew from whence the harmony came.

Abruptly, Woodget jolted and jabbed a finger across the sea.

'Look!' he hissed. 'Over there!'

His friends squinted through the glare of the shimmering water and then they saw a dark speck bobbing upon the burnished waves.

'Hello there!' Woodget called, jumping up and down and waving his arms.

At once the singing stopped and the speck sank below the surface.

Slowly the mice stirred and the world seemed paler and filled with a sudden bitterness at the loss of that ravishing sound.

'Why did you do that?' Thomas complained.

The fieldmouse stared mournfully at the unbroken waves.

'I didn't mean for the tune to end,' he said sadly. 'I wanted whoever it were to come closer.'

'That were a piece of driftwood,' Mulligan said, shaking himself out of the spell the beguiling song had woven around him. To his dismay he saw that he had left his pack unattended on the deck where they had been sitting and swiftly he ran over to it and gripped it tightly in both paws.

'And that was no voice,' he called, 'just the wind. Mighty strange things happen at sea; cold blue flames a-licking the masts I've seen and fish with wings leap from the deep, but though there are yarns of sirens who lure mariners to their doom or chant their witching songs over them to make them forget all they are – I ain't never seen nor heard one.'

He hoisted his bag over his shoulder and his face was set and stern. 'There are myths enough that are mine to contend with,' he uttered grimly. 'Aye, old tales that might yet spring to evil life. It's no time I have for other fables – the one alone is plenty for me.' He lapsed into brooding contemplation as he gazed up at the deepening blue of the sky, then shivered.

'Brrr!' the one-legged mouse said. 'It'll be cold when that sun sinks behind the waters and the stars pop out above. I'm thinking it's time to get below.'

Woodget continued to stare out at the empty waves. 'Not yet,' he muttered. 'I'd like to stay a little while. In case it does come back.'

'I'm definitely stopping,' Thomas added, swaying a little from the rum. 'I wants to get a good look at who's singing. Oh yes, oh yes – I do and there's no mish . . . mishtaking it.'

Mulligan frowned – he had remained up here too long. The deck now seemed horribly open and exposed, a perfect place for an enemy to make a sudden unexpected attack. He clutched his pack thoughtfully and longed to return to the hold which at that precise moment offered the best hope of sanctuary, even amongst those snobbish characters berthed on the cotton bales. All his instincts were telling him to return, to seek the safety of a crowd and leave this undefended place where Able Ruddaway had undoubtedly looked into the pitiless eyes of Death.

But to gain the refuge of the hold meant walking the dark length of that sloping passage and for all his bluff talk of old battles, Mulligan did not want to venture there alone.

'What about you, Dimmy?' he asked suddenly. 'Will you be staying with your two mates or would you care to keep an old rascal company? It's wearisome work tramping back down there on my tod.'

Dimlon glanced at the others, pondered for a moment then nodded with a brisk flap of his ears. 'Alrighty,' he said cheerfully. 'I'll go with you, if you're willin'.'

'That I am lad!' came the all too grateful reply.

Together they marched to the entrance of the dark passage which led down to the hold and entered its deep, clinging shadows.

For some time their sight floundered in the darkness. Away from the rich dazzling sunlight it seemed as though they had plunged into a chasm of engulfing night and they stumbled on blindly, the only sound being the rhythmic taps of the peg-leg striking the sloping floor.

Dimlon's eyes gleamed in the gloom and all traces of his former sleepiness appeared to have left him. With a smile on his face he followed Mulligan into the blackness, his gaze fixed upon the Irish mouse's back, and silently he fumbled with the buckle of his satchel.

'What's this then?' croaked a dry voice in front of them. 'Had a little party have we? That's nice, oh yes, isn't that pleasant?'

Mulligan thumped his stick on the ground and squinted as his eyes grew accustomed to the murk, whilst Dimlon's face fell.

'Who's there?' the Irish mouse demanded. 'Get here where I can see you.'

Ahead of them there was a shuffling sound and from the complete darkness ahead loomed the imposing figure of a tall rat.

The creature was plump, but the uncommon length of his arms, combined with the stretched appearance of his upper body, lent him a gangly aspect – resembling a wide-boled tree with sagging, yet sturdy branches. The rat's eyes were small, yet fiercely alive and full of sly curiosity, shifting constantly from Mulligan to the pale grey mouse at his side. His features however were not sharp or cruel, but neither were they docile or dullwitted.

Catching his breath, Dimlon studied the rat doubtfully and saw that he possessed a large pimply snout, marred by a deep scar which travelled all the way across his face, from one jowl to the other.

'Who are you?' Mulligan demanded, gripping his stick and brandishing it threateningly.

A swaggering arrogance was in the rat's bearing as he prowled nearer, alarmingly unconcerned by the weapon in Mulligan's paw.

'Mebbe you've heard my name already,' his cracked voice uttered. 'I done told your other little chum.'

'Jophet . . .' Mulligan murmured and he stared nervously at the creature's tail, but it was too dark in there to be certain. 'Spying on me is it?' he cried, rallying a little. 'I'll have none of that! You get back to the rest of your filthy kind.'

Jophet folded his long arms and slouched against the passage wall. 'No,' he replied with a forbidding calmness. 'I've a mind to stay here awhile and watch you return to the hold. I wouldn't want owt to happen to you, now would I?'

Beads of sweat pricked Mulligan's brow and he bared his teeth, preparing to fly at the insolent villain.

Then he remembered that Dimlon was there and he mastered himself once more.

'Dimmy,' he said, 'stand close to me. This vagabond won't harm us if he knows what's best.'

A smirk appeared on Jophet's face and he snickered softly. 'You call me a vagabond?' he cackled. 'Is it I who have flitted from isle to isle these past years? Tell me, Haltfoot, what quest sends you halfway round the world? What business drives you on – could it be an errand of some kind? If so then I wonder what could have been entrusted to you? A message perhaps? I think not. A treasure more tangible, I guess. Hmm, yes I wonder very much and you can stake your remaining leg that heads other than mine are puzzling over it too. What plots are you hatching? we ask ourselves.'

Mulligan's paws were shaking now; the rat knew too much.

A hissing laugh whistled through Jophet's lips when he saw how uneasy his words had made the Irish mouse.

'For your own safety,' the rat told Dimlon, 'I would not remain in the stumptoe's company. Only ruin can come of mingling with such as he.'

'Do not listen to him,' Mulligan instructed. 'We must continue on our way. Let the fool prattle his rattish nonsense with none to hear it.'

'What's in the bag, Peg-leg?' Jophet inquired with a twitch of his arched brows. 'Shall we open it and take a peep? Let me lay my curiosity aside.'

'Keep back, you vermin!' Mulligan roared, his temper finally flaring, and he thrashed his stick furiously in the air, only a hair's breadth from the rat's snout. 'I'll not be spoken to like that by one of your hellish breed. Listen to my warning and heed these words well if you value your stinking skin. If I so much as clap my eyes upon your heathen face during the rest of this voyage or at any time thereafter, then you'll feel the brunt of my rage. Your flea-bitten hide I'll tear from your bones whether you be an adept or no and leave your bloody sinew shivering in the darkness!'

Breathing hard and quivering with fury, the Irish mouse drew Dimlon closer and placed his paw upon the pale grey mouse's shoulder.

'The air reeks in here,' he muttered. 'Come, Dimmy, to the hold.'

With his eyes fixed upon Jophet's disrespectful and arrogant face, Mulligan limped by. But as he journeyed down the passage he was painfully aware of the rat's glaring and watchful eyes boring into the back of his skull.

Helping Mulligan hurry along, Dimlon glanced around and to his dismay saw that Jophet's unflinching stare was now fixed upon him. It had been a frightening and disturbing encounter and now his mind was greatly troubled and he was eager to return to his lonely encampment upon the wool sacks to consider what he should do.

Quickly the two mice gained the bottom of the sloping way and the hold opened up before them.

Alone in the passage, Jophet drew his claws thoughtfully over his snout and slipped silently after them.

'Come on, Woodj,' Thomas called.

Apprehensively, the fieldmouse grasped the rope

with both of his tiny paws and began to climb down. 'Oh dear,' he murmured. 'This is plum stupid. Don't let go now, Pipple, pretend it's only a corn stalk a-waving in the breeze at Betony Bank.'

Determined that this time, if the singing recommenced, they would be ready, Thomas had pattered around the deck rail and decided upon a reckless course of action.

Realising that if the singers did return they would be too high up to see anything very clearly, Master Stubbs's rum-addled reason knew what had to be done.

Several feet above the water line, he had espied a narrow ledge where two small mouse bottoms might just manage to perch for a while. So, with Woodget's help, he had thrown a rope over the side and proceeded to clamber down it. Intoxicated beyond reach of common sense and heedless of the great danger, Thomas hurried rashly down – humming happily to himself the whole time.

When his feet reached the ledge, he scrambled on to it, precariously rocking on his heels as he sought to steady himself and muster as much of his sense of balance that remained to him. Although the platform was proving to be a lot smaller than its appearance first suggested, somehow he managed to press his back against the hull and slither down until his legs were dangling out over the edge of the narrow ledge and he was sitting relatively securely but without much comfort.

Below him, the churning waters splashed upwards and he was now so close to them that his toes were cooled in a fine salty drizzle. But Thomas was not afraid of the gurgling death that waited for him if he should fall; he glanced only briefly at the thrashing sea, then turned his attention upwards once more.

'Come on, Woodj!' he called. 'That's it, paw over paw. Sshoon have you here.'

'I knowed how to climb, Tom!' the fieldmouse yelled back. 'But this ain't no field and I must be softer in the head than I ever did think. What's got into him – or me for that matter? I sure do regret giving him his first taste of berrybrew that night. The stuff drives out his sense.'

At that moment a sweeping fold of water smacked against the ship and its showering spray shot into the air, drenching Woodget completely, and for a perilous instant his paws slipped from the rope.

Upon the ledge below, Thomas saw his friend struggling, his fingers slipping from the wet line, and the terrible predicament he had placed him in finally shone through the alcoholic veils which had furled about his wits.

'Woodget!' he choked, as the fieldmouse wailed and scrabbled to remain aloft. 'Hold on!'

If Woodget had not wound his tail tight about the rope then he would have surely plunged into the rushing waters, but at last he was able to steady himself and held on more tightly than ever before.

'Go back up,' Thomas called. 'It's too dangerous.'

'Not on your nelly!' Woodget cried back, feeling more determined after a moment's rest – if not more confident.

Inch by inch he laboured, descending slowly to that treacherous lip where Thomas was waiting until finally he was sitting beside him.

Woodget clutched the ledge for dear life. He could not tear his eyes from the foam that bubbled and frothed beneath his feet and his ears were filled with the clamour of the rushing waves and the rumble of the ship's engines. Never had he sat in such a terrifying place, but amid the fear his excitement boiled and a fierce thrill possessed him every time the cold and salty spray touched his downturned face.

'Oh Tom,' he murmured, 'what an awful seat this is. We could tumble into the drink at any time.'

Greatly relieved to have his friend safe by his side, Thomas surrendered once more to the rum's influence and he gave one elaborate nod of the head.

'Aye,' he agreed, 'but what a switch from that stale and noisome hold. Why, you might as well be buried under the ground and a-wandering in a town of the dead as be down there. Least here you know you're alive and value every second. Did you ever breathe such air, Woodj? A mouse could die here and be happy for it.'

'Do you think the singing will start up again?' the fieldmouse asked.

'If that's what it was,' Thomas answered. 'But whose voice could it have—'

Before he had finished speaking, there it was. The music which they had imperilled their very lives to hear again suddenly began and its sound was clear like a bell of crystal ringing over a barren, tuneless land.

The mice's hearts leapt when they heard it and Woodget forgot all about the white-capped danger which rushed below him.

'Thomas,' he whispered. 'Look, do you see?'

At his side, Thomas' eyes stared unblinking out to sea and he gripped the fieldmouse's arm excitedly.

A little distance from the ship, rising from the radiant and gentle waves, the top of a head appeared.

Golden was the colour of the hair which hung in long, trailing tresses and the failing sunlight revelled there, burning in sparkling fires, and the droplets which fell from the flaming locks glimmered back into the waters like jewels of twinkling amber. Delicate shells of many lustrous colours were threaded into the glistening curls and upon the creature's brow sat a circlet of small pearls.

As yet the face of the creature had been hidden behind that dripping curtain of shining gold, but now the head was tossed back and the hair swept behind two strangely shaped ears.

Then Thomas and Woodget beheld the face and as one they sharply drew their breaths.

Never had they seen anyone more beautiful and never afterwards could their fumbling words attempt to describe that supreme loveliness.

Like a mouse maiden she appeared, yet unlike any their eyes had ever looked upon. Exquisite were the finely shaped features and the fur which covered them grey as the sea, yet at times it flashed like the bright silver of a fish's scale. A blue, flawless as a sapphire and deep as summer twilight, blazed in the large eyes, glittering with a radiance all their own – a luminous flame to scythe through the darkness of the raven deeps where not even a faint glimmer of the sun's rays could reach.

Like two shapely fins were her ears and their spine-webbed elegance served only to enhance her grace and beauty in Thomas' eyes.

But the maiden was as yet unaware that she was being observed and, inclining her head to one side as she threaded yet another shell on to a golden strand of hair, the heavenly song rose from her curving lips – climbing steadily into the mounting dusk.

'What's she doing out there?' Woodget asked in a murmur. 'Where'd she come from?'

Captivated by the vision in the distance, Thomas let out a yearning sigh, but the sound was far louder than he ever intended and was carried far across the water.

At once the lovely creature looked up and stared angrily over to the *Calliope* – the fierce blue of her eyes gleaming directly at the two mice sitting upon the ledge.

A look of astonishment and horror registered upon her face but an instant later she was gone – vanished beneath the sea.

'No!' Thomas yelled. 'Don't go! Please come back!'

A stillness settled over the waters and the rippling circles which formed when the maiden disappeared, spread ever wider until they were lost in the ship's wake.

'She'm gone, Tom,' Woodget muttered sorrowfully. 'But what manner of folk were she? 'Tweren't natural.'

Thomas was still gazing out to sea, his eyes following the last of the faint ripples.

'I don't know,' he answered in a subdued voice. 'P'raps she was one of Mulligan's sirens he spoke of – or else we both dreamed her.'

Suddenly a voice laughed at them nearby and Woodget was so startled that he almost fell off the ledge.

'What strangeness is this?' cried the faintly teasing voice. 'A fine pair of tritons, I deem. Yet the larger of the two has hardly wetted his toes and the other is more like unto a sorry-looking spratling.'

Thomas and Woodget stared, not daring to move a muscle. For there rising once more from the waters was the beautiful maiden, and a mocking smile was upon her face.

'Halia did not know that there was an audience for her song,' she laughed, 'and one so brazen that he would dare call after me. It is well that my father is far from this place, for he is ever wrathful with the discourteous and ill-bred.'

'I'm sorry,' Thomas said hastily, 'I never meant no harm nor to be rude. I just wanted to hear your music a while longer and maybe learn something of you.'

'You wish to learn of Halia?' she asked with amusement trickling from her lips. 'And what would one of the earthborn know of we who dwell in the realm of my father? For though you may draw close to the sea, you fear it still. A triton you may appear, yet you are not of that race. A soil-treader you are, a trampler of the sod and grubber in the dirt. What business bears you from the dust and clay of your home and over my country?'

'Your country?' Thomas mumbled. 'What do you mean? This is only the sea.'

A spluttering shriek of laughter issued from Halia's mouth and she shook her head despairing of the tears which streamed down her cheeks.

'Only the sea!' she wept. 'If you did but comprehend the folly of your words. Great in jest are your poor untutored wits, yet you are too high a prize for me to enjoy alone. Stay a moment longer, Master Triton, others should share your worldly view.'

With that, she dipped down below the water and Thomas turned to Woodget who had been too shy to say anything to the beautiful creature.

'What do you make of her?' he asked. 'Can it be the rum still affecting me?'

'If so then it's trickin' us both,' the fieldmouse replied, 'but whatever's the truth of it, that damsel's having some sport or other.'

Before Thomas could make any response, the golden-haired maiden emerged from the sea once more, clapped her paws together three times and called out six names.

'Dias, Enalus, Metaneira, Myrtea, Carmanor, Zenna. Come, look on what I have found.'

To Thomas and Woodget's astonishment, five other faces rose from the water. All of them were beautiful and adorned with shells like Halia but none had golden hair like she.

The tresses of one shone like silver, another was like burnished copper, two others were livid green and the fifth was white as the foaming waves.

'Dias,' Halia gurgled, beckoning one of the others to draw closer. 'See these scratchers of the mould, a triton I have named he with the red cloth about his neck, but he bears no shell to bring the storm and poorly would he fare in our waters.'

The silver-haired maiden swam close to her side and she peered at the mice curiously.

153

'Oenopion I name him,' she laughed, 'for the bloom of the wine is still on his face, but what of the other? That minnow who burns redder than the hair of Enalus our sister? What say you of him?'

Halia giggled as she regarded Woodget, her lithe form bobbing up and down with the gentle rising of the waves. 'No larger than a fat worm upon a hook is he,' she cried, 'and see how he squirms.'

'Won't you come join us, Wineface?' Dias asked. 'If it is your wish we shall show to you our father's kingdom and all the marvels hidden therein. Let your eyes be astounded by the gardens of the deep. Flowers brighter than any which grow on mortal lands bloom in our royal courts.'

Thomas shook his head. 'Many thanks,' he replied, 'but I think I'll content myself with perching here awhile.'

'But we shall guide you,' Halia cried. 'Metaneira, Myrtea – help me ease this unwilling creature into the sea. I would make a true triton of him yet. It is long since we welcomed an earthborn into our halls. We shall sing the song of oblivion over him and he shall forget his precious world and its weary clay. With us always shall he remain – an esquire of the waters to amuse us and do as we bid. Drag him down.'

Mischievously, the maidens swam forward, their green hair flowing wildly about them as their webbed paws reached up to clutch hold of Thomas' legs.

The mouse merely chuckled and swung his legs out of their grasp.

'Alas no,' he said delightedly. 'Fair as you seem, dear ladies all, I'm not yet that far soused.

Grogconcocted phantasms you are, and once I tipped into the sea that'd be the end of Thomas.'

'Thomas!' the maidens cried, taking up the name and singing it with their silvery voices. 'A fine sturdy title. Thomas Triton, we now call you. A friend of the sea-daughters. Oh what a consort he would make – a prince amongst the proud storm warriors of our court.'

Thomas chortled, and Halia turned back to Woodget.

'And your name, Master Worm?' she laughed.

'Woodget,' he answered.

The maidens gurgled in their mirth and leaped amid the swelling waves as they called out, 'Woodget Worm, Woodget Worm.'

'Oi!' the fieldmouse demanded crossly. 'You stop that.'

'But Master Worm,' Dias cried, shaking her silver hair. 'You are no triton like your gallant comrade, for do we not perceive that you bear the sea no great love?'

Woodget frowned and folded his arms tersely; it was no use arguing with these silly creatures.

'See how he pouts,' Halia laughed. 'The worm is as awkward as Zenna of the sullen face.'

She whirled around, sending a spout of water splashing over Woodget's knees as she did so, and he muttered under his breath.

'Zenna!' she called. 'Where are you? Did she not arise with the rest? Where is she? Zenna! Do not hide with the wide-mouthed fishes below, their looks may marry with thine but you are not of their kin. Come let the sun shine upon that plain face of yours – if he can withstand such a drearsome sight.'

At that the other maidens burst into laughter.

Thomas grinned to hear them, but Woodget thought it was an unpleasant and cruel sound.

Then, from the rippling surface of the sea, further from the *Calliope* than the rest of her sisters, rose Zenna.

Dark was her hair, black as a crow's wing, and no shell adorned it. Sleek and wet it clung to her broad skull, hanging lank and heavy about her narrow shoulders. Although she was not ugly, nor plain as Halia had suggested, her features lacked the grace of her sisters and in their bright, ornamental company she appeared drab and sombre.

The light that shone in her eyes was dim and the leaden hue of slate, possessing none of the vital gleam that glinted in the keen glances of those before her. Also, her ears were larger than the others, and scalloped in shape, and beneath her chin three spines curved down towards her throat.

As swift as an otter, Halia swam over to her and towed her forward.

'Join us,' she sniggered. 'I would show you one whose tongue is as pert and dolorous as thine own.'

At first Zenna resisted, pulling away from her golden-haired sister, but then her dark eyes fell upon Woodget and she struggled no more but looked quickly away and could not bear to meet his gaze.

Halia trawled her to the side of the *Calliope* and looked up at the fieldmouse. 'Here, Master Worm,' she cried. 'I present Zenna, she who is enamoured of the cold murk which lies in the northern waters and who prefers skulking in stagnant grottoes to singing in the sun and weaving shells in her hair. Although no shell would brighten that griping countenance and maybe only barnacles could endure it. Let us find a hermit's casing and lodge her slouching frame within, a happy housing for that indecorous visage.'

Again there was taunting laughter and Zenna stared wretchedly down, her mouth pulled into an unhappy scowl as she endured the spiteful jibes and jeers.

Woodget's good nature hated this scornful teasing and his sympathy for the unfortunate maiden surged within him.

'You leave her be,' he snapped abruptly. 'Pretty you may be on the outside but you're spoiled and hateful underneath. You're nowt but vain and mean-hearted.'

The laughter died at once and the maidens stared at the fieldmouse as though he had slapped every one of them. Silently, Zenna lifted her face and her dark grey eyes gleamed at him gratefully. Then, with the faintest of smiles glimmering upon her face, she pulled away from Halia and vanished back into the sea.

'It would seem our sister has found a champion at last,' Halia eventually said with a frost in her voice. 'She will not thank you for it, Master Worm. Zenna deserves our treatment of her, for she is secretive and wanders far from our father's halls and is insolent to him when pressed about her wild roamings. She adds no grace to the court and all her speech is of woe and gloom.'

'Six against one just ain't fair,' Woodget said simply and Halia pursed her lips at his stubborn defence of her unlovely sister.

Turning to Thomas she ignored Woodget

completely and asked, 'Master Triton, I put it to you once more and this shall be the final invitation, for never again shall you chance to glimpse any of our folk. Will you not descend with me, down to the many pillared chambers of the royal hall, where greater music than our mere voices can sing plays ever and without an ending?

'Light and beauty will your eyes behold and riches beyond the measure of your thought are housed there. Gold in abundance lies glittering and heaped in corners, and monstrous gems which burn with a fire at their heart lamp the collonades. Will you not consent to come down? Can we not sing the spell of changing over you so that you may breathe our fathoming airs? No regrets shall burden your heart for as one newly awakened shall you be. Come Triton, or is the memory of your clay too precious to surrender?'

Whilst the maiden spoke, Woodget looked at Thomas and prayed that he would not yield to her tempting words.

'No Tom!' he urged. 'It's drowned you'll be!'

But Thomas was still convinced that Halia and her sisters were only figments of his drunken mind and he declined the invitation. 'Nay,' he said. 'I'll not wet more than my toes this day and it's time we was returning to our bunks. A thousand thanks to you, fair ladies, for even though you're only tricks born of the drink, fairer tricks I ain't never seen and probably never shall.'

Clambering to his feet, he waved to them and one by one the lovely faces disappeared beneath the sea, their fish-like tails flicking momentarily above the waters until only Halia remained and her sublime smile was fixed upon him.

'Farewell on your voyages, Thomas Triton,' she laughed. 'May my country bear you to good fortune and keep you safe. Perhaps it is well that you refused my call, for I guess that much lies ahead of you. Valiant deeds will you accomplish and you shall win great renown. Now I must depart, for too long have I lingered here.'

As the crimson fireball of the sun dipped low upon the rim of the sea Halia sank into the waves, until only a vague shimmering mass of waving gold could be seen beneath the surface of the water.

Thomas leaned recklessly over the ledge and caught a brief flash of two bright points like blazing sapphires – and then she was gone.

'Well,' he muttered, stretching and reaching for the rope, 'right now I could do with a good kip.'

Woodget smiled – his friend still believed that the sirens were not real. 'Hurry up and climb then, Master Triton,' he cried. 'The sooner I'm away from this place and have the deck under my feet again the happier I'll be.'

Thomas chortled and began to ascend the rope, closely followed by the little fieldmouse.

Night was falling and already the first stars shone faintly in the darkening sky. As the *Calliope* voyaged beneath the deepening heavens, gilded by the last flickering rays of the setting sun, a shadow reared from the swirling waters of the ship's wake.

With her leaden eyes gleaming, Zenna turned her solemn face towards the *Calliope*, intently watching the two tiny figures labour up the trailing rope.

Brighter shone the bleak unloved light of her gaze as she saw her champion gain the deck rail and clamber to safety.

'Woodget,' she breathed, chanting the name as though it were something new and wondrous to her. 'Woodget.'

A look of bliss lifted her serious features and a rare grin divided her ashen face. Repeating the fieldmouse's name over and over to herself she twirled joyfully in the water then, purposefully, she began to swim after the great, darkening shape of the *Calliope* and was soon lost in the gathering shadows.

7

Into the Raging Squall

The following morning, Thomas awoke late and his head was pounding. Gingerly he looked about him, but Woodget had already left their quarters some hours before so, stepping carefully from the barrels, Thomas went in search of him.

Eventually he discovered the fieldmouse talking to Dimlon at one corner of the central road and Thomas was surprised to see that they were both holding mops in their paws.

'There's one for you too, Tom,' Woodget said giving the deck a swipe with the damp mop. 'Mulligan suggested we ask the captain if we could earn our breakfast, seeing as how all our grub's run out, so us three are the new swabs.'

'Couldn't we rest first and work later?' Thomas groaned. 'I don't want any breakfast. I think my seasickness is back – my head feels awful and my tongue's as shrivelled as a raisin.'

Woodget threw the spare mop at him. 'I ain't got no sympathy for you, Tom,' he laughed. 'Or should I call 'ee Triton? You just set to it, there's a week of work to do so you'd best start now.'

Scrunching up his eyes to shield them from the dim lanterns which to him were blazing like suns and stabbing into his aching brain, Thomas dabbed at the floor and his first job at sea commenced.

For the rest of that day, they were kept extremely busy cleaning up the hold and were rewarded by three square meals which they ate with the rest of the crew.

Several times, Mulligan came to watch them sweep up or wipe the timbers and during these periods he would regale them with more stories or burst unexpectedly into an old sea shanty, the choruses of which shocked most of the other folk who happened to be passing or stopped to listen.

Thomas looked forward to the one-legged mouse's visits but Woodget still felt uncomfortable in his presence and preferred to concentrate on his chores instead.

By the end of the day, the new members of the crew were absolutely exhausted. Dimlon plodded back to the wool sacks with his heavy lids drooping over his large eyes and spoke hardly a word to anyone whilst Thomas and Woodget eagerly sought their own bunks and were asleep almost before they had cast themselves down.

That night a ponderous silence filled the hold; not even the grunting of rats as they snorted and belched in their slime-haunted slumbers disturbed the tremendous quiet which charged the still, expectant atmosphere.

Through every stupefied, insensible mind, the fleeting ghosts of beloved memories or the rambling scenes of never remembered dreams coursed freely. To some, fanciful images of their final destination, built and coloured from the exaggerations of family and friends, towered large in the deep caverns of their snug rest. Bright pictures of fields and streams flowed through the homesick sleep of others, whilst stomachs bored with the same old rations inspired nocturnal visions of steaming puddings drowning in cream and the heavenly scent of freshly baked but imagined bread set many whiskers trembling and craving lips drooling.

Even the first officer who sat up on deck, supposedly on watch, had nodded and was in the arms of some fair mousemaid: Fleur of Calais, Rinda in Bombay, Nessea in Crete, little Cho Teh who dwelt by the docks in Singapore. To each of them he had confessed his undying love, and promised to return and wed them one day, but knew that he never would and they danced on their pretty, dainty feet before him, dipping in and out of the ever winding waltz of his dream.

Only one soul was still awake upon the *Calliope*. Within his tent, the hood of his cloak cast back over his head, Simoon sat before the incense burner, a pouch of soft leather clasped in his paw.

Glittering like the wintry heavens, his great black eyes fixed upon the cloud of blue smoke which gathered around him and he began to chant a string of mysterious words. From his quick tongue the rapid rhymes of a half-forgotten land poured as in to the pouch he delved, bringing out a fistful of herbs and powders which he cast at the burner.

At once the tent blazed with a vivid green light. A brilliant emerald flame crackled within and the air was filled with angry, spitting sparks until the smoke became a dark, thickly swirling, olive fog.

Into this billowing mist Simoon stared, muttering continually, and gradually the obscuring veils parted, but through the dissipating shreds he did not see the embroidered fabrics upon the far wall. Glimmering within that vaporous, ever shifting frame, as if it were a window looking upon a remote scene in the far distance, the jerboa beheld the shores of a tranquil, moonlit country rising gracefully from the shimmering sea.

All was silent save for the prophet's faint, steady breaths. No sound of the lapping deep flowed from that ethereal view, no call of gull or sigh of wind, only the dun colours of that far away island filtered through and Simoon's eyes burned stronger than ever before.

Over the sundering waters, his unswerving gaze travelled, sweeping through the breaking waves and flying high above the silvery sands. Into the deep shade of cypress trees, his keen eyes penetrated, piercing the violet darkness and crossing the hills to where a row of white, weathered columns and tumbled stumps jutted from the ground like pale and broken fingers. Grass grew over the marble floors within that ancient temple, yet many figures clad in robes of white still gathered there. Clasping one another's paws, they formed a great circle and began to slowly pace around a large central stone.

Suddenly the wheeling ring was broken and it seemed to the jerboa's eyes that a strong gusting wind had fallen upon them. From the east it came, tearing at their gleaming robes and driving them out on to the hillside. Lifting their faces to the gale, the scattered creatures were suddenly afraid and terror was graven upon them as they stared into the battering night.

Solemnly, Simoon bent his glance eastward where the far shores of that isle were tormented with storm and the waves came riding far inland. With terrible violence the tempest raged, and in its midst sailing swiftly over the sea was a dense, thunderous cloud – wreathed by countless forked and savage lightnings.

The jerboa's face darkened and his bristling eyebrows quivered as he strained to venture closer to that wild tumult. Larger its image grew in the churning smoke before him until the inside of the tent flashed and shone with every fierce bolt that snaked from the black menacing cloud. Clenching his teeth, Simoon's paws clenched into fists and the knuckles blanched as the tremendous effort to spur his will on took its toll. Through the obscuring storm he tore, rending aside the violent lashing screens to see what lay hidden within.

The prophet's jaws ground together, as he battled with the horrendous might of the unseen power and, suddenly, he broke through.

Blanketing thunder clouds gaped about him and in he swooped, though the lightning raged all around like flickering white fences.

Then he saw it, the hideous vessel concealed deep within the tempest's heart. A high golden prow rode the leaping waves and Simoon shivered at its monstrous shape. In the likeness of a ghastly, ravening serpent had the figurehead been fashioned; two huge rubies burned in its eyes and over the surface of every polished, faceted scale was the fury of the tormented weather mirrored and hurled back into the night.

Simoon quailed when he looked on the hellish, slave-worked ship, for it was crammed with countless yellow-eyed, foul-looking creatures with curved swords in their claws and long knives gripped in their teeth. Yet the most dreadful of all those infernal, misbegotten fiends stood haughty and arrogant behind the malformed figurehead.

Tall and imposing was he, a grotesque portrait of bitterness and reviling hatred. Long and raven, his hair streamed in the gale and his narrow eyes blazed black with the awful loathing of his unquenchable malice. Pride and disdain leered upon that cruel face as he held his gaunt head high and stared malevolently past the golden serpent and at the storm beyond.

Sitting upon his cushions, Simoon gazed at the venomous creature for several moments, then raised his paw to dispel the remote visions. But even as he did so, the fiend upon the prow turned its malignant head and glared through the vast distance as if it were aware of him.

A ferocious snarl crept over the lean face and the burning eyes flashed dark, slicing through the olive drab smoke, and with a frightened shriek, the jerboa fell back before the terrible force of that evil glance.

Out flew an accusing, threatening claw and the golden ship veered around until the horrific gilded serpent bore unerringly forward and the crimson glare that beat from its ruby eyes flooded the prophet's tent.

With his back against the tapestry-adorned wall, Simoon shuddered and, holding his paws before his face as if warding off some dreadful blow, he stared fearfully up at the foggy portal his own powers had created.

On came the glittering ship, its barbaric crew yammering for death and murder, and its vicious captain threw back his head to crow with devilish mirth. Larger the nightmarish figurehead loomed until it seemed as if it would crash through the surrounding mist and plough straight over the jerboa's prostrate form, crushing him beneath its horrible weight.

'Enough!' Simoon wailed. '*Arvit Netchua Karavinda!*'

Leaping to his feet, he raised his puny arms in a gesture of defiance and challenge but the fiery glare intensified and he appeared lost in a lake of steaming gore.

'*Berakka Netchua!*' he yelled. 'Begone! Begone!'

Within the swirling mists a great wave swept before the ship, surging and rolling forward until, impossibly, it burst through the magical foggy window and the seething salt water crashed into the buckling tent sluicing about the hem of the prophet's cloak, its stinging spray battering into his stricken face. Then, just as the first glint of gleaming gold pushed from the smoke, Simoon snatched up his staff and from its rayed tip a green fire spluttered into life and an arc of dazzling energy shot into the whirling mists.

For an instant he heard the screeching of the heathen

army and the vile curses of the hellish captain bellow above the din of the storm – and then all was quiet.

Only the faintest eddying threads of pale blue smoke remained in the tent but the cushion-strewn floor was awash with sea water.

Wearily, Simoon leaned upon the staff and passed a paw over his eyes as he panted and struggled to regain his breath.

'So,' he uttered in a hoarse gasp, 'the time long feared is indeed upon us. The Scale are moving once more – rampaging over the face of the unhappy world to recover the remaining pieces. Upon the wings of storm their evil is riding and who is there in this age of the world who can withstand the High Priest of the Dark Despoiler? Perhaps we have underestimated the strength of our enemies – if so then the hope of the Council is built upon sand. Only when the nine stars herald His rebirth shall we know for certain whether our toil has been in vain. Long have we waited for this chance, much has been gambled and still more will be lost 'ere the end finds us.'

Sighing, the jerboa shook his head and lay the staff down as he cast his eyes about the waterlogged tent.

'Yet for the here and now I must also take time to consider,' he mused. 'Far away the forces of the Scale are thundering over the sea, yet into the very skirts of their twisting wrath are we sailing. Verily, a calamity approaches and the morrow will be a day of doom, but Simoon the prophet must be ready when it strikes.'

Mumbling to himself, he paddled over to the wall and began pulling down the tapestries – there was much to be done.

* * *

The next day dawned bleak and grey but through the choppy, buffeting waters the *Calliope* steadily smacked and scythed her way. Within the hold, those folk who had at first suffered from seasickness were once again afflicted and even some who had thought themselves immune lay moaning in their bunks, wailing with every roll of the ship.

Much to Thomas' amazement the vessel's stomach-curdling motion had no effect upon him whatsoever and, feeling extremely pleased with himself, he set off with Woodget and Dimlon to discover what duties would be assigned to them.

That morning Captain Gabriel Hewer's orders made no mention of swabbing the decks. 'A real Devil's squall this is,' he said, 'and like as not the brew'll spoil a whole lot more afore it improves. Make certain all's secure and keep me informed of the mood below. If those scab-faced, whining rats try to scramble to the upper decks, knock their heads together and give them something real to whinge about for a change.'

In the hold the mouse families held on to each other in grave silence as the weather outside steadily worsened. Ever more powerful became the waves that smote the *Calliope* and as she ploughed further into the storm the pale daylight failed altogether, for heavy clouds blotted out the sky and, with an ominous rumble of distant thunder, the rain commenced – torrential and driving.

Whilst the ship pitched and crashed upon the swollen, wind-whipped waves, Thomas, Woodget and Dimlon ran to and fro between the crates trying to keep everyone calm. At first they attempted to take their minds off the storm by gathering those that were willing together and in desperation called upon Mulligan to sing a few songs. Initially the rousing ditties of the Irish mouse appeared to hearten them, but when a tremendous clap of thunder resounded directly above the ship all the children began to scream.

Now the din of the storm could be heard above the throb of the straining engines and any further plans to appease the passengers were abandoned.

Then into the central thoroughfare came Simoon. The small, crimson robed figure of the jerboa emerged from one of the narrow alleyways and behind him he dragged a great bundle of possessions which he had lashed together.

Without a word to anyone, and not even appearing to notice their fearful faces or indeed anything that was going on, Simoon began to tie his goods to the side of a large crate.

The assembled mouse families watched him in disbelief as the ship's movements became ever more erratic and unpredictable.

'What's the wizard doing?' the children blubbed through their sobbing tears. But their parents did not know the answer. The jerboa was evidently preparing himself for something, but for what?

When he was certain that his bundle was sturdily fastened, Simoon climbed to its bulky summit and slipped his long, kangaroo-like feet under the straps. Then he pulled the hood over his head and waited.

Clutching at a rope for support as the deck began to

tilt more wildly, Mulligan spoke to his friends through gritted teeth.

'Unnatural this is, I don't blame these folk for being afeared. In all my years at sea I reckon this'll turn out to be the blackest day of them all! May fortune guide us to safe harbour.'

Woodget stared unhappily about them. Nearly everyone was weeping and trembling with fear and, as yet another almighty wave blasted against the *Calliope*, sending it reeling and lurching through the ravaging tempest, his own spirits withered inside him.

'We will make it, won't we?' his small voice asked.

Mulligan shrugged and tapped his bag thoughtfully. 'We have to,' he muttered. 'But there's more at work here than the elements only. A fiendish power and a dark, striving mind is behind that lashing rain.'

Woodget did not know what he meant by that but there was no time to question him further, there was still much to be done. Everything that was not tied down had to be made secure and with the help of many others they set to it.

Painfully, the morning crawled by and still the storm raged, with no sign of abating. Upon the forlorn, tormented ship the evil weather vented its fury, tossing it like a scrap of driftwood over the towering, hammering waves.

The fears of the passengers mounted and recriminations reverberated throughout the hold as spouses squabbled about who was to blame for bringing them to this dreadful end. In the rat district, the scrawny inhabitants yowled with every crashing wave and many had been sick from sheer terror. Once, five of the hapless creatures tried to scramble to the passage which led to the upper deck but Mulligan had checked the stampede by standing resolutely in the way and knocking the first of the squealing brutes to the ground with his stick.

'There'll be none of you scarpering for the time being,' he shouted. 'We're not sunk yet!'

But the tempest gripped the *Calliope* more fiercely than ever. All around, the pounding waters reared into the shivering dark like mountains of despair – only to come smashing down on top of her.

In the hold an uneasy quiet had fallen – all were now too petrified to shriek or bewail their fate.

Anxiously they waited, enduring each shuddering blow that smote the hull as if it would be the last – the one that would finally bring an end to their misery.

Only the creaking of the ropes which held the cargo in place could be heard amid the roaring tumult and Thomas hoped that the crates were sufficiently fastened down.

'Green spare us!' Woodget whispered.

'Oh Aunty Lily!' Dimlon jabbered.

Suddenly, a wave more violent than any they had yet experienced rammed into the ship and as the hold tipped almost vertically, chaos and confusion erupted.

In that instant Thomas' voyage on board the *Calliope* ended, but in the years that followed he never forgot the sheer horror of those final terrible moments.

Screeching and howling, the passengers were thrown forward, tumbling uncontrollably along the main thoroughfare – falling on top of the panic-stricken, squawking rats.

Woodget went spinning head over heels down

the suddenly steep deck, his little figure bumping into Dimlon, who in turn fell against Thomas. Only Mulligan managed to save himself, snatching at a corner of tarpaulin as his fellow travellers were flung by, shrieking in terror, unable to stop themselves.

Like an insane see-saw, the *Calliope* jerked and plunged as the wild, merciless waters possessed it utterly and the passengers were shaken from port to starboard then fore to aft like jangling beads in an enormous rattle.

'If you value your necks, hold on!' Mulligan bawled. 'Or you'll be dashed to pieces. It's somersaults she'll be doing next!'

Toppling and slithering, the creatures in the hold grabbed at ropes, crates, chests – even the hull's rivets were scrabbled at in the frenzied struggles to find something to cling on to.

Somehow Woodget battled his way from the seething, wailing throng and made a frantic grab at one of the ropes.

But not all were quick enough to find a pawhold and back they fell when next the ship lurched, only to be thrust forward again as it wildly bucked and dipped.

Like a shrieking tide with flailing arms, thrashing legs and whisking tails the mice, rats, shrews, hedgehogs, stoats, voles and moles were washed to and fro. Lethal and hopeless was their plight, for no one could spare a paw to help them and those who valiantly struggled to save some poor, tumbling wretch were torn from their anchor and fell headlong into the screaming, steerless crowd.

But soon the violent, brutal shaking began to reap a horrible harvest.

Mothers screamed as children were ripped from their aching arms and went flying down the tilting deck to be lost amid the surging flow of tortured bodies. Breath was punched from lungs as feet and elbows drove heedlessly into stomachs. Many of Mulligan's snooty neighbours were already dead but their limp frames continued to be hurled across the hold. Heads cracked against the metal bulkheads and backs snapped when they struck the corners of great quivering crates. Skulls split open as they slammed into the hull and bones splintered, their fragmented spikes piercing mangled, flapping limbs.

Never in all his young life had Woodget been so frightened. It was as if they had suddenly plunged into a dark, tormented nightmare and he wrapped his arms and legs about the rope more tightly than ever. But every pitch and yaw brought new horrors as the rattling flotsam of the dead and dying flushed past him and in that snarl of bruised and fractured bodies he recognised many faces, young and old.

Despair filled the *Calliope* and the fieldmouse stared about him, sobbing with terror, searching for Thomas and the others.

'Tom!' he cried, ducking just in time as a rat's gangly, battered corpse cannoned by, almost knocking him from his perch. 'Tom! Where are you?'

Woodget's heart sank and he prayed that his friend was not amongst that jumbled multitude of the dead.

Outside, the maelstrom raged with increased savagery and from the engines there came a horrible sound of rending metal as the prop-shaft twisted and buckled.

'Over here!' Mulligan's voice called. 'We're over here.'

Separated by the central road, Woodget saw that Thomas, Dimlon, the Irish mouse and a host of others were clutching desperately at the tarpaulin.

But the sight brought little comfort, for at that moment the ship was lifted from the sea by a gargantuan wall of foaming, lightning-crowned water and hurled through the crackling air. Over and over the *Calliope* turned, flipped by the monstrous wave as if she were no more than a coin and then with a ruinous, almighty, deafening crash that jarred every one of Woodget's bones and had him squeezing shut his tear-filled eyes as tight as he possibly could, the ship returned to the sea.

In the grisly tangle of bodies which came smashing on to the deck, nothing stirred and all voices were stilled.

Whimpering, Woodget opened his eyes, not daring to hope that his friends had survived, but to his relief he saw that they were still clutching the tarpaulin.

Staring across at him, hanging on for dear life, Thomas managed a desperate nod. 'Don't worry!' he cried. 'We'll make it yet, Woodj!'

At his side Dimlon stared about him with his round eyes blinking in dismay and the three cork pendants which hung about his neck swinging violently with every jerking roll of the ship, smacking him in the face until he managed to wedge them under the strap of his satchel.

Only Mulligan appeared unafraid, yet his face was

terrible to look on for it was set and grim and as he raised his eyes to the ceiling he shouted his defiance to the Green Mouse and in that hour his mood was as black and thunderous as the tempest itself.

'This is not the end!' he bellowed. 'It cannot go down to the deeps. Hear me now, I command you, spare us from this pitiless storm!'

Then, Woodget noticed that Mulligan was only holding on with one fist – his free paw was tightly grasped about his precious bag and the fieldmouse gaped in bewilderment. Even encompassed by all this death and horror, the peg-leg was still protecting whatever secret was hidden in that pack.

'He's mad!' Woodget cried. 'Totally crazed – it can't possibly be worth riskin' his life fer.'

Outside, the typhoon screamed more viciously than ever and the *Calliope* floundered in the tortuous, rearing seas.

When another fierce wave pummelled the ship and sent it wheeling through the violent, ferocious tumult, Dimlon let out a shrill yell and his fingers slipped from the tarpaulin.

Squeaking, he tumbled down towards the mass of broken bodies but just as he thought his life was over, a rough, tattooed paw flashed out and Mulligan caught hold of him.

'Get you back here, lad!' he snapped hoisting the spluttering mouse back to safety before returning his paw to the bag.

Dimlon stared at him with a mixture of fear and gratitude in his wide eyes. For a brief instant he opened his mouth to thank him and then clapped it shut and turned quickly away.

'When will it cease?' Thomas cried. 'We can't go on much longer!'

Mulligan shook his head. 'That I don't know. But if it doesn't blow itself out soon then we're all done for one way or another.'

And then, cutting through their dread and fear a clear, resonant voice rang out above the din and the ringing words shone like a ray of hope in the pits of their despair.

Throughout everything Simoon had remained poised upon his bundle, his small seated figure never once caught off balance or off guard by any of the insane lunges of the ship. Now he lifted his head and cast back the fringed hood.

'Hearken to me!' he cried. 'There is yet a chance for us all. If you can suffer the hurts and abide your wounds but a little while more then the worst of the storm will truly have passed. Its malice is not directed towards us, yet we have dared to venture where only one vessel is permitted to voyage. Through the rim of its fury are we crossing but that will soon be past.'

Mulligan glared at him and the jerboa's great dark eyes gleamed back in acknowledgement.

'So it's nearly over!' Thomas yelled thankfully.

'No indeed,' came Simoon's cryptic and unpleasant reply. 'For soon your troubles begin in earnest.'

Thomas frowned but the prophet had pulled up his hood so that his face was lost in the shadows and he made no further movements nor would he answer any of the questions the survivors called to him.

Anxiously, but with a renewed faith for their salvation, the remaining passengers held on and though the *Calliope* continued to tip and tilt, gradually the violence decreased and the howl of the tempest began to fade.

'The phoney fortune teller was right,' Thomas muttered in disbelief.

'Course he was,' Mulligan told him, 'but it don't need no magic to predict that. Storms don't last forever, but the ship's still being knocked about out there.'

'But not half as bad,' Thomas answered. 'Why, I could even let go now and get over to Woodget.'

'You stay where you are!' the Irish mouse instructed. 'We're not through yet.'

Hearing this gruff statement, Simoon raised his head again and held up his paws.

'In that we are agreed,' he declared. 'Yet to cling on like ticks to flesh or spiders to webs, will not avail you now. The host is dying and only a few tattered strands remain of our spinning. In this evil hour we must face a new peril. Leave your moorings and head for the upper deck, while there is yet time.'

Sliding his feet from under the straps, Simoon leapt to the floor and with a small silver knife began cutting his unwieldy bundle of goods loose.

'Flee while you may!' he warned them. 'The moment of doom is nigh! Let it not override you!'

Everyone stared at him, that strange, velvet-robed creature who darted from one rope to another – hacking them in two.

'What's he doing?' Thomas murmured. 'What did he mean by "doom"?'

'The fool's addled,' Mulligan said. 'Look at him now, he's climbing back on top of his baggage.'

Sure enough, once the bundle was no longer

tethered to the crate, Simoon hauled himself back to his former position then folded his arms as if he were waiting for something.

'To look at him you might think he was simply going to fly out of this calamity,' Mulligan added scornfully, 'like a genie on a carpet.'

Further along the hold, Woodget craned his neck to see what the jerboa was up to and he wondered what he should do.

'Mister Simoon?' he cried. 'What'll happen?'

The prophet turned his head and bowed respectfully to the fieldmouse. 'Make haste,' he urged, 'gain the passage, run to the upper airs – it is your only chance.'

Such was the compelling force in his voice that Woodget let go of his rope and dropped on to the deck.

'Tom!' he cried. 'Come quick! Simoon says we must an' I believe him.'

'Don't be stupid!' Thomas yelled back. 'Be careful, Woodj, we might be thrown about again at any time!'

A soft, regretful sigh issued from Simoon's fringed hood. 'Alas,' he uttered. 'Already it is too late. The moment has come.'

Down the sloping passage there came the sound of running footsteps and into the hold tore Captain Gabriel Hewer. Wretchedly, he took in the awful spectacle of the squashed and broken dead, then called out at the top of his voice.

'Abandon ship! Abandon ship! The squall's driving her towards the rocks!'

At first the survivors merely gawped at him, doubting that the situation could get any worse, then the full horror of his words dawned on them and they leapt from their perches and bolted towards the passage as though all the servants of the legendary Hobb were pursuing them.

'Don't shove there!' boomed the captain. 'Let the wives and children go first. Hoy you, belay that pushing!'

But the passengers paid him little heed; their one consuming desire now was to gain the upper decks, to leave this appalling, grisly place where they had witnessed so many violent and needless deaths. Yet in spite of their anguish, and driven by the blindness of their terror, they ran over the fallen bodies that lay across their path, praying that there would be time to mourn for them and regret their careless tramplings later.

Still seated upon his belongings, Simoon watched them go screaming through the hold and his sparkling eyes sought for Woodget. Swamped within that frenzied mob there briefly glimmered a patch of reddish gold fur and the jerboa's thorny brows joined together as deep furrows scored his face.

Poor Woodget was caught in the overpowering flow of the screaming, stampeding survivors and was swept helplessly along, his scared little face bobbing up behind taller shoulders and upraised paws.

'Fare you well, Master Pipple,' Simoon breathed in a soft, sorrowful whisper. 'Many are the ordeals that yet await you. May such blessing as are in mine power to grant go with you. But I dread that against the trials to come their humble strength will fail. I pray that you do not.'

'Tom!' Woodget's plaintive voice cried. 'Tom!'

Further back in the surging crowd, Thomas vainly

tried to catch up with him but the crush was too fierce and he yelled Woodget's name as loud as he could.

'Wait for me!' he roared. 'Wait for me, Woodj!'

But the fieldmouse could not escape from the jostling, thrusting horde and was carried with them to the passage where they battled and kicked and forced their way in, cramming as many of their frantic, pressing bodies inside as they could.

Suddenly a tremendous crunch reverberated throughout the fabric of the *Calliope* which threw everyone to the ground, and those in the darkness of the passage screeched piteously as they stumbled over one another. Then the terror-charged air was blasted by a dreadful, nerve-shredding, scraping din as the keel was driven over rock and reef.

With its panels and timbers shuddering and groaning, the ship almost seemed to cry in agony as ugly rents were scored in her side, but still the gale slammed her to the utmost of her ruin and she was hurled against the rocks.

Once more the *Calliope* lurched but this time there came a terrible splintering of wood and metal and the hull bulged and hammered inwards.

Cracking like whips, the restraining ropes snapped around the cargo and the crates went skidding across the deck, killing all in their thunderous path. Toppling to destruction, the great wooden boxes split asunder, disgorging their contents over the floor – and then it happened.

With a deafening, grinding rip of juddering metal the hold buckled and was torn apart. Into the ship exploded a jag of solid rock that gouged up through the shivering deck like a massive black fang, and into the ship's flesh that tooth bit deeply.

At once the sea came flooding in, the clamour of its spouting greed outmatched only by the screams of those still trapped in the hold.

'Come on lads!' Mulligan bawled at Thomas and Dimlon. 'Get you above. There's lifebelts enough for all. The ship can't help us now, she's done her best!'

In the passage the thick wailing current of charging creatures climbed ever upwards but the way was narrow and their progress painfully slow.

Still caught far behind them, Thomas turned to look on the daunting sight of the deluge which was boiling and gushing its way inside. Already the stern was sinking and the wool sacks by the aft bulkhead submerged beneath a seething flood.

'Why can't they hurry?' he cried, desperate to follow Woodget to the upper deck. 'If we don't make a move soon the water'll be over our heads.'

'No, no, no,' asserted Mulligan, adding darkly, 'the ship won't stay in one piece for that long – she'll be ripped apart.'

Hopping up and down at their side, Dimlon abruptly leapt into the opening as the crowd in front flowed forward. 'Now!' he yelled. 'Hurry, get inside – we can begin the climb!'

Mulligan lumbered after him but Thomas hesitated, for there, down the central aisle, still sitting on top of his bundle of goods, was Simoon.

Already the water was racing up the crate-blocked thoroughfare and splashing towards him, but the prophet did not appear to care. His paws were resting lightly upon his knees and Thomas thought he heard the jerboa chanting to himself.

'Simoon!' the mouse called. 'Get over here – now!'

Slowly the jerboa turned to him and the dark eyes glittered as he raised a puny paw.

'Look to yourself, Master Stubbs!' he shouted back. 'Fear not for Simoon! But turn if you can from the treacherous course which lies ahead of you. Disprove my words at our first meeting. Safeguard those around you, do not betray the trust of he who loves you as a brother. Farewell!'

To Thomas' dismay the hull shivered as the gash in the *Calliope*'s belly was ripped ever wider and the angry waves came rushing up to meet the waiting Simoon.

'Tom lad!' Mulligan's anxious voice boomed. 'Get you in here!'

Thomas turned and fled into the passage but his last glimpse of the jerboa haunted him long after. With a serene expression upon his face, Simoon gazed at the endless, roaring waters as they flushed around his goods and even as the hold split in two and a wall of frothing brine came crashing in, the bundle was lifted up and the prophet was swept into the far, murderous darkness.

Outside, a jagged pinnacle of spiking black rock thrust from the seething fury of the waves and on to this awful, wrecking peak, the *Calliope* had been bitterly impaled. Now her gored, shattered bulk was plucked by the tempest and stung by the driving rain. All around, the thunder boomed and trumpeted and the blackened heavens were riven with dazzling stabs and spears of wrathful lightning.

Into this deadly storm the remaining passengers emerged, spurting suddenly on to the upper, rain-lashed deck. Immediately a vast wave came sweeping over the side and four unwary mice were washed into the sea – their squeals lost in the raging wind.

With his woollen hat pulled down about his ears but unprotected from the needle-sharp, biting rain, Woodget clung desperately to the deck rail as the torrential tides came blasting against the *Calliope*'s broken stern and everyone around him howled in terror.

No one knew what to do. The lifeboats were gone, for the official crew had abandoned the ship before she hit the rocks. All that remained were the large cork lifebelts but what hope was there in those if the full devastating might of the violent sea was ranged against them?

'What'll we do?' screeched the mice. 'We should have stayed below.'

Many of them tried to fight their way back to the passage but collided with the overpowering surge of their fellow passengers who were still issuing on to the deck – wailing that the waters were rising behind them.

They were trapped, there was nowhere else to go, but in that fearful gale they could not survive for long and beneath their very feet the ship was breaking up.

Consumed by terror and despair, nearly all of the gibbering, tremulous rats cast themselves over the side, hoping to find sanctuary from this terrible plight upon the great rock which towered upon the left. Perhaps some crevice or shelter could be found in that monument of destruction where they could escape the brutal ravages of the savage weather. But even as they hurled themselves off the edge, the wind tore at them and the poor, puling creatures were dashed against the hard rock or flung into the churning sea.

Abruptly, the deck splintered and buckled in two and the cries of the passengers increased. To face the sea clutching only a lifebelt was an insane prospect but to remain here was to meet certain death.

As the waves roared over the sides, the bravest fought their way forward to where the lifebelts were stowed and yanked them free. To the mice the circles of red and white painted cork were huge, but they could bear at least thirty survivors without difficulty.

Drenched with salt spray and beating rain but too afraid to move, Woodget could only watch as the rest of them made a dash for the seven belts and he glanced back to the passage, but Thomas and the others were still nowhere to be seen.

Around the rapidly disintegrating carcass of the *Calliope*, the sea was thick with its surrendered and plundered cargo. Barrels bounced and rolled upon the ferocious waters, wooden chests rode the inflamed tide to be smashed upon the adamantine rocks and in that confused slick of crate and keg, a small round nest was carried by a crest of foam – its occupants trembling still.

Yet upon the creaking deck, fear had bred selfishness and spite. Four of the lifebelts were already being hoisted over the deck rail, but few were those who lifted them and they would suffer no one else to join their craven crew – kicking and punching away all who tried.

With their paws clutching at the cork and their fingers gripping the attached ropes, a group of five stoats charged over the edge and plunged down into the wild sea. More lifebelts followed but none were sufficiently moused and soon only two were left and already they were being towed to the rail.

'Stop right there!' bellowed a ferocious, commanding voice and there was the captain, tearing up from the flooding passage with Mulligan and the others followed close behind.

'Tom!' Woodget squeaked. 'I was so scared. I thought you was dead!'

Thomas hurried to his friend's side then glared across at those trying to make off with the lifebelts.

'We'll all be dead if we don't put a stop to that!' he yelled.

Over the deck the skipper ran, cuffing the heads of the mice and voles who were making off with the remaining lifebelts. After him hobbled Mulligan and the peg-leg's stick went swiping across the fingers of those the captain missed. Even Dimlon was incensed and with an expression upon his face that startled Woodget and daunted those before him, the pale grey mouse waded into the rest of the cowardly thieves.

'Now!' Captain Hewer bawled when the lifebelts were liberated. 'Let the weaker folk come forward and take tight hold. That's it, as many as can squeeze on.'

In the squalling rain the passengers gripped the cork and ropes until nothing of the belt could be seen under their huddled bodies. Then they battled against the gale to the side and tumbled into the swirling waters below.

'Right,' Mulligan shouted to Thomas and the others, 'this one's the last, so take a position, lads.'

But there were too many for the final lifebelt to bear and to their dismay everyone realised that many would be forced to stay behind.

'Youngest first,' the captain commanded. 'You'll have to remain here, Mulligan.'

The Irish mouse stared at him. 'I can't!' he declared. 'I've got to get off this ship. You don't understand – I must be spared. I have to!'

'You'll do as I say,' the captain snapped back. 'Let the youngsters go, we've had our share of life. Give them a chance.'

Mulligan's face went pale and his paw clenched his stick more firmly than ever as he prepared to do what he must. But, before he could carry out the heinous plan his desperate brain was formulating, a wave greater than the others came crashing upon them.

The deck crunched and snapped beneath the dreadful, violent blow. Its timbers were dragged into the sea, leaving only a floundering, railless section wedged between the rocks. Twenty-three mice, rats, shrews and voles were thrown overboard and drowned in the deep and amongst their forsaken number was the captain. But upon that last, resolute fragment of the *Calliope* the final lifebelt was still waiting to enter the waters.

Few now were left to cling to its sides but there stood Mulligan and the others. Grimly, ashamed at the thought of what he might have been compelled to do, the Irish mouse snatched at a rope and Dimlon squeezed in behind him.

'Come on, Woodj!' Thomas said. 'There's just room enough for you an' me.'

Together they reached for the lifebelt but their paws never touched it.

At that moment a second mighty wave thundered across the broken deck and with their terrified shrieks ringing in Mulligan's ears, both Thomas and Woodget were dragged into the tempest-torn, froth-capped sea.

8

At the Shrine of Virbius

Far from the treacherous, biting rocks the two quailing mice were swept – out into the thrashing tumult which wrenched and snatched at their striving bodies. High the heaving, swollen waves lifted them, before flinging their defenceless, tumbling figures back into the deep – crashing a deluge of pounding waters over their small, gasping heads.

Unable to swim, Woodget's arms and legs kicked and flailed helplessly in the almighty, churning sea and, as he squealed for help, the choking brine flooded into his mouth.

Retching and battling futilely against all hope, the fieldmouse's gargling yells were seized by the devouring gale and scattered into the blaring storm.

Vainly he tried to keep his head above the water, but his limbs were tiring and his muscles ached. He no longer knew where Thomas was. At first, when the immense wave had plucked them from the shrinking deck they had endeavoured to stay together, but the thrusting push of the unyielding current proved too strong and swiftly the two friends were separated. With every blast of the violent, pummelling wind, the gulf between Woodget and Thomas widened until mountainous cliffs of rearing water and dense, impenetrable swathes of steaming spume and spray isolated them both.

From the black, clangorous heavens, livid spikes of lightning leapt and flashed, discharging into the flaring sea – illuminating in stark, blinding instants the immense, unquestionable authority of the vast encircling waters.

Woodget was lost, his tiny form no match for the ancient, peerless might of the roaring deeps. Gradually his panicky, frenetic splashings grew weaker and more often now did his head dip below the destroying waves. Sea water filled the fieldmouse's nostrils and glugged into his balking mouth as he gulped down his final breath. The cork talisman bobbed pathetically at his breast as the tempest beat upon him and his lungs strained for air.

It was too great a trial for one small fieldmouse who had only ever waded in the stream near his home before boarding the *Calliope*. Then the water had merely reached his knees. It had been a delicious summer's afternoon and he had thought himself marvellously daring to sit in the centre of that sweet, trickling brook and lie down to cool his sunburned ears and tail.

Now he was lost, engulfed in the fathomless expanse of the wide, beleaguering oceans, no more than a speck to be devoured and forgotten. It was useless to try fighting that cold, unconquerable realm, better to slide into the oblivious dark and cease the unavailing contest. There was no escape from the force of the unbeaten waters and no chance of release, he was theirs now. Woodget belonged utterly to that uncharted murk, it had claimed him and it was time to surrender.

Under the gale-driven waves his lolling head sank; the sea water rushed into his ears and closed over his head until the only sound was the amplified thump of the blood in his veins and the frantic pattering of his bursting heart.

Down Woodget spiralled, his tail whirling behind him. For a brief while a trail of silvery bubbles leaked from his lips, before failing completely when his lungs were finally spent. At last it was over; his bitter grapplings with life were done. The inviting deep had mastered him and, as he descended from the cares of the riotous world above, a prickling blackness crept over his limbs.

Only one glimmer of joy glowed in the closing windows of his mind. An image of that summer's day when he had gazed upon Bess with the sunlight glinting in her chestnut hair and the scintillating reflections playing over her lovely face. On that glorious afternoon his heart knew he loved her and the sound of her blissful laughter echoed faintly in his flooded ears. Then, like a spent, wavering flame, the image was extinguished and Woodget's unconscious mind flitted into the snug vanquishing void as his limp body twirled lifelessly down.

Thomas flayed his arms about him, yelling the fieldmouse's name between his gasping breaths. Yet only the howling night answered and his worst fears soared.

The last glimpse he had seen of Woodget had been many minutes ago and then his friend had been floundering amid the crashing waves – spluttering and coughing as his little arms beat hopelessly in the water. But the storm had driven them further apart and Thomas wept as he guessed the awful fate that had befallen him.

'No,' he blurted, his tears squandered in the raging tempest. 'Woodget!'

But there was no time to grieve, for his own desperate contest for survival was still being waged and his life teetered in the balance. More powerful than the fieldmouse's arms were those of Thomas but in that fierce turmoil his labours were of little use. He knew that soon his fight too would be over, yet valiantly he battled on.

Then, just when his thoughts became as clouded as the perilous night, a miraculous chance occurred and in that desperate hour Thomas' flagging spirits rallied and dared to hope for deliverance.

From the surrounding darkness, propelled upon a breaking, foaming white wave, a barrel torn from the ship's hold came rolling into view.

Not wasting a moment, in case the perfidious waters whisked it away again, Thomas used the last dregs of his strength and toiled towards it.

Anxious seconds stretched by as the mouse swam, spurring himself through the clashing waves, his eyes fixed upon the reassuring bulk of the floating cask in front. About him the lightning flickered and the thunder shook the deep calm reaches of the sea but Thomas was blind and deaf to all else now.

Before his salt-stung eyes, the barrel grew ever larger and he struggled closer – then, with a trembling, quivering wrench, he dragged his arm from the waters and to his lasting joy clamped his paw upon one of the cask's sturdy metal bands.

Sobbing in relief, he managed to haul himself from the waves then collapsed across the wooden sides – overcome by exhaustion, fear and the horrible, searing loss of his dearest friend.

'Woodget!' his whimpering voice cried. 'Woodget!'

Mulligan grunted and rolled on to his back. Drifting from the aching oblivion that had stolen over him as he clung to the gale-tossed lifebelt, his senses slowly revived.

A cool, refreshing breeze was now blowing upon his grizzled, sand-crumbed face, bearing the fragrance of wild thyme and pine trees, mingled with the pungent scent of burning grasses and acrid woodsmoke.

In the distance he could hear the dim rumour of the tempest as it travelled over the sea, the faint rumblings of thunder becoming ever softer and more remote.

Groaning, the Irish mouse realised that his left arm lay twisted beneath him and the wound in his shoulder had opened again, smarting from the salt water of his sodden fur.

Gingerly he wriggled his fingers to ensure no bones were broken then slid his sprained arm from under him and sat up, opening a bleary eye.

Above him, in a sky scoured clean and clear by the awful storm, a full moon was shining – its silver radiance flooding the world below and casting a bright path over the becalmed waters of the sea.

As one emerging from a deep, troubled sleep, Mulligan stared about him, waiting for his jangled wits to collect and order themselves.

He was sitting upon a bank of wet sand that sloped down to the water's edge where the rippling waves meekly lapped the shore. The curving coastline was strewn with all manner of wreckage. Splintered relics of the *Calliope* littered the moon-bathed sands; shards of shattered timber jutted from the beach like long, deadly thorns and fragments of broken crates floated as a thick, crusting scum upon the placid waters.

Groggily turning his head, Mulligan saw that behind him the sandbank rose gently, before levelling into a grassy upland – fringed and bound with the dark, grasping shapes of gnarled, weather-twisted shrubs.

To his surprise it all looked vaguely familiar; a curious tingling crept down his spine but the answers eluded his bewildered mind.

'I know this place,' he mumbled in a daze. 'I know it. Certain sure I am . . . I've been here before . . . and yet . . .'

Mulligan sighed, it was still too soon, no doubt it would become plain enough in time.

Turning back to the shore, his gaze fell upon his

bag that had slipped from his shoulder and was now lying almost buried in the sand.

'My pack!' he cried, lurching forward to seize hold of his precious belongings. 'Sure, it's born lucky you were, Mulligan.' Then, even as he was congratulating himself, his face darkened – what had happened to the others?

Clumsily, the peg-leg picked himself up and scanned the sands.

Only then did he realise that not all of the wreckage consisted of the mere splintered remains of the *Calliope*. Here and there, sprinkled carelessly over the beach, Mulligan saw the bodies of his fellow travellers.

Upon the damp, silent shore they lay: mice, voles, stoats, hedgehogs, moles and rats. The faces of some stared up at the bright moon with glazed, unseeing eyes while others were half hidden by torn fronds of seaweed and dusted by sand.

Sadly, the Irish mouse stepped between the scattered dead, pausing beside each of them to see if it was not too late, but in this quest he held little hope.

'All gone,' he whispered. 'Aye, for them the way was too harsh. Many more I reckon are at the bottom of that deceitful ocean now. To look at her, all flat and glasslike, you'd never suspect. As cruel as they come she is. Takes a battered old rogue like me to come safe through her perils. But a tragic, sorry loss this night has been. Am I then the only one?'

Bereft of his stick which no doubt was floating upon the great waters somewhere, he limped morosely back along the bank, engulfed in troubled thought, then he paused and his heart beat faster.

There, down by the water's edge, within a great clump of tangled weed and broken timber he glimpsed the edge of something round, painted red and white.

Urgently, he bounded down the sands and tore the weed-twisted splinters away – then gave a loud cry.

'Dimmy!'

With his paws still clutched to the lifebelt, his legs and tail submerged in the shallow waters and the satchel marked with the letter 'D' twined about his body, lay Dimlon. But the pale grey mouse was sprawled motionless and his heavy lids were closed over his eyes.

Anxiously, Mulligan fell to his knees and pressed an ear to the mouse's chest.

'By the Green's beard!' he cried in delight. 'The lad's alive!'

Hastily, he hauled Dimlon from the water and laid him upon the sands.

'You'll soon be spouting nonsense again,' Mulligan chuckled. 'Seems we've both got charmed lives.'

Grinning his lop-sided smile, Mulligan thanked providence, then slowly, as if some outside influence exerted its will upon him, he raised his eyes and gazed inland once more.

Beyond the knotted shrubs, the vague outline of a dark wood crowded the foothills of a great and lofty mountain range whose sheer, limestone crags shone milk-white under the resplendent moon. Yet rising before those shadowy heights, black and dense against the shimmering heavens, was an immense plume of dark smoke.

The smile perished on Mulligan's lips and he cursed

his jumbled wits for failing to recognise it sooner.

'I do know this place,' he uttered in a hoarse gasp of disbelief. 'Yonder are the White Mountains – the Lefka Ori! By all that's wonderful, that cursed storm has washed me to the very foot of them. I'm on Crete! It's swept me to the very spot I was headed for!'

Trembling with excitement, he stared at the immense mass of the mountains and drew a paw over his eyes. 'The Shrine of Virbius! At last I've come to the Temple of the Twelve Maidens. The sacred pillars of the Lord's birthplace!'

Astounded by this amazing chance, but alarmed by the climbing column of smoke in the distance, Mulligan took a last look at Dimlon and patted his head affectionately.

'Have to leave you now, matey,' he breathed. 'Old Mulligan's got important business to attend to, though it looks like I'm here too late. You ought to be safe for the meantime, sure – I'll come back for you when I can, so I will.'

Quickly the Irish mouse trudged up the sandbank and soon the shore was left behind as he pushed through a gap in the hedge and limped his way into the meadow beyond. Through fields filled with blue anemone, yellow flax, white crocus and pale purple corydalis he went and steadily the ground began to rise until he was lost in the shaded pine woods which skirted the mountainside.

Many years had passed since Mulligan first set foot upon the soil of that hallowed country. Here, as a boy, his father had brought him and with the wide, awe-filled eyes of an infant he had glimpsed the stones of the revered shrine where the spirit of the Green was reputed to have originally risen from the barren earth.

It had always been a beautiful haven of peace, one of the dwindling number of sites where the Divine still flourished and was venerated. Nestling upon the mountain's shoulders, the ancient temple had, through the ages, fallen into a stately decay – a graceful collection of eroded stones rearing from the verdant ground and pointing skyward. At the edge of a wide ring the pillars were arranged, girding a bowl-shaped hollow where a large altar jutted from the centre.

All his life Mulligan had loved the worn marble of its pillars and the grass-grown mosaics that covered the temple's floor. To all outside observers it was merely another time-ground ruin but there the primal forces of life and light were worshipped. Yet the only offerings placed upon the sacrificial stone of Virbius were garlands of flowers and baskets of fruit given in gratitude of the Green's bounty.

Behind the worn unroofed stones of the temple, the real shrine was located, for there grew the sacred grove where, on certain nights of the year, His glorious presence could be glimpsed shimmering under the branches like the ghostly reflection of stars upon the water.

There in the thickets of evergreen oak, wherein stood a throne wrought of leaf and bough, Mulligan had first heard his father recount the history of the Dark Despoiler and the terrible legacy that had been entrusted unto their kin. Since that far off day, the images conjured in the Irish mouse's mind as the legend unfolded had forever plagued his waking hours. Now he was embroiled even deeper inside the unending saga as it threatened to burst back into the living world.

Many times had Mulligan returned to the temple during the course of his wayfaring life and always the maidens who preserved its memory and tended the altar welcomed him, for he was the last of his line – heir to a part of the great burden which they too shared.

Now the blessed woods which had once been filled with the chanting hymns of devout pilgrims and the murmur of solemn prayers, were hushed and still. As his hobbling steps carried Mulligan beneath the high pines and cypresses, the reek of burning and destruction grew ever fiercer. Choking streams of billowing fumes coursed between the trees and through the leaves ahead he could see the angry flicker of flaming tongues.

Sternly, he spurred himself on, crashing through the final distance, until the woods opened up around him and the green sward of the hillside stretched before him – up to the Temple of the Twelve Maidens and the Shrine of Virbius.

'No,' Mulligan gasped as his eyes beheld the terrible devastation that had been visited upon the once idyllic place. 'Not here!'

Every one of the temple's weathered pillars had been hurled to the ground and set rolling down the sloping lawns, and behind it the sacred grove itself was ablaze.

Angrily, the Irish mouse lumbered on, over the trampled grass that had been flattened and furrowed by countless razoring claws, until he stood at the very edge of the ring where the pillars had stood.

Only two of the round stones remained rooted in position, but over their weathered surface vile pictures and ghastly curses had been scrawled in a red, sticky substance.

Even as he turned from them, his nostrils impressed upon him the true horror of the night.

Borne upon the scorching fumes that polluted the cool air was a frightful stink, like the iron-tanged stench of a charnel house. The awful fetor of raw, chopped flesh and freshly-spilled blood hung thick and cloying upon the ash-drifting atmosphere, catching in the back of his throat and forming a syrupy, metallic bitterness upon his cringing tongue.

Steeling his nerves, the mouse stepped down into the temple and through the swirling clouds of hot, concealing smoke.

Suddenly Mulligan let out a cry of disgust and he reeled backwards as his tormented eyes beheld the grim spectacle at the centre of that once tranquil and hallowed place.

Upon those faded, moss-encroached mosaics, he saw them – a mass of cruelly slaughtered bodies.

There, around a large stone, engulfed in a pool of congealing gore, lay many folk of the temple – but the white robes they had worn were now stained crimson and slashed to shreds. Their carcasses had been thrown into one untidy, irreverent pile, but Mulligan's horror at the sight spiralled when he saw that nine heads had been savagely hacked off at the neck and arranged into a serpentine, wriggling shape upon the ground. Beside this gruesome, snaking line, ugly scarlet letters had been daubed and Mulligan shivered when he read them.

Nine bright stars from out the void
shining up on high

It was the first part of an ancient rhyme which he knew only too well and in a low, murmuring, fearful whisper he chanted it to himself.

Nine bright stars from out the void
shining up on high
whose banished soul do they call back
and augur in the sky?
Despoiler of the ancient lands,
who baked the deserts dry.
Scarophion, Scarophion – the demon is close by.

Mulligan staggered away from the monstrous row of decapitated heads, carefully avoiding the oozing lake of blood and muttering oaths under his breath to call upon the protection of the Green Mouse to save him from the momentous evil his eyes were witnessing.

Within that repulsive heap of the butchered dead, Mulligan recognised the shapely arms of maidens and knew that, somewhere along that snaking line, their once lovely faces were now hewn and chopped.

'This is madness,' he wept, 'the madness of that foul, worming devil. The Scale have been here – those bloody-clawed, heathen murderers!'

Unable to look on that dreadful spectacle any more, he wheeled about and stared instead at the inferno which raged where the grove had once stood.

The oaks that had grown there for so many years, watching the stones crumble before them with the slow passing of the ages, were wreathed with ravaging, destroying flames and under the intense heats the mighty trees withered and blackened. Into the sky the dark pall of smoke rose, glittering with orange cinders that soared up on the violent, baking airs and floated in smouldering clouds out over the dark woodlands.

'There's nothing left here now,' Mulligan murmured desolately. 'The power of the Green has fled this place and won't never return. Is this how it shall be? Is the enemy to win at every turn? It's fearsome strong they've become if they can assail His very birthplace. What chance have I now? What chance have any of—'

Mulligan's voice drifted into silence and he looked up sharply. Above the spitting crackle of the devouring flames his ears had caught the unmistakable sound of someone weeping.

Hurriedly, he lumbered from the fume-flooded temple and climbed the three steps to stand upon the grass again.

'Hoy there!' he called. 'Who is it?'

Upon one of the toppled stones that had been cast down the hillside, crouched a hunched, sobbing figure. To Mulligan's surprise he saw that it was a mouse maiden and she was dressed in a robe of pure white but under the glare of the burning oaks she seemed to be arrayed in a single brilliant flame.

At the sound of his call, the maiden lifted her head and gazed fearfully across at him – perhaps not all of the foul brutes had departed upon the hideous ship, maybe one had been left behind to ensure that the temple folk were indeed completely slain.

She was a young, frightened-looking mouse, with

light brown fur and a face that was wet with wretched tears. Her long black hair was twined high upon her head and on her brow she wore a plain circlet of fine silver.

Quivering with emotion, she peered through the drifting smoke at the sturdy outline of the one-legged mouse and her nervous apprehensions vanished immediately. She knew that unmistakable silhouette well enough, and a surge of relief and elation rushed through her being. To see a familiar face in the midst of all the chaos and despair was beyond anything she had hoped for and gladly she ran over the trampled lawn to meet him.

'Mulligan!' she cried, her voice hoarse with weeping. 'In the hour of my utmost sorrow you have come – the Green Himself must have sent you to me.'

Mulligan limped forward and into his outstretched arms the maiden cast herself, clinging to his solid bulk like a child to its father and into his barrel of a chest she let loose the full tide of her grief.

For several minutes, the Irish mouse comforted her as best he was able, waiting until the shuddering sobs which possessed her finally subsided.

'Now then,' he began gently, 'are you up to telling me what happened here this night?'

Wiping her eyes, she pulled away from him and stared over his shoulder to where the broken temple was choked with smoke, then beyond to where the fires still blazened greedily.

'Not here,' she uttered. 'Not so close to . . . to what lies in there.'

'Come then,' he said hobbling down the hillside,

'let us be free of this reek at any rate and sit where the air is sweeter.'

Yet the maiden lingered where she stood, as if the sight of the wanton destruction and the awful knowledge of those concealed within the cloaking fumes mesmerised her.

'Did you . . . did you look on them?' she asked in a flat, dead tone. 'I was too afeared to. I cannot compel my feet to bear me inside that place, tell me are they . . . are they all . . . ?'

'Every one of them,' Mulligan answered, 'unless others escaped like you, but there's nowt we can do for those poor folk in there now, save inter them.'

Tearing her eyes from the horrible scene, the maiden turned back to him but all expression had left her face, no trace of the desolation that had wrung her could be seen now; it was as if her spirit had perished and Mulligan's heart bled to see it.

'No,' she said softly. 'I was the only one outside the temple when the . . . the attack happened. Neltemi is my name. I do not think you would recall me for I was only a child when you last visited our shores. I was but a pilgrim's daughter at the time and entered the service of the temple seven years ago.'

Mulligan gave her paws an encouraging squeeze and asked, 'How is it you survived this carnage?'

Neltemi stared over to where the dark, shadowy woods bordered the sloping hillside. 'When the outriding gales of the tempest fell upon us,' she began, 'I was abroad in the forest, searching for blooms to weave in a garland to place upon the altar.'

Her voice dropped to a throaty whisper and she sat upon the gouged lawn before continuing.

'Never had I seen such a fury of nature,' she murmured, 'yet it was not a natural storm. All around me the trees were swaying and creaking down to their roots, then it seemed to me that evil voices were carried upon that blasting gale. I became afraid and sought for shelter. Even as the rains began to batter from the thundering clouds I gained the higher ground to the west of here, and there in a shallow cave I waited for it to pass.'

'What happened then?' Mulligan asked.

'It did not pass,' she told him bleakly. 'The tempest grew worse and from my vantage point I saw a vast shadow come sailing over the sea. Like a black cloud it was, but travelling low over the water until it drove far on to the shore and then the guise lifted and I saw it, the glittering ship with its fearsome prow.'

The maiden gripped Mulligan's arm desperately. 'It was the vessel of Scarophion,' she hissed, 'and on to the sands leaped none other than the High Priest himself.'

'Are you sure of that?'

'It could only have been he,' she answered vehemently. 'Who else could radiate such evil and torment the elements so? Then, behind his loathsome form, the army of the Scale came. Beneath the lightning the steel of their swords flashed and into the trees they rampaged, their savage cries riding upon the winds.'

Neltemi glanced back at the ravaged temple and bowed her head. 'My folk were unarmed and unprepared,' she said simply. 'No battle ensued, no ringing of sword against sword. All I heard were their screams as they were cruelly put to death and the rumble of the stones when the pillars were hurled down.

'Then the grove was invaded and despoiled and the trees were kindled. But none of those heinous deeds, not even the murder of so many innocents, those whom I loved as my own kin, none of that compares with the dreadful knowledge of what they have stolen.'

The maiden fixed her gaze upon the stricken face of the old seafarer at her side and in a frail whimper added, 'They have taken it. The seventh fragment which we have kept secret and guarded these many ages has been reclaimed by the infernal legions of the Dark Despoiler. His power is waxing Mulligan, and there is nothing we can do to check it. This hallowed place has proven to be no match for their barbaric might. Why did the Council not warn us of their strength? We were told the Scale would not dare to assail us.'

Mulligan laughed grimly. 'Aye,' he said. 'I too was told the self-same thing and yet I was pursued, followed all the way from Greenwich and who knows, maybe even before that. Seems that the wisdom of some ain't as keen as it used to be. Either that or there's a traitor at work.'

Neltemi shivered, then looked at him curiously. 'And what of your errand?' she asked cautiously. 'Did you bring *it* from the Starwife's realm?'

'That I did,' he answered, patting his bag. 'The old battleaxe gave it up to me, though whilst I was kept waiting outside her chamber I thought she'd decided the nine years weren't enough and she'd hold on to it a bit longer.'

'Steeped in wisdom is the Handmaiden of Orion,' Neltemi murmured. 'Or so it is said. She would not keep the fragment any longer than she ought. Even though she was never a custodian of the other pieces, surely she is aware of the peril they bring? It is hazard enough to guard our own charges, for you know the ruin the works of Scarophion bring.

'Where each of the nine fragments have been hidden, their malignance has cultivated decay and nourished weariness until the very stones despair and crumble to dust. Deserts and wastelands have those once fair regions become, or else confined to the dim memory of history as were we. Yet the burden you bear is the mightiest of them all. Too imbued with the evil of the coiled one is that fragment and thus have your family been accursed.'

'Accursed?' he repeated. 'Aye that's the very word for it. Bearing this thing in secrecy once every nine years from place to place is no great labour, but home and hearth have been denied me. No heir have I to continue the errand and maybe I should give thanks for that. No child of mine would I wish to pass this vileness on to. No, the toils of me and my ancestors shall finish when I do.'

'But it cannot remain in any one place for all time,' Neltemi answered. 'Even the Starwife would not permit it to remain in her own land longer than was necessary. This evil must never be entombed in one region forever. Think of the damage its very presence would cause.'

Mulligan stared at his pack thoughtfully. 'I know it,' he muttered. 'But I also know that other forces are at work now. The Council bid me to carry this treacherous object here and await instruction. Why so? That is something they have never done before. What reason did they have? Who was I to see?'

'I know not,' she answered. 'If Cisseus, the head of our order, knew of it then she told no other, and now it is too late. Cisseus lies dead within the temple and I cannot aid you. Little do I know of the Council's intent, I was but a gatherer of flowers and chanter of hymns, nothing more.'

Mulligan chewed the problem over carefully. 'Well,' he decided at last. 'It is plain that this loathsome device cannot remain here, the shrine is destroyed. As you cannot advise me, then only one course can I see now.'

'The city of Hara!' Neltemi breathed. 'Yes, within its sculpted walls the final hope resides. Should that sanctuary fail then the light will indeed be doomed to darkness everlasting. If the Holy One cannot guide you then all are lost.'

'Aye, but now the time runs short,' Mulligan added. 'The Scale will return far over the seas with their hellish prize. How long is it till they come marauding again or one of their agents is successful? Is this not the year when *His* stars are to be ranged in the heavens? I guess as much from what I read back there in that place of death.'

'When the moon has waned and waxed again, the nine shall glimmer above,' she answered gravely, 'and not once in another hundred winters shall they converge again. But my heart fears that never again will they need to wait, for this is the age of *His* renewal. Perhaps all our efforts have been in vain. Nearly all our glories have faded; the cities are dwindled into the dust or jungles have devoured them.'

'Well, I'll not give up hope of it yet,' Mulligan cried, 'but it's off at once I must be going. There's passage I have to find; a long trek to India so it is.'

Neltemi rose and laid a paw upon his cheek. 'Then the last handmaiden of the temple bids you farewell,' she said.

'I'll not go till I've helped you sort this out,' he told her. 'You've no wish to see the horrors piled in yonder wreckage. I'll do what needs to be done.'

The maiden shook her head. 'No,' she said, 'you shall not. It is true, I have no desire to look upon what the temple now holds and my nerves rebel at the very thought, but there are no others to assist. You, Master Mulligan – son of Padraic – cannot afford to waste even a moment more. Go now, tarry not for my sensibilities. I will command my courage and see to the dead to ensure they are honoured in our fashion. Your task is greater and will prove the most difficult. When you see the Holy One, tell him of us, tell him the Shrine of Virbius is ended and that in the city of Hara the fate of the world now lies.'

'I'll see that he knows,' Mulligan promised, 'and who can tell? If the Scale are vanquished a second time, perhaps the Temple of the Twelve Maidens will rise again and new groves shall grow.'

Neltemi managed a weak smile, then her forehead creased into a frown and she stared fixedly at the shadowy woods nearby.

'In there!' she hissed. 'A movement!'

With his paw on his bag, Mulligan whirled around

and from the shade of the trees a thin, dark figure emerged.

'Who is it?' Neltemi asked. 'Can it be one of the heathen disciples?'

To her astonishment, the one-legged mouse laughed. 'Nay,' he answered, 'that's nothing to be scared of.'

On to the despoiled lawn the newcomer blundered, his ungainly feet traipsing a crooked path over the trampled grasses. Like a drunken owl, his head bobbed and swivelled from side to side upon his long neck, while at his sides his arms flapped in a ridiculous, flustered manner.

Neltemi stared at the peculiar stranger, and started when from his mouth she heard his high squeaking voice shout, 'Mister Mulligan! Wetan'-drenchedsandcloggeddrippynoseawfulfrighted I am! I doesn't like it. Oh, I wish I was back with Aunty!'

Mulligan raised a paw in greeting. 'Ahoy there, Dimmy!' he called. 'It's pleased I am to see you.'

'On the beach back there!' the youngster whined, hurrying over the lawn. 'Bashedbrokebitsan' deadunsallabout they was all drownded – all them mice an' voles and such. All of 'em gone and I don't know what became of Woody an' Tom. Like as not they're swillin' about somewhere too, oh it's so fritful!'

Neltemi's eyebrows arched to a point as the pale grey mouse lumbered closer, his face screwed up in misery and his satchel swinging at his waist.

'You know this one?' she whispered to Mulligan.

'Aye,' he replied. 'Name's Dimmy – and I've never known a title more suited to no one.'

'Yet he managed to find you simple enough,' she said, 'though all the isle of Crete stretched about him.'

Hearing her words as he came puffing up in front of them, Dimlon threw his arms about Mulligan's shoulders and in a wailing, gabbling voice wept, 'I seed the marks your wooden leg made in the sand and how they were headed for the smoke. Was that clever? Would Aunty be proud? It was lonely on the beach, only dunkedmoleys and coldsoppingshrews and mices, so many faces I knew. Is the harm and hurt over now – is the risk finishedan'done? Are we safe Mister Mulligan, can we stay here and be safe as castleswithdrawbridgesbigtowerslotsofbubblyoil-tothrowdownonbadnastyheads? No more boaty-bobbers for Dimmy, not never – oh but then I won't see Aunty again.'

'Don't you go bawling your eyes out,' the Irish mouse chided him. 'I've more to do than dry them.'

Dimlon sniffed then glanced at the maiden before turning to stare at the fierce burning which still raged further up the hill.

'Someone's played with fire,' he warbled, his eyes rolling in their sockets. ' "Don't you go fiddling with that tinder box, Knucklepateslopwit or you'll frazzle your ears off!" that's what she tells me. Oh but what a beautishusbigflickerysparkwhizzingblaze, and so hot – why even here my fur's a-steamin'.'

Twitching his nose he quested the parched, ash-snowing air and smacked his lips hungrily. 'Is there sausages?' he asked patting his stomach. 'Dimmy's tum's a-wagging.'

Neltemi glared at the idiotic creature in dismay, then turned hastily to Mulligan. 'Stay no more,' she said. 'Go now, begin the long journey to the city of Hara.'

'I will,' he answered, giving Dimlon a sharp prod with his finger. 'And you're coming with me if you'll keep that prattling mouth of yours buttoned.'

'But Dimmy doesn't want to go no place, not no more. He wants to eat and have a comfyheadon-pilloweightytwinker.'

Mulligan ignored him and took the maiden's paw in his as he bowed before her.

'May your fortitude not desert you,' he said gently. 'I would that my urgency was not so great. Farewell.'

Neltemi nodded. 'Green be with you,' she answered, 'and may the Scale be blind to your voyage.'

Neglected for the moment, Dimlon gazed at the broken, smoke-choked temple and the burning oaks behind it.

'Is there no one else?' he asked suddenly. 'Why is there such a big bonfire with none to see it? Can Dimmy have their jackety spuddies if they don't turn up?'

That was too much for Mulligan. Incensed by the mouse's absurd stupidity, he whisked around and shouted at him.

'Are you such a witless dolt?' he snapped. 'Can you not see what has happened here? Brainless should have been your name – or Gowk of the solid plank! The enemy has been here, Dimmy! The servants of a terror so old and so cruel it would bite away your soul if you were to hear so much as a whisper of it! No, there aren't any others here – because they have all been barbarically murdered. Butchered and gored

215

by that scurvy, pagan crew. We three are the only ones alive for miles around. We are totally alone and cut off from any help whatsoever! So pipe down your incessant squawking before I cuff your ears and crack you one good an' proper!'

Dimlon blinked and trembled under the ferocity of his outburst then took several steps back and fiddled with the buckles of his satchel.

'Are you certain you will take him with you?' Neltemi asked Mulligan. 'The boy is moon-kissed, his company can only be an affliction.'

The Irish mouse sighed. 'I feel responsible for him,' he said. 'Whilst onboard ship I thought an agent of the serpent was drawing too close, but there were a pair of brave-hearted and generous lads to whom I would've entrusted the fragment if the situation proved too hopeless for me. Those two were the friends of this poor idiot, but they were lost in the wreck. No, the fool will go with me, perhaps I can instil some sense into him.'

'Such beneficence!' rang a sudden, spiteful hiss that crackled with hatred and cut through the air like a razor.

Mulligan's face fell and he wrenched his eyes over to where Dimlon had stood.

'How selflessly noble of you,' the vile, vicious voice continued, 'to take that poor jabbering cretin under your protective wing. I would have spiked or gutted him long ago and dissected his oozing brains to find the cause of his crass imbecility.'

Neltemi clutched Mulligan's arm and her eyes shone with fear as she looked upon the evil vision which now stood before her.

'What . . . what trick is this?' Mulligan stammered. 'What fiendish devilry is at work here?'

Immersed in the diabolic glare of the leaping fires, the wide-eyed innocence now dismissed and with a deriding, scornful sneer twisting his features, the mouse he had known as Dimlon sniggered hideously.

At last he had abandoned the nauseating masquerade of the simple, likeable Dimmy and was revealed as his true, pitiless self – the cloaked figure who had watched the bungling rats try to waylay the Irish mouse upon the quayside, and the one who had murdered Able Ruddaway.

From his satchel he had taken two curved, glittering blades, fixed them on to his claws and was now waving them menacingly in front of their faces – slicing the glinting knives to and fro and revelling in the horror that shone in their eyes.

'Gullible and credulous have you been, Mulligan!' crowed the fiend that had pursued him over land and sea. 'You should have obeyed the counsel of your dotard masters and trusted no one. See to what hazard your blind faith has brought you!'

'He's one of the Scale!' Neltemi cried. 'A disciple of the Serpent!'

Stupefied, Mulligan opened his mouth then clapped it shut many times before managing to utter a sound.

'N . . . no . . .' he stammered. 'This cannot be, it isn't possible. Dimmy – Dimmy, what is this?'

A gurgling laugh answered him. The glinting blades continued to weave a taunting dance as the leer distorted his features beyond recognition and the mouse's eyes began to burn with a golden light all their own and the dark pupils shrivelled into narrow slits.

'Dimmy?' rapped the harsh, needling voice. 'How swiftly you accepted that odious simpleton! His contemptible, chattering character was but an invention – a device to inveigle myself into the loathsome company of that guileless fieldmouse and his tedious associate and so finally into your own. And oh – how easy it proved. You were so eager to gain their confederacy that you failed to question the identity of this absurd, donkey-witted oaf who dangled at their tails.'

Screwing up his horrendous face, he assumed for a moment Dimmy's incredulous voice and taunted Mulligan all the more.

'Feebleheadedincompetentpegleg – hah! Are you not ashamed to have ever believed in such a ludicrous façade? There is no Dimlon! No brutish Aunty Lily – only I and my consummate, lying tongue.'

'And who might you be?' murmured Mulligan faintly, although he knew only too well.

'Dahrem Ruhar,' hissed the other, 'loyal servant of the Black Sovereign, dedicated unto Him when from my recanting mother's womb I was gladly freed. And you – dear, terrified weed-picker, you were quite wrong, for I am no ordinary disciple.'

At that he flicked his tail and brought it snaking around before him. Then, as Mulligan and Neltemi stared, the tip of its writhing, worm-like skin suddenly quivered and a dark pink line appeared, dividing it in two until the halves curled backwards and the malformed shreds shook apart, twitching into a repulsive fork of flesh.

'An adept!' cried Neltemi. 'He's an adept of the Scale!'

With his mutilated tail switching to and fro, Dahrem bared his teeth and they saw that they had grown into hideous yellow fangs.

'Now you are mine, Mulligan!' he roared. 'Long have I dogged your crippled shamblings, for the secret of your gutterbred family I suspected. Over the globe you have flitted, wallowing in the bottle and carousing in dockyard dives. Yet I knew that one day you would lead me straight to that which we all are seeking – and then it happened.

'Into the land of the drab of the firmament you were received, in Greenwich, and there my guesses were confirmed. I knew then that from that place you bore a valued prize and even the pretended ignorance of Dimmy could not fail to have recognised the truth. So, that is what became of the ninth fragment. Many years have our scholars studied the ancient records gathered from the pathetic temples of our enemies and pondered over its fate.'

Cackling, he stalked closer and Mulligan's fingers tightened over his bag, but the servant of Suruth Scarophion had him trapped and there was no escape.

'The location of the others we have long known,' he hissed, 'for who can hide the creeping desert and the wild wastes that spring from such hidden treasures? Yet where the final piece was bestowed, none of our arts could reveal. But now I have it. Dahrem Ruhar shall take it back to its rightful place and he shall rise high in the Dark One's favour when He is reborn.'

'You'll not lay your scurvy claws on the cursed evil

my family have fetched and ferried over the seas for countless generations!' Mulligan told him, his old tenacity returning. 'I'll not end our terrible legacy by passing it straight to one of your hellish and profane crew!'

When he heard this, Dahrem threw back his head and let out a hooting shriek of mocking laughter.

'And who will prevent me, Master of the Rumswillingguts? Not you certainly, and as you so stupidly pointed out, there is no one left alive here to come to your aid. We are completely alone, we three, and you are far from any chance of rescue. My brethren have done well, they have taken the seventh fragment which this ramshackle shed of a shrine has been hiding – and do not think that we are ignorant of where the eighth is secreted. That has ever been known and soon, before the stars that herald His return begin to flame in the sky, that too will be assailed. But now your time is over and my own star is about to rise. Surrender the fragment unto me.'

He opened his blade-bound claws but Mulligan drew back.

'It's through me you'll have to pass before you'll see so much as a wink of it!' he growled.

'Oh believe me, I shall be delighted to oblige,' the grotesque creature replied with a malignant chuckle. 'Do not think that because you saved my life on board the *Calliope* that I will spare yours. No, your life will I most eagerly take to win my prize.

'Do you desire to see the other powers granted unto an adept of Sarpedon – My Majestic Lord? Should I slough this raiment for your harrowing and most awful benefit? I think not, your blood would freeze if

I were to reveal my unhallowed grandeur. No, it would be better for you to yield up the fragment without my having to wrest it from your paws and, just to make it more amusing, I know just the way to compel you.'

With a flash of gold, the claw reached out, seized Neltemi by the paw, then wrenched the maiden from her feet and dragged her close to him. Before Mulligan could do anything she was held fast in the treacherous mouse's grasp, his wiry arm crooked beneath her chin – glittering blades resting threateningly upon the fur.

'Make no attempt to save her,' he spat maliciously, 'for you cannot. The talons of Scarophion are steeped in the vessels which house His black blood. One tiny snick of the flesh and she is doomed to a torment greater than your pickled mind can grasp. Now, open that precious bag of yours and give the fragment to me.'

'No, Mulligan!' Neltemi gasped, throttled by the crushing strength of Dahrem's sinew. 'I am nothing. Run now – you must try.'

The adept of the Dark Despoiler squeezed her throat a fraction tighter and her rasping voice became a shrivelled squeal.

'You ask the peg-leg to run!' he snorted. 'And how far do you think his hobbling could get him before I pounced to rend and rip? Keep silent little flower puller, or my talons may grow weary of your squeaking and snip into that lovely neck to carve out your windpipe and let it flap from the gash to whistle in the breeze.'

'Don't!' Mulligan cried, dragging the bag from his shoulders and opening it hastily. 'Take what you want!

Just do her no harm – I beg you. She's scarce more than a child.'

The jagged fangs ground together in Dahrem's jaws and a feverish light gleamed in his horrible, reptilian eyes as he watched Mulligan take from the pack a peculiar object covered and bound by many strips of dingy grey cloth.

'Remove the wrappings!' he urged. 'I must see it before I release her.'

'No!' Neltemi shrieked, battling to drag the powerful arms from under her chin.

But Mulligan ignored her protests and bent over the parcel, his fingers tugging at the bindings.

A horrible grin like a row of pointed gravestones appeared on Dahrem's face and, while the maiden continued to writhe in his grasp, he stared at the unravelling bundle in Mulligan's paws.

'Don't!' Neltemi wept. 'Please!'

The Irish mouse glanced up at her for a moment. 'I must,' he said. 'I know what torture would be yours if I did not submit. I will not have that evil upon my conscience. Let the thing go, let him and his infernal mob take it. The time of our guardianship and custody is over.'

Tearing another ribbon of cloth away from the object in his paws, Mulligan's face was suddenly illuminated from beneath by a rich gleam of burning gold and a deep, emerald green.

'The ninth fragment!' Dahrem yelled. 'Give it to me!'

But imprisoned in his deadly embrace, Neltemi stared down at the terrible thing which Mulligan held and even now was lifting up to give to him.

Desperately the maiden sobbed and snapped her eyes closed, then with a shudder, she called 'Take this chance I give to you Mulligan – flee if you can!'

Gripping the two curved blades in her paws, she yanked them down towards her and they plunged deep into her throat.

'NOOO!' Mulligan bellowed, leaping to his feet.

Snarling, Dahrem hurled Neltemi from him and his twin knives flew across her back in rage as she collapsed on to the lawn.

Wailing, the maiden felt the venom race through her veins and already it began to eat into her flesh as from the great, ugly wounds the blackened blood frothed and spouted.

Aghast at the sacrifice she had made, Mulligan gaped down at her thrashing form as it convulsed and buckled in agony, then he stared across at Dahrem.

The ghastly mouse was tensing himself, preparing to spring. The muscles rippled under his pale grey fur and upon his claws the lethal blades scratched at the air.

But Mulligan was too quick for him. Inflamed by the screams issuing from Neltemi's foaming mouth, the peg-leg loosed a deafening yell and with all his strength, lunged forward, striking Dahrem full in the face with his pack.

Howling, Dahrem tumbled backwards and Mulligan's lumbering weight came trampling over him, punching the breath from his lungs until he wheezed and gasped for air.

'Scum!' the Irish mouse bawled, raising his fist and striking the winded creature's jaw with a resounding smash of knuckle and bone.

Dahrem yammered in pain as one of the fangs splintered in his mouth. Then another almighty crack smote the side of his head and when the third impassioned blow pounded into his face his yellow, snake-like eyes fluttered shut and he knew no more.

'Right!' Mulligan raged, reaching for the abominable creature's knife-clad claws. 'This is one nap you'll not wake up from, Dimmy lad! You foul savage wretch. I'm goin' to take off them poisoned blades and shove them into your lying, treasonous mouth. It's eating them filthy razors you'll be doing and while you're at it I'll cut out that deceitful tongue of yours! Let's see how long your blood takes to turn black and burn you from within! That'll open them viperish gogglers again I'll be bound, just long enough to see me laugh in your face and watch the skin melt off your bones.'

Overwhelmed by hatred, Mulligan fumbled with the fastenings that held the golden weapons in place. Nearby the cries of Neltemi were failing and tears filled his eyes for he knew there was nothing he could do to save her. Once the venom entered the blood, the die was cast and the abhorrent fate sealed.

Carefully, he removed one of the curved knives and set about untying the second. But in his anguish and trembling from the hideous screams that clamoured in his ears, Mulligan's fingers slipped.

To his despair, the one-legged mouse's paw jerked along the base of the blade and his thumb accidently pressed against the razoring edge.

Yowling, he stared at the drop of blood that blobbed up from the broken skin and, in that awful instant, knew that he was finished.

Of all the perils Mulligan had prepared himself to face over the mounting years, never had he suspected that in the end his death would be due to such a clumsy, senseless blunder.

He who had fought in so many ferocious battles, who had been captured and taken to the dens of the Scale in Singapore and shown there the terrifying instruments of torture as the chisel-featured high priest and his blubbery, powdered consort looked on in callous disregard. There, even as they manacled him to the rack, he had torn himself free – leaving his leg still fettered in the irons as somehow he managed to fight his way out, though the pain threatened to overwhelm him.

Many times had Mulligan the mariner thwarted the designs of the dreaded enemy but now, here at the last, his own carelessness had doomed him and from the black venomous blood of Sarpedon there was no remedy or salvation.

Suddenly the dying cries of Neltemi fell silent and the Irish mouse stared over to her steaming body.

'So the last of the twelve maidens passes,' he breathed, 'and soon I shall follow her.'

Desolately, he staggered to his feet, not wishing now to kill the unconscious figure that sprawled under him. Only one thing mattered at that precise moment, only one thought loomed large and great inside his stricken mind. The fragment – everything else dwindled into insignificance, only that mattered. It must be taken away, cast into the sea, if that was the only choice left to him.

'Green grant me time,' he mumbled, taking a final, shivering look at Neltemi's blistering remains. 'My wound is small, perhaps the venom will take longer to work its evil. The ninth piece must not be left out here for any to find. Here at the end of my life's labour I must do what I can.'

Wretchedly, he stooped to snatch up the object he had taken from his bag and removed from the many layers of wrapped cloth. Then, with long lumbering strides, Mulligan raced over the lawns and disappeared into the dim shade of the pine woods.

In the brooding silence that followed, a groaning murmur disturbed the peace and Dahrem opened a dimming eye as gradually he slipped back into wakefulness.

A brief pang of terror washed over him when he found that one of the blades had been removed from his claw and he waited for the first searing agonies to commence. Yet no poison had invaded his lifeblood and when he realised that, the merciless mouse marvelled.

'The fool!' he whispered. 'What lunacy of his rum-drowned wits made him spare me?'

Then, from some distant reach of the obscuring trees there came a fearful shriek as Mulligan felt the venom begin its grisly work and Dahrem sprang up.

Hooting with ghastly mirth, he set off in pursuit – fixing the knife back on to his claw.

9

The Passing of the Burden

All was dark beneath the waves. Far above the storm was raging, but in the turgid deeps no force of wind or rain could penetrate the tranquil peace.

Through the cavernous, rippling gloom a solitary figure fell, turning slowly through the shrouding shade, like an autumn leaf lazily spinning from the tree.

Down went Woodget – his little body limp and silent. No thought stirred in his blackened mind; he knew only peace and an end to his sorrows as deeper he drowned.

Yet in that hollow chasm, two points of soft grey light glimmered, faint in the distance. Swiftly they advanced and around them a face formed in the dim darkness.

Concern and sadness scored the ashen brow and

the tangled tresses of her sable hair flowed like ink about her forlorn face.

Through the tideless waters Zenna came: seventh daughter of the king under the sea, whose understanding surpassed the groping thoughts of earthborn races. Princess of the remote cold regions beyond the province of her vain and frivolous sisters, her territories were the ice-locked north and the biting cold of the southern wildernesses.

In those desolate wastes only the hardiest and oldest of living things dwelt, biding out the passing ages in winding caves at the roots of the world. Unto those very foundations of rock and earth, right to the source of all that now moved through the ocean or walked upon the land above, had Zenna ventured and from those nameless spirits and cloistered intellects she learned much.

Since that evening when Woodget had defended her from her scorning sisters, she had followed the *Calliope*, hoping for another glimpse of the small land creature. Then, when the storm commenced and it was plain that the ship was in danger, she had fled to her father's halls and pleaded with him to bring calm and still the wrath of the waters. But the squall had not been of his making and there was naught he could do. Over that part of his realm where the tempest boiled across the sea, a power greater than his held sway.

So back she raced, only to behold the *Calliope* smashing upon the pinnacle of rock and to hear the screams of her passengers.

Now, torn with anguish, she hurriedly reached the fieldmouse's side and the light of her eyes dimmed when they beheld him.

'Woodget,' she breathed, though no bubbles rose from her mouth.

In mourning, she raised her webbed paw and caressed his furry cheek.

Quickly she drew the paw away, then stared at him – the light burning more keenly in her eyes. Somewhere, deep within the fieldmouse, an indomitable spark of life still glowed, but even as she sensed it, the ember waned.

Hastily, Zenna touched Woodget's temples with her delicate fingers and put forth the power that was in her.

From her lips a wondrous, plaintive music began and the haunting melody was full of enchantment and invocation.

Round and around the divine notes entwined them, growing in might and splendour with every yearning chord until its strength bound them close and all through the vast oceans the sublime echoes of her heavenly voice were heard. Those who listened to the blissful airs were moved to both grief and jubilation.

Louder and more forceful became her song, and although there were no discernible words, it was filled with the knowledge of all living things. Of the weeds that grew beneath the sea her music sang, to the verdant grasses which thickly covered the cloud-brushed hills and the brightly coloured, burgeoning flowers that rose to greet the warming sun. From fallen seed to towering tree, her glorious harmony told. Of the egg to the bird, infant to adult, from weak to strong. The unquenchable force of pulsing, unfurling life beat forth from her being and in that chill, secluded darkness a dim green light began to glimmer, until it shone bold and bright throughout the limitless waters.

Suddenly, the fieldmouse in her arms twitched and his chest heaved as he jerked his head from side to side.

A triumphant grin split Zenna's face and the music ceased.

'From the brink have I brought thee, my little champion,' she murmured, her voice frail and her strength diminished by all that she had imparted to him, 'and for a brief time only thou may breathe as do I, yet to the surface must Zenna now bear thee – and fleetly. Ah, but much do I crave for thee to remain and end my solitude, yet were I to sing the full song of changing to keep thee at mine side even a short while longer, then the memory of who thou art and whence thou came would burn from thy mind.'

Drowsily, Woodget shook his head, but his eyes remained closed. Though she had fanned the dying spark within him into a steady flame, he was still very weak and the numbness that had crept over his limbs had not yet passed.

Smiling wanly, she propelled him up through the darkness. Back to the churning pull of the upper tides they ascended – up to where a bulky shape rocked upon the waves above.

Zenna gazed up at the fat silhouette over their heads, but before she lifted Woodget into the turbulent air, she wavered and brought her face close to his.

Tenderly, her lips touched his pink nose – then the tempest was about him once more.

Woodget choked and the water coughed from his lungs.

Close by, her eyes watching over him, Zenna waited as the fieldmouse squeaked and lashed about with his arms, crying shrilly, and her gaze turned to the large floating cask and the figure that still clutched to it.

Thinking himself tormented by guilt and the terror of the storm, Thomas raised his head and there – to his amazement and overwhelming elation – he saw Woodget.

Quickly he squirmed over the barrel and held out his paws, shrieking at the top of his voice.

'Woodj! Take hold – you're safe! You're safe!'

Shivering and retching in the fierce salt water, the fieldmouse lunged forward and felt Thomas' strong fists clench about his paws.

'Up you come, Pipple!' Thomas shouted, dragging him from the sea and desperately hugging his spluttering frame. 'Oh Woodj – I thought you was a goner. Praise to the Green that you've been spared. We're going to make it out of this you an' me, we will – I promise.'

Beneath the rain-lashed sky, Thomas clutched fiercely to Woodget and upon their bulky craft that tilted and jerked at the mercy of the driving ocean, they were carried out under the eaves of the destroying storm and eventually into calmer, safer waters.

Immersed in the waves, Zenna turned away. She had lingered too long and a staggering fatigue now consumed her. Down to the darkness she descended – down to the restful halls of her father.

Thomas looked up at the mountains that reared in the distance and wondered at the column of smoke which polluted the clean air – even as Mulligan had done several hours before.

Up to the debris-strewn shore, almost to the very spot where the lifebelt lay half covered with seaweed, the barrel had borne the two friends, bobbing gently in the shallows amongst the rest of the *Calliope*'s shattered flotsam.

Still holding on to one another, the mice had fallen into an exhausted swoon and only when Thomas had begun to slide off the cask's curved sides did he splutter awake and find himself up to his waist in water.

Rousing Woodget, he had waded on to the sands and there they now stood, gazing about them curiously, lamenting the bodies of their drowned fellow passengers yet at the same time thanking the providence that had spared them from the ravages of the tempest.

'I remember music,' Woodget began slowly. 'All was dark but there was a voice a-singing – least I thought there was.'

'You was dreaming,' Thomas told him. 'Next you'll be saying it were them rum-inspired sirens again.'

The fieldmouse sighed. He was certain that he was not mistaken but he was too weary to continue and merely said, 'Right you are, Master Triton.'

'Don't call me that,' his friend replied. 'It's a stupid name and I don't like it.'

Woodget looked up at the snowy slopes of the White Mountains. 'Tom,' he murmured in a small voice, 'where does you think we is?'

Thomas shrugged and scratched his head. 'Could be anywhere,' he answered. 'There's no way of telling how far that gale pushed the ship off course and what happened to us after that. I don't know how long we was asleep for either, but I reckon the dawn won't be long in coming. See over there, behind them rocks that run down to the sea, the night's growing fainter, the moon's dipping and the stars are failing.'

Removing the neckerchief from around his throat he wrung it out and flapped it a few times to shake off the last drops before tying it back in place.

'One thing I do know, however,' he said gruffly. 'Looks like we're the only ones who made it. Look how many others didn't.'

Woodget pulled his hat from his head in respect. 'What do you think we should do, Tom?' he asked quietly. 'How are we ever gonna get back home?'

'There must be someone up by that fire we could ask,' his friend replied. 'But first things first, there's nowt we can do till we've laid these dead folk to rest. I ain't leavin' them exposed on this beach when the sun rises. The gulls'll only find 'em and start their greedy pecking. Wouldn't want that now, would we?'

The fieldmouse shuddered and shook his head, repelled at the very thought.

'Tell you what,' Thomas began in a forced, cheerful tone. 'Why don't you start lookin' about for something we could use as a shovel? There must be plenty of useful bits in all this wreckage.'

'What'll you be doin'?'

Thomas scowled and stared along the shore. 'I'll

find all I can and carry them over,' he said. 'One great big grave'll have to suffice. It's better'n being gull bait.'

And so Woodget began to search amongst the bric-a-brac of splintered clutter that was heaped along the sands, whilst Thomas set about the grisly task of heaving the drowned bodies up to where the shore met the twisted shrubs and laying them in a row upon the coarse grasses.

When nearly half an hour had passed, Woodget had already commenced digging and the number of drowned corpses which Thomas had brought over had grown to seventeen.

'There's still at least twenty of them as far as I can see,' he said gloomily as he came toiling up the bank with the body of a rather plump mole hoisted over his broad shoulders. 'Probably an awful lot more further along the coast too, but I'll need a rest soon or I'll be falling in that trench of yours myself.'

Woodget leant upon the flat piece of wood that served as a spade and gazed at his blistered palms, but remained quiet and thoughtful.

A pallid, grey light was edging up over the rim of the sea and when he had lain the mole upon the ground, Thomas stretched and peered at the horizon.

'The sun's rising,' he uttered impatiently. 'That means the gulls'll be squawkin' and crying overhead any time soon. Better get a move on.'

Quickly he hurried down the sands and as Woodget watched his burly figure go foraging amongst the wreckage, he was relieved that he did not have to perform such a grisly and unpleasant task. Then, before he returned to his own labours, the fieldmouse glanced at the glimmering horizon and rubbed his eyes.

In the great dim distance – where the silvering sea joined the fading night – a band of grey vapour was rolling over the waters. At first Woodget thought nothing of it and dismissed it as he did the early morning mist which gathered in the dells of Betony Bank. But when he next looked up from his digging, the dense cloud had moved with uncanny speed across the waves and was now much closer.

In the ashen light of the encroaching dawn, his sharp sight could plainly discern the swirling skeins and curling wisps that crept from that wide, swiftly flowing fog bank. That great and bloated vaporous wall was driven by a single purpose, as though a determined urgency was sweeping it over the sea, steering the concealing mists straight towards the shore and, as a wave of fear gripped him, Woodget threw down his makeshift spade to run after Thomas.

'Tom!' he cried, waving his arms in the air. 'Tom! Tom!'

Turning over a large, brine-saturated plank, Thomas cautiously peered beneath. He had volunteered for this gruesome duty in case, among the debris, there were the bodies of Mulligan and Dimlon. He did not want Woodget to stumble across the carcasses of their friends, but it was a chilling and macabre search and he wished it was over.

Hearing the fieldmouse's calls he raised his head and wondered what all the shouting was about.

'Over yonder!' Woodget cried, jumping up and down as he raced towards him.

Thomas stared at the shimmering sea and squinted at the dense cloud that sped over the waters.

'Bless me,' he muttered as Woodget came puffing up beside him. 'What is it? 'Tain't no ordinary fog – look how fast it's moving and there ain't hardly a breeze.'

'I don't like it, Tom,' Woodget whimpered. 'I fancy there's summat inside that thick cloud, summat that don't want to be seen – an' it's headed straight fer us.'

'But what could it be?' Thomas breathed.

'I doesn't know an' I doesn't want to find—'

Abruptly breaking off, the fieldmouse pattered down to the water's edge where he tilted his head to one side and strained to listen.

Over the sea the mist came swiftly on, moving like a great island of white smoke whose ethereal hills were constantly shifting in a turgid, heaving dance. Over its changing, gaseous bulk the rays of the approaching dawn glimmered and shone, tinting the undulating outline with delicate, flickering shades of rose, blended with vibrant streaks of peach and deep veins of shimmering gold.

With his eyes fixed upon this mysterious yet curiously beautiful spectacle, Thomas came to stand beside the fieldmouse, whose large and sensitive ears had obviously heard something beyond the range of his own, and in a low whisper he asked, 'What is it?'

Woodget turned to stare at him with a mixture of confusion and fear written upon his face.

'Tom,' his woeful voice cried in alarm. 'There is summat in there – I done heard it! Muffled by the thick fog it is, but plain enough to my lugholes.'

Thomas gripped his friend's shoulders. 'Tell me,' he said.

The fieldmouse glanced back at the advancing vapour. 'Lurkin' in there, deep inside its very heart, there's the sound of a girt ship a-ploughin' through the waves. Oars are dippin' in the drink and pushin' it on to the beat of a thumping drum, and there's voices too – I can hear folk callin'.'

'A ship?' Thomas murmured. 'That's not possible. How could the mist cling to it like that?'

'Like I said,' Woodget muttered, 'I doesn't want to find out. Some witch's magic or other, I'll be bound.'

Thomas held his breath, then he too caught the vague noise of waves crashing against a hull and the monotonous throb of a pounded drum.

'You're right, Woodj,' he admitted. 'But I don't think we should stay here and wait for whoever's inside that fog to get any closer. The rate it's travellin' it'll be slap bang on top of us afore we know it. Whatever it turns out to be, it don't seem clever to stay out here in the open for all an' sundry to see. Let's you an' me get off this beach and dart up into them meadows, p'raps even to the trees.'

Together the mice scurried over the shore and up the sloping bank as the mist flowed ever nearer, growing larger with every passing moment.

Past the incomplete grave Thomas and Woodget ran, then through the shrubs and into the flower-filled field beyond.

'Have to finish buryin' them folks after,' Thomas panted. 'It's the living we've got to take thought for now.'

Suddenly Woodget skidded to a halt and he grabbed his friend's arm desperately.

'Stop!' he yelled. 'Tom! Wait!'

Thomas stumbled and whirled about.

'What is it now?' he demanded.

Woodget pointed towards the trees and held up a paw for his friend to be silent.

From the pine woods there suddenly came a frightful scream that was shrill with agony and torment, and the hearts of both mice stopped as they listened.

'What were that?' Woodget murmured when he recovered from the initial shock. 'Oh Tom, what is this horrid place we've a-come to? Full of weird nasties it is: first there's rollin' fog, now terrifyin' wild beasts. I ain't goin' no further.'

To their dismay another scream issued from the trees. It was a terrible, soul-rending screech and the fieldmouse covered his ears in a vain attempt to blot it out.

'You don't have to go no further,' Thomas muttered. 'That's coming this way too. It's crashing through the woods, whatever it is. Sounds like all the devils in the pit are torturing the creature. But one thing's fer certain, we can't go forward nor back – we're trapped, Woodj.'

'Oh Tom,' the fieldmouse whined, turning around to stare at the shore. 'The fog's closing now, it's almost here.'

Thomas followed his gaze and sure enough, tendrils of the unearthly mist were already groping their way along the gently breaking waves and over the floating debris of the *Calliope*. Then, like an avalanche of swirling steam, the great island of fog came rumbling after.

Curling fingers of searching mist had already crept ashore and were stealing up the sands when, within the dense cloud, the drum beats suddenly ceased and Woodget heard the unseen oars being lifted from the water and an anchor go splashing into the waves.

From the pine woods the screams continued and with each hideous yell the horror of them intensified.

'That thing's at the edge of them trees now,' Thomas muttered. 'Listen, it's out in the meadow!'

Screened by the spring flowers which were already opening in the brightening sunlight, the source of those infernal shrieks came charging. The two mice could hear it rampaging towards them and they drew close to the shrubs which bordered the sandbank.

Trembling, Woodget looked over his shoulder to where the immense wall of mist obliterated the shore and he nudged Thomas urgently.

'Tom,' he whispered. 'There's summat movin' in that fume down there – see, there's figures wadin' out the water.'

His friend grimaced. Within the depths of the churning fog, indistinct but large, grey shapes were lumbering through the shallows.

Yet now the wailing screams were very close and the fieldmouse shivered. Every screech was a fresh torrent of misery and anguish – so fierce and dreadful that it wounded the spirit and drove deep into his mind like a biting, murderous spike.

Now the meadow was engulfed by the ghastly cries. Over the clumps of white crocus and blue anemone they rang, and Thomas knew that at any moment the maker of those grotesque screeches would burst upon them. He hunted over the ground for something to protect them.

Lying beneath the shrub where Woodget had flung it, he discovered the makeshift spade and Thomas flourished it in his fists as suddenly the bellowing creature came crashing through the yellow flax.

Behind him, down upon the sands, where the outlying wisps of mist flowed between the scattered wreckage, seeping into every hollow and splintered crevice, three dozen stern-looking figures stepped from the sea.

As the fiery disc of the morning sun reared above the horizon, their steel-shod feet trod upon the shore and the brilliant light was mirrored in their silver armour – casting dazzling, bouncing reflections before them like beacons blazing in the gloom.

Tall and proud were those newcomers. At their sides they carried great spears with tapering, burnished blades – adorned with scarlet beads and crimson tassels in imitation of the blood they had skewered from their enemies.

With grim expressions, they glared up at the mountains where the black smoke still reared in the now dim blue sky then turned their attention to the meadow and heard the terrible, suffering screams clamouring from it.

At the front of the armour-clad strangers, the tallest of them raised a gauntleted paw and, with the great spears raised, they charged up the bank towards the place where Thomas and Woodget stood behind the twisted hedges.

'Tom!' the fieldmouse cried. 'No!'

Thomas let the weapon fall from his fingers, for he

too recognised the figure that had come lumbering upon them and he opened his mouth in shocked astonishment.

'Mulligan!' he yelled.

Through the pine woods Mulligan had staggered, hurrying from the Shrine of Virbius as fast as he could, before the venom that had entered him could execute its lethal work.

Yet the Irish mouse had not gone far before the first bitter pains began. His right paw turned black and from his punctured thumb there dripped a foulsmelling ooze which withered the undergrowth when it splashed over the ground.

Further along his arm the pricking, shooting agonies travelled and from his dissolving tattoos the dark blood bubbled – forming ghastly, frothing pictures over his withering flesh.

But for a long time Mulligan denied the pain, holding out against the excruciating torments that ravaged his arm, clenching his teeth as he hurtled on. Through the trees he bolted, his wooden stump smashing against snaking roots and ripping through the ferns and grasses, but never once did he falter or fall.

Only a single thought burned fierce in his mind, outshining the pain that bit into his shoulder and crept across his chest – the fragment had to be taken as far from the ruined temple as possible and he knew that he would die in the attempt.

In his left fist he clutched it, the thing which had cursed his family throughout the ages, and he was determined never to let it fall into the enemy's grasp whilst there was a breath still in his body.

Then, when the eaves of the wood were within his

swimming sight, the venom found his heart and the poison flowed swiftly in. That was when Mulligan cried out. It was too much to endure in gritted silence and his tortured voice flew high and shrill over the treetops to herald the rising dawn.

Such was the savagery of the blistering, scalding pain that his convulsing spasms hurled him against the trunk of a stately cypress. The wound in his shoulder that the rats had inflicted upon him in Cornwall gushed with steaming blood and his shrieks cut through the cool airs.

In his paw the green and golden device slipped from his loosening fingers. Then amidst his racking anguish, he heard a voice come hissing from the woods behind him.

'No escape, Peg-leg!' it called. 'Your office is over.'

'Dahrem,' Mulligan gasped. 'I should have killed him when I had the chance.'

Goaded by the threat of the evil, pursuing mouse, Mulligan seized hold of the fragment more firmly than ever and threw himself from the tree trunk and darted for the meadow.

But the insidious, chilling voice grew louder in his ears as Dahrem came hunting, gaining upon his hobbling progress and hissing his hatred.

'I can hear your sweet agonies, Peg-leg,' he cackled. 'Do I not know that delicious sound too well? Thus did the bosun perish. Soon your eyes will boil, Peg-leg. Give up – the contest is ended. I and my beloved Lord have beaten you. The time of the Green's insipid sovereignty is over! The darkness is falling, just as it now veils your stinging sight. Yield to the majesty of Sarpedon.'

Another, bellowing scream issued from Mulligan's throat, but this time his voice was cracked and gurgling, for the venom was filling his lungs.

Behind him the adept of the Scale leapt from the pines and his swivelling, reptilian eyes scanned the meadow for his stumbling prey.

A malevolent sneer distorted the pale grey mouse's face as he beheld Mulligan's tormented form struggling through the flowers. The fool was his now, his to toy with before the final piercing agonies snatched his unworthy and wasted life away. How amusing it would be to wrench the ninth fragment from him whilst he yet lived.

'For him to go yammering to his doom knowing that his puny efforts have all been in vain,' Dahrem hooted. 'Such sport must not be denied.' And with a whoop of malicious mirth he hared after his hapless victim.

Even though it seemed as if the end had indeed come and his labours proved unavailing, Mulligan forced himself on. Choked from the rising, poisonous bile that frothed up his throat, the Irish mouse staggered towards the tangled shrubs that fenced the meadow. The breath rattled in his breast as he strove to gulp down the sweetly perfumed air, but each gasp was shorter than the last and his dissolving lungs were almost utterly consumed.

Before his streaming, rolling eyes the world was falling back into night and to him the sun's glimmering rays were like the shadows of death. Then, as he went crashing through the last swathe of growth that separated him from the hedge and the shore, two blurred figures reared in front of him.

At first Mulligan thought that they were more vile members of the heathen cult and he tried to barge past them but his good leg collapsed beneath him and within the wooden stump of the other the flesh liquefied and, like ink, his lifeblood welled up – spilling over the earth.

Thomas and Woodget stared down at the awful apparition that had blundered into them and the fieldmouse yelped in fright and horror.

Upon the ground, writhing in his unnumbered agonies, Mulligan yelled and squealed. In his paw he clasped something bright and gleaming but it was as if he was mortally afraid of his two friends and tried to ward them off with ghastly screeches and frail thrashes of his shrivelling arms.

'Mulligan!' Woodget whined pitifully. ''Tis us – Tom and Woodget! What's happened? What is it?'

The Irish mouse screeched as the vile, foaming toxin flooded into his mouth and spurted from his nostrils, then as if the veil had been torn from his eyes, he saw a brief, clear vision of the two mice standing over him.

Hope soared in Mulligan's twitching heart and the ghost of a grin haunted his face as he reached up with his paw and pushed the loathsome treasure into Woodget's astonished grasp.

'T . . . Take it!' he commanded, through his final torments. 'To . . . to Hara . . . to the . . . the city of the Holy One. Swear to me . . . swear!'

Woodget stared down, tears welling up in his eyes. 'I . . . I swears,' he stammered.

A tremendous sigh galed from Mulligan's lips. There was still a chance to cheat the unholy fiend and he bowed his head in gratitude.

'My . . . my thanks,' he murmured.

'What can we do to help?' Thomas asked, distressed by the horrific sight of the once solid seafarer whose quivering frame was dwindling before their eyes even as they watched.

'Keep back!' Mulligan warned in a grotesque, poison-babbling gargle. 'Don't . . . don't come near – the . . . the serpent has bitten. Beware my friends, beware . . . of him.'

'Who's done this to you?' Thomas cried angrily.

With his last strength, Mulligan pointed a shaking finger back over the meadow, but before he could utter the name, the venom claimed him. Emitting a strangled gasp, he slumped into the grass like a salted slug; threads of oily smoke streamed from his ears and the slime-filled sockets that had once housed his eyes crumbled and caved into the decaying skull.

So perished Mulligan, the last in his line and penultimate custodian of the ninth fragment. But in the end he had not been vanquished and the toil of his ancestors had not proven worthless, for the evil had at last been passed on and he died with a triumphant smile traced upon his flaking, rupturing lips.

Appalled and aghast, Woodget wailed and threw his arm before his face to hide from the nightmarish scene, whilst at his side, Thomas stared dumbly down as the hideous, steaming corpse was completely destroyed by the virulent, devouring, black blood of Suruth Scarophion.

'Save us!' he whispered.

'Mister Mulligan!' the fieldmouse wept. 'I don't

understand. Tom – what's happenin'?'

Backing away from the stinking pool of dark, oozing sludge of grizzled fur and glistening, black putrescence, Thomas shook his head wildly. 'I don't know!' he cried, his voice unnaturally high with terror. 'I feel sick.'

Dragging the back of his paw over his eyes, Woodget turned away then gazed at the thing the Irish mouse had entrusted to him.

'Thomas,' he murmured in a hushed, awe-filled voice. 'Look, this must be what he had in his bag all that time.'

Rebelling against the mounting waves of nausea that threatened to overwhelm him, Thomas gazed at the object in the fieldmouse's paws and blinked in wonder.

In Woodget's fingers was a large piece of curved jade and, under the morning sun, the countless hues of rich swirling green that spiralled within its ravishing depths appeared to move and pulse with an inner light all their own.

Yet, surmounting the splendour of the precious jade were carved bands and curling patterns wrought of the purest gold. In glittering fronds and sweeping arabesques, the gorgeous metal wove an intricate design that encased the livid mineral entirely – bordering the irregular edges of its peculiar, fragmented shape with cunning and skilful craftsmanship.

'What do you reckon it is?' Woodget asked. 'Some kind of bowl it looks like, but if so then one fit fer a king.'

'It'd be a broken one,' Thomas observed. 'It looks

to me like a piece of something bigger. A vase maybe?'

'You think Mulligan did steal it after all?' Woodget muttered, daring to gaze back at the horrendous, smoking remains of the Irish mouse.

Before Thomas could answer, a cold, brutal voice resounded in their ears. Woodget dropped the treasure in surprise and they whirled around in astonishment. In all the confusion and despair surrounding Mulligan's death they had forgotten about the figures emerging from the mist down on the shore behind them.

'Take them!' the savage voice snapped. 'Take them!'

Over the sands the armed warriors had come, following the sound of Mulligan's dying howls, and now there they stood – towering over the frightened mice, with no expression in their eyes save icy condemnation and bitter enmity.

Twice the height of Thomas stood the leader of these strange creatures. His sharp, pointed head was mostly hidden beneath an ornate helmet, fashioned in the shape of a snapping maw and decorated with the colourful plumage of exotic birds. But under the shadow of this and above the mouthguard which protected his snout, his eyes glinted bleakly and as fiercely as the polished silver armour which covered his menacing bulk. Even his long, powerful tail was covered in sections of jointed, beaten metal, although tufts of brindled brown fur could be glimpsed poking through the narrow, flexing gaps.

In his fist a tall, tassle-adorned spear was firmly gripped and he glared at Thomas and Woodget, snorting with disgust as though the very sight of them repelled him.

Around him the other warriors were regarding the mice in a similar, detesting manner then, as if he could stand to look no more, the leader gave a curt signal and at once three of the great, snarling ogres rushed forward to seize them.

'Be sure to bind their claws,' the tallest spat as he glowered down his barbed snout at the mice. 'Then haul them on to the sands and hack off their treacherous heads!'

Kicking and struggling, Thomas and Woodget felt their paws being tied roughly behind their backs and they were plucked from the ground and carried through the twisted shrubs on to the sandbank.

'Stop!' Thomas cried, squirming for all he was worth. 'Put us down!'

'Listen to the maggot-folk cheep,' roared the one carrying Woodget.

'They'll not be wriggling for much longer,' rejoined another. 'Chattan will set their heads up for all to see in this hateful place of death.'

'Make the ending swift,' the leader barked, glancing across the meadow to the pine woods and beyond to where the now faint trails of smoke rose before the mountains. 'There may be more of this detestable breed lying in ambush. Karim – wield your sword!'

On to the sand the two mice were thrown and kicked until they rolled on their stomachs with their necks stretched out, ready for the execution.

'Wait!' Thomas yelled.

But it was no use, there came the ominous ring of

metal as a gleaming, curved sword was drawn from its sheath and into the air it sliced – tracing a brilliant arc of white light before it came scything down upon their necks.

10

The Legacy of Mulligan

'Hold!' the leader bellowed. 'Stay your stroke Karim!'

Above the two mice, the creature with the sword growled impatiently and waited for the order to complete the execution.

But from the gnarled shrubs bounded the tallest of the armour-clad warriors and in his steel gauntlet he grasped the glittering fragment of gold and jade that Mulligan had given to Woodget.

Nudging Thomas with the toe of his boot, he scrutinised his tail then turned his attention to Woodget and did the same to him.

'Adepts can cleave the halves together at will,' Karim whispered.

His leader ignored him and gave Thomas an annoyed kick.

'Raise your eyes!' he commanded. 'What have you to say of this? How came it into your possession?'

The mouse turned and a green and gold radiance fell upon his face.

'I don't know what it is,' he said gruffly. 'It was given to my friend here. That's all I can tell you.'

'Given!' the leader roared sceptically. 'Such horrors as this are not simply given away. Always they are dearly bought, now – answer me with the truth, or Karim's blade shall drink of your worthless blood.'

Thomas glared up at him. 'You're going to kill us anyway,' he said belligerently, 'so that's not much of a threat, is it? What I've told you is true, but if you're too stupid to realise it then it's your fault not mine!'

The leader snarled and the other warriors murmured indignantly.

'Permit me to kill the insolent whelp, Captain Chattan!' Karim demanded. 'The tail of the beast may not be cloven but its unholy tongue is surely forked.'

'Thomas ain't lying!' Woodget piped up. 'Mister Mulligan done gave that sparkler to me afore he died. We doesn't know where he got it from, nor who it belongs to – that's the Green honest truth.'

Towering over them the leader sharply drew his breath, then crouched down to inspect the prisoners more closely.

'What know you of this Mulligan?' he demanded. 'Describe him to me.'

Woodget's fears seemed to be confirmed; Mulligan must have stolen the object from some fabulous palace and these fearsome soldiers were obviously in search of him.

'He ... he were an Irish mouse,' he began, 'who

liked a tot of rum now and then. Gettin' on a bit he was, with tattoos down his arms.' Woodget's description faltered as he recalled Mulligan's final tortured moments and he fell into silence.

'He had a wooden leg,' Thomas finished for him. 'Look, if that thing belongs to you then take it and leave us alone. We don't want it, all we want is to find a way back to our home – that's all.'

'This Mulligan,' the armoured creature asked. 'He was a friend of yours?'

Thomas glanced across at Woodget and wondered what he should say for the best, but it was the fieldmouse who answered and in a bitter, forceful voice.

'Yes he were!' Woodget cried. 'Mulligan was our friend, an' if you don't like it, Captain Chattan – then it's just too bad!'

A soft chortle issued from behind the mouthguard of the helmet.

'I believe you,' the leader replied, but now his tone was gentler than before.

Lifting his gauntleted paws, he carefully removed his plumed headgear and scratched his tiny ears.

The captain's head was small but it sat upon a thick and brawny neck that was covered in the same brindled brown fur that poked from the segmented armour which encased his tail. Down the length of his pointed muzzle however, and across the width of his eyes, was a patch of darker growth which gave him the startling appearance of someone wearing a mask. Yet the finely shaped features of this warrior were genial and kind and a faint smile was traced upon his lips.

In spite of his predicament, Woodget found himself liking that face. It was stern yet trustworthy and again he wondered what manner of creatures these soldiers were. To him they looked like a large breed of weasel, but he had never seen anyone quite like them before.

Thomas however was still not certain; he was full of questions and impatient for answers.

'Who are you?' he asked. 'Why are you treating us like this?'

Chattan's eyes fixed upon him for an instant. 'We are the enemy of he who was vanquished in the first pages of history,' he told him, 'and are sworn to destroy all who still worship that base and faithless father of despair.'

Turning to his troops, he nodded and said, 'Remove their bonds, I do not think we have anything to fear from these two. My judgement tells me that here are no members of the evil brood.'

In a moment the ropes that tied the mice's paws were cut and they sat upon the sand, rubbing their aching wrists.

'Thank'ee,' Woodget said.

'My fingers are numb,' Thomas muttered ruefully. 'Your folk weren't too gentle with the knots.'

'They had excellent reason,' came the sharp reply. 'For it is well known that the Scale dip their claws in venom.'

Woodget's thoughts returned to Mulligan once more and he hung his head sorrowfully. 'What do this poison do?' he ventured meekly. 'Do it eat at you and turn your blood black and foaming?'

The leader's face darkened. 'How do you know of this?' he asked.

'That's what happened to Mulligan,' Thomas answered with a shiver. 'But he said he'd been bitten by a serpent. He shrivelled right in front of us. It was horrible! Poor Mulligan – I . . . I can't . . .'

'Then alas, I see that he is indeed slain,' the leader lamented. 'This is evil tidings. He was a most valiant and praiseworthy hero of your kind.'

The mice stared at him. 'I thought you was hunting him!' Woodget declared in astonishment.

'Did you?' came the soft reply. 'Then you were much mistaken. The one-legged nomad was most welcome in our city, and held in high esteem by those who sit upon the Green Council. He will be sorely missed by all who knew him and when we return to our city there shall be a day of mourning in remembrance of him. Ashes shall be strewn in the winding streets and his likeness carved above the thousand steps that climb the holy mountain. Our poets will compose verses to praise him, for his was a wearisome burden but he complained never.'

Chattan's eyes stared into the distance and he became lost in a memory that returned the smile to his lips.

'For my part,' he said with a sigh, 'my grief will be tempered with the recollections of the times he honoured me by sharing the contents of his flask.'

Stirring from his reverie he looked back at the two mice.

'It is obvious to me that you have much to tell,' he said, 'but such tales must wait. We came only to give aid and do battle with our foes, yet we have come too late. The enemy has departed over the seas and what harm they have done here, well it does not take the book-learning of one of our scholars to imagine the slaughter that awaits our fearful vision.'

Lowering his sharp-nosed face, he gazed down at the glittering fragment in his grasp, then stared up at the White Mountains which were gleaming in the sunlight and narrowed his eyes at the spiralling smoke that still climbed above the trees.

'First we must make certain,' he said, rising to his feet and pulling the helmet back on to his head. 'Though these folk are harmless, it is clear that within this region there are still members of the Scale. Now we must march to the Temple of the Twelve Maidens and see in truth the terrible deeds that have been committed in that most hallowed place.'

The warriors lifted up their spears and shouted dreadful war cries, but before leading them away, Captain Chattan instructed Karim to remain with Woodget and Thomas until his return.

'For your own safety,' he assured them. 'Our armour may protect us from the darts and claws of our enemies, but you would wither at the first stroke. Do not despair of Karim Bihari's company; to friends he is more gentle than his appearance suggests. Have no more fear of losing your necks. Now that he knows you are not a follower of the Coiled One, my lieutenant shall guard you with his own life.'

With that he led the others away and they marched into the meadow and towards the pine woods.

Alone on the shore with the mice, Karim returned his sword to its sheath and sat down with a jangling clank of his armour.

'I have no wish to see what awaits them,' he said, driving the shaft of his spear into the sand. 'We were delayed too long to be of any use here. The Scale have preceded us, only death will they discover.'

'If you don't mind,' Thomas began, truculently folding his arms and frowning at the warrior, 'I think it's time you told us who you lot are and what you're doing.'

Karim's eyes twinkled at him from inside the helmet. Then, with a sweep of his arms, the warrior removed the headgear and they found themselves looking at a creature similar to Chattan.

But here was a chubby face covered by dark red fur and a grinning mouth filled with large white teeth. Upon his forehead were stripes of ochre-coloured paint and a mane of ginger hair flowed down the back of his powerful neck. About the jovial jowls grew a thick, russet beard that was plaited into three short knots and in both of the small ears there was a row of silver hoops and studs. When he took off the gauntlets the mice saw that upon the large paws there were also many rings and silver bangles that rattled and tinkled at his wrists.

'You have never seen a mongoose before?' he cried in amusement. 'Where have you been hiding? Are there none of my kin in your country?'

'Mongoose?' Woodget replied, repeating the unfamiliar word until he became used to it. 'No, there bain't be no mongeeses by Betony Bank. Not that I ever heard – only a gaggle of scruffy ordin'ry goose birds with honking beaks what me and our Cudweed used to pester and tease.'

'Betony Bank,' Karim uttered. 'That is a curious-sounding land, outside of my experience. Upon our ship there are many charts; you must declare to me in which ocean this place lies.'

Thomas glanced at the water's edge where the borders of the great island of fog still curled over the waves.

'Is your ship in there?' he asked.

Karim nodded. 'Yes,' he said, 'in the centre of that enchanted mist the *Chandi* is moored. She is the finest of our fleet.'

'But why do it lurk in that there fog?' Woodget chirped.

'So we may cross the seas in secret,' Karim answered with a laugh. 'How else ought we to journey? The servants of the Scale are everywhere, it is not well for them to know all our ways and destinations. Always have the ships of Hara voyaged cloaked within vapours woven by our wise folk. Yet this, like so many other of our works, have the disciples of Gorscarrigern copied and turned to their own accursed purpose. A ship of their own do they possess, a golden vessel whose gilded timbers are tempered in blood and whose hideous prow inspires terror and dread.

'Within the eye of a storm does *Kaliya*, their slave-worked ship, travel and when its thunderous passing mars the waters, no other craft, unless some powerful sorcery protects it, can endure the violence which rages in its wake.'

The mongoose gazed around the shore, at the wreckage of the *Calliope*, and sighed forlornly.

'I would guess that is what became of these poor folk,' he muttered. 'On our voyage we saw the tempest's fury in the distance and, recognising the evil

258

within, Captain Chattan steered the *Chandi* straight at its heart. But the Scale did not linger here, soon their hellish vessel veered aside and the storm drove east then south to avoid us.'

Tutting to himself, he sucked his teeth and preened the orange feathers that adorned his silver helmet.

'Many of us thought it would have been better to pursue that heathen crew to the bitter end of their journey,' he added, 'but our captain would not have it so. To these ravaged shores he delivered us and here we found you. Forgive my earlier eagerness to separate your heads from your bodies, it has been a long voyage and there was hope of battle at its end. I fear my enthusiasm got the better of me.'

'Hang on,' Thomas interrupted. 'Where did you say you sailed from – Hara, was it?'

Woodget blinked and stared at his friend in surprise until Karim put down his headgear and asked, 'You have heard of my city?'

'That's where Mulligan told us we were to go,' the fieldmouse announced. 'To see "the Holy One" – ain't that right Tom?'

Karim stroked his knotted beard thoughtfully. 'Chattan will wish to hear your tale in full when he returns,' he said, 'and you had best wait until then for the account of it, in case it grows stale with a second telling.'

'Mulligan made me promise to take that golden thing to your city,' Woodget confessed, 'but I haven't even got it no more – your captain still has it.'

Karim eyed him keenly. 'Have no fear for that treasure,' he muttered. 'Chattan Giri has no desire to steal it from you. When he learns your story I am sure he will return it to your care. Only a fool or a member of the Scale would lust after such an unwholesome device.'

'The Scale,' Thomas murmured. 'But I thought . . .'

Above them a seagull suddenly burst into a raucous squawking as it rode the air and Thomas sprang to his feet.

'While we're waitin' for your lads to come back,' he said quickly, 'me and Woodj'd like to finish off buryin' them what's dead, if that's all right with you.'

'So, you bury your dead in the land of Betony Bank,' Karim remarked. 'In Hara we inter them in the tombs cut under the mountain, if they do not die in battle away from our walls. But I respect your custom and will assist you in the labour, if you will allow me.'

'Course we will!' Woodget cried. 'The more the —'
Abruptly the fieldmouse coughed as he realised what he was about to say and trudged off up the sandbank, grieved by his lack of thought and consideration for his deceased fellow travellers.

When nearly three hours had passed and the late morning was growing uncomfortably hot, Thomas and Karim had found all the bodies that lay scattered upon the beach and into the wide grave they had reverently been placed.

'Green guard and keep you,' Thomas murmured as the last spadeful of sand was patted down on top of them and the grave marked by a notice written upon one of the *Calliope*'s timbers.

With the dark, poisonous sludge that remained of Mulligan, neither mouse knew what to do and they feared to venture near it again. But they desperately wished to honour him and lay his soul to rest, so steeling their nerves, they took up their shovels again and stepped into the meadow.

'Wait,' the mongoose told them. 'There is nothing you can do for the Irish nomad. Be content that his agonies are over. To bury that putrid slurry would only lock the venom into the ground and the soil would die utterly. In such cases it is best to leave it to the action of sun and rain. Let the weather destroy the blood of Gorscarrigern. In time only a bald patch of earth shall be here but who knows, maybe plants will grow again – then will Mulligan's spirit be truly appeased.'

'But we can't just leave him like this,' Woodget muttered. 'He can't go unnoticed for folk to trample by and not know he lies here.'

'Then build a mound of stones beside the reeking mire,' Karim suggested. 'Yet take care not to go too close. The very fumes can spin the senses and cause you to fall into its foulness.'

And so they collected a great quantity of large and heavy pebbles and piled them high, near to the spot where Mulligan's life had ended. Then, upon a large piece of wood, Thomas scratched the peg-leg's name, wedged it in place for all to see and dismally the mice bade their travelling companion farewell.

Woodget closed his eyes and offered up a silent prayer, then blew upon his calloused and blistered paws.

Wiping the sweat from his forehead, Karim leaned upon his makeshift spade and puffed out his round cheeks. As the strongest of the three he had done most of the hard work, except in the building of the stone mound, for that was a personal tribute and although he revered Mulligan as a valiant figure, the grief of Thomas and Woodget was deeper and more intimate and he did not intrude upon their solemn toil.

In the short time he had known them, the mongoose had grown increasingly fond of Thomas and Woodget. The mice who dwelt in his city were so serious and po-faced that he had never considered them to be an interesting race worthy of attention – with the exception of the Irish nomad – but this pair were far different from them.

Although the fieldmouse had not mentioned it to anyone, his tender paws were causing him much pain, but diligently and without a murmur of complaint he had pushed himself as hard as his little strength allowed. Karim admired him for that and was touched by his insistence on the matter of Mulligan's epitaph.

As for Thomas, the lieutenant was amazed at how many of the dead he had already carried up the sandbank. For such a small creature he was deceptively strong and capable. He approved of the way the mouse was not daunted by any task and marvelled that he did not balk at the hideous work, but stoically plodded on with it until the job was over.

'You have the hearts of mongooses,' he complimented them when all was complete. 'Now, let us return to the sands and talk no more of death for a while.'

So from the vicinity of the freshly dug graves they walked in silence, all three lost in their own thoughts, and returned at last to the place where they had sat before. But they were not there for long when Woodget's acute hearing detected the return of

Captain Chattan and the others.

Hurriedly Karim struggled back into the armour which he had discarded in the heat of the digging and stood to attention as they waited for the company to emerge from the meadow.

Presently the sound of their marching grew closer and through the twisted hedge they came. Even though the plumed helmets still covered their heads, Karim could tell that their faces were drained and horror shone in their dark eyes.

Captain Chattan greeted his lieutenant with a hollow, stricken voice and Woodget and Thomas wondered at the change that had come over him. He seemed shrunken, bowed by a great weight, and they noticed that the paw which gripped his spear was trembling.

'You did well to remain here, Karim,' Chattan uttered, 'for the shrine was defiled and the grove burned. As to the maidens who tended the place . . . we built a great pyre and now the sacred grove burns anew.'

He cleared his throat then turned to the warriors behind him and gave a signal. 'Bring him forward,' he cried. 'Let us see if the idiot's claim is true.'

From the rear of the company two mongooses came, holding some wriggling thing between them and, although he could not see over the plumed heads of those who barred his view, Woodget clapped his paws in delight when he heard a familiar voice whimpering in woeful dismay.

'Oh Lordy, you've landed yerself in enough hot water now to boil an effylump – a right picklingfixbunkeredholepinchingcleftstick this is and no mistake. Oh my, oh my, oh my! What'll become of me?'

'Dimmy!' Thomas and Woodget shouted with one voice.

Before Captain Chattan, Dahrem Ruhar was hauled, but into the innocuous and unassuming role of Dimlon, the simple young mouse, he had once again slithered and slipped.

As Mulligan had lumbered through the meadow, spilling his frothing blood over the spring flowers, the consumately vicious and irredeemably evil servant of the Dark Despoiler, Dahrem Ruhar, had crowed with devilish glee and leaped after his staggering prey.

Then, through those lidless, reptilian eyes he had seen the one-legged mouse stumble straight into Thomas and Woodget and his fangs glistened in the early sunlight as Dahrem contemplated the sport he could have with two further victims.

Flourishing the curved blades upon his claws, he had stolen through the grasses, saliva dribbling from his jaws in eager anticipation of the ghastly entertainments that would be his to relish. First Thomas would feel the deadly swipe of his talons but the fieldmouse was another matter – what delight there would be in harrying that puny yokel.

Cackling softly to himself, Dahrem imagined the plaintive cries as the irritating bumpkin pleaded for his life, and when he tired of his squeaky grovelling, he conjured up a hundred horrendous horrors to inflict upon him before he perished.

But, even as the infernal disciple of Scarophion had crept closer, glimpsing the faces of his enemies through the stems of the yellow flax and preparing to pounce and strike them down, his schemes were dashed and toppled in total ruin.

Up the sandbank, the armoured warriors came striding and through the hedge they burst with their spears blazing in the sun. Hastily, Dahrem withdrew, squirming back through the grasses, slinking upon his belly like a wriggling serpent, and a bitter curse hissed from his quivering lips.

Away from those fierce soldiers he fled, for he recognised them well enough and knew from whence they came. But now his malicious strategies were in disarray and the triumph that was so nearly his was fading fast. There was no way he could fight such a company of armed warriors from the city of Hara, so he organised his malignant wits and set his treacherous mind in motion to plot and consider his next move.

Swiftly that base, iniquitous brain worked and when he formed a grotesque and guileful plan, like a repulsive spider, Dahrem took up a position at the edge of the wood and there he waited in a cringing, curled up ball – ready for the troops to discover him.

There would be time enough later to contrive a way to fulfil his ultimate goal and claim the ninth fragment. Cunning and stealth had always won him his desires and this would prove no great challenge; even warriors needed sleep and attacks were always best received when least expected. No, for the present at least, his dignity would have to suffer further affronts and injuries as he reforged the disguise he had worn upon the *Calliope*.

The two halves of his forked tail joined together

again and his reptilian vision dimmed as his eyes changed back into Dimlon's innocent, heavy-lidded and docile features.

Now, when the guards brought him before Captain Chattan, he was staring wildly in mock fear at the bright spears that surrounded him and his head lolled feebly upon his long neck.

'Oh Dimmy!' Woodget rejoiced, rushing forward to fling his arms about the pale grey mouse's neck. 'I didn't think I'd ever be cheered on this awful day, but I'm so glad to see you I could burst!'

'However did you manage it?' Thomas cried, shaking him vigorously by the paw and clapping him on the back.

Dahrem squeaked with feigned joy to see them, whilst at the same time he laughed inside, scorning their friendship. Those fools were his guarantee of safety from this proud, parading rabble; they would confirm his false identity and so place him beyond the suspicion of that haughty captain.

How ironic that these self-same creatures whom he had been most eager to slaughter would now be his deliverers. Yet still Dahrem yearned to murder them and he prayed to his foul master that the opportunity would present itself again. Even while Woodget hugged him, the desire to rip out his throat burned within his black heart and he ached to drape himself in Thomas' entrails and lop off his snout.

But such luxurious pleasures would have to wait; for the moment he had to humble himself once more and wear the guise of Dimlon.

'W ... W ... Woody!' he cried, gibbering with fake emotion. 'And Tommy too! It's a miracle, a blessuspinchmewakefulstonkingwonder this is – a real finominy! I thought you pair were goners for sure, me an' old Mulligan both did.'

With his suspicious gaze trained upon Dahrem's expertly elated face, Captain Chattan spoke to Woodget and Thomas, but not once did his eyes leave that beaming mask.

'Then this dunceling is known to you?' he addressed them. 'We found him by the eaves of the wood, quivering like the spawn of the swamp frogs. I did not believe his tale – he claimed to have been washed ashore with the Irish nomad and together they ventured to the Shrine of Virbius. There they were attacked by a single member of the Scale and Mulligan was wounded, but this craven lout did flee and soon became lost in the darkness.

'He says he knows nothing of what happened to Mulligan after that, nor what became of the enemy who assailed them. His speech is peculiar and I soon tired of it but I do not trust him. There are ramparts of deceit behind his eyes – he knows more than he says.'

Thomas laughed and shook his head. 'Don't go accusin' poor Dimlon of conspiracies an' such,' he told him. 'Why, there's nothing sinister 'bout him. We should know, we've travelled with him fer days. Your trouble, Captain, is you're too busy lookin' for enemies at every turn – you done forgot what friendly folks are like.'

'He's right,' Woodget put in. 'Dimmy's as harmless as we are – more so in fact, and Mulligan done trusted him.'

The mongoose stared at the prisoner a moment more, then gestured to the guards to release him and at once Dahrem hugged the others in a show of deliriously happy greeting.

Lifting his paws, Captain Chattan held up Mulligan's precious fragment and studied it with a morbid fascination as though he was looking on something hideous and thoroughly evil.

'I do not need to tell you that the piece long kept within the Shrine of Virbius had been taken by the pagan curs,' he breathed to Karim, 'so now their High Priest possesses seven of these baneful things. If we had departed when I first desired that might not have been.'

Breaking off from greeting Thomas and Woodget, Dahrem turned to look at the device in Chattan's gauntleted paw and the livid light that pulsed within the gold-encased jade inflamed his black and merciless being.

There it sparkled, the ninth fragment – the missing piece that for so long had confounded the lore masters of his infernal brotherhood. No trace of it could ever be found in any manuscript ransacked from the temples they had despoiled, and far over the globe had the murderous agents ranged to discover word of it.

Now that very fragment glittered before Dahrem's eyes, yet it was out of his reach. How he longed to put on the poisoned talons that were hidden inside his satchel and cut off those defiling paws which held the hope of his insane, fanatical kind.

If he could only return to the Black Temple, where the glorious statue of Scarophion reared in demonic splendour and dreadful majesty, with this, the long lost answer to all the empty years without their Lord.

Then would there be a new High Priest to overthrow he who stood behind the prow of the golden ship and ordered the rising of the tempest. A new tyrant under the command of the Coiled One would emerge and all would wither before his pitiless armies.

Dahrem blinked and dismissed the delicious daydreams; there would be time for such fancies later when the skulls of his enemies lay piled about him. Now he must remember the role he had set himself and, with a shake of the head, become Dimlon again.

'Right,' Thomas was saying, facing the mongoose captain squarely, 'time for some answers. I want to know exactly what's going on and what is that thing of Mulligan's anyway? All this talk of Dark Despoilers – we done heard that afore, yet we was told it were nowt but a legend from ancient times. Me an' Woodj got a right to know and we won't be fobbed off no more.'

Captain Chattan smiled faintly.

'There is much we both wish to learn,' he said, 'but first let us sit and eat. Tales are digested better if they accompany more tangible nourishment. Come, we shall prepare a meal and you three shall sit with me.'

Thomas could not argue with that. He suddenly realised how hungry he was and agreed to wait a fraction longer to discover the answers to his nagging questions.

So, upon the shore, five fires were lit, made from the shattered wreckage of the *Calliope* that had already dried in the baking sun. Around the flickering flames, groups of warriors sat and from their mist-enshrouded ship, the *Chandi*, provisions were fetched and cooked over the scorching heats.

Woodget, Thomas and Dimlon sat in the largest group of nine mongooses, which counted Captain Chattan and Karim amongst its number, and the fieldmouse hummed happily to himself as a great iron pot was filled with vegetables, herbs and wonderfully fragrant spices that tingled in his nostrils when he sniffed them.

As Thomas began their story, Chattan and the other warriors listened attentively, the captain halting him on occasion to question him more closely about some point or detail. When Thomas touched upon Simoon, the prophet, a curious expression flitted across the mongoose's face but he made no comment and let the mouse continue. Thus the entire journey, from the skirmish upon the quayside, right to the destruction of the *Calliope*, was related and at the end of the tale Karim let out a low whistle of admiration.

'Then an agent of the Scale was indeed aboard your ship,' Chattan murmured. 'It is clear to me that Mulligan was aware of this. No doubt he intended all along to entrust the fragment to you should anything befall him.'

'Now it's your turn,' Thomas prompted. 'Just what is going on?'

The captain stiffened and his face became grave. 'A desperate road have you travelled,' he began, 'and some horrors have you witnessed along the way. Yet they were but glimpses – the merest snatching glance at the great turmoil which confronts the present world. A corner of the fearful curtain which cloaks that evil from prying eyes have you twitched upon your voyage, but no one I fear is strong enough to behold all the secrets which it conceals.

'Yet know this and be glad that the sun is shining for the recounting of it – for the dark is no place to hear such nightmares.'

At that he paused, for the meal was ready to eat and Karim served it into bowls which he passed around the group.

Woodget's pink nose thrilled at the aromatic scent which steamed from the stew, but he was too enthralled by Chattan's words to attempt any sampling mouthful and he waited for him to resume.

'Whilst generations of your families have slept at peace in your remote, contented land,' the captain murmured, 'a stinking blight has crept over the other regions of the earth and if it is not checked, one day it shall reach even your blissfully ignorant shores.'

A loud slurp interrupted him as Dimlon sucked on his spoon and the loathsome creature actually managed to blush before returning to the meal with more dainty manners, but all the while his ears were alert and he revelled in the discomfort the tale of his glorious brotherhood brought upon those who sat beside him.

'In secret has the peril grown down the uncounted ages,' Chattan told them, 'spreading like a black, creeping fungus over the face of the land, but now openly does it go to war and our defences are found wanting. Can you but imagine a tenth of the evil that now rises in the East?'

'Are you really telling us that this snake god is still worshipped?' Thomas muttered sceptically. 'Even the jerboa said it happened ages ago and I didn't believe all that stuff he told us anyway. Demon serpents – it's all rubbish isn't it? Like the myths about Hobb and

271

the two-headed ratty thing in Deptforth or wherever, back home.'

'Oh I don't know, Tom,' Woodget broke in, blowing upon his first spoonful of stew to cool it. 'Simoon was pretty convincin' – had me believin', he did.'

The mongoose shook his head. 'Doubt is ever a ready weapon of evil,' he declared to Thomas. 'Only when it is too late does the cynic realise his folly and thus is he brought to ruination. Know now the truth of Suruth Scarophion. He whom we in Hara name Gorscarrigern – the Coiled One. You have said that Simoon the prophet told you some of the tale. Let my tongue relate it all and you will understand the events in which you have been embroiled.'

Thomas and Woodget put down their bowls and, although he was famished, Dahrem copied them. It was strange hearing the ancient scriptures from the mouth of this filthy snake-biter – but he swallowed his revulsion and assumed the same rapt expression as the others.

'Upon the steps of his most ghastly temple was Gorscarrigern finally assailed,' Chattan uttered. 'Then, by the enchantments of the many worthy sorcerers and cunning folk that dwelt in that age of the world, his terrible might was bettered and into the tumbling ruin of his shrine did he flee. Then were the spells which knitted his repulsive flesh finally broken. His black blood was spilled and, caught in that gushing tide of death, the magicians and seers who had wielded the power of the Green were cruelly slain.'

'Like Mulligan . . .' Thomas breathed in consternation.

'Just so,' the mongoose starkly affirmed. 'For later it was discovered that the few detestable disciples who survived the bloody battles of the time crept back into the unroofed temple when the hosts of the Green had departed, and from the reeking corruption of their slain master's carcass they gathered up the venom. Undoubtedly, after all these ages they must still have great store, for the self-same poison was used upon the Irish nomad.'

'Then the Scale do exist,' Thomas whispered.

'Assuredly they do,' Chattan said. 'Nothing is more certain to we who dwell in the Eastern Lands. For many years now we have known that the heathen creed were multiplying and baptising more newborn unto their evil cult. I fear that somewhere, in some secret, distant region a new temple now stands and the rites of Gorscarrigern continue under the auspices of the cruel priest and priestess.'

Narrowing his eyes until they became dark slivers, he lowered his voice as though enemies surrounded them and muttered, 'Yet the worst horror I have still to tell. For now I speak of Mulligan's burden and you too shall know of the dread that has plagued our thoughts for centuries.'

Woodget shifted uncomfortably. He was not certain that he wanted to know after all, but he couldn't very well ask the captain to stop now. So, with his mouth dropping open and a chill creeping up his tail, he learned the awful truth about the glittering fragment and his flesh crawled as though a horde of ants was swarming beneath the skin.

'When Gorscarrigern had finally expired,' Chattan told them, 'and the terror of his momentous corpse's ghastly presence had dimmed, the bravest of the Green host which had surrounded the barren, scorched hill upon which the vast, unsanctified temple now stood in ruins, stole forth. Into that terrible place they crept, avoiding the rivers of venom which still flowed from the corrupting flesh of the gargantuan demon, and made search amongst the destruction for any members of the Coiled One's retinue which might have survived.

'So it was they discovered a hidden stair that wound deep into the earth and countless dungeons and cavernous pits did they find. Then, housed within the bottommost grot was unearthed a hideous, great altar and there the most ancient and jealously guarded secret of Gorscarrigern was finally revealed.

'Atop that pagan altar which flowed with hot fresh blood and the hearts of those sacrificed, was kept his last and greatest hope.

'Long had he laboured over it, instructing the countless high priests who served him down the years upon its construction, and the skill of thousands was poured into its making. From the bowels of the earth, from the bones of mountains and the flesh of stones was it crafted.

'Nine segments of precious jade, carved and polished by dedicated claws, did he command to be brought before him. Nine priceless pieces in tribute to the nine stars which burned in the heavens during the length of his blaspheming reign and which blaze still when his unquiet, banished spirit draws closest to the living plane.

'In the dark years of his hateful sovereignty, when his power was waxing, he weaved terrible spells about those fragments – instilling his inglorious might into each and every one.

'Then was gold gouged from deep mines and in the furnace of his throat he smelted it and spewed it over the ground for his wrights to work into the shapes of his malevolent desiring. So were the fragments of jade clad in gilded traceries, and when the puzzling pieces were brought together his devoted servants knew what they had built.'

'What was it?' Thomas urged.

Chattan held up the fragment that Mulligan had kept hidden for so long and everyone gazed at it, mesmerised yet repelled by its uncanny beauty.

'See the intricate golden fronds that twist and bud around the edge,' he said, tracing the shape with his finger and grimacing unconsciously. 'Profane arts wrought them and the other eight pieces are similarly devised. But it is written that when the nine are brought together, the gold writhes with life and the carven images reach out and join until the final shape of Gorscarrigern's unhallowed design stands whole again and is sealed with neither crack nor gap.'

Dahrem pretended to look afraid and in a quailing voice asked, 'So what is this shape? What does Mulligan's baublingsparklytrinket become – what is it a part of?'

'It is the hope of his followers,' the captain replied. 'For before his flesh was vanquished, the Coiled One vowed to return. But only when the Green host discovered that infernal pit did they realise his threat was founded in truth.

'Upon the gore-dripping altar, guarded by the last of his adepts, they discovered the united fragments –

and the joy of their victory was diminished.

'For there, nestling within the scarlet bodies and drenched in their hot, fresh blood was a sight to darken the doughtiest of spirits. At last the grand schemes of the Dark Despoiler were revealed to those outside his priesthood and in that desperate hour the ancestors of all free folk were mortally afraid.

'Fashioned in jade and covered with ornate patterns of furling gold was the object that would cheat them at the last – a great green and golden egg!'

'An egg?' Woodget cried. 'How come – what fer?'

'From his withering corpse, the foul spirit of Gorscarrigern had meant to flee and into that glittering shell he no doubt purposed to enter and thus would his fleshly body be reborn into the miserable world – refreshed and seething with new, burning life.

'Yet his striving with the magicians upon the temple steps had weakened him more than he had bargained for, and their mastery had sent his dark soul out into the cold void from whence it originally came. So, when that final cavern was reached, the warriors of the Green host found that the egg was still empty – nurturing naught but stale air and the hopes of his remaining disciples.

'Then was the altar thrown down, but in the ensuing destruction the egg would break only into its nine elements and no hammer nor force of violence could smash them.

'To the upper airs were these invulnerable pieces taken and the decision was made to keep them separate and divided, for then the Coiled One could have no chance of returning.'

Chattan turned Mulligan's secret treasure over in his paws and frowned deeply. 'So it was,' he muttered. 'Eight pieces were entrusted into the care of the mighty kings and generals who were gathered there and their armies bore them back to their cities in triumph. Yet little faith was put in the enduring strength of fortress walls, for time levels all strongholds and they knew that the influence of the fragments would speed the decay.

'Thus did they resolve that the ninth and largest piece of the egg should not remain in any lone place forever and into the custody of one faithful to the Green was it given. Such was the unending doom placed upon that loyal house; every nine years it was decreed that the fragment must be conveyed to another place of sanctuary – one year for each unhallowed element. So, throughout the tireless ages, that is what the descendants of that virtuous bloodline have done, voyaging across the globe, visiting each holy shrine in turn – bearing this glittering thing of dread.'

Thomas sucked his teeth and scratched his head, bewildered. 'Are you telling us,' he began, 'that Mulligan—'

'Mulligan was the last of that honourable ancestry,' Chattan said firmly, 'heir to the terrible burden of the ninth fragment.'

Woodget stared down at the ground, immersed in a terrible rush of guilt for ever having doubted the Irish mouse's motives. How could he have suspected him of stealing? Everything he had done since they had first met now became clear and he reproached himself bitterly.

'But,' Thomas uttered in a wavering voice, 'you said that the Scale now have seven of these bits. Are they really trying to find them all?'

'They will not stop until the egg is reassembled and their demonic master is reborn,' the mongoose told him.

'Is that really possible?'

Chattan fixed him with his eyes. 'Oh yes,' he answered in a sombre, sepulchral tone. 'For though the unclean spirit of Gorscarrigern has long been exiled and shuttered from the world, there are times, when his constellation shines in the night and we brush close to the realms of the dead, when the way opens for him to return.'

'So where's the eighth piece?' Thomas breathed.

Chattan glanced at Karim before answering. 'In the city of Hara,' he said simply.

Thomas chewed his bottom lip. 'Mulligan told us to go there,' he murmured.

'Indeed,' the captain nodded, 'and when we set sail you shall accompany us aboard the *Chandi*. But now I have spoken long and the food is growing cold. Yet before we eat, I must return this foul thing unto its rightful custodian.'

Lifting the golden fragment, Chattan reached across and placed it in Woodget's cringing paws.

'To you the Irish nomad entrusted this horrible legacy. Guard it well and let no member of the Scale discover your secret. To my city you were bidden to journey, yet what counsel you shall be given there, it is not my part to judge. May the Green watch over you, for in the terrible time to come I fear you will need His blessed protection.'

Woodget stared aghast at the gold-encrusted jade that sparkled in his grasp and with a look of fear upon his stricken face he gazed up at Thomas, whilst at his side, Dahrem Ruhar smiled slyly to himself.

11

The City of Hara

In a subdued silence the meal was finally eaten, but neither Thomas nor Woodget were in any mood to savour the new and unfamiliar flavours of the eastern spices. They ate merely because they knew they had to, all thoughts of hunger had gone and any enjoyment they might have had was lost.

Both were too absorbed in what Captain Chattan had told them to pay attention to anything else. The world now appeared to be more full of shadows than before and they almost wished they had never met Mulligan. It was he who had opened the entrance to this dark and sinister world and they found themselves yearning to slam the door shut again and escape to some carefree land where none of these horrors had ever been heard of. Yet even as they considered this, they knew that should Suruth

Scarophion ever return then nowhere would be a refuge from him.

Miserably, the mice emptied their bowls and stared dolefully into them as if the solution to their troubles might be hidden there.

Eventually Thomas lifted his eyes and, turning to the captain, said, 'If we have to go to this city of yours, then we'd best make a start. The sooner Woodj and me get all this over and done with, the better.'

'And me!' Dahrem pleaded. 'Don't forget D – what'd he do stuck out here all on his lonesome? Let me come with you.'

'Come then!' Chattan declared, rising to his feet. 'Karim, see that the fires are doused, whilst I take our honoured guests to the *Chandi*.'

Down the shore the captain strode, towards the waiting wall of mist and, with his gauntleted fingers, he beckoned the three mice to follow.

'Do not be afraid,' he told them as he stepped into the outlying wisps that flowed over the sands, 'the fog is but a simple enchantment and will not harm you.'

In spite of his assurance, Thomas and Woodget ventured forward cautiously and Dahrem eyed the vapour with trepidation. What if the magic arts of this uncouth rabble were capable of detecting his true identity? Would that cloaking mist permit a member of the Scale to pass?

There was only one way to find out. Chattan was already becoming lost in the enshrouding fog, fading to a vague outline, and so, with his paw clasped upon his satchel, Dahrem rushed forward and leapt after.

Thomas coughed nervously as the pale grey mouse

was swallowed up by the obliterating cloud, then with a nod to Woodget they both entered the swirling mist and its furling fingers wrapped close about them.

Woodget shivered. It was cold inside that encircling fog, where the hot Cretan sun failed to penetrate, and it was as though he had been struck by a sudden blindness. Only a dense, white blankness reared before him and at his side even Thomas' sturdy shape was veiled and blurred.

In his paws Mulligan's fragment grew chill, the gold glinted like ice and the pulsing light dimmed within the jade.

'I doesn't like this, Tom,' the fieldmouse murmured, but his voice fell flat and dead against the billowing cloud.

'Don't worry,' his friend uttered, although the sound seemed to come from a long distance away. 'Just keep on walking.'

Woodget obeyed, faltering only when his toes found the water's edge and he jumped back in alarm.

'It's freezy!' he cried.

Thomas' dim silhouette was a little way ahead of him. 'You get used to it,' he promised, wading a little deeper into the water, 'but I don't think there's much further to go. The mist's breaking up here.'

Ignoring the goose bumps which prickled over his body, Woodget went splashing after until the waves were lapping against his middle then, suddenly, the fog parted and he emerged into the warm sunshine once more.

'Oaks and ivy!' he declared, gazing around him in wonder.

Before him, bathed in a shaft of brilliant sunshine,

Thomas stood spellbound by the sight that met his eyes and, beside him, Dahrem was similarly transfixed – yet envy and malice gnawed at his heart when he looked on the lovely spectacle unveiled before them.

Only Captain Chattan turned when the fieldmouse emerged from the mist and he grinned at him with a proud light twinkling in his dark eyes.

'Behold the *Chandi*,' he said.

The fog bank was in the form of a great, wide ring and in its centre, sitting with immeasurable grace and symmetry upon the glimmering sea was the most beautiful ship Woodget could ever have imagined.

A quarter of the size of the *Calliope* was she, for here was a galley built by the shipwrights of Hara, whose only crew were the folk of that great, fabled city.

White as winter frost were her shapely timbers, resembling an exquisite sculpture chipped entirely from a single and immense block of ice. Over her slender prow and bluff stern, an intricate, overlapping latticework of images, symbolising the beneficent powers of the world, clustered – richly embellished with the brightest silver.

Two great emeralds which burned with a fire like the unstoppable, bursting might of spring, blazed in the eyes of the large and lifelike figurehead that was carved in the shape of the Green Mouse, and they shone brightly over the sea, guiding the *Chandi* through any waters, however fierce the weather or dark the night.

All around the elegant vessel, seeming to hem it within a fence of upraised spears, the long, lean oars pointed out and upwards and from the deck, like tall and stately trees, three masts rose into the clear blue sky. Each tapering trunk was bound with further examples of the silversmith's art and from the ornate bands a delicate web of fine rigging was strung.

Yet surmounting all of this and sitting atop the main mast, was a crescent moon, also of silver, and it sparkled and glittered above the rest of the ship like a fallen star, whose glare was so bright that it pained the eyes to look on.

'She's beautiful,' Thomas marvelled. 'Makes the *Calliope* look like a rusting bucket.'

Captain Chattan laughed, then he raised a tiny whistle to his lips and blew three short blasts upon it.

In response, from the galley there appeared a small rowing-boat which swiftly came towards them. At the oars of this craft there was another mongoose but this one wore no armour, only a light blue cape and a belt to which was attached a long, pearl-handled knife.

'Hail, Mahesh!' Chattan declared. 'See, I have brought three guests to accompany us on our return.'

When the rowing-boat pulled alongside the captain, its occupant stared intently at the mice but said nothing and merely bowed politely.

'Now my friends,' Chattan told them, 'you must climb into this craft if you are to board our ship. Let me assist you.'

One by one the mice were helped into the rowing boat. First went Thomas, then Dahrem who made a ludicrous fuss as he scrambled over the side and nearly capsized it entirely before finally sitting down. Then, with Chattan's aid, Woodget clambered in beside him and the captain joined them.

With an expert dip of one oar into the sea, the boat

was whirled about and the serene shape of the *Chandi* grew larger as they swept towards it.

Into the centre of the open space, which lay concealed from all outside eyes within the mysterious bank of fog, they went and soon the white timbers of the galley's smooth hull filled the mice's vision until their little craft came to a halt with a gentle bump.

From the deck above, a rope ladder was lowered and Captain Chattan ascended it first in order to show them how it was done.

Eventually they were all standing upon the *Chandi's* upper deck, where the rest of her crew were gathered in two regimented lines awaiting the return of their captain.

All wore blue capes about their shoulders and, to Thomas and Woodget's surprise, they saw that, as well as mongooses, there was a complement of small, long-tailed creatures, with dark bars striping their fur, which they later discovered to be palm squirrels whose agility in the rigging was unparalleled.

Once he had introduced the three mice to the curious crew, Chattan gave instructions for the other rowing-boats to return to the shore and bring back Karim and the rest of his warriors.

'Well my young friends,' he beamed at his guests, 'you are most welcome and the freedom of the ship is yours.'

Thomas and Woodget thanked him, and with an ingratiating grin fixed upon his face, Dahrem babbled idiotically.

'Splendiforouscruisydreadnoughtslooper!' he yapped, wagging his head up and down. 'Lor – if only my Aunty Lily could see her Dimmy now!'

'What I don't understand,' Thomas began, staring round at the enveloping mist, 'is how you manage to see where you're going?'

At that Captain Chattan laughed out loud. 'The *Chandi* knows all waters,' he replied, 'yet her mariners have many charts to consult if she should stray and there is still the sky above, for we steer for the most part by the stars.'

'But I still don't see,' Thomas grumbled. 'How do you know where the shore is? How do you avoid the rocks and reefs?'

The mongoose grinned. 'When we set forth I shall show you,' he promised.

Just then Woodget, who had been scowling to himself as his thoughts troubled him, asked, 'How long will it take afore we reach your city, Captain?'

'My land is far from here,' he replied, 'yet the *Chandi* can travel with great speed when the wind fills her sails. If we are fortunate then the journey will not take much more than fifteen or sixteen days.'

'As long as that?' the fieldmouse murmured unhappily and, clutching the fragment, he wandered to a corner of the deck that was covered with a canopy of white silk and sat down upon a heap of cushions.

Chattan watched him then turned to Thomas who was standing with his head tilted right back, admiring the towering masts and shielding his eyes from the glare of the sun.

'It is a difficult burden that has been given to your friend,' he said.

Thomas looked at him then peered over to where Woodget was sitting with his chin in his paws. 'Oh it isn't Mulligan's treasure, nor what lies ahead that's bothering Woodj,' he commented. 'Once he says he'll do something that's it and no complaining. No, the Scale and all the dangers we might face are the furthest things from his mind at the moment. I know what's bothering him, he figures that it'll be at least a month before he can get home and see Bess again. Poor Woodj, if it wasn't for me none of this would've happened and he'd still be back at home.'

'Do not condemn yourself too sternly,' the mongoose told him, 'for I believe it was meant to be this way. Destiny has a way of guiding the paths of those she requires to do her bidding – if you had not led him to this point she would have found another method.'

'All the same,' Thomas shrugged, 'I wish Mulligan had given me the fragment instead, then Woodj could've returned home straight away.'

Chattan's eyes narrowed as he considered the little fieldmouse and he shook his head slowly. 'No,' he said. 'He would not have deserted you, even as you do not desert him.'

Listening to all that they had said, Dahrem suddenly bounded forward. 'I'll go sit with Woody!' he cried. 'Dimmy can cheer him up.'

'Wait!' Thomas snapped, pulling the pale grey mouse back. 'Let him be for a while.'

An obedient grin spread over Dahrem's face but he raged inside and he wondered how he could bear to remain upon this hateful ship with the ninth fragment so tantalisingly close without being able to claim it.

'A chance will present itself,' his seditious mind thought. 'A moment will come when the vigilance of these fools is wanting. Then shall I strike and the agonies of My Lord's blood shall eat into them.'

But Dahrem was not permitted to dwell on these delightful musings, for Karim and the others were climbing aboard – their armour clattering and clanking as they hoisted themselves on to the deck.

Then Captain Chattan called for the anchor to be raised and the sails to be unfurled and Thomas watched the crew set about these duties with great interest, wondering if during the length of the voyage they could teach him some of their skills.

With a ruffling of the canvas overhead, the wind filled the sails and the mice saw that they were of the purest white and embroidered with a pattern of intertwining green leaves about the edge. Then, gracefully, with the surrounding mist moving with her – the *Chandi* began to skim through the water.

'Just think, Dimmy,' Thomas murmured excitedly to the evil creature at his side, 'we're setting off again, to a land I've only heard of in old tales, one of the most mysterious and fabulous places there is – India.'

A distinct sneer formed upon Dahrem's face before he could stop himself, then he gave a theatrical sigh and said, 'Yes, but who knows what might happen 'tween here an' there?'

In the days that followed, the white and silver ship of Hara steered first towards Egypt and passed secretly through the great canal one early morning, like a shred of dawn mist.

Yet its crew and three passengers saw little of the lands that they voyaged past. Only the snowy walls of the enchanted fog which enveloped their vessel could they see, and the mice quickly tired of it.

But, keeping his promise to Thomas, Captain Chattan showed them how they could peer through the cloaking vapours if they so wished. To a place directly behind the figurehead he brought them, and where the light that shone from the emerald eyes touched the ethereal, obscuring curtain in front, they could see vague images as if they were gazing through a hazy window. Dim outlines of desert hills they saw and enormous figures hewn from stone, worn smooth by the scouring of thousands of years and abrasive, sand-filled winds.

But the temperature became horribly hot and both Thomas and Woodget were amazed that the mongooses could even contemplate doing any work, let alone pull on the oars when the breeze dropped – for all they were able to do was lie beneath the silken canopy, wiping the sweat from their foreheads and panting wearily.

Dahrem however was unaffected by the extreme heat. He was well accustomed to arid climes and with his heavy lidded eyes, he slyly spied the ways of his enemies, contemplating what his next action might be. To his overwhelming disappointment he soon realised that a constant vigil was kept upon the deck and even in the middle of the night five mongooses stood fore and aft – alert and watchful.

No, to consider taking the fragment by force whilst surrounded by this despised throng was an insane notion and he bided his time, amusing himself with thoughts of murder and hideous cruelty.

Down the Nile, the *Chandi* journeyed – then out into the Red Sea.

When the sun dipped below the rim of the

enshrouding fog and the air became cooler, Thomas would wander around the galley and chat to the crew, learning from the squirrels the art of rope weaving and, with much merry laughter at his expense, how to hitch up the sails.

Sometimes Woodget accompanied him, and the fieldmouse excelled in climbing the rigging, but mostly he preferred to stand behind the figurehead and hear tales of the foreign lands they had passed from any who was willing to tell him. Occasionally the galley would drift over shoals of brightly coloured fish and once a porpoise delighted them all by leaping in and out of the mist, seeming to derive much amusement from the curious, chill cloud. For an entire afternoon, it travelled alongside the ship, calling up to the faces which gazed down upon it and emitting a high-pitched chatter in its peculiar clicking voice. Then, after accompanying them for many miles, it gave a final call of farewell and plunged out through the fog – never to be seen again.

At night the temperature dropped dramatically and, when the starlight glimmered cold and white upon the deck, the captain would join his guests and tell them stories of his city. But it was Karim who brought the stories to life, colouring them with descriptions of those who dwelt there, and Woodget's homesickness ebbed a little as he looked forward to the prospect of visiting the fair-sounding place.

Of Hara's history and legends they learned much, how it was founded many ages ago in the deeps of the Coiled One's reign by a wealthy warrior king who wished to build a stronghold in the mountains. But coming there, he beheld a vision of the Green and thereafter the monarch renounced his riches and power, and though his kin built the city around him, he remained on the mountain communing with the Green spirit until the day he died.

'Always in the years after,' Chattan continued, 'has there been a Holy One – a sadhu – at the top of the thousand stairs. They are a most blessed order and the one who sits there now is counted amongst the wisest.'

'Some say he is the embodiment of the Green himself,' Karim put in. 'The mother of my dear wife believes him to be a divine spirit clothed in mortal flesh, but then she is the sister of Nakir, the fruit merchant who once spent three months living in the banana trees to see if he could catch a glimpse of the Green spirit.'

'And did he?' chortled Thomas.

Karim pulled a woeful face. 'Poor Nakir,' he murmured drily. 'He eventually returned with a raving tale of whispering voices and insisted that the bananas spoke to each other in the night, plotting how to take their revenge upon the macaques who devoured them. Ah – you may scoff, my little friends, but to this day no one has ever seen Nakir eat a banana and he will not suffer the very name to be mentioned in his lunatic presence, neither does he sell them upon his stall.'

Woodget smiled, then became thoughtful. 'Do you think your Holy One will know what to do with Mulligan's fragment?' he asked.

Chattan nodded. 'If the sadhu does not, then no one can,' he answered. 'For he is the head of the Green Council and all revere his words – they are few and seldom, yet never without value.'

And so the days melted into weeks and across the Arabian Sea the *Chandi* voyaged. Then a day dawned when there was much excitement, for through the enchanted mist a distant coast had been sighted and their charts told them that there at last were the shores of their homeland.

For the rest of the morning the squirrels leapt about the rigging, ensuring that the sails caught every breath of wind to speed them on their way, and the vast strip of land upon the horizon gradually grew closer.

Standing behind the figurehead, Thomas, Woodget and Dahrem looked on the breathtaking sight in silence. It seemed as if a limitless continent of solid darkness was spreading over the sea, stemming the wide expanse of the immense waters, declaring an end to the deep's untame realm and usurping it with another, equally wild and hazardous region.

'That is my home,' Captain Chattan's voice breathed softly behind them, 'a land most beloved in my heart. Never can my eyes look on her without great emotion stirring in my breast. Lovely is she, yet deadly to the unwary traveller. The forests are filled with monstrous beasts of tooth and talon, but the main peril creeps along the ground or swims through our rivers – even the sea writhes with them.'

'The Scale?' Woodget asked nervously, gripping a leather bag that Karim had given to him and in which he now kept the fragment.

'Not they,' Chattan assured, 'yet in every country do the servants of Gorscarrigern have a foothold. I was speaking of the lesser serpents, though they can still maim or kill with fang and constriction. Yes, my homeland is plagued with such base creatures; in all places do they thrive, all perhaps save one.'

Breathing deeply, as if he was able to inhale the airs that flowed down from the as yet unseen mountains of his country, the mongoose half closed his eyes. 'But in the haven of Hara,' he said, 'the paradise that the Green fashioned in the beginning of all things has come to pass once more. No serpents stray too close to its outer walls, for the virtue of our city repels them and keeps their slithering evil at bay. That is well for they have ever been the instruments of the Scale, for that foul creed exert a horrible influence over them and can instruct them to do their bidding. If the power that sustains our fortress should ever perish then I tremble to think what would befall us.'

'But what if the forces of the Scale themselves attacked?' Thomas asked doubtfully. 'Could you keep them out?'

'They have never tried,' came the pensive reply, 'but our sentries would sight their approach before they came within many miles of Hara and our defences are strong.'

Dahrem raised his eyebrows and, summoning a casual tone, to disguise his true scorn, muttered, 'I does feel a tidy lot safer knowin' that.'

The *Chandi* made good progress and the great continent that spread over the waters slowly became a lush and verdant green and beyond the immense shores there began to form ghostly blue hints of forest-covered mountains.

By the late afternoon the galley had almost reached the coast and Chattan told the mice that they would soon enter the mouth of the Periyar River.

With the sun setting behind them, saturating the circling cloud with deep hues of crimson and rose, they could see its rays moving over the tall trees that covered the hills of the Western Ghats and Chattan declared that hidden deep within those steaming forests lay the stronghold of Hara.

With his chin resting upon his knuckles as he leaned on the carvings behind the figurehead, Thomas watched entranced as tall, spindly palm trees reared around them and a sultry breeze fanned into his face.

'Where's Dimmy?' he asked, turning to Woodget. 'He should see this. We're finally here.'

The fieldmouse looked back to the galley's stern and saw that their pale grey friend was slouched over the edge, seeming to stare glumly into the water that rippled in the *Chandi*'s wake.

'I reckon he's feelin' a mite homesick too,' he murmured. 'Best leave him alone.'

Leaning upon the silvered stern, Dahrem Ruhar gazed down into the darkening waters that flowed into the estuary of the Periyar River, but not a single thought concerning the mythical life he had invented for Dimlon occupied his mind. No, at that precise moment he was taking a great risk and if the others had discovered him then his true hideous nature would certainly have been revealed.

A fierce golden light was burning in his eyes and his pupils had narrowed into needle-like slits once more, for down in the water, churning through the ship's wake was a large and repulsive sea snake.

With lithe and powerful movements of its glistening, flat-tailed body, the serpent easily kept pace with the *Chandi*, yet from the waves it had raised its head and was gazing up at Dahrem – transfixed by the baleful forces that beat out from the mouse's gleaming eyes.

'Hear me, little brother,' Dahrem hissed down to it, 'seek out the disciples of Scarophion, tell them that the time to assail the walls of Hara has come at last. Tell them Dahrem Ruhar – the double-faced master of artifice – has sent you and that he will be waiting with a prize which will bring an end to the Green's insipid and inglorious reign.'

The ugly head of the sea snake swayed from side to side as the instructions drove into its brain. Dahrem's strength of will was overwhelming and the authority that rang in his repellent voice was absolute. The serpent was utterly his to command – even if he ordered it to destroy itself, it would obey without the slightest flicker of rebellion. Such was the vile art of Scarophion's adepts. Control of all others was their black ambition, and with a jerk of his head, Dahrem dismissed this newly devoted messenger.

Into the waves the snake dipped its head and, with a furious thrash of its body, sped quickly away.

A horrific leer formed on Dahrem's face before the golden glow diminished in his eyes and he became Dimlon again.

When he returned to the others a bright half moon was shining in the heavens, turning the enshrouding mist to a milky silver, and the air was filled with the strange calls of wild beasts and the alarming shrieks of native birds.

The sound of the sea, which had become so much a part of their lives over the past weeks, was now forgotten and left far behind as the noises of the jungle rose about the forested banks of the Periyar.

'I ain't never seen trees like those,' Woodget was saying to Captain Chattan. 'Them's so dense and huge. Be black as pitch under that leafy roof. You'd not get me setting so much as a toe in there, and like as not I wouldn't last more than a minute – what with tigers and spiders as big as me and more.'

Hemmed in on all sides by the lofty, jungle-clad hills, the river wound slowly southwards, glimmering like a mirrored thread through the darkness until the captain shouted an order and the galley turned midstream.

Towards a narrow tributary she veered, but it was a grim, dreary-looking place, overhung with drooping branches that formed a tunnel of leaf and bough and about which swarmed a choking cloud of mosquitoes.

Both Woodget and Thomas' spirits sank as they understood that the *Chandi* was going to venture into that forbidding entrance, for no chink of moonlight filtered through the matted evergreen ceiling and it looked as like a monster's lair as they could imagine.

'Here we press into the very deeps of the jungle,' Chattan told them, 'and from here the secrecy of the concealing mist will hinder rather than aid us. Presently it shall thin and disperse and your view will be obscured no longer. Here our sails will be of no avail so our progress will be up to the strength of those who pull on the oars. But the way ahead is heavy with gloom and though we shall light the lamps, perhaps you would prefer to retire beneath the canopy, for the flames will draw many creatures to us and hungry insects may drop from the branches overhead.'

This unwelcome thought mortified Woodget and set

him itching immediately, but he did not want to appear afraid and, as Thomas did not wish to miss any stage of their journey, the fieldmouse remained at his side.

Into the leafy cave mouth the galley sailed and for several, uncomfortable minutes the mosquitos flew thick and angrily about those on board, buzzing shrilly in Woodget's ears, but he clamped his eyes and mouth shut and waited until they were clear of the awful swarm.

When he opened his eyes again, he saw that the surrounding mist was already dissolving and being stripped away by the gnarled boughs of drooping rhododendron trees that they journeyed beneath. Like wizened and arthritic crippled claws, the twigs snatched at the shredding vapour, capturing it within the knots of their branches until all of the enchanted fog had been torn away, and behind the *Chandi* it clung in tattered skeins over the gurgling water, resembling the mournful spectres of ancient willows.

Gazing around at the darkness which now pressed in around him, Woodget suddenly felt horribly visible to this hostile world. When Karim came striding up with a great silver lantern, the fieldmouse wanted to rush over and extinguish the light that was announcing their presence so brazenly and a tide of panic mounted within him.

'I really doesn't like this,' he uttered miserably.

'Do not fear,' Chattan said kindly. 'It is not far.'

Thomas took hold of his friend's trembling paw and gave it a gentle squeeze, but at that moment a tremendous, trumpeting roar shook the very air and a chorus of agitated cries reverberated throughout the jungle.

'What be that?' Woodget whimpered in horror.

Hanging the lantern from a hook on the main mast, Karim chuckled. 'Only the bellow of a bull elephant,' he laughed. 'Old Tusker likes to hear his fine booming voice now and again, that is all.'

'An elephant,' Woodget echoed, his fears pushed aside. 'I'd like to see one of them. Hey Dimmy, did you hear? There be elephants near here. Didn't you want to take a statue of one back to your aunty? Now you can tell her you actually heard one!'

Dahrem looked at him blankly, as though he did not have the first idea what Woodget was saying, then he gave a gushing giggle and nodded enthusiastically.

For nearly an hour the galley journeyed through the tunnel of leaves and, with a growing sense of unease, the mice gradually became aware that they were being watched.

In the corner of his eye, Thomas thought he saw small figures dart through the branches and once Woodget caught a glimpse of two tiny eyes gleaming down at them.

Disturbed, they voiced their fears to Karim who grinned broadly and told them that what they had seen were only the scouting sentries of his city who observed everything that moved along this stretch of water.

Then, abruptly, the overhanging boughs cleared, the forest became less dense and, as they followed the narrow river around a twisting bend, both Woodget and Thomas let out gasps of wonder.

'There is Hara,' Chattan said proudly.

Surrounded by a prodigious, high wall that was fortified by lofty towers and whose smooth, lime-washed stones gleamed pale and white under the moon, a bare mountain of rock swung into view and climbed into the night – its jagged summit appearing to touch the vaulted heavens.

All about the slopes of that rearing peak clustered the dwellings of those who lived within the confines of the city walls, and though the buildings were still a great distance away, the passengers and crew of the *Chandi* could plainly see the cheering glow of the lighted windows and their cares were eased.

But over all there was a faint, livid glow that Thomas could not understand and when he questioned the mongoose about this, Chattan merely told him that he would see soon enough.

Ancient was the city of Hara, one of the true hallowed places upon the Earth – built in the deep shadows of the past to glorify the spirit of the Green – and, as the river curved around further, Thomas and Woodget gazed up in dumbfounded amazement.

Above the winding streets and the huddled rooftops, a flight of steps had been cut into the mountainside and high that zig-zagging stair soared. At last it ascended to an incredible sight that was carved into the solid rock and which made Thomas and Woodget shake their heads in disbelief and gawp like idiots.

There, hewn into the mountain and towering over the city, was an image similar to the one which stared out from the prow of the *Chandi* – but a hundred times greater.

Many ages had the masons and sculptors of Hara

toiled over the gargantuan spectacle that gazed across the jungle roof. For, looming above the city, like a guarding sentinel to inspire hope in the hearts of its people and dread into its enemies, was a magnificent, almost worshipful portrait of the Green Mouse.

To the East its graven eyes stared, forever locked within an expression of challenge, towards that place whence the threat of Gorscarrigern had first arisen.

Inside its open mouth a fire burned constantly, tended and fed by the daily gift of a stick of fuel from each of Hara's inhabitants. Over the city the light of this beacon leapt and danced, steeping everything in a delicious warmth, yet above the flames a second source of illumination glimmered and glowed and it was this that had sparked Thomas' curiosity.

Set in the middle of the immense, sculpted forehead of the monumental Green Mouse was a single green stone that Thomas reckoned must have been at least as tall as Chattan. The livid, bleak light which shone from its depths reached every corner of the city, and not even the furthest, cramped alley-way was free of its pervading light.

A look of comprehension appeared on Dahrem's face when he saw it and though he detested the very sight of the mountain he stared at it unflinchingly.

But it was Woodget who put his thoughts into words.

'That light,' the fieldmouse whispered, ''tis the same as the one what shines in Mulligan's fragment.'

Chattan nodded. 'Yes,' he said. 'Behind the jewel that sits upon our Green Lord's brow there is a chamber gouged into the mountain and there the eighth piece has been kept these untold ages.'

'Yet not only were chisels used to forge his holy likeness,' Karim continued. 'It is written that the enchanters who did battle with the Coiled One upon the steps of the Black Temple, and who perished in the spilling of his black blood, came to this place ere they took that desperate road and by their arts blessed the mountain and aided the masons in their labour.'

Chattan nodded. 'So, of all the shrines which harboured such evil as lies inside the nine fragments,' he said, 'our city has remained unharmed. Although outside its walls the jungle has become wild and filled with peril, we have been spared the fate that claimed the other sanctuaries.'

Then the vision of the mountain was denied them, for the galley had rowed up to the city's walls and barring their way was a huge gate of iron set into an enormous stone archway that spanned the entire width of the river.

Flanking the sides of the arch were tall figures carved in stone depicting heroes and kings of old, and Woodget was intrigued to see that amongst the bold warriors and stern-looking mongooses were many images of mice.

But he did not have time to study the figures further, for above them, at the apex of the archway, there came a rusting squeak and a metal shutter was thrown open.

From a small window, a furry face was peering down at them – holding aloft a guttering candle.

'Who comes to Hara in the dead of night?' called the stranger.

Captain Chattan strode into the light of the silver lantern and in a loud, formal voice declared, ''Tis I, Chattan Giri – returned with the *Chandi*.'

'Speak the passwords,' demanded the gate warden.

'From Sagara, through Vana have we journeyed,' the captain sang out. 'Tirtha we have passed and now we would seek Parvata.'

A peevish grunt echoed down from above and at the top of the archway the shutter was slammed shut once more.

'What be happening?' Woodget asked Karim.

The portly mongoose grinned. 'That was Fikal Khatmal,' he replied, 'a tree shrew. Most seriously does he take his duties, and so he ought for this is the only way to enter the city unless the walls are clambered and breached. Yet the small fellow has no humour in him – vinegar is sweeter than he. For thirty-seven years he has attended the Eastern Gate and seldom leaves his post. Yet my dear wife's mother has heard that in all this time, Fikal has never bathed and I am thinking that if she is correct in this, then when his time is over, who will be brave enough to take the gate warden's place? Not I for one, for they say that even the flies refuse to enter his quarters.'

But all further talk was hushed, for there came the sound of cogs and wheels being turned with a slow grating of rusted, scraping metal, followed by the rattling clink of heavy chains and, with a juddering motion, the iron bars of the gateway began to lift from the water.

Up, into the stone arch, the barrier was hoisted and beneath it the crew of the *Chandi* pulled on the silver-tipped oars and the galley journeyed back to the place where she was first constructed.

As the ship rowed into a tranquil, crescent-shaped harbour, the spectacle of the mountain reared once more before its passengers and crew and behind them the iron gateway came rattling back into the water with a resounding splash.

Woodget jumped and glanced back at the barricaded way, but Thomas was already staring about the harbour with great interest. It was crowded with many vessels: from those of comparable design to Chattan's ship – although none were as large or as ornately embellished – down to the humblest river boat with awnings of woven straw.

'What a place,' was all he could find to say.

Presently the galley drew up alongside the quay and the mice saw that a second, inner wall surrounded the city, but this was not a smooth fortress of impenetrable, unscalable stone like the first – this obstacle was crusted and laden with a myriad carvings, all jostling for attention.

Whilst they tried to absorb the countless patterns and likenesses, Captain Chattan leapt ashore and, as was the custom of the Haran mariners, bowed in gratitude to his crew as they filed past him.

Bringing up the rear came Karim and the three passengers, and when he had thanked everyone for bringing the ship safely back to port, the captain led them all up to a pair of great wooden doors set into the ornate, inner wall and situated at the top of a wide flight of white marble steps.

Discs of beaten silver studded the imposing entrance but, even as they climbed the stairs to reach them, the doors swung open and the crew gave a great cheer – for the streets beyond were filled with their families and friends who rushed forward to meet them.

Joyous cries rang through the steeply sloping

streets as mothers met sons, and the warrior husbands threw their arms about wives and children. Reunited families of palm squirrels leapt high into the air and above them, from high, garlanded balconies that were strung with many tiny, tinkling bells, marigold petals were thrown and they cascaded down like a sumptuous blizzard of golden snow.

Karim's wide bulk was obliterated by a horde of eight youngsters who pounced upon him – squealing deliriously to see their father again.

His great, rumbling laughter rang throughout the adjoining streets and with two infants clambering on to his shoulders, another trying on his plumed helmet, three more squabbling over who could hold the spear and the remaining two tugging at his paws, the chubby mongoose was a joyful sight.

Thomas smiled as Karim threw one of his daughters into the air and caught her again in his powerful arms. Then Woodget nudged him and pointed at two females who stood waiting for the children to move aside. One was roughly the same age as the lieutenant, but the other was elderly and clucked to herself disapprovingly.

'That'll be his ma-in-law,' the fieldmouse giggled.

But Thomas was looking around them at the unfamiliar buildings that towered over the steep and narrow street, admiring the detail of the carving. Nowhere was spared the skill of the sculptor; statues of every living creature covered all available space and in between them ran beguiling patterns or groupings of stone fruit and flowers.

What Thomas found peculiar however was that no sense of scale had been used, meaning that upon the crammed walls elephants were the same size as small birds and voles rubbed shoulders with rhinoceroses. It was one great, extravagant jumble of images, where even fanciful beings flourished in abundance. There were rats with six arms and two-headed leopards and he even discovered a three-eyed mouse amongst the thronging sculptures.

Thomas' mind reeled at the thought of how long it must have taken to build. Even the steps on which the streets were founded were inlaid with gold – it was a staggering, ostentatious display and he thanked his stars that he had not missed it.

'Isn't it glorious?' he shouted to Woodget above the din of the merrymaking crowd around them.

'I'll never be able to describe it proper to Bess,' his friend replied. 'What do you think, Dimmy?'

Dahrem had often heard of the magnificence of this much-vaunted stronghold of his enemies yet he had never believed half of it. Now, looking on the opulent grandeur, his malice boiled within him and he lusted to hurl down every stone and bring death to all these witless fools. Yet he found malicious satisfaction in the knowledge that the end of their precious city was already assured and he sniggered to think of how these winding streets would shortly overflow with blood.

'Oh,' he burbled, 'a real bobbydazzlin'spangly-dog'sdinner this is. I'm sure to buy Aunty summink realposhshutuptheneighbours here.'

'But first,' came Chattan's voice behind them as he stepped out from the happy assembly, 'we must climb the thousand steps to the Holy One. I have no doubt that he will wish to speak with you this night.'

'That suits me,' agreed Woodget. 'Sooner he tells us he'll take old Mulligan's fragment off me the better. This is a fair city you got here, Captain, but I'd still prefer to sit out the rest of my days in the field back home.'

'Come then,' the mongoose instructed. 'We shall leave the festivities and ascend.'

So, up the sloping streets the captain led them and gradually the mirthful sounds of the celebration they had left behind grew fainter. Always there was something new and wonderful to delight their eyes, whether it was a pretty little courtyard decked out with colourful hangings, a fragrant, flower-filled garden or the elfin gleam of small, multi-coloured and faceted glass lamps which were occasionally strung across the confined alley-ways.

Each new turning brought them a further fresh perspective of the city and though their path led only upwards, the mice's heads were soon confounded as to the way back and they knew they would never be able to retrace their route to the main doors without assistance.

High the spiralling way took them, and it was not long before their legs began to ache. Then, as they passed under a marble archway decorated with the likenesses of two pouncing tigers, the ornate dwellings suddenly came to an end and the bare mountainside rose before them.

'Here begin the thousand steps,' Chattan declared. 'Far above, behind the fire that burns within the idol's mouth, the Holy One sits.'

'Lordy!' Dahrem squeaked as he stared up at the stairs cut into the rock. 'I's breathless already. Dimmy won't never make it up all them clamberers, he ain't no billygoatingdanglebeardedbuttingbottom.'

'If you wish we can rest a while until you are recovered,' the mongoose suggested.

Dahrem shook his head emphatically. 'No, no,' he insisted. 'Dimmy can't face it. You three go climb – I'll stay here and wait till you come down. The very thought of goin' so high up makes Dimmy's head spin and his tummy go poorlysick.'

'Very well,' Chattan said, but he turned to the others and asked them if they desired to rest a moment.

'I don't,' Thomas answered. 'Let's get on with it.'

Woodget agreed. Although his little legs did ache, he knew that of all of them it was he who had to go up there and speak with the Holy One.

'I doesn't reckon this'll take long, Dimmy,' he told Dahrem, 'and we'll be back as soon as ever we can. You sure you'll be all right here on your own?'

'Course I will!' Dahrem announced. 'I hasn't got anythink to be fritted of in this place. Safest I've felt in a long time I feels here. I might even have a nice little dozeynapper while you're gone.'

And so Chattan, Thomas and Woodget set off up the thousand steps and as soon as they were out of sight behind a bank of solid rock, Dahrem whirled around and hared off back into the city, clutching his satchel and cackling to himself.

12

The Holy One

It had been a long and strenuous climb, but eventually Thomas and Woodget found themselves at the summit of the thousand steps and were standing upon a wide, rocky ledge. Above them the huge stone face of the Green Mouse towered upwards and from the great open mouth, where the beacon fire constantly crackled, there blazed a bright flickering light which glinted in the mice's fur and shone over the polished surface of Chattan's armour.

With his heart pattering in his chest, Woodget gazed around him, leaning against the wall of sheer, solid rock to support his wobbling legs.

'That were some hike!' he exclaimed. 'We sure are far up, Tom! Look, you can see clean over the forest from here.'

Thomas was too out of breath to answer and so,

still puffing for air, he gave a feeble nod.

The top of the thousand steps afforded an excellent prospect of the city which shimmered way below. Its cramped, narrow ways and ornamented buildings seemed childishly small when viewed from that giddy altitude and Woodget's head began to spin as he realised just how high they had climbed.

Wrenching his eyes away from the seemingly miniature rooftops, he fixed his gaze to a point beyond the outer defences where, from that towering height, the dark mass of the crowding jungle appeared no more than a wild, untended garden.

Taking deep breaths of the thin, warm air which flowed and eddied about the mountains, the fieldmouse's sensitive nose tingled to the fragrance of sweet-scented burning wood. Lifting his face, he saw that from the idol's great open mouth a plume of smoke was gently rising, floating high into the night where it became a livid green as it wafted before the glowing stone set into the sculpture's brow. Then up it soared, winding around the craggy peak's tapering spire – to drift and curl before the bright half moon.

'Come,' the mongoose told them when he saw they had regained their strength. 'The Holy One will be waiting.'

From the ledge, a ramp of stone led up to the carved mouth and into this large, fire-lit cave where the beacon steadily burned, Captain Chattan led them.

With his paw before his face to shield him from the intense heat of the leaping flames, Woodget peeped around the large, light-filled cavern and saw that it had been shaped into a perfectly smooth dome. But ages of unrelenting, scorching smoke had smothered the stone with a thick mantle of soot that occasionally crumbled to the floor to form a soft, black carpet.

'Why don't nobody never sweep up in here?' the fieldmouse asked. 'It's so deep it looks like I got me a pair of black socks on now.'

Chattan stared briefly into the flames before offering any reply. He put down his spear and unfastened the sword which hung at his waist and leaned it against the wall.

'The fire which burns here is sacred,' he eventually said in a reverent tone. 'Since the founding of Hara, it has blazed here, springing from the very torch the first Holy One bore when he explored the mountain and beheld the vision of the Green. Should the beacon ever be utterly quenched then my city shall fail.

'But every nine years, in tune with the errand of your friend Mulligan, the mouth of the idol is cleansed – yet the soot is not discarded. When mixed with cement it is used in the strengthening of our homes and boundaries and even the ash which is raked from the heart of the flames has a purpose, for it is deemed by us to be a most holy substance.'

'What do you use that for?' Woodget asked.

'You shall see,' the mongoose answered, turning and stepping carefully through the down-like, sooty dust, and leading them to the rear of the cave where a low archway opened into a low passage which divided into two tunnels.

Thomas and Woodget glanced at them both; the left path descended into darkness but the other sloped upwards and was lit by lanterns suspended from the rocky ceiling.

'That way leads down through the mountain,'

Chattan said as the mice peered into the blackness of the unlit tunnel, 'into the silent tombs and out to the rear of the city. But let us not talk of cold graves or the chill marble effigies which lie down there. Our road leads us upward still, for the sadhu abides in a chamber above us, behind the eyes of the great likeness, within the very mind of the Green, if you will.'

Up the well-worn, twisting path he then took the mice until the winding way turned a final corner and ended abruptly. Before them a richly embroidered curtain was draped across the rock and Chattan cleared his throat to call out and announce their presence.

Yet before he could even open his mouth – a dry, wheezing voice barked out from the room beyond.

'Enter and be blessed, Chattan Giri.'

The mongoose hung his head respectfully and, with a glance to Thomas and Woodget that told them to follow him, he drew the ornate drapery aside and passed within.

After him the mice trailed and found themselves inside a small, sparsely furnished chamber that was entirely enclosed by the mountain – with no window or opening to the outside world and illuminated only by the light of one meagre lantern. Upon the floor, palm leaves were strewn and, piled in a corner, with flowers arranged around it, was a heap of grey ashes. Across one wall another tapestry had been hung, but that was the only decoration in the solitary hermitage, which did not even boast a table or any manner of chair.

Yet sitting in the middle of the bleak, secluded

room, upon the ground with his legs crossed and his paws placed lightly upon his knees in an attitude of meditation, was the Holy One.

There he sat, the head of the Green Council, he who was counted amongst the wisest of all living creatures and who, above all others, purported to know the will and intent of the Green spirit.

For many, many long years, since the building of the city in the dark age of Scarophion's reign, a Holy One had resided in that very chamber and learned the ways and mind of the divine life-giver and he who occupied that most revered position in the time of Thomas' youth was held in great esteem.

A great span of years, beyond the number accorded to lesser mortals, was granted to those who were chosen for that most venerated calling, but it was a solitary existence which few could endure. When a Holy One assumed the exalted office he had to renounce his past and all former attachments to live in austere and dedicated isolation for the rest of his life, seeing his ministers only at times of trouble and seldom dispensing counsel even when it was desperately sought.

Such was the separate and estranged nature of the Holy One, all respected him and the folk of Hara were extremely proud of the present incumbent, yet not one of them envied his lonely, disciplined existence.

Now he sat in the centre of the room, he who had first climbed the thousand steps nearly three hundred years ago when the echoes of the horn which sounded the death of his predecessor were still resounding over the jungle, and to Woodget's consternation he found that the sadhu's eyes were fixed upon him.

The fieldmouse had never seen anyone like him before and so he stared straight back – greatly intrigued.

The head of the Green Council was a loris, a small kind of lemur. Once the fur that covered his withered, mottled flesh might have been a pale brown but now it was patchy and white and made even more startling by the application of ashes, for over every part of his body, the Holy One had rubbed and smeared the ash taken from the beacon fire – to purify him and bring him closer to the Green spirit.

As a pale, crouching phantom he appeared; a colourless, shrunken spectre that patiently sat through the endless passage of time, growing old with the mountain and wasting with the world.

Two great, saucer-round eyes, that were dimmed and clouded with age, occupied most of his flat, white-whiskered face, and upon his crown, his long snowy hair had been wound into a tight ball which was encircled by a garland of dried marigolds and beneath the small, crabbed mouth a long wispy beard trailed on to the floor like a ghostly column of smoke.

Beneath the small, papery ears and around his bent shoulders, the Holy One wore a necklace, or mala, made of amber beads which symbolically protected him from the distracting influences of the outside world, but as far as Woodget could see the creature did not appear to have any neck. The gaunt head seemed to be attached directly to a stunted body from which two long arms, so emaciated that they resembled hairy sticks, sprouted – ending in wrinkled paws that clicked and crunched with rheumatism at the slightest movement.

The toll of prolonged years weighed heavily upon the withered creature's back, for it was bowed and hunched and the upper body dwindled down to narrow, bony hips and a pair of thin, spindly legs.

When they had entered, the Holy One raised a paw and dangling from a cord that was bound about his scrawny wrist was a large rusted key that swung like a pendulum.

'Less than a moon has passed, Chattan,' his dry, whispering voice began as his staring eyes scrutinised the mongoose captain. 'Hardly any time at all since you gainsaid my advice and took to your ship to follow in the wake of *Kaliya* – the golden ship of our enemies.'

The mongoose stiffened and Thomas realised that here were the smouldering embers of an old argument. Karim had hinted that their captain had set off after the marauding worshippers of Scarophion without the proper authority to do so and it was now clear that he had done this against the wishes of the Holy One.

'Yet our quest was not in vain,' Chattan protested, abandoning his deference and humility. 'If we had not departed, then never would we have discovered the companions of the Irish nomad.'

Before he could say any more, the frail loris held up both paws.

'Please,' he murmured, gesturing for his guests to join him upon the floor, 'sit with me. It pains my joints to have to stare up at you in this fashion.'

Chattan and the mice did as they were bid and the captain placed his fingertips upon his brow when he next addressed him as though he were at prayer.

'Sadhu,' he began in a calmer and more respectful manner. 'I bring grave tidings—'

'I know all you have to say,' the Holy One interrupted. 'The Temple of the Twelve Maidens has been defiled and the seventh fragment stolen. So the doom which we all dread creeps a step nearer. Did I not tell you it would be foolish to pursue the ship of the Scale? What did you achieve, Chattan Giri? Naught became of your wilful determination to prove my counsel false. The Shrine of Virbius was destroyed – I knew you could not prevent it.'

'Yet that is not all,' the captain continued. 'Mulligan is slain but the ninth piece did not fall into the claws of the enemy.'

To his surprise, the Holy One chuckled softly to himself. 'Chattan,' he muttered. 'Do you think the sadhus of Hara have sat within this mountain these many years, blind and deaf to the turmoils of the world? I know all that has passed, more so than you do yourself. I may be old, Captain – my sinews might be shrivelled, my bones dry and brittle and when I walk I have need of a prop to support me – yet that does not signify that my mind has mouldered also.

'Every day the attendants come in here to fuss and ensure I am well, but I need them not and I know what is in their thoughts. Though they dissemble and are pretty of speech I can read them well enough. Always they wonder how much longer I can endure and marvel that I have not yet taken my place in the tombs under the mountain. But for the present sadhu of Hara there are still many years above the ground, perhaps even long after you have charged into your last battle, Chattan Giri – captain of the *Chandi*.'

The mongoose stared remorsefully at the ground. 'Forgive me, Sadhu,' he begged. 'Always you have proven your great wisdom.'

'No, no, no,' the Holy One muttered, with a weary shake of the head. 'There is naught to forgive. You have done well, Chattan, and may your heart rejoice in what you have accomplished, for indeed nowhere in my foresight did I glimpse these two most honoured guests from a distant land. So be at peace. You were fated to set forth and bring them here and perhaps other forces beyond my vision were at work.'

Slowly shifting his weight upon the ground, and wincing as if the movement caused him pain, the aged loris finally turned to the two mice and raised a paw to them in greeting.

'Hail to you, Master Stubbs,' he said, 'and to you, Master Pipple – you must excuse the rantings of such a terrible beast as I. Age strips one of much and gracious manners are amongst the first to be lost. I ought to have welcomed you sooner but my over-ripe concern was directed solely upon the captain here. Now I remember the courtesies and crave your pardon.

'I am the sadhu of Hara, a seeker after truth and one who wishes to understand the mind of our noble Lord. I am well versed in all the unhappy misfortunes and ill chances that have dogged your unwary footsteps since the festivities of spring. You have deserved better than to be met by such a cantankerous old terror as I.'

Thomas fidgeted with his neckerchief, feeling a trifle awkward, but the round eyes of the loris were trained upon Woodget and the fieldmouse was not at all comfortable under their intense inspection. It was as if the creature was weighing him up and delving into his mind – probing deep inside his thoughts and challenging him. Then, with a shiver, the unnerving sensation was over and the Holy One was smiling at him kindly.

'So fieldmouse,' he breathed. 'Unto you the Irish nomad entrusted the terrible burden. A curious choice, yet Mulligan and his line were no less curious.'

'That's why we be here,' Woodget said shyly. 'Mister Mulligan told us to bring it to you.' Gingerly, he dragged the leather bag on to his knee and began untying the fastenings, but the Holy One stopped him with a click of the tongue and a stern expression furrowed the hoary face.

'No,' he said. 'Do not bring out the fragment yet. Come, Chattan, I have need of your arm.'

The loris's joints creaked and the gristle snapped in his hip, but eventually, with the mongoose's help he rose to his feet.

'The time has come,' he declared, 'for you to see that which few have ever gazed upon, the topmost chamber – where the Green Council first assembled long ago and where the burden of our city is bestowed.'

Across the room he went to where the second tapestry was hung, and with his gnarled paws he dragged it aside.

Beyond lay a dark stairway, worn down by the accumulated footfalls of every sadhu since the city was founded and, still clinging on to Chattan, the Holy One began to climb, closely followed by Thomas and Woodget.

At the top of the stone steps was a wooden door with sturdy iron hinges and from the keyhole of a large and secure lock there streamed a fine pencil of green light.

Woodget stared at it thoughtfully, then, from the cord which bound his wrist, the loris lifted the rusted key.

With a snap, the mechanism turned and when the Holy One pushed it, the door juddered open with as much creaking protest as his own arthritic joints.

At once a sudden radiance flooded out into the dark stairway, bathing everything in a ghastly, putrid light that chilled the blood in their veins and Woodget clutched his bag in astonishment, for it seemed to him that it gave a violent jerk and tried to work itself free of his paws.

Into this new chamber Chattan strode, followed by Thomas who noticed by the expression which had crept over the captain's face that this was the first time he had ever ventured there. Then, behind them, clutching tightly to the bag's leather straps, Woodget hurried after.

Like the inside of the idol's mouth below the sadhu's chamber, only far larger in size, this room had been carved into a perfect dome. Yet here the concave surface had been covered with enormous sheets of burnished bronze and, opposite the doorway where they all stood, the curved, gleaming wall was dominated by a great oval translucent stone. Then the mice understood that they were now standing behind the green jewel they had seen at the centre of the immense sculpture's forehead.

Yet all eyes were drawn into the middle of the

cavern, for there was a pool of gurgling water and, rearing like a glittering stalagmite from its centre, was a plinth of solid crystal – carved with mysterious symbols and spells of abatement and restraint. Surmounting this was a silver dish and Woodget let out a little gasp when he beheld the object which stood upon it.

Encased within a complex tracery of gold, was an irregular shaped piece of jade.

'Yes,' the Holy One declared. 'Here is the eighth fragment of the shell Gorscarrigern made in the deeps of time. To Hara it was brought when the Dark Despoiler's fleshly body was finally destroyed and here, wrapped about with such enchantments as were in the power of our ancestors, it has remained.'

'It's just like Mulligan's piece,' Thomas breathed.

'You are mistaken,' the loris corrected. 'The ninth fragment which the Irish nomad bore is the largest of them all. That is why it could not remain in any one region permanently, for its corrupting influence would lay the land waste with more speed than all the others.

'Great was the hope in those early times after the Coiled One's downfall, all thought the world was free at last – but one by one the sanctuaries decayed and the strongholds vanished into dust. All the groves and shining cities – crumbled and plundered by the heathen hordes. The hallowed places are lost and only we are left – one bright glint of light and reason. Here in this beleaguered corner of the world Hara stands alone and around us the darkness has returned.'

Woodget stared at the fragment and shuddered, for it was the source of the livid green light which filled the chamber and when he dragged his eyes away he found that the loris was studying him again.

'Now it is time, Master Pipple,' the Holy One said coaxingly. 'Bring out the legacy of our departed friend Mulligan.'

Nervously, the fieldmouse unfastened the top of the bag and reached inside, closing his wary fingers about the cold treasure which the seafarer had given to him.

Into the repulsive glare the ninth fragment was lifted and at once the unwholesome radiance was doubled as from the gilded jade in Woodget's paws a second brilliance welled up.

'Step a little closer to the pool,' the Holy One instructed. 'I would have you witness the foul arts of our great enemy.'

Tentatively, Woodget moved towards the babbling water and with every movement, as the fragment in his grasp drew nearer to the one upon the plinth, he became aware that a horrific change was taking place.

Fearfully, he stared down and let out a frightened squeal.

'Woodj!' Thomas cried. 'What is it?'

The fieldmouse turned a stricken face to him then held the fragment a little higher so that he could see and Thomas shrank away – sickened.

In the horrible light, to his disbelief and revulsion, he could see that the intricate golden latticework was actually moving. The twisting fronds and curling arabesques which covered the jade shell were rearing up and wriggling like glittering worms. It was as if they could sense that the eighth piece was near and were straining to reach it.

Thomas grimaced and his skin crawled, but then

he saw that upon the silver dish, the other fragment was behaving exactly the same. Each segment of golden scrollwork was writhing abhorrently and the entwining patterns blindly groped the air – striving to join together and be one.

'It's hideous!' Thomas blurted.

Hastily, the fieldmouse stuffed the object back into the bag and the harsh green light was immediately diminished. As he moved away from the pool, upon the plinth the eighth fragment ceased its frantic squirming and the golden designs returned to their former state and were motionless once more.

Captain Chattan folded his arms and nodded grimly. 'So it is proven that the evil might of Gorscarrigern has not decreased over the ages – its potency is still strong.'

'The power of the living gold is certainly unaltered,' the Holy One muttered with a peculiar, almost delighted gleam in his large eyes.

'Was it ever in doubt?' the mongoose cried. 'Never shall the world be free of his threatened return whilst the pieces remain in existence.'

Woodget finished tying up the bag and bit his bottom lip thoughtfully.

'What is to become of Mulligan's fragment now?' he asked. 'Tom and me have brought it to the city like I promised, but what next?'

The wizened loris took a deep, rattling breath and in a resolute voice announced, 'The fragment shall abide here.'

'Here?' Chattan repeated in disbelief. 'What are you saying, Sadhu? I know the lore of Gorscarrigern as well as any.'

The Holy One held up his paw and Chattan fell silent.

'If you would permit me to finish, Captain!' he said tersely. 'You are not privy to all the schemes of the Green Council so you cannot comprehend our intent. I have said that the fragment shall remain here and so be it. There is yet a chance of which you are ignorant, but in which we have poured all our hopes.'

'What chance?' the mongoose asked and a trace of scorn crept into his voice. 'This evil can never be vanquished, or do you propose to send it back over the waters to the land of Greenwich? Would the Handmaiden of Orion receive it and keep it there forever – or until the forces of the Scale besiege and destroy her realm? I see no chance or hope in that.'

The aged creature glared back at him and the atmosphere in the chamber became charged with tension until at last the Holy One looked away.

Always Chattan pushed and strained to know more than his rank warranted and the sadhu knew that the mongoose would have to be dealt with cautiously. It would be a grave error of judgement to disclose too much to this obstinate captain, yet to deny him utterly might prove even more calamitous.

'A little only am I permitted to impart,' the loris finally murmured in response. 'Did you not wonder why the Irish nomad was travelling to the Shrine of Virbius when it was not the appointed time? His journey was at my instigation. There at the temple he was to have met with one who might have put an end to our anxieties.

'You, yourself, have already touched upon it, Captain – when you spoke of a world free of this fear which plagues our existence. If but one of the fragments were to be destroyed then the Coiled One would forever be denied entry to this plane. Reflect on that. Is it not a most wondrous thought?'

Chattan frowned. 'I do not understand,' he said stubbornly. 'The pieces are impervious to any violence. Are you suggesting that it is now possible to damage that which was made in the dark years? Who is this one of whom you speak? How can you believe this unlikely claim?'

The shrivelled creature at his side shambled unaided towards the great oval stone set into the curved wall and gazed through its rippling translucence, down at the blurred, indistinct shapes and lights of the city that were vaguely visible far below.

'His name is already known to you,' he muttered, 'and, I think, familiar to our young guests. Although I was pronounced head of the Council, he is not lesser than I – in fact in some ways his strength is the greater.'

Thomas glanced at Woodget and shrugged, but the eyes of the fieldmouse were sparkling.

The Holy One fingered the mala about his neck. 'I speak of the wanderer of the ancient pathways,' he chanted, 'obeah pilgrim, far seer, chanter of spellcraft, mage and prophet.'

'Simoon!' Woodget declared delightedly.

The Holy One nodded.

'That jerboa!' Thomas exclaimed incredulously. 'But that's ridiculous – why, he's no more than a bogus fortune teller and common trickster!'

'There is nothing common about the treader of the

forgotten track,' the Holy One reprimanded him. 'You have seen only that which he has permitted you to see.'

Woodget clapped his paws excitedly. 'I knowed it!' he cheered. 'I knowed old Simoon was an honest-to-goodness magician! He bain't no phoney after all, oh that do make me happy – on account of the fortune he told me.'

'Well even if he isn't a sham,' Thomas said slowly, 'there's nothing he can do for anybody now. I saw Simoon get washed into the darkness when the *Calliope* went down.'

'Did you indeed?' the Holy One murmured, growing a little tired of Thomas' doubts and objections.

Chattan narrowed his eyes. 'Sadhu,' he said, 'are you saying that Simoon is not drowned?'

'The briny deeps will never claim that one,' came the answer. 'Our two visitors and the friend they have left at the bottom of the thousand steps – yes, I know all about him – they were not the only survivors of the tempest. Others escaped and Simoon was one of them.'

'Then we should have remained on Crete a while longer until we found him!' Chattan said. 'If the jerboa has truly found a way to destroy the fragments he must be brought here without delay. I shall rouse my crew and set sail with the dawn to fetch him.'

The mongoose hurried past Thomas and Woodget but, with a commanding snarl that was impossible to disobey, the Holy One called him back.

'Captain, Captain,' he said. 'Always you steam ahead and go haring off without thinking. Simoon was not washed up on to the Greek shores. He is far from those waters now and is at present bound for Singapore.'

'Then I must go to him,' the mongoose exclaimed.

'No you will not,' the Holy One said tetchily. 'When Simoon has done what he intends, and only then – he will come to us. He needs no one to convey him hither, certainly not you, Chattan Giri.'

The captain looked at the floor abashed. 'I desire only to see our city delivered from the threat of the Scale,' he explained apologetically.

Listening to all that had been said, at that moment Thomas muttered sceptically, 'What I don't see, is why Simoon didn't just go up to Mulligan when they were both on board the *Calliope*?'

To his dismay the Holy One's response was alarming.

'Be silent!' he snapped, his frail frame trembling with anger. 'The sadhu of Hara will not be questioned in this fashion. You should give praise that you are ignorant of the great matters which darken my waking thoughts and torment my dreams!'

Scowling, the loris drew a paw over his eyes, then mastered his temper and, when he was calm, chided himself for his harsh outburst.

'Again I crave your indulgence,' he said to Thomas, 'but I am worn by this great care and an end is approaching which we have long looked for. Of the Council's plan I can say no more. Here at the culmination of our designs it is vital no mistakes are made.'

Brightening a little, he shuffled forward and laid his paws upon Thomas' shoulders. 'Yet this much I can tell you, Master Stubbs. Your role in this hazardous undertaking is finished and you may depart for your home as soon as you are ready.'

Thomas looked at Woodget uncertainly and the Holy One knew what he was thinking.

'The fieldmouse is also liberated from all obligations,' he said. 'Now, Master Pipple, the time has come for you to lay aside the burden Mulligan entrusted into your care. Place it here upon the floor, as far from the eighth fragment as is possible. It will be safe enough there. If we can but keep them from the clutches of the enemy a little while longer, until the constellation is come and gone, then all will be well again, for a time at least – until the next appearance of the nine heralding stars.'

As he said this, the Holy One became lost in thought and an expression of overwhelming remorse settled within the deep lines that scored his age-ravaged face.

'Sadhu,' Chattan said, concerned. 'Are you unwell?'

The loris peered at him as though through a mist then muttered thickly. 'Alas, there are times when my mind remembers that it is joined to this decrepit body,' he explained.

'We have fatigued you,' the mongoose observed. 'Come my friends, the audience is over. By your leave, Sadhu.'

'Go with blessings upon you,' the Holy One said. 'Leave me here to meditate on the peril we all face. I shall make my own way back to my chamber.'

And so Thomas and Woodget bade the withered creature farewell and he thanked them for all that they had done.

'Will we see you again before we go back home?'

the fieldmouse asked as he headed for the door.

'You may,' came the cryptic reply. 'You may indeed see me before the end, Master Pipple.'

With that Woodget followed the others down the stairs and the Holy One was left alone in the glimmering room.

'What we have done is for the good of all,' he whispered to himself as he raised his shaking paws to the mala and began running the amber beads through his bony fingers. 'We agreed it was the only solution. I cannot quail now. In the past my heart was resolved and so it must remain. Ignore the fears, expel the mercy from my breast. The decision is already made and sealed, it is only my part now to conclude it – once and for always.'

'Even though you know the cost?' came a sudden, but not unexpected, croaking voice from the doorway.

The Holy One turned and framed in the entrance was a tall, gangly shadow.

'Did you hear what was said?' he asked.

The figure nodded. 'I did, I was standing at the foot of the stairs listening and hid when they returned. You did well to assuage the mongoose's suspicions; I feared for a moment that he would ask more questions than you could answer.'

'Chattan is a valiant warrior,' the loris admitted sorrowfully, 'and he loves this city above all else. If he so much as guessed the truth of our plans then he would have attempted to put a stop to them.'

'And that would never do, would it?' the rasping voice muttered.

'No,' the Holy One confessed. 'Better that he knows naught of the carnage that is to come.'

Into the domed chamber the figure came and the glare of the eighth fragment glinted in the rat's beady black eyes.

'It would've been better if you hadn't dragged the jerboa into it,' he muttered. 'It was a stupid risk telling the captain where he'd gone.'

'Chattan Giri is not a fool,' the loris said. 'A sprinkling of the truth was the only way to alleviate his doubt. But you heard me, I made no mention that Simoon's destination is where the Black Temple has been built once more. No doubt if I had, then the impulsive captain would have mustered our strength and set sail without delay – and we cannot afford to have our warriors alerted this night. Let them carouse a while longer and be lulled off their guard. Though even now my heart screams that I should warn them all and turn aside from this heinous path.'

'It's a bit late to start dithering now,' the rat remarked.

The Holy One looked at him, then shook his head in a resigned manner.

'Yes, you are correct,' he said hollowly. 'The lot is cast, there is now no turning back. The remaining two fragments are here waiting to be taken, and already the adept of the serpent, whom Chattan and the two mice unwittingly brought with them, has paid a murderous visit to the gate warden.'

The loris's voice trailed off and he closed his eyes as a bitter tear trickled down his wrinkled face and disappeared into the fine whiskers of his beard.

'Fikal Khatmal lies slain,' he uttered hoarsely. 'Even now his corpse is withering as the black blood of Gorscarrigern devours it. As I speak, Dahrem is operating the mechanism which raises the barrier from the river, leaving the harbour open to attack. This night the forces of the Scale will storm through the outer defences and assail the inner wall and find it undefended. I have given orders that the sentries should keep a vigil elsewhere. They do not question the wisdom of their sadhu, never has it proven false – not until now.'

The rat sucked his teeth and grunted. 'If I'd known that grey mouse was an agent of Sarpedon,' he said, 'I would have let him get to Mulligan sooner.'

'It would have changed nothing,' the loris answered, 'except perhaps those two merry friends from a distant land might have been spared this horror, but the plundering of Hara was inevitable.'

'Be a proper night of slaughter,' the rat stated coldly.

'I know it,' the Holy One whispered with dread. 'Help me to the steps, there is one final task I must complete. No, say nothing, the deed is mine to accomplish, this I determined from the beginning. Earlier this night I told Chattan that I might outlive him – that is a prediction I shall take great pleasure in disproving. I have betrayed my sacred trust and therefore go to my death gladly. My final act is to be one of ultimate treachery, and so the sooner I embrace Death the better. Now, come!'

Reaching out his spindly paws, the ancient loris clasped the other's strong arms and Jophet, the rat, helped him to the doorway.

Woodget stirred in his sleep then found himself wide awake and sitting up in a darkened room.

At first the unfamiliar surroundings confused him

but, as he waited for his eyes to grow accustomed to the gloom, he heard the reassuring snores of Thomas rising from the other side of the bedchamber and he quickly recalled all that had happened since the audience with the Holy One.

On their return down the thousand steps, the mice and Chattan had discovered Dahrem waiting for them and, in the gabbling guise of Dimlon, he quizzed them on all that had taken place.

Passing back into the city streets the mongoose had offered them the hospitality of his home and they accepted gladly. The Giri household was a two-storied, lime-washed building with flowers spilling from the balconies and there they were greeted and made most welcome by a pretty mongoose maiden whom they learned was the captain's sister.

After a bite of supper they mulled over all that had occurred, but it was not long before Woodget began to nod and so the guests were shown to their rooms.

Now the fieldmouse wondered what had awoken him, but he suspected that Thomas must have given an extra loud, piggish snore and he hoped he would remember it in the morning so that he could tease him.

It was a warm night, but Woodget snuggled back under the sheet and plumped up the pillow as he tried to get comfortable again and return to sleep.

After several restless minutes, to his annoyance, he was still wide awake and sitting up again, he hugged his knees.

'Must be all the excitement,' he murmured, careful not to disturb Thomas. 'P'raps my poor noggin can't quite believe that it really is over and soon I can head back home. Well, Woodget lad, you've seen a tidy bit more of this 'ere world than you ever thought was likely. Still, you'll be a lot happier with one of your mum's hot dinners inside you and a certain pretty paw a-holding yours.'

The fieldmouse twitched his whiskers; it was no use trying to get to sleep. His head was too stuffed with thoughts and he tutted in vexation.

'Maybe a little stroll and a breath or three of air will bring on the drowse,' he decided, and so he slid from the sheets and padded noiselessly over to the door.

Past the room where Dimlon was apparently sound asleep he pattered, then down the stairs and in a moment had slipped out of the house.

The night was still and strangely silent. No jungle noises were carried upon the slight breeze and the deserted city streets were engulfed in shadow. All the buildings were dark and blind. No cheery glow shone from the picturesque houses, all the windows were shuttered – their occupants deep in slumber – and even the twinkling glass lamps which were strung overhead had burned themselves out.

Yet over all, the baleful light that shone out from the jewel, high upon the mountain, cast a ghastly sheen and Woodget's meandering steps instinctively led him away from that reminder of his recent burden.

Down a narrow alley he wandered, keeping track of the way he had come so that he would not forget and spend the rest of the night lost in some remote quarter of this sprawling city.

His pace was slow, for he was not anxious to explore; the excursion was merely an effort to induce sleep, so he was able to study the buildings around

him in detail and appreciate the skill of the folk who
had built them.

It was undoubtedly the most beautiful and
harmonious place in all the world and he felt content
that he was soon to return home, for nowhere else
could ever compare or match the wondrous city
of Hara.

Just when he thought it was time to start retracing
his steps, the sweet sound of running water came to
his large ears and he determined to press a little
further to discover its source.

Beneath an archway festooned with flowers
he went and, to his delight, found himself standing
in a charming, high-walled garden with a silver
fountain in its centre – surrounded by trees that
bore all manner of different fruits and from
which dangled delicate wind chimes that jingled
faintly in the breeze.

For some reason the ghastly pallor of the eighth
fragment did not invade this pleasant area and over
everything that grew there – the vines which covered
the walls, the deliciously scented blooms, the heavily-
laden trees, even the lichen that sprouted between the
paving stones – shone the bright, milky radiance of
the moon.

Stepping between the fruit trees, Woodget gazed
at the water that flowed from the fountain. It was
sparkling with frosty stars, catching and reflecting the
moonlight and dappling the garden with soft, argent
ripples.

Enchanted, and realising that he was thirsty, the
fieldmouse walked through the lush, daisy-speckled
grass and cupped his paws, noticing as he bowed his

head to drink that the fountain was fashioned into the shape of a horn of plenty.

The water was icy to the touch and he drew his breath sharply, yet when it passed his lips Woodget felt a marvellous peace and contentment flood through his being and he wiped his mouth, chuckling unaccountably.

'You are far from your field, little master.'

Woodget jumped and peered around him to see who had spoken.

The voice was rich and softly spoken, and though he was not afraid in that fair garden, the fieldmouse was perturbed that he was unable to find anyone nearby.

'Who's there?' he asked.

'Do you not know me?' came the silken reply and there was a quality in that voice that reached deep inside Woodget's soul and instilled a sublime feeling of awe.

'Few have ever found their way to my garden,' the voice continued, 'and fewer still have quenched their thirst at the fountain.'

Woodget glanced into the dim shadows behind the trees. 'What you be hiding fer?' he called.

'On such a night as this even the greatest may hide and not be ashamed,' came the response. 'For in the dark before the dawn, terrible deeds shall be committed and there is naught I can do to prevent them. My pity reaches out to the folk of this city and yet how can that avail them?'

'What does you mean?' Woodget asked, straining his eyes towards the farthest corner where he thought the owner of the voice was lurking. 'What be going to happen?'

Around him, the leaves of the trees rustled upon the branches, the fruit quivered on the bough and the wind chimes jangled in discord.

'Much that I do already lament,' the velvet voice said forlornly. 'The path of life is strewn with many perils and the folly of knowledge is one of the greatest dangers. Wisdom is a treacherous weapon, little master, for it is sundered from compassion. All too often the end of the journey gains more import than it should and the wise become blind to the road and the method of their passing.

'Thus it is here, and I mourn the act which will be done in my name. Remember this, you wanderer who have drunk at my fountain; it is the journey itself that matters and how you fare upon the road. If you falter and cannot gain the end of the path it is no failure. I am watching, I gather all unto me – whether they stumble or no.'

Woodget scratched his head. 'Well I does want to get to the end of my journey,' he said, ''tain't nowt more important to me – I doesn't know what you be blatherin' on about and I doesn't want to know neither.'

'Then perhaps there is hope for this land yet,' returned the voice and Woodget fancied that its sorrow was now tinged with gratitude.

'Well I can't be stayin' here for what's left of the night, gabbin' to someone who I can't even see,' he declared. 'Goodnight, whoever you is.'

'Till the next time we meet, little master.'

Shrugging, Woodget gave a cursory wave, stepped through the trees once more and passed under the flower-covered archway.

Behind him, within the deep shadows that lay beneath the rambling vine, a pair of gleaming, green eyes shimmered between the leaves and the garden suddenly burst into blossom, before fading into nothingness – returning to an empty, neglected courtyard where the faint jingling of wind chimes hung briefly upon the air before that too disappeared.

About the city the darkness deepened as storm clouds rolled across the stars and, from the depths of the jungle, there began the solemn beating of many drums.

13

The Betrayal of Hara

Returning through the empty streets, Woodget plodded, his small shape dwarfed by the tall, sculpture-encrusted buildings which hemmed in the cramped, slanting ways. It was all so grand and marvellous but he doubted if he would ever learn who the figures that clustered around the doorways and upheld the balconies represented. Despite his travels and adventures he still felt lamentably rustic and untutored and, as he continued to wend his solitary way, a terrible sense of loneliness and insignificance overcame him.

Now the adventures were over and soon he would be returning home to startle and amaze Bess with his incredible tales. But he reflected that, in the years to come, these terrible events would fade into the past and be only a dim memory of his reckless youth which perhaps in time even he would begin to doubt as his mind became fuddled with age.

'Least I been a part of summat exciting and important,' he told himself. 'Though I don't s'pose I'll ever know what'll happen in the end. Not unless the enemy wins o' course, then we'll all find out right enough.'

In the ghostly light that beat from the jewel in the mountain, his russet-coloured fur was ashen grey but soon the shadows began to deepen as the moon was hidden behind the rolling clouds. Then Woodget's sharp ears heard the distant, rhythmic pounding of drums and he wondered what they could mean.

To him the unceasing beat sounded unpleasant and even threatening, but perhaps such noises were commonplace here in this strange land. All the same, the desire to return to the Giri household became uppermost in his thoughts and he consciously quickened his pace.

Overhead, the dense clouds continued to drift and gather – blotting out the stars and circling about the craggy peak of the mountain.

'A nasty old storm's a-brewing,' the fieldmouse muttered to himself and he considered that the relentless drumbeat might be a warning, telling everyone to beware the approaching severe weather.

Then the first rumbling of thunder boomed out over the jungle and beyond the city walls the horizon flared white with a crackle of lightning.

Woodget hastened down the sloping paths that led to Chattan's dwelling and another flash exploded in the thick clouds above. For a blinding instant the city flickered beneath the harsh glare and the darkened streets were flooded with a shivering light.

At once the fieldmouse stumbled to a halt and he stared ahead in disbelief.

For an instant, revealed under the jagged lightning, he thought he had seen the frail and shambling figure of the Holy One hobbling slowly down the stepped street which led to the great doors of Hara's inner defences. Then just as quickly the scene was engulfed in shadow and the fieldmouse tutted at his own credulous senses.

'You be a-dreamin', Pipple,' he mumbled, "twere only the lightning a-playing tricks. What would the likes of he be a-doing out tonight? You'd best get in afore the downpour starts.'

Hurriedly, he darted aside and found at last the home of Chattan and his sister. Pushing open the door, he silently crept inside and gingerly climbed the stairs.

A minute later, Woodget entered the room given to him and Thomas and, after fumbling around in the gloom then stubbing his toe on one of the bedposts, slipped back into bed.

'Where've you been?' asked a sleepy voice from the other cot.

'Only out for a walk and some fresh air,' the fieldmouse replied. 'Did I wake 'ee Tom?'

'Probably,' his friend grumbled, 'but I don't mind, I was having horrible dreams. I thought we were back on the *Calliope* again – right in the middle of the storm.'

At that moment another dazzling bolt of lightning blistered from the skies and through the fenestrated shutters which covered the window there stabbed countless brilliant rays that punched into the room like shooting spears of intense white flame.

'Good grief!' Thomas exclaimed loudly, his face momentarily caught in silhouette before the darkness sprang back.

A second later there came the sound of heavy raindrops clattering on the roof slates as the deluge fell from the heavy clouds – followed by a tremendous clap of thunder.

Outside the bedchamber, across the landing, they heard footsteps, followed by a gentle knocking upon their door.

'Is all well with you my friends?' Chattan's voice asked. 'I heard you cry out.'

Woodget giggled. 'That were just Tom being scared of the storm,' he answered.

'There is nothing to fear,' the captain's calming voice told them. 'Often the weather changes without warning. It will swiftly pass.'

'I was not scared!' Thomas hissed but Woodget was not listening.

'Well I done heard a warning,' he chirped. 'I done heard them drums a-beating out yonder in the forest.'

At that, the door opened and Captain Chattan entered the mice's room with a lighted candle in his paw which he lifted until its gentle beams played over the fieldmouse's face.

'Drums?' he asked, a slight frown puckering the dark mask of fur around his eyes. 'What do you speak of?'

'Afore, when I went out for a stroll,' Woodget answered, not liking the anxious tone that now rang in the captain's voice, 'there were a beatin' an' a bangin' of drums.'

In the glimmering candle glow, Chattan's face clouded with concern – his eyes now almost completely hidden beneath the deep scowl which furrowed his brow.

'You ought to have awoken me at once,' he said crossly. 'Let us pray no evil will come of this. It may yet prove to be nothing and you were mistaken, but now my heart is uneasy and I must go seek out the sentries on watch to hear their tidings.'

'I'll come with you,' Thomas suggested.

'And me,' added Woodget, feeling horribly guilty as if he had failed the trust the captain had placed in him.

The mongoose stared at them a moment then shook his head and bid them to remain.

'If there were indeed such drums as you claim,' he told the fieldmouse, seeing the nervous, anxious look on his little face and trying to reassure him, 'then the guards would most certainly have sounded the trumpets to alert the city.

'No, most likely it will prove to be no more than the beginnings of the storm which you heard. I will not be gone long and I would rather you were here in case the thunder awakens your friend Dimlon and my sister.'

With a nod to each of them, he left the room and closed the door behind him.

'Tom,' Woodget whimpered unhappily. 'I knowed what thunder sounds like and what I heard weren't that. Them were drums out there in the jungle – I be certain of it.'

Thomas clambered from his bed and opened the shutters, ignoring the rain that splashed into the room and fell on to the back of his head as he gazed down into the street.

'I hope you're wrong Woodj,' he murmured. 'For all our sakes.'

Girding a sword about his waist, Captain Chattan descended the stairs. There was no time to struggle back into his armour, so he simply wrapped a light blue cloak around his shoulders to ward off the worst of the rain, then out into the city he went.

The stepped streets were already flowing like mountain streams as the rain rapidly gushed down them and, glancing around him, the mongoose saw that here and there, in the surrounding buildings, lights began to glimmer in the windows as the thunder continued to crash overhead.

Turning left and cutting westward across the city, he ran – heading straight for the inner boundary wall and the nearest sentry tower.

Like a pale phantom, driven by the ravaging squall, his cloaked figure darted – the ankle-deep rain-water splashing wildly around him as he charged through the narrow, rushing rivers that the streets had become.

Then he saw it, the inner wall, carved with the images of countless exotic creatures and, rising high into the turbulent night, a round tower covered with a foliate pattern skilfully chiselled from stone and painted a warm orange, delineated with broad white lines.

Squinting up into the battering rain, he gazed at the high, covered ramparts, straining to see the sentries – but upon the silver-roofed platform at the topmost turret, not a soul was stirring.

With the thunder blasting in his ears, Chattan barged through the entrance at the base of the tower and glared around the guardroom.

There, slumped across the mess table, fallen from stools or slouched against the walls, were over a dozen mongoose sentries and to his anger, each one was fast asleep.

In nearly every paw there was a drained goblet and upon the flagged floor were pools of spilt wine. Chattan ground his teeth together furiously – the guards were drunk.

Wrathfully he strode up to the table and slammed his fist down upon the board. With a shudder, a goblet leapt into the air, losing what was left of the wine it contained and, though the heads of the snoring mongooses jarred and jolted under the violence of the captain's blow, not one of them stirred.

'Get up!' he bawled, cuffing the closest to him about the ears. 'How dare you leave your posts! Up I say!'

The inebriated sentry did not move and, in a rage, Chattan kicked the stool from under him and the mongoose dropped heedlessly to the floor, his chin striking the ground with a horrible crack.

Yet still he was not roused and Chattan's outrage turned icy cold as a dreadful suspicion formed in his mind.

With growing unease, he snatched up one of the goblets and sniffed it warily. Masked by the rich fruity scent, it was impossible to tell, but his instincts told him that this was no ordinary intoxication which had overwhelmed the guards.

'How many others have supped this way tonight?'

he asked aloud, staring accusingly at the drinking vessel as though it might answer. 'How many other guardrooms bounding the city contain this same terrible scene? Are there no patrols outside our borders – are they lying drugged also?'

Frantically, he hurled the goblet to the floor and rushed to the spiralling steps that ascended to the look-out turret. Yet all the while his misgivings grew and he feared that the worst nightmare of all the folk who dwelt in Hara had at last become a reality.

Breathless, he lunged through the trapdoor which led to the high platform at the top of the tower and, with blinding spikes of lightning erupting in the troubled heavens all around him, flew to the western side which overlooked the wide, orchard-filled gulf between the outer defence and the inner boundary.

All was lost in the obscuring torrent of rain that lashed from above, but with every livid, electric flash, the horrific scene was finally burned in upon his senses.

Where the outer wall curved around, towards the crescent-shaped harbour, he beheld a great, golden ship come sailing under the stone archway.

About its hideously shaped prow, the threads of storm which had survived the tangled passage of the overgrown river still rampaged and bolts of energy went hissing into the water.

'*Kaliya*,' Chattan croaked in horror, 'the ship of the Scale has come. It has passed the iron gateway – what treachery is this?'

A horde of ugly, yammering creatures filled the slave-worked vessel's upper deck, and they jeered at the top of their raucous voices, brandishing bright

swords, flaming torches and curved scimitars in the air – thirsty for blood and slaughter. But behind the ghastly figurehead, standing silent and sinister as he looked up at the reviled city which rose before them, was the cloaked figure of Gorscarrigern's pitiless High Priest.

Long had he waited for this moment and, closing his bright yellow eyes, he breathed deeply to savour the unholy rapture that consumed his sable soul.

At last the impregnable refuge of the vainglorious Green was about to fall and he let loose a shrill cackle of evil, gloating laughter.

High in the sentry tower, immovable as the marble sculptures which crowded the inner walls, all Captain Chattan could do was look on in despair.

Into the harbour the *Kaliya* came and the water boiled and steamed with her passing. At first Chattan thought that was merely because of the lightning which snaked about her glittering hull, but then he saw that dark shapes were swimming alongside and toiling in her putrid wake.

Under the stone arch poured a thousand disciples of the Dark Despoiler, with knives and daggers clenched in their teeth, and flanking them, churning their wriggling bodies through the frothing tumult was a seething mass of cobras, pythons and sea snakes – all under the High Priest's command.

Then, bringing up the rear, drifting like fallen, ulcerous trees, came fifty monstrous shapes whose bulging eyes barely skimmed the surface of the water. Into Gorscarrigern's service the High Priest had seduced the crocodiles of the Periyar River and their mighty tails pounded against the stonework of the archway as they streamed through the Haran outer defences.

For several minutes, the captain watched them, too aghast and stunned to move. Past the white fleet of the city the loathsome *Kaliya* sailed, ploughing straight through the small barges and straw-canopied river craft which were moored in her way until finally she reached the quay – coming to a juddering stop alongside the *Chandi*.

At that instant, the horror that had rooted Captain Chattan and frozen his limbs, suddenly thawed and he knew what had to be done. There was still a chance. If his folk could be roused then the inner walls might yet be defended.

Leaping to the turret's central pillar he wrenched a silver-tipped horn from its hook and, running to the eastern window which looked out on to the city, blew three piercing blasts upon it.

Gulping down the tempest's pummelling air he put the instrument to his lips a second time and again the blaring notes trumpeted across the roof tops.

Then his thoughts flew to the main entrance. In their endeavour to break in, the Scale would launch their first attack upon those two great doors and his mind reeled as he tried to calculate how long they could withstand the battering fury before they were splintered and torn from their hinges.

Looking south he strove to see what was happening, but the entrance was hidden behind the huddled roofs, so, sounding the horn three times more, he leapt for the stairs and fled down them.

Through the guardroom where the sentries still slept soundly, unaware of the peril that assailed the city, he hurtled. Then out into the pelting rain, noticing with scant satisfaction that several more lanterns had been lit in the surrounding windows and in a fierce, shrieking voice he cried a further alarm.

'The Scale are here! The Scale are here! Awake folk of Hara! The hour we have long dreaded is upon us! We must fight!'

As he sped down the spouting, flooded streets, those who had not partaken of the wine that night came scurrying out, with spears and bows in their trembling paws and frantically they charged after him to defend their city.

Startled and afraid, Thomas and Woodget had heard the horn blasting over the city and, peering from their window, had seen the captain go racing by in the street below.

Fearfully they scampered down the stairs and hurried outside, where they were quickly joined by the mongoose's sister and, with a wicked sneer threatening to erupt on to his face at any moment – Dahrem.

The adept of Scarophion had remained awake throughout the night, listening to the approach of his hellish brotherhood and relishing every dark moment. Now he was eager to look on the slaughter that would ensue, but another, more appealing thought loomed large in his malignant mind and so he determined to remain as Dimlon a little while longer.

'What's happening?' Thomas cried to a nervous-looking musk shrew that went puffing by with a quiver of arrows in one paw and a bow in the other.

'The enemy have come!' came the urgent, squeaking reply. 'Nearly all our great warriors are drugged, only a handful and we smaller ones are left to defend the walls. Arm yourselves – come aid us.'

Thomas stared at Woodget then looked back at Sobhan.

'Are there any weapons in this house?' he asked grimly.

The mongoose maiden made no reply but raced indoors and returned, bearing a long knife for each of them and a sword of her own.

'Bless us!' Woodget whimpered, gripping the knife in his little paw and staring at the glinting blade.

'Stay by me, Woodj,' Thomas told him. 'I'll make sure those devils don't get you.'

Into the streets they ran, joining the throng of frightened mice, shrews, marmots, voles and palm squirrels that rushed after Chattan.

Down toward the main entrance, the captain raced; already he could hear a squawking clamour of evil voices as the nightmarish host of Gorscarrigern leapt ashore and surged up the steps behind the fearsome menace of their High Priest.

With his heart hammering upon his ribs, the mongoose heard a thin, hideous cry cut through the thundering storm and the great doors reverberated with a thousand blows before an ominous silence fell that was followed by a single, horrible, shivering crash as a battering ram smashed against its silver-studded timbers.

It was not far now, Chattan thought, leaping through the deluged streets – around the next bend the gurgling thoroughfare dipped sharply and he would see the main entrance rise in the sloping distance.

With his saturated cloak flapping madly behind him and his sword in his fist, he hared around the corner – but the sight which met his eyes caused his bounding stride to falter and he slithered to a standstill.

A long, agonising time it had taken him, and the journey had been slow and painful. Every brittle joint complained and pronounced its grinding protest but finally he was here. Soaked to the mottled skin, leaning upon a short staff, his fine wispy beard hanging like dripping, bedraggled threads and his long, scrawny legs bowed almost as much as his back – was the Holy One.

Many years ago, he had resolved to do the deed which now lay before him and nothing, save a blade in the breast, could have stopped him now.

As Chattan and those who flowed into the street behind him watched, the ancient loris shuffled through the rushing flood-water, right up to the huge double doors.

'This cannot be,' Chattan breathed, staring at the scene, unable to comprehend what he was witnessing. Into his unblinking eyes drove the stinging rain but still he could not wrench his gaze from the awful, deranged spectacle and all around him the stricken crowd whispered in fear.

'What's he doing?' Thomas muttered. 'I don't understand.'

Behind him Sobhan's grip tightened on the hilt of her sword. 'He is betraying us all,' she said bitterly.

Around her the other folk had also guessed what the Holy One intended, yet no one wanted to believe it.

The colossal doors of the city were barred by

three stout and sturdy beams, but the manner of their release had been conceived by the same minds who constructed the iron barrier which spanned the river. Thus each of those mighty shafts could be drawn by the pulling of a single lever, positioned in the stone to the right of the entrance – and it was to this mechanism that the Holy One now shambled.

'NO!' Chattan yelled and he plunged down the stepped street with his sword raised, ready to strike down the aged sadhu if he had to.

But it was no use. He had not travelled half the distance when the wizened loris took hold of the operating lever in both bony paws and, summoning the last reserves of his withered strength, threw it down.

Iron wheels turned and the ages-old apparatus began to clank inside its stone housing.

With a blank expression upon his rain-stung face, the Holy One picked his way to a point directly behind the sweep of the doors and waited – waited – watching as the first of the massive beams was drawn across the timbers and slid into the gargantuan wall.

'He is in league with the Scale,' Chattan murmured wretchedly. 'Our sadhu has surrendered us to the enemy!'

It was too late now to attempt to reach the entrance and reverse the mechanism; already the second beam had rumbled free of the doors and in a moment the third would follow.

Chattan thought wildly and strove to quell his panic. All that was left to them was battle, but of that he held little hope. Behind him the assembled city folk had crammed into the winding street like so many tightly squeezed sheep and he knew that if something was not done, then their foes would find them easy prey. They had wedged themselves into a confining space which would take precious time to clear and the captain's dismay came close to mastering him.

But if they were to die then it would be as warriors and in a mad, screeching voice, he bawled.

'Make way there! Disperse the ranks. Take up your arms! We must stand and fight – this night shall decide all our fates. Into the jaws of death we are staring but let us not waver or show the hated foe any sign of fear.'

The faces that looked to him, however, were truly frightened. But there in the crowd, the captain saw a chubby, red-bearded countenance that was flushed with anger and he cried aloud in rejoicing.

'Karim!' the mongoose called. 'A thousand blessings upon you! My heart soars to see that you did not drink of the wine this night.'

Through the crowd the lieutenant came, arrayed in his gleaming armour, wielding his spear and his sword, and a defiant, deadly fire blazed in his eyes.

'Captain!' he bellowed. 'My blade is yours to command. Many of the heathen filth shall fall before I do.'

Even as he said it, the third shaft was clear of the doors and with a dreadful creak they swung open.

All eyes were trained on the ever-widening space that lay between them; many small voices wailed with terror and knives went clattering to the ground as the horrific legions of the enemy were gradually revealed.

With torches held above their heads, the flames spitting in the rain, thousands of red-rimmed eyes were shining in amazement at the opening doors, fearing some unexpected trick. Poised outside the entrance, blinking suspiciously and licking their fangs, the assembled forces of the Scale were an abhorrent, petrifying sight.

Standing in an avenue of dagger-wielding creatures, a hundred great rats held a huge battering ram in their claws but their dribbling jaws lolled open at the sudden unbarring of the entrance and they stared upwards and about them for any hidden traps.

Behind them the first of the crocodiles had already clambered from the harbour and were glaring into the city, and all around their repulsive, scaly feet twisted a knot of venomous snakes whose reared heads were swaying from side to side as their tongues flicked in and out of their mouths to taste the unfamiliar airs.

But standing before the entire host of this pagan, murderous rabble, with a hood overshadowing his face, stood a figure of infinite menace and eventually all eyes, those of Hara and those of Scarophion's followers, were drawn to look on him.

Hissing in the shade of his cowl, as the lightning blasted overhead, the High Priest peered across the threshold and looked on the frail form of the Holy One who stood there – shivering from the great age of his bones rather than from fear.

For over a minute the two sides, good and evil, regarded one another and not a voice uttered a word. Only the thunder and the noise of the teeming rain disturbed the silence. It was a balancing moment of fate – a destiny that had long been awaited by both forces, and the march of advancing doom was felt by everyone present.

Then, with an arrogant swagger, the High Priest strode forward until he was standing in front of the Holy One and the unnatural calm was shattered as his shrill voice mocked the ancient sadhu.

'Witless ape!' he shouted with a hissing scorn. 'Your line has ended and the time of your false, grubbing deity is over. Death has found you out at last – you and the rest of your squalid rout who infest these dirty, middenish hovels!'

With that he raised his claws from the folds of his cloak and all saw that upon them he wore two golden talons.

'The Lord Suruth Scarophion is the one true god – may every unpledged mind tremble at His worshipful name!'

Screeching with hideous laughter he lashed out, but the loris did not flinch and when the poisoned blades ripped through his throat it was exposed and ready for them.

Like a rag doll, the Holy One crumpled to the floor but with his last breath he gave thanks and then perished – his blood mingling with the seething rain-water.

Crowing in ghastly delight, the High Priest sprang aside and leapt on to the base of a nearby statue then, with a high-pitched yell, gave the order to attack.

At once the demonic army came charging through the entrance, whooping and screaming bloodthirsty oaths.

But before them, at the summit of the stepped thoroughfare, Captain Chattan had not been idle.

Quickly he had made his plans and, whilst the High Priest was cackling with foul glee, he barked instructions to Karim.

At once the lieutenant led a division of spear-bearing voles and the handful of other mongooses down an adjoining alley-way. Swiftly they hurried along, for the path wound around a block of two-storied buildings, emerging once more half-way down the sloping street, where they lay in ambush ready for the marauding devotees of the Serpent to go stampeding by.

Then Chattan ordered a detachment of squirrel archers to climb on to the balconies above and shoot at the enemy from there. The rest of his host he told to stand firm and beware the blades of their foes.

Yet that was all he had time to say, for the enemy was already upon them.

Up the stepped street the invading disciples of the Coiled One surged, slashing the lightning-rent night with their scimitars and shrieking with savage voices.

Into their beserking midst a hail of arrows fell from the bows of the palm squirrels who began leaping from balcony to balcony to evade the barrage of missiles and poisonous darts which immediately ensued. In the street below, ten of the fork-tailed devotees were slain, with feathered shafts buried deep in their necks and over the fallen bodies of their dead confederates, the infernal horde rampaged – trampling and crushing the corpses under their relentless, screaming advance.

As a thickly flowing tide of claw and cutlass, the hideous creatures came rioting up the thoroughfare and crashed viciously upon the city's defenders.

Into the soft flesh of tree shrews their poisoned knives swiftly sank; arms were hacked from shoulders and faces raked with venom.

Yet Chattan was at the forefront of the assault and his slashing sword wove a barrier of steel that none could pass.

Before his bloodied blade, seven great rats had already fallen but more came leaping to take their place and their scimitars rang against the mongoose's sword, chiming and clashing with powerful strokes – the razoring edges barely missing his face.

At his side the shrews were faring less successfully, and many died in the first horrific moments of the battle. But as soon as any breach was made in the Haran barricade which blocked the street, another of the small animals jumped in to replace the dead and their little swords proved just as deadly as the weapons of the enemy.

Several rows behind the main conflict, Thomas and Woodget prepared themselves for the onslaught as the ranks began to thin and the ferocious army of the Scale drew ever closer.

At their side, Dahrem eyed the brutal proceedings with intense interest – it was immensely satisfying to see the dark forces drench the marble stairs with blood and when they had charged through the entrance he had had to bite his tongue to prevent himself cheering. Yet now he was faced with a difficult problem and he sought for ways to solve it.

It was he who had discovered Mulligan's fragment and he certainly wasn't going to let anyone else steal the credit for that. But how could he flee to the mountain without being challenged?

'Dimmy's mortalafearedfraidycat!' he whined piteously. 'He ain't no soldier. He can't stay here, he wants to go and hide in darkcubbyholeunderstairsorindraughtylofty. Let him go, let him through.'

'Keep the fool silent!' Chattan's sister demanded, pushing forward to be at her brother's side. 'Behind our lines there are infants and babes in arms with more courage than he.'

Thomas glowered at the pale grey mouse. 'Pipe down!' he shouted. 'Where d'you think you could go anyway? There's no escape from these horrors. Just do the best you can when your time comes.'

At that moment the evil host sent up a great clamouring as Karim sprang his ambush and, at the head of the mongooses and voles under his command, plunged deep into the right flank of the vile, scrambling horde.

The creatures dedicated to Scarophion shrieked in confusion as this unlooked-for hazard drove clean across the narrow street and those caught between the two Haran forces squealed in dread. Ahead of them Chattan and his sister were dealing out death to any who dared lunge at them and even those hateful little squeakers at their side were doing nasty damage with their sharp daggers. Now a new front had opened behind them, cutting them off from the rest of their kind and Karim's tassled spear had already impaled four burly rats whilst his sword had hewn the arms off another and chopped the legs from under a sixth.

But their snarling panic at their perilous predicament only fuelled the fires of their madness and they threw themselves upon their enemies with more savagery than before.

Dodging the mongoose captain's sweeping sword strokes, a large, slavering, black rat burst through the defending shrews, his claws raking their tender flesh as his snapping jaws bit out their throats. In a crimson-spattering instant he was behind the front line and, standing in his ravaging path, gazing up into his hate-filled eyes, was Woodget's small and frightened form.

With a thrash of his forked tail and a curdling screech of delight, the brute dived straight for the fieldmouse's head, his claws outstretched – ready to rend it from his body.

Woodget squealed and woefully held up his knife, but before he knew what was happening, Thomas dragged him aside and grimly took his place.

Yelling hideously, the black rat cannoned into him and Master Stubbs collapsed beneath the crushing weight of the vile-smelling beast, yet even as the venom-soaked claws came reaching for his neck, he thrust up with his dagger and pushed the blade clean through the fiend's windpipe.

A horrific, bubbling gurgle issued from the beast's choking maw but to Thomas' dismay his stroke had not been fatal. Rearing off him, the rat grasped the knife's hilt, wrenched it from his throat and a fount of hot blood went flowing over his matted fur.

Groggy, but inflamed with cruel purpose, the creature raised Thomas' own knife and, lying sprawled and winded upon the flooding street, the mouse knew the end had come.

'You leave him be! You scaly heathen scurvy scum!' Woodget's high voice shouted, his fright blossoming to courageous fury and finding Mulligan's favourite curses the only words suitable in such a dreadful plight.

Baring his teeth and gripping his own knife vehemently, he pounced upon the rat's upraised arm, jabbing him in the side and biting the scabby skin until he could taste the unclean blood in his mouth.

Enraged, the wounded creature flung its arm wide and the fieldmouse went spinning through the rain-lashed air, landing bruised but otherwise unharmed, way up the street and a dozen anxious paws helped him to stand.

But it was too late. The rat was now towering over Thomas and there was nothing his friend could do to save him.

Then, to Woodget's astonishment, Dimlon jumped to Thomas' aid, flourishing a silver-hilted sword retrieved from one of the fallen shrews.

'Keep back!' the pale grey mouse blurted.

At first the rat chuckled darkly, and then a strange, shocked expression struck his ugly face as he leered at Dahrem and he blinked in bewilderment. Then his lips trembled and he opened his jaws to speak.

But whatever he had been about to utter was swiftly curtailed, for the treacherous mouse squeaked in mock horror and swiped the sword across the rat's neck. A moment later, a lifeless body slumped to the ground as the severed head went tumbling down the street to bounce back into the throng of his comrades.

'The villain were goin' to get us!' Dahrem sobbed, throwing the sword down as though it, and what he had done, appalled him.

Thomas scrambled to his feet and muttered his

thanks, as Woodget came running up to fling his arms about them both.

'You was so brave, Dimmy!' he cried admiringly. 'Weren't he Tom?'

But Thomas recalled the last expression that had formed upon the rat's face as he peered at their companion. It was not that of a callous, taunting killer, but fear had registered there and, unless Thomas was mistaken, a look of recognition.

Around them however, the uproar continued to blare and, unable to dwell on the ghastly experience, Thomas picked up the sword Dimlon had cast aside and dashed across the rat's headless body to stop up the breach. But the number of hellish disciples trapped between Chattan and Karim was dwindling and overhead the squirrels' arrows found many foul targets.

Yet their fortune could not last much longer. Behind Karim the remaining host of the Dark Despoiler were too great a number to hold back and around the stout lieutenant many of the mongooses in his company had been killed and the complement of voles had diminished to under twenty.

Yet despite the odds, Chattan and Karim met across a mass of corpses and with renewed vigour they meted out death to all who came.

Beside her brother, Sobhan fought as well as any warrior but when her sword crashed against a heavy axe wielded by a yellow-throated weasel, the steel blade splintered in a flurry of sparks – yet she drove the remaining shard into his breast and he toppled backwards bowling over those who yammered behind him.

Desperately, Sobhan searched for another weapon but Chattan pushed her back.

'We cannot win this!' he cried. 'They are too many.'

'I will die at your side!' she shouted defiantly, wrenching a scimitar from a dead rat's claw.

Her brother glared round at her. 'You would do better to spend the last moments of your life elsewhere!' he yelled. 'See to the city's children. Take them from this peril if you can – you might yet escape this foulness.'

The maiden stared at him but even in the heat of that awful moment saw the wisdom of his counsel. Blinking away her tears, she sought for words but there were none to express this parting and so with a brisk movement, she touched his arm in farewell then disappeared behind the lines and hurried back up the sloping street.

Plunging his spear deep into a powerfully built mole's gullet, Karim heard his captain's instructions and prayed that his own infants would be spared the violence of this night. To allow them time to escape was the only thought that consumed him but even if they did, what manner of world would they find? When the nine stars next appeared in the sky to herald Gorscarrigern's approach, his loathsome servants would possess every fragment of his diabolic shell and into the living plane would his soul be reborn.

Bellowing like a trumpeting elephant as he battled on, Karim shouted to his captain.

'This night all our hopes shall fail!' he boomed. 'But you could still cheat the designs of the Coiled One.'

'I?' Chattan answered, splitting the skull of a

ravening rat. 'What riddles do you speak, Karim? Against this filth we cannot prevail.'

'Maybe,' the lieutenant barked back. 'Yet what of the evil treasure they have come to claim? Are we to let them steal it so easily?'

'The fragments!' Chattan cried. In the height of the battle he had given no thought to the remaining pieces.

'They must be taken from this place!' he roared. 'Yet who can I send to bear them away?'

Karim staggered backwards as a cudgel rammed into his breastplate but he rallied at once and the club dropped to the ground still clutched in a dismembered fist.

'None!' he bawled in answer to his captain's demand. 'So send yourself and take the three mice with you if all still live. Their fates are bound up with the fragments, that much is plain to me.'

'I shall not desert and flee the battle!'

Just then, agonising screams issued from the attacking host as through the gaping entrance lumbered the largest crocodile and up the narrow street it came trudging, heedless of the creatures in its determined, destroying path – squashing everything beneath its pounding, splayed feet.

With its immense, tooth-filled jaws it callously scooped up seven shrieking cult members and devoured them with a toss of its head.

Standing a safe distance away, upon the base of a statue, the High Priest rubbed his claws together triumphantly. The lesser servants were dispensable, they had served their purpose. Now the inhabitants of Hara would see that their paltry struggles were in vain and with the unholy power that was in him he spurred the huge, grotesque reptile on.

Chattan drew a paw over his brow as the grinning apparition advanced. Then, at the crocodile's side, he saw the heads of fifty serpents rear above the screeching mob, their lidless eyes fixed upon the animals of the city and, as one, the cobras stretched wide their eye-patterned hoods.

'We are lost,' Chattan muttered.

Karim whirled around and shook him by the shoulders. 'Then keep our memory alive!' he begged. 'Gladly will I give my life if I can hope you have denied them what they wish.'

The captain looked at him. Already the ground was shaking beneath the approach of the great crocodile and the cobras were spitting their venom at the squirrels who quailed upon the balconies before dropping like ripe fruit into their tangling midst.

'In the Green hereafter, your place shall be set high, Karim Bihari,' Chattan said quickly.

The lieutenant held his gaze then nodded briskly. 'Go now,' he instructed. 'I will hold them for as long as I am able.'

Swiftly, Chattan leaped from the front line and shoved through the squealing shrews behind, calling for Thomas, Woodget and Dimlon.

Skulking a short distance away from the battle, Dahrem heard the urgent summons above the rumbling thunder and splashed forward to bring the other two from the fray.

Thomas was proving to be most proficient with the sword, and with every parrying thrust or slicing blow, his skill and confidence soared.

Hovering behind him, feeling completely inadequate and miserably insignificant, Woodget hopped from side to side, brandishing his knife in readiness. But no further incursions into the defences had as yet been made and his courage was rapidly subsiding as he beheld the terrible abhorrence which came marching towards them.

'Quick!' Dahrem cried to him, pulling on the fieldmouse's arm. 'Mongoosiecaptain calls for us. Listen! Tell Tommy!'

Woodget whisked about and saw Chattan beckoning to them feverishly.

'Tom! Tom!' Woodget squeaked. 'This way! This way!'

Locked in combat with the enemy, Master Stubbs did not hear his friend. His arm was tiring and with anguish, he wondered how long he could continue. He too had glimpsed the advancing nightmare but was too afraid to look upon it fully. Better to swipe and hew the rats and weasels before him, until he perished by their swiping claws, than contemplate such a horrendous apparition.

'Tom!' Woodget cried again.

Thomas glanced over his shoulder.

'The captain needs us!' the fieldmouse called.

Master Stubbs gave a final, scything sweep with his sword then sprang back and his place was immediately filled by two valiant musk shrews.

'Hurry!' Woodget urged, following Chattan's retreating figure through the petrified crowd.

At his side Dahrem pranced excitedly, babbling in Dimmy's plaintive tones about how glad he was to be leaving this awful place.

Hurriedly they caught up with the mongoose captain and, sombrely, Chattan told them where they were headed.

'We go to the mountain,' he said. 'Though the city of Hara might flounder, the forces of the Scale must never take the fragments. Here at the end we shall deny them the sweetness of their unhallowed victory.'

With his satchel slung about his shoulder, Dahrem said nothing but the hour of his greatness was fast approaching and when Suruth Scarophion was reborn into the world, it would be due to him.

From the grisly scene of the battle, through the pouring, lashing rain, the mice and Chattan Giri raced, vanishing into the storm-drenched darkness – ascending the terraced paths that wound about the slopes of the mountain.

Below them, within the beleaguered street, the repellent form of the crocodile finally reached the Haran forces and with a croaking hiss, it swung its massive head from side to side, shattering the bones of those not quick enough to get out of its way. Then, the enormous mouth gaped open and into its crunching jaws it shovelled a dozen, shrieking defenders.

Only one stood his ground, undaunted by the oncoming terror, and when the shadow engulfed him, Karim Bihari called upon the Green for aid. Then as the reeking, dripping maw yawned closer, he leapt over the gore-gouted teeth and, standing upon the scarlet-stained, fleshy tongue, rammed his spear straight into the monstrous reptile's throat.

Braying in torment, the horror thrashed wildly, its mighty tail crashing into the ornate buildings

– smashing through the stone sculptures and demolishing the houses.

Around its flailing torso, nearly a hundred followers of the Serpent were utterly crushed and in the ruin of the toppling masonry, countless more perished.

Scrabbling at its own jaws, the crocodile flipped over, exposing the pale flesh of its belly, and seizing their chance, the surviving archers strung the last arrows to their bows and took aim.

In the volley of feathered shafts that followed, the monster screamed once more, then his struggles ended. But from his lolling jaws the broken body of Karim Bihari tumbled – his pulverised armour twisted and rent about his mangled corpse.

From his vantage point upon the base of a six-armed statue, the High Priest looked on the horrific scene with no emotion save amusement and summoned through the entrance further abominations of scaly hide, who went waddling up the death-strewn street, clambering over the carcass of their vanquished brother.

At last the age-old city of the Green was defeated and the time had come to claim the eighth fragment for the glory of his master. So, leaving the main body of his infernal host to finish slaughtering the inhabitants, he took a legion of rats and poisonous snakes and with his dark cloak whirling about him, set off towards the mountain.

Up the thousand steps Chattan and the mice had hastened, not pausing for breath nor to glance down at the turmoil which ravaged the city streets below.

The steep mountain way had become exceedingly treacherous for the rain cascaded down the stone stair, forming a rushing waterfall, causing their feet to slither and slip, and many times Thomas and the others lost their footing.

Now, with the fierce gale plucking and dragging at their fur, those dangers were behind them, for they had reached the summit where the rocky ledge led to the great carving's open mouth.

But within the sooty cavern all was dark for the sacred fire had been extinguished by the gusting rains of the unnatural storm. The mouth of the Green Mouse's likeness was flooded with water and the ash floated in a thick, charred scum upon its turgid surface.

Through this, Chattan waded and the mice followed him to the rear of the cave where the passage divided into two tunnels, one leading up to the Holy One's chamber and the other plunging into darkness.

'The downward road must we take,' the mongoose told them. 'It leads deep into the mountain's roots, through the catacombs – then out beyond the inner boundary. There we must trust to providence and avoid capture, for what we shall carry from here this night is beyond price.'

'The fragments,' Thomas muttered. 'If you stay here on watch, me and Woodj'll go and fetch them.'

Chattan drew his sword once more and shook his head. 'No, Master Thomas,' he told him. 'You have proven your skill with a blade and must remain with me – lest the Scale are swift in pursuit. We must buy time for the fragments at the price of our own lives if need be.'

'S'all right Tom,' the fieldmouse said. 'I can manage on me own.'

The mongoose narrowed his dark eyes. 'One fragment is burden enough,' he warned. 'Dimlon can go with you. Give the other evil to him and be as quick as you can. There is no time to waste.'

'Oh no,' Dahrem nodded deliriously. 'Dimmy not dawdle – he help Woody gladly.'

And so the fieldmouse scurried up the spiralling path that led to the windowless chamber above, and at his side, with his black heart rejoicing in the knowledge that the two precious fragments would soon be his, went the adept of Sarpedon.

When they had gone, the mongoose ran back into the flooded fire chamber and peered out of the stone mouth – to look down upon the troubled city.

Breathing a sigh of relief, he saw that as yet, the thousand steps were clear and he turned to Thomas who came splashing after him.

'It is better than I hoped,' he said. 'We have put a good distance between ourselves and the Scale. If we can but keep the pieces from their possession a little longer, the next conjunction will pass harmlessly.'

'I don't fancy turning into another Mulligan,' Thomas muttered despondently. 'Flitting across the globe, lugging those evil things in tow.'

'Perhaps it will not come to that,' Chattan told him. 'Unless all of the sadhu's words were false.'

Thomas looked at him quizzically but then, cutting through the air above them, there screeched a horrendous, terrified squeal.

'WOODGET!' the mouse cried, spinning around

and charging back through the cavern. 'What's happening up there?'

As the fieldmouse's screams floated out into the night, Captain Chattan brandished his sword, but before he followed Thomas, he saw that far below, dark shapes were racing towards the bottom of the thousand steps.

14

The Adept of Sarpedon

U p to the Holy One's chamber, Woodget had led Dahrem. Then through that bare room they had hurried, pulling aside the tapestry curtain and climbing the flight of stairs beyond where they discovered, to the fieldmouse's relief, that the wooden door was unlocked.

Into the livid green glare he scampered, over to where his bag lay propped against the curving wall.

'Here be the piece old Mulligan kept,' Woodget declared, peeping inside to check it was still there. 'I'll take this, you get the other one, Dimmy.'

As one in a beautiful dream, Dahrem stole into the domed, bronze-plated chamber, his pale grey fur steeped in the ravishing glow which beat out from the eighth fragment in its centre.

Bathed in the cold gleam, flickering starkly as the

lightning continued to crackle about the mountain, its flashes blazing through the large oval stone set into the far wall, he crept forward – entranced.

Dahrem's outstretched paws quivered with emotion as he beheld the gorgeous spectacle of the wondrous treasure. Here at last was the culmination of his yearning desire – the fulfilment of every, fantastical wish and his eyes sparkled greedily.

To the middle of the chamber he went, crossing to the circular pool and reaching over to the silver dish that stood upon the crystal plinth.

From the days of his infant youth, ever since he had been dedicated into his master's profane service and his tail mutilated upon the altar, Dahrem had tried to imagine what it would be like if Sarpedon were ever truly to return. To that glorious end, every zealous member of the cult had toiled over a thousand generations but he suddenly realised that he had never quite believed it would happen, or that he would live to see it if it did. Now his lord's rebirth depended solely upon him and his eyes grew moist at the awesome prospect.

Wrung with emotion, he gazed on the splendour of the eighth fragment which the early inhabitants of this accursed city had stolen and carried back here in triumph.

Although over many years the Scale had managed to reclaim most of the divided pieces, only the high priests and priestesses had been permitted to look on them and Dahrem often lusted to steal into their private sanctum to gaze on the mysterious fragments.

Now, to his adoring eyes the cunning work of his beloved, dark sovereign was the most beautiful sight he had ever seen. Even the great, golden image which dominated the Black Temple was nothing compared to the exquisite, spellbinding skill that had gone into the making of this. The intricacy of the scrolling gold was bewitching and the lurid light that pulsed from the jade instilled him with pride and an avenging passion to destroy all who opposed Sarpedon the Mighty.

Holding his breath, Dahrem opened his twitching fingers and the moment he had longed for throughout his wicked life took place.

About the twisting lattice of gold he closed his paws and the touch of the cold metal tingled through his palms, invigorating and exhilarating his corrupt soul – inspiring him to fresh acts of violence and despair.

Reverently, the pale grey mouse lifted the eighth fragment from the dish and, closing his eyes with pleasure, hugged it to his breast.

'Hurry up, Dimmy.' Woodget's voice intruded upon his black bliss. 'We bain't got time for you to dilly-dally.'

Dahrem wheeled around and the faintest glimmer of gold gleamed in his heavily lidded eyes.

'Stay a moment,' he uttered huskily. 'Dimmy must put this in his satchel. He'll be quick, you'll see – you won't be kept waiting long. I promise.'

The fieldmouse grudgingly consented as Dahrem began unbuckling the flap of his satchel and, worrying over what might be happening outside, Woodget scuttled to the great oval stone set into the bronze and pressed his little face against its glassy surface.

Behind him, Dahrem reached inside the bag and

carefully fitted two curved, glittering blades on to his fingers.

'Nearly ready,' he said with a hiss. 'Dimmy's just about done now.'

Oblivious to the adept's actions and innocently unaware of his murderous intent, Woodget was busily squinting through the translucent stone and down upon the huddled rooftops far below.

Behind him, Dahrem took a prowling step closer, his eyes fixed upon the leather bag gripped in the fieldmouse's paws and where the baleful glow glinted in the razor-sharp talons they cast bleak slivers of light across those small vulnerable shoulders.

'You finished?' Woodget called.

'Oh yes,' came the sibilant reply, 'the time to end many things has come.'

Woodget turned around but his first, unsuspecting thought was that Dimlon had not put the fragment in the satchel after all, for its ghastly light was still glowing in the chamber and he scowled at the simple mouse's silliness.

'What be you a-playin' at?' he began. 'There bain't—'

The fieldmouse's voice died on his lips as he saw the glittering knives and his face was a portrait of blank incomprehension.

Dahrem was almost unrecognisable. Infinite malice disfigured his countenance and a repellent snarl twisted over his mouth, drawing the thin lips back over the deep red gums.

'Dimm . . . Dimmy?' Woodget stammered fearfully.

Dahrem gave a sniggering hiss. 'Dimmy was never here,' he taunted. 'His character was but a mask I wore to gain your trust. How easily you accepted him, but then you were almost as much of a prize fool as he. Now it is time to curtail our acquaintance.'

'Dimmy,' Woodget implored. 'Stop this, it bain't funny.'

The adept of the Serpent stalked a little nearer – a mocking cackle rattling in his throat.

Woodget shrank against the oval stone and his eyes grew wide with terror as, behind the pale grey mouse, he saw the switching tail slowly unpeel into two separate halves.

'No,' he cried, 'it ain't true! Green save me!'

At last the fieldmouse understood and his squealing shriek echoed around the domed chamber.

Viciously, Dahrem swept the gleaming knives before his face and the yell was silenced as Woodget shuddered in fear.

'Such arrogance!' Dahrem spat. 'To think you could deny us the last two fragments. When His Unhallowed Majesty returns, no other creed will thrive in any land. Now, surrender to me the ninth piece, or must I tear it from your poisoned corpse?'

Tears of anguish welled in Woodget's eyes. 'Then it were you who killed Mister Mulligan,' he sobbed.

Only a repugnant cackle answered him and the fieldmouse knew that as soon as he handed the bag over, he was dead.

But then, as the blades shone before his face, from somewhere deep inside him there swelled a fierce resolve. Set against the awful doom which awaited the world, his life was unimportant. If he could only delay the evil creature a minute or two more, if only he could alert Thomas and the captain.

Trembling, he lifted the leather bag that contained Mulligan's life-long burden, remembering the vow he had made to the dying Irish seafarer. Never would he yield the ninth fragment to a servant of the Scale.

Without a thought for his own safety, the fieldmouse suddenly lunged forward and, using all his strength, shoved the bag in Dahrem's face – screaming at the top of his lungs.

Caught off guard, not expecting his petrified victim capable of such a desperate action, Dahrem staggered backwards and, still yelling for all he was worth, Woodget fled past him – swinging the bag in his fists as he raced for the door.

But Dahrem rallied swiftly and, screeching with fury, bounded across the chamber to cut off Woodget's escape.

In an instant he had leapt to the entrance and with a perilous rumble growling in his throat, glared at the fieldmouse who skidded to a stop before him.

'Keep away!' Woodget wailed.

But Dahrem's anger was boiling and his breathing became guttural and wild as he watched the frightened fieldmouse go scurrying back around the chamber. Over his large eyes flowed a film of gold and his pupils shrank into slits as the dark power which coursed through his veins seized control.

Throwing back his head, he let out a horrific, bestial shout then sprang after his prey.

Woodget's short legs were no match for his great, leaping strides and a moment later he was plucked from the ground and sent hurtling through the air.

With a juddering smack, the fieldmouse's flailing

body struck the great oval stone and he fell to the floor in a wriggling heap.

Crowing with laughter, Dahrem loomed over him, with the eighth fragment grasped in one set of claws and the curved knives glittering upon the other.

'Shall the blood of the Almighty Lord burn and froth within you?' he hissed. 'Or will I dash out your feeble wits first?'

Callously, with the back of his claws he gave Woodget a battering blow across the face and the fieldmouse let out a pitiful whine. But he huddled over the bag in defiance as Dahrem bent over him, and the cruel creature began to tortuously stroke the back of Woodget's neck with the golden knives – tormenting him with the imminent threat of horrendous, agonising death.

'I must conclude this pretty play,' he sniggered insidiously. 'If this is how you wish to die, grovelling in the dirt, then so be it.'

'SPAWN OF THE SNAKE!' bawled a sudden, ferocious voice.

Dahrem whisked around and standing in the doorway, with Thomas at his side, was Captain Chattan.

'Dimlon!' Thomas spluttered. 'What's happening? Woodj – are you all right?'

The mouse hurried forward but Chattan pulled him back. 'Look at him!' the mongoose snapped. 'We have been deceived. We have been harbouring a disciple of the Coiled One in our midst.'

'Dimmy?' Thomas mouthed silently, and he stared in disbelief at the forked tail which Dahrem thrashed behind him, then beheld with revulsion the shining, reptilian eyes.

Upon the floor Woodget wept with joy to see his friends but Dahrem's menacing figure was standing before him, preventing his escape.

Sucking the air through his teeth, Dahrem regarded the mongoose haughtily. 'Tell me, Captain,' he hissed, 'how does it feel to know the full measure of despair? By the morning your proud city will be in ruins and only vipers shall garland the broken walls to plague the ghosts of your kith and kin. All your paltry struggles have been as dust in the wind. You and all your kind have failed. Sarpedon has proved victorious.'

'Lay down the eighth fragment,' Chattan commanded grimly. 'I will not permit you to take it.'

'Permit!' Dahrem roared with derision. 'You have no authority here! Do you not have eyes to see? I am no common disciple of He who was banished long ago. An adept in His service am I – with all the power and privilege granted to that glorious and most august order.'

Chattan stepped forward, his sword raised, but Dahrem merely grinned hideously and beckoned him closer.

'A contest?' he chortled darkly. 'You are as idiotic as the fieldmouse. Presently my brothers shall swarm up the mountainside – if you fled now you might just escape them. Is it your wish to die needlessly, Captain? For against an adept of the Scale there is no deliverance.'

'You waste your final breaths,' Chattan barked. 'Are you afraid to face me? Is your courage confined to frightened folk smaller than yourself? What mettle is in you – accursed creature of the Dark Despoiler? None I would guess. A craven worm are you, like all members of your blasphemous, loathsome cult.'

As he spoke, the mongoose stabbed out with his sword, taunting the foul grey mouse, and Dahrem's laughter was stilled.

'So be it,' he swore. 'The blade of Hara against the teeth of Sarpedon. May the venom bite you slowly.'

With that he flew at Chattan, lashing out with the golden knives. But the mongoose jumped aside and brought the flat of his sword slapping smartly across his opponent's back.

'A little quicker next time,' the captain suggested archly. 'Not as easy dealing with someone who's armed, is it?'

Incensed by these jibes, Dahrem spun around and the rage blazed in his eyes.

'Prepare to meet your precious Green!' he shrieked, spitting with hatred.

Like one demented, he sliced the air before him and pounced forward but Captain Chattan's sword came singing to meet the knives and with a screech of metal the weapons clashed together.

As gold rang against steel, Dahrem pushed his head forward and his snapping jaws bit into the mongoose's chest.

Chattan yelled in pain and Dahrem spat a bleeding chunk of flesh on to the floor.

Fiercely, Chattan thrust the creature away but at once he flew back, the knives razoring madly for the mongoose's face, before the sword parried and knocked them aside.

Still standing in the entrance, not knowing what to do, Thomas watched the battle breathlessly. His own sword was gripped in his paw but he knew that any attempt to help the captain would only hinder him.

Dahrem was a nightmarish adversary, his poisoned talons ripped murderously for the mongoose's throat whilst his jaws sought to rend and tear. Fortunately for Chattan, the eighth fragment was still gripped in his other claw or the struggle would have been twice as brutal and savage.

Sitting beneath the oval stone, Woodget wiped his eyes. He longed to scurry over to where Thomas was waiting and flee down the stairway, but whilst the battle raged about him, he was too afraid to budge.

A dreadful chiming clamour resounded throughout the domed chamber as the weapons smote each other. Then, with a burst of strength, Chattan hurled the adept from him and when he came marauding back, flung his arm wide and the tip of the blade cut a scarlet arc across Dahrem's body.

Screeching, the creature stumbled back and glared down at the blood which soaked his fur.

'Very well,' he seethed. 'You wish to carve the skin from me. See now the splendour afforded to an adept of the Black Master. Look on me and die!'

With that he raised his claws and, to Chattan's dismay, began to tear at the crimson wound.

Cackling vilely, Dahrem clutched the bloody edges and with a deliberate wrench, tore the fur apart.

By the entrance Thomas lowered his sword, unable to believe the gruesome spectacle unfolding before his eyes. Dahrem was insane. The treacherous mouse was tearing his hide clean away, pulling viciously at his own flesh, and a horrendous splitting noise issued from his back as the fur fell in two hideous, shredded scraps.

From his legs the skin snapped as he yanked it loose, shedding it like a snake, and with a final rip, he tore the covering from his head and on to the ground threw Dimlon's pale grey face – ears, whiskers and all.

Woodget cried out and buried his head in his paws but Thomas could not take his eyes from the apparition which now stood facing Captain Chattan and the bile bubbled in his throat.

There, his true, inner nature revealed at last, stood the thing that was Dahrem.

As a lizard he appeared, yet it was an abomination of creation. Wet, slippery, dark green scales covered his repugnant body – from the tips of the forked tail to the squat crown of his square, grotesque head.

Two great lidless eyes bulged from the sloping brow, set above a serpent-like snout, and within the scale-ringed mouth were rows of needle-like teeth, rooted behind a pair of saliva-trickling fangs.

Yet upon his great claws the knives still glittered and he raised them threateningly, the tatters of his mouse's skin clinging about the wrists.

Such was the heinous gift granted to the adepts of Gorscarrigern, for when they willed it they could slough off their mundane, warm-blooded raiment and parade their profane devotion in his honour.

Thomas' terror and revulsion finally overwhelmed him and he staggered through the doorway, unable to gaze on that detestable spectre any longer. On to the stairs he blundered, struggling to master the nausea

swelling inside him, and though he cursed himself, he could not compel his feet to take him back into that chamber.

Down the steps he ran, shaking uncontrollably. Never had he been so afraid and he threw himself into the Holy One's room, sobbing with fright and shame.

Above him, Chattan looked on the hissing abhorrence of Dahrem and his sword quivered, betraying his fear.

From behind his fingers, Woodget peeped out at the dreadful scene and saw the reptilian fiend take a purposeful step forward, beating the cloven tail upon the floor with relish.

'You do well to quail,' Dahrem spat, his tongue flicking between the fangs. 'The wrangling is over and death has claimed you.'

But Chattan's face grew dark and his loathing for the enemy only increased. Seizing the hilt of his sword in both paws, he charged forward but the apparition swerved nimbly and the stroke missed him.

Then Dahrem lunged, his large, smooth head hunched into his powerful shoulders as his haunches bounded over the floor.

The mongoose whirled about, just in time to meet the golden knives with his steel but, divested of his weak guise and waxing in foul might, his opponent was now possessed of an unnatural strength and the captain was driven back towards the wall where Dahrem intended to impale him.

Gritting his teeth, Chattan pushed the blades aside and ducked under the reaching arm, darting behind the crystal plinth which supported the now empty dish.

After him the reptile sprang and, with the pillar separating them, they fought about the circular pool, the captain valiantly matching every mighty stroke. Then, at last, his blade slipped against the raking gold and went crashing into the column of crystal which chipped and shattered – casting a thousand sparkling diamonds into the pool.

But Chattan's sword lodged in the splintered stump and, before he could wrest it free, Dahrem gave a triumphant hiss and the golden knives scored the mongoose's arm.

'Captain!' Woodget cried.

Chattan winced in agony as the venom began its lethal work. Already the blood was frothing from the twin wounds but he steeled himself against the pain and snatched his sword from the fractured crystal.

'Put down your weapon,' Dahrem warned him. 'Such folly will only speed your demise. Feel the poison gnawing at your fibres, Captain – soon it will devour you utterly.'

But the mongoose's face was set and grave and the determined expression caused a flicker of doubt to register on Dahrem's ghastly face.

'I know I am to die,' Chattan snapped. 'But you at least I shall take with me!'

With a yell, he leapt forward, cleaving the air with the sword. Before him, the adept prepared to strike a second time but the tenacity of death possessed the mongoose and his sweeping blows were wild and savage.

Dahrem tried to counter, his glinting blades flashing brightly. But against Chattan's fury there was no withstanding and the captain's sword came scything down upon his wrist.

Screeching, the reptile recoiled but the curved blades fell to the floor with the rest of his severed claws and the screams of his anguish shook the chamber.

Yet the effort had proven too much for the captain. The stinking venom was foaming from his arm and his sword clattered to the floor beside Dahrem's knives.

Then, with a groan of despair, he toppled to his knees and collapsed.

Above him, the adept nursed his bleeding stump and spat upon his withering victim.

'Now we see who is mightier. Your usurping Green has proven to be weak. Go now to his garden in paradise – you will find it rank with thorn and weed.'

At his scaly feet, the captain flinched and the torment of his wounds consumed him.

Then, breathing feverishly, Dahrem turned and his gaze fell upon Woodget.

Still huddled upon the ground, the fieldmouse stared forlornly up at the horror which approached him. The eighth fragment was still clutched in the reptile's claws and its gleaming eyes were fixed upon the bag which contained the ninth.

Woodget's glance shifted to the captain's writhing form and his ears rang with his agonies. Where was Thomas? Why was he not here?

'Give it to me,' Dahrem's hissing voice demanded. 'Your custodianship is ended.'

Woodget gazed at him, then scrunched up his little face as he clung to the leather bag.

'Never!' he wailed.

Dahrem growled, the pain of his truncated wrist had killed any joy this moment might have held. All he wanted was to take both fragments back to the Black Temple – he was not in the mood for any further sport.

'Can you not see the torture that your noble captain is suffering?' he rapped. 'Do you desire the same miserable fate? Shall I retrieve my talons and spike your yokel skin?'

Shivering, Woodget made no answer but waited for the deathblow.

Dahrem sneered. No, he would slay this contemptible maggot without resort to poison. Baring his fangs, he drew a deep breath and lunged for the fieldmouse's neck.

A strangled scream echoed from the mountain and the domed chamber quaked at the dreadful sound.

Quivering, Woodget stared upwards, his terror bursting into relief.

Above him Dahrem's snake-like face bristled with woeful astonishment as he gazed down at the silver blade which now thrust out from a wound in his breast.

Behind him, his courage mastered at last, stood Thomas.

Woodget sobbed for joy and bolted past the incredulous, gasping reptile to be with him.

But Dahrem was neither finished nor beaten; with the mouse's sword still lodged between his ribs, he turned slowly.

'Save us!' Woodget cried. 'He ain't dead.'

'You think you have won?' the choking voice demanded. 'Only Sarpedon conquers all.'

Glowering at them, he took a heavy step forward, flourishing the eighth fragment above his head, and the livid light which beat from the depths of the ancient jade made him appear filled with a power greater than any who breathed mortal airs, and Woodget shrank close to Thomas.

'Into this world His splendour shall come again!' the nightmare exulted. 'His black grandeur shall rise renewed and not a corner of the globe shall be free of His excellent dominion. Nations shall fall and under the Dark Despoiler's guidance I shall govern. Slaughter and death will prevail and He will be supreme. At last the night is falling – an endless darkness to kill the light and this time none shall dare assail Him!'

Hooting with vile laughter, Dahrem threw back his head – yet in that moment, as the fragment blazed with evil glory, his labours proved too much.

The golden treasure became a weight that was too heavy to bear and it pulled him off balance, dragging him backwards. His tail lashing about him, he went crashing against the oval stone which he slammed into with the full force of his stumbling fall.

A tremendous, deafening note sang out as the fragment smote the glassy stone. There erupted a shower of fiery sparks and with an ominous shudder, the great jewel moved. Within its bronze setting the stone shifted, and a cloud of dust and stones poured into the chamber as it began to rock precariously upon the crumbling lip of granite beyond.

Outside the mountain, in the middle of the great likeness's forehead, the glimmering gem trembled and shook.

Inside the domed chamber, Dahrem staggered to his feet. The hilt of Thomas' sword had been driven deep into his back but with fearful eyes he stared up at the tremulous mass of shaped translucent stone that reared above him and lurched as it juddered and tilted dangerously inward.

Suddenly, Thomas rushed forward and, spending all his strength, gave the reptile an almighty shove.

Back Dahrem floundered, his scaly body crashing against the stone a second time and with that his fate was sealed.

Out from the rock the great oval jewel fell and, flailing wildly upon the edge a moment longer, with the eighth fragment still in his grasp, Dahrem toppled after.

Down the mountainside the enormous stone tumbled, smashing on to the immense, sculpted face of the Green Mouse, and a tremendous crack split the night as an entire side of the gargantuan features shattered. With a thunderous clamour of crumbling rock, half of the enormous face dropped down on to the steps far below – hurling tons of rubble into the air.

Thomas and Woodget hastened to the gaping portal, through which the rain was now blustering, and peered down.

Dahrem's hideous, reptilian form plunged through the night – the glare of the fragment gleaming like an emerald flame in his claw.

His terrified screech carried on the gale, he plummeted down, spinning helplessly, until the squalling rain gusted across the mice's vision and they could see no more.

Far the adept of Suruth Scarophion fell, the rushing air screaming in his ears and his forked tail whisking wildly about him. Above him the shattered stone face of the Green Mouse dwindled in the sky but always he kept tight hold of the unhallowed fragment and, bathed in its baleful light, his body struck the bottom of the thousand steps.

At the foot of the mountain, all the forces of the Scale were now assembled. Many were already ascending the stone stairs when the great jewel came thundering down and the sculpture's face split asunder – falling in ruin about them.

In terror they scattered as the steps were broken and buried in an avalanche of rock, then before they had recovered, to their astonishment, they saw a bright green star come falling after and with a bone-crunching crash, Dahrem's shattered body pounded on to the rocks.

Yammering in fright, the cult members gathered around his broken form, recognising it to be one of the great adepts. Even they feared to look on him or venture too close, but down the battered, buried steps the High Priest came and he pushed his way through the clamouring press of the mob to gaze upon Dahrem's corpse.

Into the shadows of his dark hood, the glare of the pulsing jade gleamed and the High Priest let out a covetous hiss.

'The fragment!' he cried.

Stooping over the battered, reptilian body, the High Priest tore the jade shell from Dahrem's claws but even as he held it aloft, to the foul cheers of his followers, Dahrem stirred.

Though the veils of death were gathering about him and his frame was smashed beyond repair, the one who had portrayed Dimlon so cunningly and inveigled his way into the trust of many, let out a gargling sigh and the High Priest raised his claw for silence.

At once a hush fell.

'You have done well, my devoted agent,' the cloaked figure said. 'Your name will be written in the blood of our enemies above the doors of the temple. Our quest is nearly ended. All that remains is to find the ninth and final piece.'

At that, a malignant smile formed on Dahrem's cut and bleeding face.

'The end is indeed here,' he uttered, his speech riddled with pain. 'The last fragment is there – high in the mountain.'

Spinning around, the High Priest squinted up through the darkness then, leaving Dahrem to perish, he swept up the stairs and a legion of Sarpedon's disciples raced after him.

Alone, but surrounded by a circle of his gawping brethren, Dahrem died – his golden eyes staring fixedly up at the damaged vision of the Green Mouse and his dark, seditious soul went shivering into the void.

High above in the domed chamber, as Dahrem gasped his last, another, more tragic, scene was taking place.

Thomas and Woodget knelt by Chattan's side. But there was nothing they could do for the mongoose. Tormented by the agonies of the venom, the captain of the *Chandi* was slipping mercifully into unconsciousness and, pulling the woollen hat from his head, Woodget wept over him.

'Oh Tom!' he cried. 'He's nearly gone – he can't last much longer.'

Through the great oval hole in the curved wall the wind was howling in, tugging at their hair, and Thomas solemnly rose to his feet.

Splashed by the teeming rain he whispered a remorseful prayer over the captain's body then told Woodget to stand.

'We can't stay here,' he said.

But the fieldmouse did not want to leave Chattan, not while there was still a spark of life in him.

'Tom!' he protested. 'Us can't abandon the captain to die on his own. He might speak again afore he goes.'

Thomas leaned down and grabbed Woodget by the shoulders – shaking him forcefully.

'Listen!' he declared. 'It's up to us now. We're the only ones left to keep them horrors out there from getting Mulligan's fragment. Do you think Chattan would want us to linger and get caught?'

Woodget flinched under Thomas' scolding and he shook his head miserably.

'Look Woodj,' his friend said more gently, 'I know this is all my fault. I was the one who made you leave Betony Bank in the first place and sent us both into this mess – but we're here now and there's no way out.

'We can't just go home and forget what's happened. There's a job still to be done and there's no one else but us left to do it. They've all gone – all those who promised to guard us and take this peril off our paws.

392

It's back to you and me now and we can't let them down. Everything's depending on us Woodj – do you understand? Everything!'

Woodget rose and wiped the tears from his eyes. 'Right you are, Tom,' he agreed, wrapping his fingers about the bag's leather straps and hoisting them over his shoulder.

'Let's take that passage through the mountain, but where to then, Tom? Where'll we go then?'

Thomas hurried to the doorway, stooping to pick up the mongoose's sword as he ran. 'There's only one place we can go!' he shouted.

'Where's that?' Woodget cried, racing after him.

At the top of the stairs Thomas paused. 'Singapore,' he said flatly and proceeded to descend to the Holy One's chamber.

Before he followed, Woodget took one last look at Chattan's shrivelling form.

'Goodbye to 'ee, Captain,' he murmured softly, then down the stairs he fled.

15

The Lotus Parlour

*M*other Lotus, or Ma Skillet as she was more commonly called by her customers, sat in her creaking chair behind the bar and puffed on the long stemmed clay pipe she held in her podgy claws.

A hazy fug hung in the claustrophobic, stuffy air, made all the worse by the pungent reek of her smouldering tobacco, and she dabbed a scrap of lace about her fat, sweating neck, then tried to cool herself with a colourful paper fan.

It was a humid June night and the Lotus Parlour was stifling and sticky. Narrowing her thickly lashed and almond-shaped eyes, her gaze roved about the dim room, making sure everyone had something in their cup then she pursed her vermilion lips tartly.

The proprietor of the sleazy establishment, where the riff-raff of the Singapore River came to drink cheap liquor or gamble in one of the discreet alcoves, was a bloated, middle-aged brown rat. Yet the fur which covered her flabby face was powdered white with flour and three beauty spots peppered her left cheek. Fixed in the hair at the back of her head, above the straggly pigtail which dangled past her broad shoulders, was a lustrous blue butterfly, impaled upon a golden pin and through one of her nostrils she wore a silver ring.

It was nearly forty years since she had first arrived on the island from her native China and by now she knew all the sordid histories of each of her regulars. Only when a ship came into the busy port and its unofficial passengers disembarked, did she ever see anyone new come through that grimy door. Yet they were all of the same type: rats and gutter vagrants with meagre coins seeking gut-rotting grog or shady characters who went to whisper in darkened corners.

Drowning their sorrows or carousing drunkenly within the Lotus Parlour's grubby confines, the dregs of Singapore could usually be found. It was a seedy den of a place – the only permanent fixture of the scruffy shanty town where desperate, destitute creatures from all over the globe eventually found their way.

Set into the harbour wall, lost in the deep gloomy shadows of a rickety wooden pier, just above the mud bank and the level of the highest tide, it was a place of ill repute – haunted by cut-throats, pirates and those sorry souls who were past caring what became of them.

Lengths of old sailing canvas, painted with bright and garish colours, festooned the smoke-stained ceiling and hanging from fine threads was a veritable shoal of tropical fish. But all were dried and withered and their natural iridescent colours faded with the accumulated dirt of many years or hidden beneath haphazard splodges of gaudy pigment.

Upon the walls was a kaleidoscope of what were once brilliant macaw feathers, arranged in rayed patterns – but they too were dulled and sullied with layers of dust.

Suspended directly behind the wooden entrance was a pottery bowl that dripped with stalactites of greasy wax. Within its molten interior a bright, tapering flame steadily burned and when any new arrival stepped through the door, their eyes were immediately dazzled so that the patrons could get a good look at them before deciding whether to remain, scurry through the back door or fling a knife at the unwanted interlopers.

The rest of the bar was dimly lit; only a few paper lanterns glowed upon some of the tables, creating cosy caves of subdued colour – but sinister shadows flitted about the cramped niches which were screened by curtains of glass beads, and where unpleasant deals were being made, contraband exchanged and the spoils of river piracy divided.

That night the Lotus Parlour was relatively quiet; the all too familiar ugly rogues were huddled over their drinks: a muttering group of bamboo rats, a filthy, squint-eyed ermine, three sly-looking weasels with scars on their faces and knives in their belts, a Burmese water vole who'd had rather too much of the shady establishment's liquor and several black bilge rats who kept to themselves and spoke to no one.

Ma Skillet viewed them all and yawned. Still, there was always a chance that some fresh, unknown face would come through that door, for a cargo vessel had entered the harbour nearly an hour ago and she knew that eventually its complement of low-life would find its way here.

Drawing on her pipe, she closed her eyes and two wisps of smoke drifted from her nostrils as she thought of the great ceremony that would take place later that night. In a few hours she would have to close up the premises and she reflected on the celebrations that lay ahead. But her reverie was interrupted as a slurring voice was suddenly raised in song.

Pouting with displeasure, she glared through the cloying reek and across the room – to where the Burmese water vole was lifting his wooden beaker and crowing some half-remembered ballad.

Ma Skillet rapped the fan upon the slop-spilt bar, but the vole was too far gone to notice and, removing the pipe from her mouth, she looked around for the young rat she had recently taken into her service.

'Kiku!' her clipped, impatient voice rapped. 'Kiku! Get you here!'

From behind a ragged curtain which covered the entrance to a rancid-smelling kitchen, the face of a handsome rat maiden appeared and Ma Skillet jabbed a fat claw in the direction of the burbling vole.

'Him!' she cried. 'Out you chuck!'

Kiku grinned, not understanding her meaning, and nodded affably.

Ma Skillet fizzled with exasperation and slid from her chair in annoyance. Pulling her frayed silk dressing gown tightly about her so that it bulged and ballooned even more than usual, she lumbered over to where Kiku's pretty face was still beaming and spitefully pulled out one of her whiskers.

The rat maiden squealed and sprang back inside the kitchen, only to be hauled out again by her mistress's strong claws.

'You watch!' Ma Skillet scolded. 'Mother Lotus, she out chuck him.'

Waddling between the tables, the proprietor of the Lotus Parlour blustered towards the vole who greeted her with a rousing chorus of his warbling song until she snatched the cup from him, and seizing the scruff of his neck, frogmarched the bewildered creature to the door where she pushed him out on to the slithering mud.

Clapping her paws together, she returned over the sawdust-covered floor of the bar and said to Kiku, 'You understand?'

The other nodded. 'Ahh, yes Mamma Lotus, he no good – ack! Kiku, she see now, oh yes.'

Ma Skillet rolled her eyes and wondered why she bothered trying to train someone so stupid. There were plenty of others clamouring for the humble bed and board the lowly work offered. Too soft-hearted, that was her failing. Still, keeping such a guileless fool and putting up with her feeble grasp of the common speech amused her regulars and besides, it kept the illusion going for any newcomers and that was all that mattered.

'Empty cups,' she shouted to her, as if by saying it loudly, Kiku would understand it better. 'You fetch them – go.'

The rat maiden had been there long enough to know

what that instruction meant, so pulling the curtain aside she pattered into the bar whilst Ma Skillet settled herself back into her seat and puffed on the pipe.

Through the tables Kiku went, peering into every beaker – scowling at a customer if there was only a drop left in the bottom and nudging him to finish it.

The rough clientele muttered and grumbled under their breaths, but they knew her mistress's eyes were upon them so they made no complaint and yielded their vessels grudgingly.

Kiku collected all she could and returned to the bar where the patrons had to come and pay for them to be refilled.

The young rat maiden was a lovely addition to the Lotus Parlour and that was another reason Ma Skillet put up with her. When she sidled by the tables, those eyes which were not glazed with drink followed her about the dim room.

So far her brief life had been filled with unhappiness and when she had arrived in Singapore, Kiku was alone and down on her luck. Many troubles and heartaches lay behind her and there was nowhere left to run. All she had ever wanted was to find peace and live amongst the friends she had never had, where a warm and gentle sun, that did not scorch or bake, shone over a tranquil corner of the world – that was her dream.

Yet for the moment it seemed impossible and she was grateful for the scraps her mistress left her and, though she did not comprehend all that was said, she strove to learn and improve her comprehension.

Humming to herself, Kiku looked to Mother Lotus to see if there was anything more she could do, but the bloated rat dismissed her with a flick of her paper fan.

Kiku bowed and pattered back into the foul kitchen.

Clenching the pipe between her teeth, Ma Skillet drummed her claws on the bar and those patrons with no cups came sidling over to reclaim them. Smiling, Ma Skillet held out her open palm and not until she had received payment would she refill the beakers with a stinking brown liquid and permit the customers to return to their tables.

Stuffing the coins into a bulging purse attached to the belt of her dressing gown, she leaned back and dreamed of the festivities that she would join later.

Again her musings were curtailed as the entrance swung open and into the light radiating from the suspended candle came two figures.

The bar's buzzing talk died immediately and every ugly head turned to eye the newcomers with suspicion.

Ma Skillet leaned forward, inhaling a deep breath of tobacco smoke as she too scrutinised the two strangers.

They were dressed in long, dark cloaks, their faces concealed by deep hoods, and for several moments they stood by the door blinking in the harsh light until their hidden eyes grew accustomed to it.

The proprietor of the Lotus Parlour arched one of her charcoal-drawn brows. The figures obviously did not want to be recognised, yet she was certain, merely by their stature and bearing, that she had never seen either of them before.

Both were shorter than her usual patrons, so she guessed that they were not rats. The larger of the two seemed quite burly under that mantling cloak but his companion was no bigger than a shrew and curiosity began to burn inside her ample bosom.

Thomas peered about the murky room, his eyes watering in the malodorous atmosphere, and looked for an empty table. At his side Woodget gathered the abundant folds of his hood about his crinkling nose, whilst keeping a tight hold of the bag slung over his shoulder.

Twelve days had passed since their flight from the forces of the Scale in India and looking back over that desperate time they could hardly believe they had managed to survive and evade capture.

Whilst the High Priest and his followers were still searching the mountain, the two mice had hastened down the pitch-black tunnel until they finally came to the city's catacombs. There, among the cold marble effigies of the embalmed dead, they eventually found a climbing road that led to the far side of the city – emerging close to the edge of the deserted harbour.

Fearing they would be sighted at any moment, they daringly stole a small river boat and sailed under the stone archway and into the overgrown waterway.

Behind them in the city, the cult members continued to rampage, burning the buildings, sticking the decapitated heads of the Haran folk on to spears and drinking the blood of those not slain by poison.

Yet in the mountain, though the High Priest hunted and searched, destroying everything in his path, he could not discover the ninth fragment and only when it was too late did he realise the route it must have taken, and in fury he dragged his forces from their revels before they had time to gorge themselves or explore every chink and corner.

On to the *Kaliya* they piled, but by that time Thomas and Woodget had put a great distance between them and concealed by the lashing rain escaped at last to the coast.

Wary of everyone they met, the mice finally sold the small Haran craft at the nearest port, where they then boarded a ship. Now, two vessels later, they had arrived in Singapore and were both extremely weary for the strain of their adventures bore heavily upon them.

The unfriendly silence which greeted their entrance continued long after their vision adjusted to the change in light and they had made their way to the place recently vacated by the unmusical water vole.

Uncomfortably aware of every hostile glance, Woodget sat down but did not let go of the bag's leather straps.

Since departing Hara, neither he nor Thomas had trusted anyone; every creature they met was a possible member of the serpent cult, so they kept their own company and talked seldom in voices above the level of a whisper for fear of being overheard.

'A likelier band of cut-throats I never did see,' the fieldmouse murmured.

Thomas agreed, 'Aye, so remember to leave any talking to me.'

'Does you really think we'll find him here?' Woodget asked doubtfully. 'This don't look the sort of place he'd be at all.'

'No, but someone's bound to have seen him. There can't be many like him I'll warrant. No, if Simoon is in Singapore like the Holy One said, then this is as good a place to start asking as any. But if he's as gifted in the ways of prophecy as everyone seems to think, then he ought to know we're here already.'

'And what if he ain't?' Woodget muttered desperately. 'What does we do then? We can't keep this 'ere nasty bit of goods secret all our lives. Oaks an' ivy Tom, them evil snake worshippers'll find us one day! There bain't no escapin' 'em – they's everywhere! One slip o' the tongue is all it'd take and that's it, we'll end up stone dead.'

Thomas' eyes glittered in the shadow of his hood. 'I know,' he answered solemnly, 'but for the moment there's nowt else we can do. If we're unsuccessful here then we'll just have to go somewhere else.'

'But where?'

'There's always Greenwich, I suppose,' Thomas said softly. 'That's where Mulligan had just come from, remember. He said he'd been to see the Starwife – if we can't find Simoon then she really is our last hope.'

Woodget sighed. 'Least that's back home,' he said, 'an' old Mulligan did say as how it were a good restful place.'

'Well I'll bear that in mind,' Thomas commented.

'But it's a long way back. A long way to keep this 'ere nasty a secret and who knows what Dimmy might have told the rest of his foul folk? Does they know our names? Are they hunting for us?'

'*Maafkan Saya!*' rang a sudden, terse voice behind them.

Startled, the mice looked up and there was Ma Skillet – standing with her claws folded on her breast, her white face staring at them truculently.

'Good evening,' Thomas said politely.

'Ahh,' the fat rat declared, 'you are Britlanders. Many Englishers come here, buy liquor. But they no can stay if no buy liquor.'

Thomas understood and reached inside his cloak for the last of their money. 'Forgive me,' he said, 'we have journeyed far and are very tired, we were not thinking. Could me and my friend have a drink, please?'

The rat pursed her lips; the stranger's manners amused her but she was not to be thwarted in her prying quest for knowledge. The cloaked newcomers interested her and she was determined to discover both their identities and their purpose before closing the bar that night.

'Mother Lotus get good strong quenchers for you,' she said. 'Mister . . . ?'

Thomas pulled the hood from his head and Woodget followed suit. The rosy light from a pink paper lantern fell upon their careworn faces and the rat gurgled with mirth.

'Mouselets!' she cooed and at once the babble of voices recommenced and the uncouth-looking characters around them returned to their business. Mother Lotus had accepted the strangers and that was enough to assuage any suspicions.

'Very splendid strapping fellows,' she continued. 'With good Englisher names, yes?'

The mice looked at one another and Thomas cleared his throat. 'This is Master Cudweed,' he announced, much to the fieldmouse's chagrin. 'And I'm—'

'He's Mister Triton!' Woodget broke in quickly.

404

Ma Skillet bowed to them both, but gave Thomas a lurid wink. 'Triton,' she repeated, relishing the sound on her tongue. 'Very pretty,' and with a chuckle, she trundled away.

'She didn't ask what sort of drinks we wanted,' Woodget hissed.

'I should think they'll only serve one sort anyway,' Thomas replied. 'And what'd you have to go an' tell her I was called Triton for? You know I think it's a stupid name.'

'Least you ain't called after your sister,' the fieldmouse countered. ' 'Sides it suits you. I told 'ee I likes it better'n Stubbs.'

Thomas shook his head. 'Well let's see if she's heard of a travelling fortune teller hereabouts,' he murmured.

Carrying two wooden cups which frothed over with a horrendous brown scum-covered concoction, Ma Skillet returned.

'Mouselets travel big distance,' she said. 'Liquor of Mother Lotus make you strong – send away tired feeling. You drink, you like.'

Thomas took the proffered cup and lifted it to his lips, blowing a clear space through the foaming head before attempting to sample the noxious brew.

Woodget did the same but the large rat's eyes were only turned to Thomas so he merely pretended to drink and hastily put the cup down again.

Ma Skillet watched with delight as Thomas spluttered and choked after his first mouthful and clapped him roughly on the back. 'It's good, yes?' she said proudly.

'Delic . . . delicious,' he lied with a wheeze.

'Clever mouselet,' she laughed. 'You very beautiful fellow. Mother Lotus like you.'

Thomas shifted on his seat and fumbled at his neckerchief. 'Oh?' he mumbled nervously whilst kicking Woodget under the table.

'What you do in Singapore?' she asked, stroking his fine hair in her claws. 'Here, you have more drink.'

She pressed the cup to Thomas' lips and swigging a second detestable mouthful he shuddered and said, 'My friend and me were looking for someone. Weren't we Cudweed?'

Woodget was too busy enjoying Thomas' discomfort. Even after all the terrible perils they had been through and all the hideous sights he had witnessed, he was still able to laugh and had to be asked twice before answering.

'What? Oh yes, that be right,' he said.

'Who you seek?' the rat asked. 'Mother Lotus, she know every peoples.'

Thomas coughed. 'Well,' he began, 'while we were on the cargo ship, we were told there's a fortune teller – a prophet – somewhere roundabouts.'

'Who tell you this?' Ma Skillet asked.

'Oh er . . . a big stoaty chap, weren't it, Master Cudweed?'

The rat took hold of Thomas' paw and held it close to the lantern light. 'You no need teller of fortunes,' she told him with a smile. 'Mother Lotus, she know what lady fate has in store for you.'

Thomas pulled his paw away and quickly took another drink.

Twiddling with the chewed-looking ends of her

pigtail, the rat saw that his cup was nearly empty and went to fetch some more.

'I think we'd best go,' Thomas muttered. 'Let's try somewhere else.'

'She's took a real shine to you, ain't she?' the fieldmouse chortled. 'But you're right. This were a daft idea comin' in here to begin with.'

Rising, they were about to head for the door when Ma Skillet's stern voice cried, 'Where you go? Pretty Triton no have other drink yet. You not leave till you drink. No need pay, Mother Lotus – she buy.'

'That's very kind,' Thomas called, edging towards the entrance. 'But we have to go I'm afraid.'

The corpulent rat smacked the bar with her fist and at once the other customers leered threateningly at the two mice.

'You'd best sit down an' have that other sup of grog with her, Tom,' Woodget murmured. 'We can't get into no fights, we can't afford to have no one stealin' this bag, now can we?'

Thomas struggled to manage a thin, half-hearted laugh and they returned to their seats.

Ma Skillet grunted in satisfaction. The mouse pleased her and although she had no illusions about her own attractiveness, there were ways to get around that.

Pouring a further cupful of brown liquor, she reached under the bar and took from a shelf a small glass bottle containing a fine grey powder which she secretly sprinkled into the drink.

'Now mousey do anything Mother Lotus wish,' she cackled to herself. 'He be liking she very much.'

Whirling around, she sailed back to the table and

pushed the brimming cup into Thomas' paws.

'You drink – then you go, my beautiful mouselet,' she told him.

Thomas took the cup from her and raised it to his mouth.

As soon as the first drop passed his lips, the rat began to whistle a peculiar, haunting tune between her teeth.

It was a mysterious, jarring melody and as she whistled it, her claws weaved through the fug-filled air, tracing weird signs in the drifting smoke.

Woodget watched her curiously. The fat old rat was completely cracked and he wished Thomas would hurry up and finish the horrible mixture so they could get out of there.

The vile-tasting liquor burned in Thomas' throat, but after the first swig the wretched flavour didn't seem half so bad and by the third it was almost palatable. Yet all the while he drank, the eerie trilling tune treacled and seeped into his ears and a prickling sensation tingled over his body as though he were lying upon a bed of nettles.

Draining the beaker to its last dregs, he placed it woozily upon the table then stared about him in a daze.

The pink light that radiated from the lantern appeared brighter than before and flooded a blushing glow into his swimming vision. From some great distance away, or so he thought, he heard Woodget's high voice filled with mounting concern call out, but a wondrous feeling of contentment was seeping into his spirit and there was nothing he could do but yield to its marvellous warmth and welcoming joy.

'Tom!' the fieldmouse cried in consternation when he saw his friend's eyelids droop and a foolish expression spread across his face. 'What be the matter? Wake up, Tom, this ain't time fer a doze. Tom! Tom!'

But to his dismay, Thomas sank deeper into the trance Ma Skillet was weaving about him and she chuckled softly to herself.

'What you doin' to him?' Woodget demanded angrily. 'Ho, Missus, stop. Bring poor Tom out of it.'

The rat glanced at him and the whistling ceased. 'I not harm the pretty mouselet,' she assured him. 'Mother Lotus like have play with he first. He hers now. My tune – it owns him. When I whistle he obey.'

Turning back to the mesmerised Thomas, she brought her face close to his and blew lightly upon it.

'Master Triton,' she called coaxingly. 'Who you see before you? What fair face you keep in heart?'

Thomas' head nodded and swayed as he tried to focus on the flabby visage in front. But the rosy, romantic light crowded in on him, creating an aura of splendour about Ma Skillet's unwieldy features, flickering and lapping over them until they melted and dwindled into a familiar and beloved countenance and he gasped in marvelling surprise.

'Bess,' he murmured.

Woodget stared at his poor friend in misery; how could the rat be so wicked as to torment him in this fashion?

'This bain't right!' he cried. 'Stop it!'

'The amusement end only when Mother Lotus she is bored,' came the harsh reply.

Around the other tables, Ma Skillet's regulars guffawed into their cups to see her toying with the newcomers. The proprietor of the Lotus Parlour might be formidable and they had reason to fear her, but there were infrequent occasions when she provided a riotous and entertaining cabaret.

'Tom!' Woodget tried again. 'Tom – listen to me. This ain't Bess.'

Ma Skillet cackled softly. 'He no hear you,' she said. 'Triton, his ear just for me. When he in trance only my voice and my command do he obey. See how happy Mother Lotus make him.'

A glad smile had alighted upon Thomas' face and with his mind's eye he gazed on the wondrous vision that continued to grow and unfurl before him.

There she was, Bess Sandibrook, sitting in a sunlit meadow of waving grasses and beautiful wild flowers, but no bloom was as lovely or as rare as she.

In her fingers she twirled her glinting, chestnut hair and the light that flashed and gleamed across her mousebrass revelled in her soft brown eyes.

'Hello, Tommy Stubbs,' she greeted in his dream, tossing her head to one side and grinning at him. 'Why'd you go off and leave me all alone like that? I missed you terrible sore I did.'

Thomas' whiskers drooped and a note of distress crept into his whispering voice.

'But I promised you,' he uttered thickly. 'I said I'd go after Woodj. You know that.'

'Well I changed my mind,' the captivating angel told him. 'It's you I want, you're the only one I could ever love, Tommy.'

Woodget turned away as tears streamed down his friend's face and he threw the rat a despising look.

Yet around them the other customers were

hooting and thumping their claws upon the tables in encouragement.

'Forget about Woodget,' the rapturous vision continued. 'Kiss me Tommy – you know you want to.'

Thomas held his breath and reached out to caress the mouse maiden's comely face, but all he touched was the flour-plastered fur of Ma Skillet who leaned forward, puckering up her lips and fluttering her heavy, soot-daubed lashes.

Still under the hypnotic spell, Thomas kissed her revolting lips, unable to smell the stale stench of her fur or the fetor of the rat's putrid breath, and did not see the flour flaking from her face and fall in crumbling deposits upon the floor.

Braying whoops of delight issued from the other patrons and Woodget glared at them murderously.

'Quiet!' he cried angrily. ' 'Tain't funny!'

But they only laughed all the more at his pious squeaking and stamped their feet for further entertainment.

Thomas leaned back dreamily, his nose and cheek covered in white dust and his beaming mouth besmeared with the greasy, vermilion lipstick.

Ma Skillet smacked her lips gleefully and stared around the bar proudly, rocking backward and forward – revelling in her callous teasings.

'You let him go now,' Woodget commanded.

The rat considered Thomas a moment or two more, then shrugged. She had had her fun and there were other, more important matters to think about and arrange.

'Just so,' she nodded. 'Mother Lotus set Triton free.

He must like this damsel very plenty, yes?'

The fieldmouse said nothing but watched sullenly as she lifted her claws before Thomas' face to break the enchantment.

'Bess!' Thomas blurted suddenly. 'I want to come home! When we get rid of this evil, let me come back to you – please!'

Woodget spluttered and stared at Thomas aghast.

'But I'm scared, Bess,' Thomas continued, oblivious to the fieldmouse's calls for him to be silent. 'We've got what the enemy's after. I don't want to be caught and be poisoned like the others. I wish we'd never seen the ninth fragment!'

All around Woodget the room seemed to darken and he swallowed nervously. What had begun as a cruel, teasing game by Ma Skillet had ended in disaster. Now everyone in the bar knew who they were and the evil that they were carrying.

Every hostile face turned in his direction as the raucous mirth ceased, and at last Mother Lotus shifted her gaze to look on Woodget with a steady, deadly light shining in her almond eyes.

'Your friend Triton has big mouth, yes?' she muttered but her feverish breathing betrayed the excitement that was mounting inside her.

Woodget grinned sheepishly. 'Poor old Tom,' he gabbled. 'Gets a bit carried away sometimes, he do. Wunnerful tales he comes up with. You don't want to go a believin' any of them Missus.'

But it was too late and he knew it. The rat drew herself up to her full, squat height and, without taking her eyes off the fieldmouse, clicked her claws.

Immediately the stools and chairs of everyone

else in the bar scraped upon the floorboards and the customers rose behind her – standing tall and threatening in the gloom.

Ma Skillet pointed at the leather bag.

'You show Mother Lotus what you keep in there,' she said coldly.

Woodget scrambled to his feet and gave Thomas an urgent shove. 'Tom,' he cried. 'Quick – Tom. Your sword!'

But Thomas was still under the spell; all he could do was gaze lovingly up at the ugly, bloated rat and murmur shyly to her as though she were the lost sweetheart of his life.

'You give Mother Lotus the bag,' she snapped, a horrible edge grating in her voice.

At that, her brutish clientele began to creep forward, their eyes glinting a bloody red in the lantern light.

Woodget backed away. 'I won't!' he answered flatly.

Ma Skillet sneered and, behind her, the sinister crowd hissed. Then to his horror, the fieldmouse saw that each of their tails was cloven in two. The rats, the ermine, the weasels – each and every one of them was a member of the serpent cult and Woodget felt faint from fear.

The white-faced rat laughed horribly as, from beneath the silk dressing gown, her own tail twitched into view and with a loathsome peeling of flesh it divided – just as Dahrem's had done.

'So,' she crowed hideously. 'From Hara you escape and straight to me you run. Such empty heads you is. Did you not know? Did the big warriors not tell you? Was the tongue of Sadhu still? Know now, here the Black Temple has risen again. You have fled to

414

Sarpedon's own land, Master Cudweed.'

Woodget choked and staggered against the wall in shock. Instead of taking the last fragment to safety, he and Thomas had delivered it straight into the serpent cult's clutches.

Now Ma Skillet's blubbery bulk stood between him and the doorway and he glanced fretfully at the horrendous figures behind her – there was no chance of escape.

'The fragment!' she insisted. 'Mother Lotus will see.'

Advancing with her claws outstretched, the rat checked herself, then tittered as a more entertaining thought struck her.

'But wait,' she chuckled insidiously. 'Poor mousey afraid. If you no give bag to me – then perhaps to Triton you will.'

Turning back to Thomas, Ma Skillet commanded him to stand and still under the sway of her foul arts, the mouse obeyed.

The almond eyes glimmered with a golden light as the rat bent her power upon him and slowly, Thomas drew the sword from under his cloak.

'No,' Woodget cried as his friend advanced towards him with closed eyes. 'Tom! Wake up! It's me – Woodget Pipple!'

Ma Skillet cackled. 'You give bag to Triton,' she told him.

Thomas strode closer and the tip of the sword blade was brought ever nearer to the fieldmouse's chest.

'Now,' the rat uttered viciously, 'stab he through the heart.'

Woodget stared into Thomas' face, but he was totally dominated by the infernal influence of Mother

Lotus and the blade pressed painfully against his breastbone.

A trickle of blood pricked from the fieldmouse's skin and seeped into his reddish gold fur as his bewitched friend prepared to thrust the blade deep into his body.

'Tom . . . !' Woodget wailed. 'Please!'

Not knowing what he was doing, Thomas drew back the sword and plunged it forward.

At once there was a blistering light as the sword burst into blue flame and, before it could pierce the fieldmouse's flesh, the steel vanished in a shower of silver stars, leaving Thomas to stumble forward – blinking and shaking his head in a confused daze.

Woodget wept and rubbed the shallow wound in his chest then turned to Mother Lotus who was shrieking in fury.

'What happen?' she squawked. 'Where sword go?'

Behind her, in the bar, the group of bamboo rats suddenly began to snarl and as one they lunged forward – only to fall back in dismay as a burst of emerald light flared into the gloom and tongues of turquoise flame came leaping into their midst. Yowling in terror, the creatures cowered from the scorching fires which formed a searing and impenetrable barrier between them and the entrance.

Confused, Ma Skillet whisked around at their yammering, amazed at the supernatural inferno which separated them – then above the din a resonant voice rang clear and defiant.

'Be still, servant of the twining tyrant – lest you are thrust into the hottest part of the flames and your wickedness melted clean off your bones.'

416

At the sound of that voice, Thomas was released and he rubbed his eyes to stare about him. 'What's going on?' he cried.

But Woodget was hopping up and down with joy and punched the air with his small pink fists.

Standing in the open doorway, with a great, bulging pack upon his back, was a diminutive and startling figure, but to the mice his presence was more welcome than a whole legion of Haran warriors.

Clothed in the familiar crimson velvet gown, embroidered with golden symbols – was Simoon.

In one paw he clasped his staff, whilst the other was raised to ward off anything that might be hurled at him, magical or otherwise.

Ma Skillet glared at the jerboa with absolute contempt. How dare he interrupt her? Who was he to interfere in the business of the Scale?

Compared to her flabby bulk, he was little more than a sand flea, yet she could see that about the rayed stars which surmounted Simoon's black and silver staff, a pale light glowed and glimmered.

Obviously there was more to him than his outer appearance suggested, yet she was not afraid or daunted – the same was true of her also.

'I am come to liberate my young friends,' Simoon's calm, assured tones told her. 'Do not hinder me or your hide will shrivel.'

Ma Skillet planted her feet wide apart and took from beneath her dressing gown a golden dagger, decorated with the image of a twisting serpent – engraved with words of power and control.

'It is you should fear,' she hissed menacingly. 'You foolish to enter here.'

Growling, she strode toward him, but the jerboa merely chuckled and tapped his staff upon the ground.

To the rat's astonishment, the dagger flew from her claw and went flying across the bar, plunging through the flames and over the heads of her frightened and scorched patrons, before embedding itself deep into the far wall.

Incensed, she sprang at him but, with a wave of his paw, her bloated body was thrown back by an unseen force which propelled her into a stack of chairs that came crashing about her head.

Ma Skillet slithered to the ground where her obese weight pounded upon the floorboards. Then, with a smile lighting his enigmatic face, Simoon bowed to Thomas and Woodget.

'Come,' he told them. 'Whilst the creature composes herself and her crew are held back by the flames, let us depart.'

The mice hurried over to him. 'See Tom!' Woodget cried. 'I always knowed he were a real magician. Mister Simoon, we got the ninth fragment—'

'Hush,' the jerboa instructed, 'save the tale for friendlier surroundings. Your plight is not yet ended – this is a hazardous place and you might have done great evil by coming here. To thine own land you should have returned and taken the Irish nomad's burden to the Handmaiden of Orion for safekeeping and wise counsel – not into the very den of the enemy and certainly not on this most perilous of nights. Let us pray we can yet repair the damage wrought by your folly.'

'Alas,' came a shrill voice, 'the harm is done and you have lost.'

Simoon and the others turned and striding through the open doorway came the dishevelled figure of the water vole whom Ma Skillet had previously thrown out.

Yet now all traces of intoxication were banished from his bearing and a haughty disregard was upon his face.

'Did you truly believe your journey from Hara was unmarked?' he asked Thomas incredulously. 'The lidless eyes of the Scale are not so blind. It was I who allowed you to venture here unmolested, but now the trap is sprung and your emissaries ended.'

Woodget eyed the ragged-looking creature curiously; there was a vile, deriding quality to that voice which was strangely familiar.

Then the vole raised its paw and, over the threshold, dim threads of gloom came seeping. Into the Lotus Parlour they streamed, to entwine and curl about the stranger, gathering into an inky darkness which swiftly enveloped his unkempt form until his shape began to shimmer and stretch.

'Green's grace, deliver us,' the jerboa murmured, and to Thomas and Woodget's consternation there was fear in his voice and his paws were trembling.

Before him the unnatural column of swirling blackness reached up to the ceiling and then, with a trembling of the air the blackness fell away in light strangling ripples, but the vole was nowhere to be seen.

Woodget caught his breath, for there, in the creature's stead there now towered a menacing and sinister figure swaddled in a black, hooded cloak.

With a sweep of his powerful claws he cast the

garment from his head and lit by the glare from the crackling turquoise flames, a hideous, sadistic face was revealed and the mice gasped in fright.

Like a piece of the blackest night, he appeared – a living embodiment of darkness, the essence of the deepest well of shadow given visible form and clothed in mortal flesh.

A sable from the remote northern wastes was he, and his sharp, arrogant features were richly clad in his sleek, luxuriant fur.

Within the glossy darkness of that gaunt, raven visage, the two narrow slits of his eyes burned a fierce yellow and gold – blazing with monumental malice and unquenchable hatred.

Above his glowering brows reared a high, domed forehead and scraped tight over his skull, a mass of dark hair fell about his shoulders.

Disdainful and sneering, his awful, wedge-shaped face distorted with pride and unbridled conceit as he stared down at the three forlorn figures and when his thin lips parted, a row of savage, cruel fangs shone white and sharp.

'At the last we meet,' his malevolent, nasal tones addressed the jerboa and the mice cringed at the sound of it for now they recognised that pitiless voice. Upon the steps of Hara they had first heard its discordant bragging – for there, standing before them, was the High Priest himself.

'Many times have I sensed your presence,' his foul voice continued to snipe at Simoon, 'striving to part the veil in your furtive yet clumsy attempts to seek me out from afar and observe my movements. Such childish antics you do engage in. I trust my deeds have kept you entertained – for assuredly they have not assisted you in any way.'

Simoon stared up at him, jutting out his chin defiantly. 'Hold your duplicitous tongue, shadow of the serpent,' he cried, but his voice was thin and woeful. 'Meddle not with the wanderer of the ancient pathways; the treader of the forgotten track will not be merciful to such a one as you. Yet even now it is not too late. If you abandon the hellish ways of your foul demon and embrace the true giver of life and hope then even you could be spared.'

'Into the eyes of your death do you gaze!' the sable snorted. 'Yet you persist in this puerile cant! You have wasted enough time, old one, the days of your flitting across the oceans and weaving your asinine webs are over. The end of your reviled world has come and the second reign of the Glorious Master is dawning.'

Glancing over to where the turquoise flames still blazed, the High Priest muttered under his breath and at once the fires were doused.

From the floor, amid the splintered wreck of the chair stack, Ma Skillet picked herself up and waddled over to bow low before him.

'Forgive me Brother Priest,' she said feeling awkward. 'Mother Lotus, she not know you before.'

The sable returned the bow. 'You were not meant to,' he replied in a boastful drawl. 'When the High Priest of Sarpedon walks in the guise of another, no eyes may pierce the shadows of his deceit. Do not upset yourself, sister. Though perhaps one day I might return the discourtesy of that rude expulsion, the High Priestess has done well. The Mighty One will be most pleased. This fateful night the rejoicing will be greater than we ever imagined.'

Tracing a curious sign in the air with his claws he held out his palm, then, from the far wall, her dagger jerked itself loose and came floating back for him to catch and he returned it to the corpulent rat, before looking back at Simoon.

'Such simple feats are mere party tricks,' he cackled scornfully. 'But is that the height of your wisdom, little burrower of the sand? You ought to have remained in the dry desert instead of daring to come between the Dark Despoiler and his rebirth. That was a task beyond the measure of your base talents.'

'Beware the wrath of Simoon the prophet and obeah pilgrim,' the jerboa told him. 'If you will never renounce the Coiled One, then the ninth and final fragment of Gorscarrigern's most infernal work I shall withhold from your grasp. By the power of the Green I deny it to you and though the nine stars may blaze for an eternity, neither you nor your descendants will ever see the egg made whole nor witness any rebirth of ancient horrors.'

Lifting his staff above his head, he called out in a loud, ringing voice, *'Neri Arkitchu Berakka!'* and at once the room was ablaze with a dazzling explosion of fierce blue energy.

Ma Skillet shrieked in dread as the blinding bolts blistered about her, and the rest of the cult members recommenced their yammering.

Clasping his paws together, Woodget stared about him, transfixed and enthralled by the fabulous display of the jerboa's strength and at his side, Thomas was finally convinced that the magician was no fraud.

All about the seedy bar the searing spikes of sapphire flame rampaged, driving the rats, weasels and ermine insane with terror, but in the middle of the miraculous, fiery spectacle, encompassed by Simoon's unleashed might, the High Priest loomed tall and unafraid.

Summoning his dark strength, he reached up with his claws and his eyes were shot with his own diabolic, blighting flame. Throwing back his head, he let out a hideous string of words and the jerboa cried out in alarm.

For a terrible moment the two powers grappled with each other. Around the High Priest, black lightnings burst into existence, clashing ferociously with Simoon's blistering forces, and the prophet yelled in anguish as though tormented with great pain. On they battled and the room erupted with both brilliance and absolute night – but in the end, it was the High Priest who had the mastery and with a piteous wail, Simoon fell back defeated.

With a spitting of black sparks, the tip of the silver-spiralled staff split asunder and even as the jerboa clutched at it for support, the magical device withered and crumbled into a heap of ashes upon the floor.

Darkness returned to the Lotus Parlour and Woodget stared at Simoon in despair.

Out of breath, his strength and power spent, the prophet wilted and fell senseless to the ground – leaving Thomas and Woodget to face the High Priest alone.

The sable laughed, but it was a hollow, mirthless sound and the mice shivered before it.

Licking the blade of the dagger, Ma Skillet eyed

them hungrily and her stomach rumbled.

'Curb your appetite,' the High Priest warned. 'These two unpledged morsels who have carried the ninth and final fragment must be given over to Our Lord at his renewal. Their blood shall slake his age-old thirst. Take them!'

Obediently, his followers scurried forward to seize Thomas and Woodget by the wrists and with a triumphant leer upon his imperious face, the sable tore the leather bag from the fieldmouse's paws.

'You can't have that!' Woodget squealed, but it was no use.

Violently, the High Priest struck him across the face and even as Thomas flew at him with his fists raised, they were gripped by the three scar-faced weasels and the fieldmouse was held by two great bilge rats.

'Bind the stupid fools and take them to the boat,' the High Priest said coldly, 'and be certain to bring the poor, infirm prophet along. I should like him to witness the magnificence of this night.'

And so, kicking and struggling, the mice were dragged from the Lotus Parlour, then one of the bamboo rats cut the straps of Simoon's pack and hoisted his unconscious form on to a bony shoulder before following the others outside.

Alone with Ma Skillet, the High Priest lifted the fieldmouse's bag and, closing his eyes to savour the moment, reached inside.

With a sudden livid radiance, the sickly light that glowed from the jade fragment shone out within the room and the sable let out a great, glad sigh as it flowed over his hatched-like features.

Languidly, his eyes opened and he gazed

enamoured upon the meticulously crafted segment in his claws.

'So, little Dahrem was right,' he murmured. 'He did indeed discover the whereabouts of that which our enemies have long kept secret. It is well he perished in Hara for never would I have permitted him to claim the honour of finding this most beautiful thing. Now it is my name that shall be written in blood above the pillars of black marble, my name that Suruth Scarophion shall praise above all others, for now I am the instrument of his deliverance.'

At his side, the bloated, white-powdered rat took a wondrous breath as if trying to inhale the loathsome loveliness of that most miraculous sight.

'Now the tally, it complete,' she uttered. 'The Black One – he return.'

A foul grin split the sable's crow-black face and he stared out of the door into the shadows that lay beneath the wooden pier, then beyond to a patch of the clear ebon night.

'Nine bright stars from out the void, shining up on high,' he chanted in a whisper, 'whose banished soul do they call back and augur in the sky? Despoiler of the ancient lands, who baked the deserts dry. Scarophion, Scarophion – the demon is close by.'

Mother Lotus hung her head respectfully. 'This night he come back,' she murmured reverently. 'The Dark Sovereign, he return.'

'Yes,' the High Priest answered, caressing the gleaming gold traceries with his claws, 'after all this long, lonely time, the ages of his exile are complete. The fate of the world is set and a new darkness is about to commence. Come, to the Black Temple!'

Swirling his cloak about him, he strode into the night and, stealing a final glance at the place she had endured for nearly forty years, gathering information and claiming the itinerants whom no one would miss to feed the sacrificial altars, Ma Skillet waddled after.

An unusual quiet descended within the bar; the place which normally buzzed and seethed with the dark underbelly of Singapore life was silent and still. Only the candle flame as it guttered in the breeze which streamed through the open door made any sound, its wax dripping a steady tattoo upon the floor.

Then, at the rear of the dim, lantern-lit place, a movement stirred the ragged curtain and from the rancid kitchen the face of Kiku emerged and fear was frozen upon her features.

Hiding in the back, forgotten by all, the rat maiden had heard everything that had transpired and, peeping through a rent in the curtain, had seen the nightmarish and frightening events that had occurred since the arrival of the High Priest.

In paralysed terror she had remained out of sight and mind but now she roused herself and crept through the bar, mortally afraid.

Even in Morocco, the country of her birth, she had heard the rumours and legends of the serpent cult and though she did not understand everything that she had heard tonight, she had wits enough to piece the meaning together.

Warily, she pattered to the entrance and peered out, pulling her head smartly in again as she saw a long rowing boat being pushed down the mud towards the river's edge.

Out on to the Singapore River the vessel was drawn

426

by the great bilge rats until it was caught by the tide and lifted upon the water. Before Ma Skillet's considerable figure, the High Priest sat, his dark form already invisible in the murk, and at the front of the craft, trussed up with many ropes and cords – were the small outlines of Thomas, Woodget and Simoon.

As the bamboo rats took hold of the oars and dipped them into the dark water, the boat pulled away from the muddy banks. Into the dim distance it sped and the doom that awaited them all gathered each one into its grim and terrible charge.

When she was certain the danger was past, Kiku looked about her, wildly wondering what she could do and where she could go. It was plain that her brief existence here was over and after everything that she had witnessed there was nothing that could have induced her to stay. Then as her mind raced, she noticed the jerboa's large pack lying on the ground and cautiously, she scurried over to examine it.

Presently, the prophet's precious and peculiar belongings were scattered about the bar as she hauled each new piece of mystical paraphernalia from the pack to scrutinise and speculate on its esoteric function.

Draping a length of richly embroidered material about her shoulders and inspecting the pictures drawn on Simoon's cards, she shuddered to think to what terrible end his uncanny profession had ultimately guided the unfortunate jerboa.

In spite of her urgent fears, Kiku wondered what her life would have been like if she had been granted the divine gift of foreknowledge. The rat maiden drew the patterned cloth about her, assuming a superior, all-knowing pose as though she were cloaked in a mantle of mystical power and sorcery – possessed with the fathomless wisdom of the ancient magicians.

Then the fantasy ended and the embroidered fabric fell from her shoulders as she stood stock-still for she was struck by a sudden revelation and in that instant everything became clear to her.

To all intents and purposes these marvellous things belonged to her now. It was no use expecting the jerboa to come back for them, not where he was heading. She could take off with them and who would decry her? Her life could blossom anew; this was her chance to start again and her blissful destiny would soar to staggering heights. The map of her life spread out before her and she knew the path she must tread. A fortune teller she would become; no one could possibly know that she was ignorant of such arts for now she had all the apparatus she needed to fool them. With her sharp wits she would be able to bluff her way through anything and, if the fates were kind, perhaps one day she would be given true power.

Hastily, Kiku stuffed as many of Simoon's magical possessions as she could into a sack, then hurried to the entrance.

A pang of guilt rankled her conscience as she saw the vague shape of the boat dwindle in the distance. But what could she do for the three prisoners it held? In this savage place there was nothing but brutality and though for a brief moment the wild fancy entered her head that she could follow her former mistress and rescue those unfortunates by herself, with a click of her tongue she dismissed the thought as madness.

428

To add to the captives' deaths with her own would achieve nothing. No, Kiku would flee – escape that friendless and barbaric region where the fork-tails lived.

Glancing once more at the darkness that lay over the river, the rat maiden left the bar and scampered away, filling her remorse-ridden mind with anything she could think of in order to blot out the awful thoughts that were forming there. A hideous fate awaited those two small mice and the jerboa, but she tried not to dwell on such horrors, for she knew that they would only torment her. So, concentrating instead on the new life that she envisioned for herself, she hurried into the gloom – dreaming up impressive sounding titles for this excellent vocation.

Her real name she would keep, even though Mother Lotus could never pronounce it correctly. But although it was exotic enough, her title needed extra flourish and flair, a grandiose term to impress her clients – similar to the distinctive 'Mother Lotus'.

'Gypsy?' she muttered, running under the rickety pier's shadow and scuttling along the shore. 'Sayer of sooth? Ack – no. Lady, Witch, Princess, Madame? Hmmmm . . . yes, Madame – it sound good.'

And with that, Madame Akkikuyu disappeared into the night, leaving the terror of the Scale behind her as she embarked upon her new and lifelong career.

As the rowing boat journeyed out of the river, into the bay and on to the sea beyond, Thomas looked up at the foul face of the High Priest and was engulfed in despair.

At his side, Woodget was sniffling, thinking about

how bitterly they had failed. Everything they, Mulligan, Chattan and the entire population of Hara had striven for had come to nothing. The battle to keep the fragment from the disciples of Scarophion had ended calamitously and as Thomas' forlorn gaze travelled upwards to the black, cavernous night, his desolation and hopelessness deepened.

Overhead, glimmering in the heavens, shining wanly in the radiance of the bright full moon, nine points of pricking light were gleaming in a twisting, serpentine constellation that he had never seen before.

The stars of Sarpedon were already beginning to blaze, heralding the return of the Dark Despoiler's spirit to the living plane and in that bleak hour, Thomas' spirits were utterly vanquished.

The cult of the snake had beaten them all.

16

The Black Temple

O ver the waters the rowing boat sailed and when they were far from shore the High Priest unfurled his cloak and gazed lustfully upon the ninth fragment once more, imagining the glory that awaited him under his unhallowed sovereign's slaughterous regime.

Into the night the lurid glow pulsed, flickering in the gentle waves that surrounded the small craft and, by its ghastly light, Thomas saw the sable's hideous face flood with an expression of supreme, malevolent delight.

Unable to look upon him any longer, Thomas tried to turn away, shifting his bound body on to its side and in that uncomfortable position, with the ropes that bound him biting into his arms and wrists, he peered over the prow of the boat and stared curiously ahead of them.

Beside him, in a meek and fearful voice, Woodget asked, 'Where they takin' us, Tom? I be real scared. There bain't no hope fer us, be there?'

'No, Woodj,' Thomas replied sadly. 'None at all this time, we're reaching the end of our voyage at last. I'm sorry I let you down.'

The fieldmouse wriggled his nose. ' 'Tweren't your fault, Tom,' he lamented, 'even old Simoon weren't no match fer that there villain. Does you think he'll recover before – before whatever they got planned?'

Thomas looked across him to where the jerboa still lay in a swoon and muttered under his breath, 'It's probably better if he doesn't.'

Directly behind them, the bilge rats continued to heave on the oars and the boat shot unerringly through the dense night until Thomas began to see black shapes appear in the shadowy distance. As they drew closer, he saw in the soft moonlight that they were jagged spears of rock which reared up from the ocean bed, clustering in a lethal, bitter reef.

Yet straight towards them the rowing boat sped and with every pull on the oars the danger swept nearer. Such was the hazard of the barbed, biting rocks that many of the outlying perils lurked just below the surface of the waves, as if they were deliberately waiting to rip and tear into an unsuspecting hull. But beyond them, others reached from the water in deadly, spiked pinnacles; some were so large that they were almost like craggy islands and upon their ridges and within the gaping clefts, sea birds nested.

Up to the perimeter of the submerged stone teeth the rats steered the boat, yet this was a journey they had made a thousand times and their wicked, cunning minds knew the location of each murderous rock. Skirting around the edge of the unseen snags and spines, the craft veered in a wide circle until, with a sudden raising of the starboard oars and straining upon those of the port side, they jolted to the left and shot into a natural channel which divided the reef in two.

In spite of his dread, Thomas was forced to admire the skill with which the rats navigated their way through the deadly formations which now reared from the sea around them as they pressed ever deeper into the centre of the rocky continent.

Through narrow waterways, between spires of stone, the little boat went, winding through a maze of secret shallows, and not once did the keel touch or scrape against any of the savage, lurking boulders.

With his head twisted to the front, Thomas eventually saw an island of rock, larger than the rest, emerge from behind the surrounding, jagged fences and it was this which they were heading towards.

Like a hill of bare, uneven stone the island appeared, a great and solid mass that sat hunched and immovable in the ocean. Situated at the centre of the vast reef, surrounded by the forest of its inferiors it was as though that titanic bulk was the grandsire of the lesser formations, as if they had sprung from its vastness.

Thomas hated the sight of it; the island repelled and frightened him. It was as if a dark, malice-filled spirit possessed the very stones of the place; horror and evil flowed across the water from its clefts and crags and, trembling, the mouse hung his head.

Stark and black against the milky moon, the huge,

brooding island was crowned with turrets of needling rock that gleamed like the upraised spears of a barbaric host. Over its grim surface, dark caves gaped like sightless eyes and, yawning over the water like a massive, screaming mouth, stretched the entrance to an immense and cavernous interior.

Up to this pitch-dark mouth the rats rowed the boat and as soon as they passed into its sombre shadow both Woodget's and Thomas' flesh crawled and they were chilled to the marrow.

Yet under that terrible entrance the little craft journeyed, vanishing into the obliterating gloom as the rock towered over them and all Thomas could see were the eyes of the High Priest glinting with a pale, greedy light.

Deep into the island they travelled and the sound of the oars splashing in the water echoed wildly around the enormous, night-swamped space.

Then Thomas began to see strange shapes glimmering in the darkness. Around them there were the vague outlines of other vessels, all moored to the rocky wall, and finally their own boat sailed beneath a great ship with golden timbers and high over the mice's heads reared the prow of *Kaliya*, the ship of the Scale. But its decks were deserted and its glittering anchor cast out upon the rocky bed far below.

'Where are we, Tom?' Woodget's plaintive voice whimpered.

'Some kind of harbour, I reckon,' his friend answered. 'This must be their lair.'

With a jarring bump, the boat drew alongside the roughly hewn wall and the rats and weasels yanked in the oars.

Then, as the ermine was tying the craft to a rusted iron ring set into the rock, the High Priest rose and his cloak-enfurled figure sprang on to a flight of stone steps which led up from the water's edge.

Clumsily, Ma Skillet lurched to her feet and the boat tilted alarmingly as her great weight rocked it. Quickly, one of the bilge rats helped her out and with a toss of her pigtail, she gracelessly disembarked.

Ascending to the top of the steep flight, as Ma Skillet lumbered after, the High Priest turned and pointed to the three captives who remained below.

'Bring them,' his shrill voice commanded, and with that the sable spun on his heel and, with his bloated High Priestess waddling in pursuit, he vanished into the darkness and there came a resounding clang of metal.

In the boat, Thomas and Woodget saw the ugly faces of three bamboo rats come leering into view above them and claws as sharp as knives bit into their skin as they were hauled up and flung heedlessly over their shoulders before being heaved up the steps, their heads smacking against the rats' bony backs.

In single file the rats went, clambering up the stairs, following the path their comrades and their leaders had taken. Along the narrow ledge that ran around the dismal harbour, they went: the rat bearing Thomas going first, then the brute who bore Woodget and finally the one carrying Simoon's limp and senseless body.

'Ha – you poxy maggot!' cackled the green-fanged rat in the middle, speaking in their own foul language and jiggling the fieldmouse upon his shoulder as he pinched him cruelly. 'A fine treat yer in fer now, though I don't suppose it'll be to your dainty taste.'

'What's that, Belto?' called the ragged-eared one carrying the jerboa. 'An' you think it'll be to yours? Didn't you see what the High One robbed from these three bits of wholetail scum?'

'Gnyarr!' the rat snarled back. 'What of it, Seska?'

'It were only the last bit of that treasure they an' all their blood-curdling adepts have been searching fer all this time. Pyerr! Didn't that old soak of a father ever tell you owt before he was gutted by Ma Skillet for sickin' on her floor?'

'So they found what they been looking fer,' Seska snapped back. 'Should make it all the easier fer us. Maybe now we'll get a bit of a rest – some proper grog for a change, not her dishwatery slops.'

Belto snorted and spat a glob of yellow phlegm down into the water. 'Always were gormless, weren't you!' he muttered. 'The fighting won't stop now. The wars are only beginning. Don't you know what them shiny fragments are?'

'I only does what I'm told,' Seska replied. 'It's best not to go pokin' your snout into the High One's affairs – I seen too many get spiked by the great adepts fer doin' just that.'

Belto grunted. 'You're a fool,' he declared. 'From tonight it'll all change, an' fer the worse – cause *Him*'s coming back. Yes, the snaking devil himself. All them old tales, all that plaguey history they ram down our throats at these musterings, where you get soused on blood an' liquor – they're all true and tonight you'll see it fer yourself.'

Seska said nothing, but Woodget could feel him quaking and found it terrifying that even the servants of Gorscarrigern feared the thought of their infernal lord's return.

The rats lapsed into silence but they did not venture much further before the ledge ended and the way was barred by an iron door.

A clangorous report echoed about the cavernous harbour as the rat bearing Thomas gave the door a fierce kick and it swung open to reveal a slightly wider passage beyond which was lit by flickering torchlight.

Into this dipping way the prisoners were carried and the path twisted and turned for some distance before abruptly, when they turned a corner, a fierce radiance welled up and the tunnel opened out into a monstrous chamber.

Thomas squirmed in the rat's grip to see where they had been brought and his eyes grew wide in amazement.

In the very heart of the great, lonely island, generations of the serpent cult had toiled with chisels and hammers, quarrying out the rocky centre, expanding the existing caves and creating a monumental cavern in which they had raised again the altar of Suruth Scarophion – dedicating it with the blood of his enemies.

Here then, was the second Black Temple – a shrine of despair to replace the profane cathedral which was destroyed in the great long ago when the combined host of the Green conquered and slew the serpent god's mortal flesh.

Since that distant, cataclysmic time, the followers had worked long in secret and as their numbers swelled, the devotees and skilled paws of their slaves had laboured with unceasing fervour to recall the diabolic glory of that first and most terrible of heathen temples.

From the floor of solid rock, a wide flight of steps, which spanned the entire length of that gargantuan space, rose with regal majesty to a raised platform where four massive pillars of black marble towered upwards to support the lofty ceiling.

Wide as the trunks of ancient trees was the girth of those mighty columns and bands of gold encircled their stupendous heights. Beyond them, in the main sanctum of the unholy shrine, the walls were set with precious gems and the hellish glare of a hundred ruby-encrusted lamps bathed the place in a scarlet light.

To the rear of the temple, upon a raised dais that was black with the age-old gore of countless sacrifices, stood the altar stone and high above that, where the vaulted roof towered out of the reach of the garish lantern light, the chamber was open to the sky.

A vast and perfect circle gaped in the chiselled rock and through it streamed the light of nine bright stars.

Yet the whole panorama of this awesome, reviled spectacle was nothing compared to that which dominated the entire, horrible scene and Thomas cringed when he beheld it.

Rearing higher than the towering pillars, up to where the roof melted into the darkness, was a colossal and nightmarish statue.

Over the marble floor its sculpted body writhed – coiling about the columns, its tail tapering into a twisting loop before the altar. Yet rising to the ceiling, the arched neck touched the rock then curved down again to culminate in an abhorrent fearsome head which surveyed the temple below with fiery eyes.

Here was the gigantic image of Sarpedon the Mighty – the Dark Despoiler of the Eastern Lands whose name meant Death and whose reign was darkness.

Fashioned in loving, dreadful detail, the likeness had taken longer to construct than the temple which housed it. Each of the innumerable scales were painstakingly wrought from the purest gold and the patterns which adorned the length of its frightful body were picked out with emerald and sapphire.

Never had Thomas witnessed such a foul monstrosity as the head which loomed through the central pillars. As great in size as *Kaliya*, the ship of the Scale, was that repulsive, glittering aberration. The rubies which shone in place of the eyes were as large as himself and the open jaws were crammed with teeth of black steel. But the two huge fangs which protruded from that horrendous mouth were tipped with diamonds and from the depths of the throat a great black smoke issued, for fires were constantly kept ablaze in the serpent's belly and the reek streamed upwards – obscuring the ceiling in a canopy of choking fumes.

Before the face of that hideous idol, the worshippers of Gorscarrigern would fall to their knees and offer up their blasphemous prayers, for it inspired them with terror and the very mention of His evil, exalted name was enough to instil them with dread. It was said that this ghastly image was but a fraction of their lord's true horror, that His earthly form was many times the greater – and that thought alone filled them with devout, demented despair.

Staring up at the terrifying spectacle, Woodget shut

his eyes and turned away, back to the relative darkness that spread before the wide marble steps upon which their captors were standing. Yet when the fieldmouse opened his eyes again he uttered a whimpering groan – the unbounded gloom which stretched below the temple was not empty.

Within that pagan place, crammed inside that tremendous cavern, the assembled host of Gorscarrigern's followers was gathered, and the sight made Woodget's blood run cold.

Thousands upon thousands of squint-eyed, malignant creatures were jostling and squirming in the murk. In that great, hollow space their thronging, stinking bodies were crowded and not a chink nor a gap of room was there between them.

With a putrid light their eyes sparkled, glinting in the reflected glare of the fiery lanterns, and as a shimmering, stagnant sea it appeared.

Never had Woodget seen so many diverse creatures massed together before. Towards the front the smaller creatures had congregated and in the infernal glare he recognised rats, stoats, squirrels, shrews, martens, weasels, ermine, mice, voles and marmots – to his mournful surprise he saw that there were even some mongooses down there. But behind them, the larger members of the despicable cult were crouched – waiting for the ceremony to begin.

There he saw foxes and hyenas, even a number of monkeys – yet in the deep darkness beyond, his sharp glance picked out the squat shapes of four crocodiles and his mind flew back to the attack on Hara.

Shifting his gaze, he saw that the walls of the cavern were carved into terraces and there too the hordes were pressed and wedged in tightly. Then lifting his face, he saw high above, perched upon shelves of rock, were many flocks of carrion birds.

At appointed times in the year the host of Scarophion's worshippers would make their way to this unhallowed place to hear the fearsome words of the High Priest as he read the black scriptures and witness the dreadful rituals of their nightmare lord.

That night they had all come expecting the revels to be high and overflowing with blood, for never in any of their lives had the constellation of Sarpedon appeared in the firmament and their pledged souls thrilled to the knowledge that the nine stars meant their evil sovereign was close to the living plane.

The atmosphere within the enormous chamber was rank and stale. The hot, stinking breath of the expectant congregation mingled with the burning reek that flowed from the golden idol's mouth and the corrupt foulness was so strong that Woodget could almost taste it.

When the pagan multitude saw the three prisoners carried from the doorway at the side of the great steps they jeered and sent up a vile clamouring – yelling gruesome curses and horrific oaths then laughing to see the mice's terrified faces.

Thomas looked on the mustered legions in dismay; their calls rang in his ears and he wished that he had been spared the sight of them, envying Simoon's unconscious state. All he, Woodget and the jerboa could possibly hope for now was a swift and painless death but he knew that such a blessing would be denied them. The High Priest would not end their lives so mercifully; no, most likely he would cast them to the mob to be torn to shreds by their claws or perhaps he had contrived an even more terrible fate for them.

Without ceremony the three rats carried the captives up the steps until they were standing between the two central pillars with the ghastly golden head of the statue rearing directly above them. Then the mice and Simoon were thrown to the floor and the rats went scampering back down the stairs to join their comrades below.

Lying face down upon the cold marble, Thomas strained at the ropes that tied him but they held him tightly so he rolled over and managed to raise himself to a sitting position.

Close by, Woodget was attempting to do the same, but all he could manage was to flounder upon the ground like a stranded fish and the crowd roared to see him struggle in vain.

'Tom!' he wailed. 'I can't move, these knots be too tight – I doesn't want to get killed a-grovellin' on the floor.'

'Hush,' Thomas said gently, 'don't show this scurvy crew that you're afraid. At least we're going together, Woodj, and the next life can't be any worse than this one.'

Suddenly, there began the beating of drums and the sea of hideous faces which stretched from the bottom of the steps into the distant dark ceased their raucous shouts and an eerie silence descended.

The fur on the back of Thomas' neck prickled – the eager, apprehensive stillness was even worse than the previous clamouring and he wondered what the steady pounding rhythm could mean.

But he and Woodget were not kept in suspense for long.

To the right of him, where the near wall of the temple's inner sanctum rose into the smoky gloom, there was a large, ornate entrance, studded with jewels and, as he stared, the door was swept open.

Louder rang the incessant beating din and from that entrance marched six voles with drums of taut skin about their necks and slender bones grasped in their claws.

Sharp and unharmonious was the harsh noise of those strident drums and into the shrine the voles came, bowing before the altar. Then down the steps they strode, halting midway where their drumming mounted in intensity until with a fierce yell they stopped and raised the bones above their heads.

Thomas grimaced at Woodget, then from the entrance others came and he shrank against the base of the nearest pillar when he beheld them.

Into the temple strode the great adepts – chosen creatures with the power to slough their skin and walk unclad in the scales of their true nature. Dahrem had been one of their number but with his death the count of their order was reduced to eight. Yet even though they entered as beings of mortal flesh, the congregation still feared them and ripples of horror echoed about the cavernous gloom.

Proud and haughty they were, those select few, whose skill and knowledge of the base, occult arts had elevated them to such an infamous rank. The first was a great and odious-looking mole, whose misshapen face held a permanent sneer, and in his massive claws he carried an object wrapped around with many peeled and dried skins.

After him the other adepts came: a stoat with a circlet of gold upon her head, a lemur whose chattering jaws lunged tauntingly at Thomas when he swaggered by, followed by an Assam rabbit covered in dark brown bristles with grotesquely long teeth. One by one the adepts entered – a squirrel, a twitching palm civit, a long-eared hedgehog and, bringing up the rear, an Indian ratel.

Like the mole, they each bore a bundle of skins and in a semicircle they gathered around the altar and waited.

Woodget stared at them fearfully. 'What they doing, Tom?' he asked. 'What they got in their fists?'

Thomas had already guessed, but there was no time to answer, for at that moment the drums rolled again and into the temple came the High Priest and after him, Mother Lotus.

To the edge of the wide steps, the cloaked sable paced and the flabby rat trundled up to be at his side.

With a triumphant look illuminating his sleek, black face, the high priest regarded the silent masses below and held up his claw in greeting.

'Servants of Sarpedon!' he shrieked and his shrill voice went slicing through the dismal murk, echoing around the deep, vaulted cavern.

'You have come this night to celebrate the rare blazing of the nine stars in heaven – yet the tidings I bring outshine even their magnificence!'

In the darkness the assembly muttered and stirred approvingly. Most had heard the rumours of Hara's downfall and they thirsted to hear the salacious details of the vicious battle.

'Know now that the fortresses of our enemies have been utterly conquered!' the sable cried. 'The Shrine of Virbius has been despoiled and the city of the Green is no more. From those squalid dens of our weakling foes the seventh and eighth fragments of Our Lord's precious work have been restored unto our keeping.'

At this the multitude roared with exultation – yammering the Dark Despoiler's praises and cheering the victories of the High Priest.

Basking in their screaming tributes and adoration, the sable stepped aside and with a flourish of his claw gave a signal to the adepts.

As one, they tore the preserved, furry wrappings from the bundles they held and there in their clutches they held the eight plundered fragments.

At once the baleful glow of so many pieces welled up within that hellish place and their livid effulgence burst out into the cavern – drowning out all lesser sources of light until even the darkest cleft was flooded with a sickly, green radiance.

Thomas screwed up his face at the loathsome glare; it was many times greater than the light which had filled the domed chamber in the Holy One's mountain and hurt his eyes. It was as if the moon had sickened in the sky and had fallen into the temple to shed corrupt and gangrenous beams upon the earth and he felt unclean and sullied at the sight of it.

But when he turned away, the full extent and measure of the infernal cult's forces was revealed under the repulsive, putrefying incandescence and his mind recoiled at their countless number.

Below him, and covering every available space into the furthest possible distance, the massive congregation were blinking and holding their rancid breaths as they saw for the first time the exquisite designs of their maleficent master.

As the deathly light pulsed and beat from the eight, separate pieces of jade, the chosen ones raised their claws above their heads and gasps of alarm and unease issued from the stunned, thunderstruck crowds.

Thomas glanced back into the intense, unwholesome glare and saw that, within each fist, the fragments were moving.

Surrounding the diseased splendour of the flaring, shining jade, the golden traceries became molten and were imbued with a frightful life of their own. Around the irregular edges the scrollwork was writhing and the intricate lattices were peeling away to search and grope in the air like the raised heads of serpents.

Crowing with dark joy, the High Priest threw back his head.

'Eight pieces we had!' he yelled. 'Yet this very night, providence and my own guile and artifice have rewarded these long empty years of waiting. For here, at this critical hour when the heralding stars swing in the sky, I have delivered unto this sacred place, the sanctum of the Black Master, the ninth and final fragment!'

Casting aside his cloak, he brought out the remaining segment which Mulligan and his ancestors had kept safe and secret throughout the ages and brandished it high for all to see.

Like a septic sun, the fragment shone and the

gathering shrieked with insane voices.

'At last!' the sable screamed. 'The time has come – the Lord Suruth Scarophion shall be reborn. His shell shall be remade whole again and this night of the great conjunction will witness a return to the dark years of the past. No dawn shall rise with the morning – His black strength shall blot out the light and under the ravishing shadow of His being all things will turn to us or rot and be forgotten in the dust and slime of His ruinous wake.'

Thomas stared up at the forbidding figure of the High Priest and winced at the madness that distorted those sharp and cruel features. The absolute devotion to the evil serpent god was horrific to see but he could not tear his eyes away now, for the moment that would pronounce the doom of the present world was fast approaching and he steeled his nerves to witness it.

Flourishing the ninth fragment in his claws, the High Priest whirled around and strode to the centre of the adepts, stepping on to the blackened, blood-stained altar stone and, as though they were controlled by one single mind, the eight creatures closed in around him.

'Too long has His Dark Majesty been banished from the waking world!' he cried, his voice rising to a crescendo of fanatical jubilation. 'Too long have our enemies denied us the means for His deliverance! But now the hour is upon us! Sarpedon will rear amongst us again, the eternal night has come at last!'

Lifting the fragment over the altar, he shrieked with rapture and the chosen ones moved their radiant charges ever closer.

Thomas watched aghast, as the golden edges of

the reunited pieces thrashed feverishly. With every passing instant that the jade fragments drew nearer to one another, the glittering, encasing metal strove and flailed more violently until, finally, the snaking arabesques seized hold of their opposite numbers and with a resounding discordant note that went chiming through the cavern and out through the portal in the ceiling, the fragments locked together – flying from the adept's clutches with the violence of their union.

Trembling with ecstatic emotion, the High Priest stared at his empty claws then down at the altar where the great and fabulous shape of a huge, glowing egg now stood.

Over its gorgeous surface, no trace or hint of the edges that had divided the nine individual segments could be seen – only a marvellous and worshipful whole. And, leaping into the air, the High priest let out an elated roar.

'Behold!' he screeched. 'The vessel which will receive Our Dear Lord's spirit! After all this time – His ancient plan to cheat the forces of the Green has succeeded!'

The congregation threw their knives and cutlasses into the air – shrieking in demented voices. 'SARPEDON!' they howled. 'SARPEDON! SARPEDON! SARPEDON!'

Throwing back her head, and twirling in a wide, inelegant circle, the wobbling bulk of Ma Skillet squawked with gladness.

'Mighty Serpent!' she exulted. 'Your peoples await! Come – be with us!'

Quaking with excitement, the High Priest gazed up at the expanse of night visible beyond the circular opening in the roof and his face was split by a raving, maniacal grin.

High above, in the clear unclouded heavens the constellation of Scarophion was shining fiercely. The nine, snaking stars which heralded the demon's proximity to the living plane were blazing with brilliant, silver fire and against their frosty flames even the moon could not compete.

'Hear me!' the sable ranted, flinging his arms open wide and falling to his knees in subjugation. 'Hearken now to the words of thy ambassador upon this mortal earth! The restraints that bind you in the void are at their weakest – break forth and array yourself in godly flesh once more. Return to us, your devoted disciples!'

Around him the adepts fell upon their faces and before the temple the assembled legions did the same – yet on all their lips was their master's name and they chanted it continuously as they waited for his return.

With horror upon his face, Woodget looked up at the circle of night and the fierce stars that dazzled there. Then, to his astonishment and distress, their cold light flashed in the midnight sky, and a profound rumbling, like the deepest, calamitous thunder, shook the heavens and the island quaked beneath it.

From the lofty, vaulted ceiling, a deluge of stones rattled down and the pillars that upheld the temple shifted with a tremendous grating of marble over rock. Yet the foul cult members were oblivious to it all; they were possessed by the thought of their lord's dark return and even if the ground had opened up to swallow them they would not have noticed.

Then, as Woodget and Thomas stared heavenward,

they saw nine rays of searing light come streaking from the Constellation of the Serpent. Through the empty reaches of the void, the flickering beams raced – streaming straight towards the unhappy world. Down over the oceans the spearing flames plummeted until at last they shone through the open portal cut into the rocky island's jagged peak and into the Black Temple their icy splendour burst.

As an immense column of pure light, the rays shot into the unhallowed sanctum, bringing with them the freezing winter of the infinite void and upon the altar, their frosty fires crackled and sparked.

Over the surface of the great jade and golden egg, the blinding hoary beams flickered – playing over the glowing shell, lapping the twirling arabesques of the precious, living metal with rime.

Thomas shuddered; the mingling of the jade's livid gleam with the harsh, brumal starlight was a chilling and unlovely spectacle – a corpse flame to awaken the long-cold decayed dead and condemn unrepentant souls to perdition.

Now the egg was wreathed in the lurid fires, completely enclosed within their bleak, glacial tongues. Then Thomas heard Woodget's small and desperate voice call out.

'Tom – look! Simoon he be coming round.'

Thomas wrenched his eyes from the awful scene by the altar and turned to where the jerboa's limp and sprawled body lay upon the marble floor.

In slow, painful movements, the prophet was awakening, returning from that dark forgetfulness to which his grappling with the High Priest had dispatched him.

Wearily, he lifted his sandy-coloured head, his brambling whiskers twitching as he opened his large black eyes and beheld the terrible sight before him.

Then, in a small, frail voice, Simoon murmured, 'Finally the end has come. Our labours are completed and the doom of many is nigh.'

Shaking his head, he slumped back on to the ground and beside him, realising suddenly just how much faith he had put in the prophet, the fieldmouse wept bitterly.

Yet still the cold fires crackled about the great egg – as the demonic, exiled spirit descended from the celestial confines to enter into the shell which he himself had ordered to be constructed in his former existence. Into that enchanted symbol of rebirth and creation that he had steeped in his own evil arts during the dark years of his reign, Suruth Scarophion, the Dark Despoiler – Gorscarrigern, the Coiled One – stole back to the mortal world and before the altar, the High Priest rose to his feet and spun around to face his followers.

'Arise!' he commanded. 'For all who adore Our Lord should witness His return.'

In silent reverence the crowds obeyed and lit by the wintry light, the adepts and Mother Lotus lifted their faces to the wondrous, miraculous vision.

As they watched, breathing rapidly in their suppressed fervour, the glacial flames about the egg began to diminish and, far above the earth, the nine stars were waning.

'See!' the sable screeched. 'Our Lord is amongst us once more.'

To Thomas' disgust, as the glare dwindled,

becoming the pale green glow of disease once more, he saw that within the great egg, behind the curving surface of the glimmering jade, something was moving.

In the heart of that hideously beautiful shell, a dark shadow had formed and already it was wriggling and contorting its squirming worm-like shape.

'Sarpedon!' the High Priest cried bowing before the altar. 'Your servants await you.'

'Tom!' Woodget whimpered. 'They've done it – the snake god's really here!'

Within the egg, the shadow jiggled and thrashed, growing larger with the passing moments. Soon it would break out of the shell and a nightmare more repellent than anything Woodget's innocent mind could ever imagine would breathe the fetid air, filling its new-born lungs with gargling gasps as it gazed upon the devoted subjects who prostrated themselves before its unhallowed and absolute authority.

'Feel the Sovereign's might and majesty!' the High Priest called. 'Let His sublime power flow through you all – let us greet Him in the essence of our devotion. At this hour all shall be granted the gift of change and transformation. Honour your master, declare to Him your fealty!'

The assembly stared at him in confusion but all could feel the horrible influence which beat out from the pulsing egg and to their stupefied bewilderment their matted hides began to itch and buckle, tearing from their flesh and falling in shreds of fur and feather upon the floor.

Innumerable nightmares were suddenly revealed – grisly lizard-like ogres with luminous eyes and spiny

ridges sprouting down their necks forming horrendous distortions of scale-covered, bowed backs. Webbed claws raked the air and spindly haunches rocked the squat, slimy bodies from side to side as the last vestige of their hot-blooded flesh was ripped loose and cast upon the ground.

Quickly their initial, startled fright was transformed to joy and they revelled in their true, scaly natures – singing the praises of their peerless tyrant in gutteral hissing voices.

Thomas closed his eyes and twisted his head away from that despicable sight. Before the steps, the host of the Scale had fulfilled their infernal goals and were now truly dedicated to their monarch's service. In grotesque imitations of the Dark Despoiler they had shed their flesh and were revealed as the vile creatures they had become.

Before the altar, the adepts were rapidly sloughing their skins, and a heap of furry, bristling pelts lay piled upon the black marble as they paraded their ghastly characters – flinging their glistening arms in the air, dragging their newtish tails behind their gruesome, spine-spiking bodies, ogling the egg with fish-like eyes, flicking their tongues in and out of their wide mouths and shrieking in demented screeches.

Watching them, and clapping with approval, Mother Lotus cackled, then she tore off her silk dressing gown and with it the abundant folds of her flesh until finally she ripped from her head the flour-powdered face.

Like a vast, pot-bellied toad she appeared, with great, bulging eyes and a pale, blotch-covered throat.

Beneath her obese, reptilian body, two stunted legs

supported the grievous weight and they tottered and staggered to and fro as she croaked her obedience to the wriggling shadow inside the egg.

Of all the servants of Scarophion, only the High Priest refrained from revealing his inner self, for he desired the demon to look upon him first of all and know him to be his main and trusted disciple. Then, when he had made his position plain and secured the high office under the Dark Despoiler, he would cast off his luxuriant coat and display his utter loyalty and allegiance.

Yet when the black deity's head broke free from the shell it would need nourishment and he turned to the three prisoners who for so long had been neglected.

'Mother Lotus!' he commanded. 'The infant Sarpedon will need sustenance. Fetch to me the smallest of the captives – the fieldmouse. He who dared to withhold the final fragment will be the first flesh upon which Our Master shall feast.'

The bloated, scale and wart-ridden horror that was Ma Skillet stooped to retrieve from her dressing gown the golden, snake-adorned dagger and with a foul giggle issuing from her lipless mouth she waddled towards Woodget, her splayed feet slip-slapping upon the floor.

Nearly fainting from terror, the fieldmouse watched her lumbering approach, the flabby reptilian hide quivering like a sour and mouldering jelly.

The clamour of the scaly multitude drowned out his own voice as he cried out with fear and around him the eight adepts strutted their abhorrence, urging the High Priestess to slit his throat and pour his hot blood into their newly born master's gullet.

Nearer the fat apparition came, her grunting gurgles terrifying him even more.

'Spike he – stab he!' the cracked, hissing voice taunted. 'Rip the sinew from bone for His delight. Mother Lotus – she provide good quenchers – oh yes.'

Up to the shivering fieldmouse, the corpulent spectre stalked until her belly bulged above his head and she pointed the dagger at this throat.

Thomas couldn't look. He hung his head as the priestess lurched to murder Woodget and waited for his friend's death cries to resound in his ears until his turn came.

But the fearsome shrieks never sounded.

Instead a clear, resonant voice rang through the excited, fervent yammering and Thomas snapped his eyes open in wonder.

'Misbegotten horror – adipose abomination! Again I say be still!'

Ma Skillet's toad-like bulk shuddered uncontrollably and with an astonished squawk, she was hurled backwards – landing in a forlorn, squealing heap on top of her plentiful, sloughed skin.

'Simoon!' Thomas yelled.

Lifting his head from the ground, the jerboa nodded at the mouse in acknowledgement, then muttered a word of release. The cords that bound all three sprang apart and fell in tattered threads about them.

Woodget's eyes were shining and he sobbed with relief as the robed figure of the prophet rose to his feet and pointed an accusing finger at the gathered host.

'Dismal followers of Gorscarrigern!' he declared, and at the sound of his authoritative voice the revels ceased and everyone turned to stare at him.

'To this desperate end – I, and the other members of the Green Council have guided your felonious footsteps. This is in truth the end of one world but not the dawning of the infernal realm of your desiring. See now how your plots are destroyed and the schemes of your tyrannous overlord are beaten into the mire of your own making!'

Glowering at him, the High Priest bared his fangs to pounce and silence the squeaking upstart once and for all – it would never do to have his distracting cries irritate the newly born master.

Yet even as he lunged forward, the jerboa threw up his paw and an invisible wall was flung between them.

Snarling, the sable raised his claws to dispel the paltry trick but behind him the adepts were muttering in consternation and he whirled around to see what had upset them.

'Now do the hopes of the Council and the efforts of many generations come to fruition!' announced Simoon. 'For we have always known that a day would come when the enemy would wrest from us the nine fragments and attempt to restore their profane deity to harry the world. That is why we have done what we have done and may it prove well for now is the moment of dread and we shall see if our designs and sacrifices were not in vain.'

'No!' shrieked the High Priest, tearing at his hair and grinding his teeth together. 'What base treachery is this? What madness do my eyes see?'

Upon the altar, the light which beat from the great egg was fluctuating. Its ghastly pallor flickered unsteadily and within its depths the wriggling shape was twitching and jolting as though racked and stabbed with pain.

'This we decided in the great long ago!' the jerboa proclaimed for all to hear in a voice that transcended the smallness of his stature and rose into the stifling airs to pierce the furthest reaches of the hollow, rocky island.

'For,' he continued, 'though the honourable order of magicians and enchanters who worked for the Green's greater glory were slain within the first temple, not all perished. There was in their number one who never stepped inside the evil shrine to beard the demon in his lair.

'Too slow and small was he to ascend the temple steps with the speed of the others and so was spared the black venom which spilled from the demon's carcass.

'So was *Simoon* – obeah pilgrim, far seer, mage and prophet, treader of the forgotten track and guardian of the old rituals – left alone – the last of that noble order.

'Yet in that sorrowful, triumphant hour when the Dark One was slain and the egg was found, Simoon knew what had to be done and the solution, as with most things, was simple.'

The High Priest hardly heard him, for the movements within the egg were failing and with a final twisting spasm, the worm-like shadow became still and died. With a final pulsing glow, the light within the jade was quenched and a solemn darkness engulfed the temple as hairline cracks appeared across the shell.

With a sickening, splitting sound, the egg began to

fall to pieces. On to the floor the jade crashed and into a mildewed dust it exploded. Fragment by fragment the shell collapsed and then, revealed within its centre was a monstrous, slug-like abomination that slithered squelchingly from the decaying egg and flopped lifeless from the altar.

When it hit the floor, the disgusting horror ruptured and burst – over the black marble there spilled a stinking, putrescent mess that smoked and festered and a faint sound, like a sigh, issued from its deformed and rotten mouth.

Speechless with grief and fury, the sable turned to look on the jerboa. 'What have you done?' he demanded. 'Sarpedon! He is . . . He is . . .'

'Sarpedon's corporeal form is once again destroyed,' Simoon told him. 'Never again can his blasphemous spirit knit slime and sinew together, for the work of the past is shattered. The shell is broken unto dust and can never be repaired.'

'How?' the High Priest cried, taking a step towards him and, in his wrath, banishing the magical barrier the jerboa had placed between them. 'The fragments were invulnerable – no harm could come to them.'

Simoon clasped his paws together and laughed.

'But no hurt nor harm was done to them!' he declared. 'Quite the opposite. For I knew that the only way to prevent Scarophion's return would be to injure him whilst he was still within the shell and so I counselled that the ninth and greatest fragment should be moved continually about the shrines of the blessed Green.

'In the unfolding years the evil was washed clean and the spells of the Dark Despoiler were turned about. The fragment was in fact hallowed. In short, we made certain that when the pieces were finally brought together again – the egg was addled.'

A terrible growl issued from the High Priest's throat and he rushed forward to destroy the sanctimonious creature. Before the steps, the congregation were screeching in dismay – nothing was left to them now and they lusted for vengeance. Yowling in abject despair, the adepts clawed at their hideous scales and shrieked into the darkness for doom and death to take them, and three of them tore out their own throats rather than exist in a world without Scarophion.

Yet Simoon seemed unperturbed. Lifting his paw again, an invisible force cannoned into the High Priest and he was sent hurtling to the far corners of the temple – crying shrilly in fright. Then the jerboa held up both paws and continued.

'Now you who have displayed your fidelity to the fallen deity, remain in the form you have chosen so that goodly folk may see you for what you are and shun you. Shrink back into darkness and never wear the raiment of warm flesh again.'

At that he reached into one of his many pockets and cast a cloud of blue powder into the air which immediately burst into a spluttering display of fiery sparks that crackled and exploded – showering down on to the rocky floor, where the tiny sizzling stars bounced and hopped, multiplying as they went.

Into the crowding hordes the magic of Simoon cascaded and leapt and to the dismay of the reptilian apparitions which were gathered within the cavern, the sparks jumped on to the cast-off skins and buried themselves into the matted hides – kindling suddenly into raging fires that devoured the sloughed pelts completely until only ash remained.

Before the altar, the remaining chosen ones were also shrieking, for their furs were burning and though they tried, they could not extinguish the supernatural flames.

Making the loudest noise, pounding up and down and blowing upon her withering skin, Ma Skillet went screeching through the bejewelled entrance, leaving a trail of ash and smoke behind her.

Observing all that was done, and finding it to his satisfaction, Simoon turned to the mice who were still sitting upon the floor and helped them to their feet.

'Now it is time for us to depart,' he said. 'Whilst the panic and fear is still upon these wretches, let us take a boat and return to Singapore – there you will find a ship which will bear you to your home.'

Thomas looked around them, not knowing what to say, but Woodget was bouncing up and down with unrivalled joy.

'I knowed you was a great magician!' he cried. 'I knowed it all the time!'

The jerboa chuckled, then looked up sharply as if he had heard something that alarmed him. 'Perhaps,' he muttered apprehensively, 'yet not all schemes are infallible. There are some eventualities which even I might have overlooked. Come – we waste valuable time!'

With that he hared down the great steps and made for the door which the rats had originally carried them through and Thomas and Woodget raced after him.

At the rear of the temple, crawling from the place Simoon's powers had thrown him, the High Priest looked on the chaos of his followers and knew the meaning of defeat. All his hopes, all his dreams of serving Sarpedon the Mighty, had come to naught and all that was left was a demented host of scale-covered horrors.

Bitterly, as the pandemonium erupted about him, he picked his way through the cinders of the adept's skins and gazed upon the black, oozing mess that had ruptured from the dead slug, and wetted his parched lips.

If he were to dip his claws in that stinking sludge and drag them across his tongue, then his vanquished life would end. He did not care for the agonies that would ensue. All he wanted was to leave the world which, without the possibility of his lord's return, was empty and devoid of hope.

Despondently he made up his mind and so, bending down he reached for the dark, venomous slime – then froze.

High above him, there came the sound of creaking metal and with his heart palpitating in his breast, the sable stared upwards.

Surely it could not be, surely even the Dark One could not perform such an astounding feat?

Breathlessly, with the shrieks of the legions screaming in his mind, as they slew each other in their madness, the High Priest gazed up and his eyes glittered, not daring to hope yet hardly able to contain the rejoicing in his foul heart if it were true.

Rearing into the darkness the gigantic, golden image of Scarophion was shuddering and, as he watched, there came the dull scrape of gold upon gold and, to his marvelling amazement, the massive, repulsive head twisted and shook and the jaws clanged open and shut.

Within the cavern the assembly fell silent as all wondered what this new miracle might mean, but over the marble floor, the High Priest ran until he stood upon the wide steps and the immense, glittering head towered straight above him.

'My Lord!' he yelled. 'My Lord – Master! Scarophion the Mighty, I, your High Priest, welcome your blissful return!'

With a clanking grinding of precious metal, the enormous idol lowered its gigantic head and the rubies that blazed in the eyes shone with hellish fires, as the infernal spirit which now inhabited the statue, looked upon the rejoicing, exultant sable.

At the last, the Dark Despoiler had indeed cheated the designs of the Green Council, for though he was not clothed in flesh, his iniquitous spirit had fled from the egg and seized possession of his own mammoth likeness.

'SPEAK.'

The strident voice commanded and the sound of it blasted down upon the High Priest like a thundering gale from a mountain top.

Up into that dreadful face, the sable gazed and his eyes became filled with anger and hatred for the one who had so nearly ruined everything.

'First, My Lord,' he cried, 'you must deal with your enemies!'

The golden jaws sprang open and from the titanic throat there streamed a strangling black vapour.

Through the tunnels Simoon and the two mice ran until, breathlessly, they came to the dark harbour and the jerboa cast around for a boat small enough to take them.

Quickly, he pattered down the various flights of stairs leading to the water and surveyed the craft that were moored there until he finally discovered a small rowing-boat and called to the others to climb aboard.

'Make haste, Master Stubbs!' Simoon instructed. 'Your arms are stronger than mine so you shall have to take the oars, I will hold the tiller. Quickly untie the rope – we must be gone.'

Thomas obeyed and, as Woodget settled down within the craft, the fieldmouse giggled merrily. 'He bain't called Stubbs, Mister Simoon,' he said. 'From here on in, old Tom's called Triton – bain't you, Tom?'

'Ssshh!' Simoon hushed him. 'I fear the danger is not yet passed. I did not reckon upon this chance – the enemy is treacherous indeed and I have underestimated him.'

Sitting down in the boat, Thomas grabbed the oars and dipped them in the water, heaving hard upon them.

Slowly the craft pulled away from the harbour wall and past the other vessels they sailed.

'Faster!' the jerboa urged. 'Put your back into it!'

Thomas strained and dragged the oars through the water as fast as he could and the boat began to pick up speed – scooting out towards the island's gaping entrance.

Outside, a faint, grey light was glimmering on the horizon as the first gleam of the early dawn climbed above the rim of the world and Simoon sighed with gratitude.

464

'It is well the day is here,' he said. 'It encourages me, yet I fear what its light may show to us.'

Woodget looked at him and the lighthearted cheer that had sprung from the relief of being rescued, guttered inside him. The jerboa's face was troubled and an edge of panic had crept into his voice.

'What be a-worritin' 'ee?' the fieldmouse ventured.

Simoon shook his head. 'It may be nothing,' he replied. 'And yet . . .'

Out from the island the small boat sped, but a more pressing concern was worrying Thomas. 'It's no use!' he cried. 'You'll never be able to navigate through the reef. We'll run aground in no time. I saw it when we arrived, it's a maze out there.'

'You give up too easily, Master Triton,' Simoon declared, delving into his robe and bringing out a small glass jar. 'We shall not falter – the correct path will be found.'

Gripping the tiller in one paw to steady himself, the jerboa rose and removing the stopper from the jar, threw it before them.

Woodget stared at the dark waters, then to his delight, there appeared upon the surface a patch of clear silvery light that radiated out in a twisting path between the rising spires of rock and beyond, to where the submerged reef lurked below the waves.

'There is our route,' Simoon announced. 'Now, you pull on the oars and I shall steer us.'

Thomas laughed, but then from the island there echoed a tremendous roar and the oars skipped futilely across the sea as the mouse shivered with alarm.

'Green's Grace!' he cried. 'What was that?'

Simoon pressed his mittened fingers to his wiry temples and closed his eyes in an effort to calm himself.

'Ignore it, Triton!' he commanded. 'All you must concentrate upon is getting us away from this accursed place.'

Woodget looked at the jerboa in surprise, then turned around to gaze at the vast, rocky hill which loomed from the waters behind them as another horrible, booming roar resounded from it.

'As I feared,' Simoon whispered to himself. 'He is not beaten.'

Again the air shook with the muffled, baying screech and the fieldmouse frowned in puzzlement. 'Sounds like them snaky folk are blowin' upon a load of cracked trumpets back there,' he muttered. 'What do 'ee make of it, Mister Simoon?'

'Much,' the jerboa replied darkly.

Woodget's frown became a deeper scowl at this cryptic remark and he was about to question him further when the cacophonous blaring sounded again, but this time when he stared back at the island, the fieldmouse's face fell and he whimpered in fright.

At the summit of the great, rocky mountain, where the spears of stone spiked around the circular portal that looked down upon the altar, a plume of smoke was rising and, rearing amid the reek, was a great and hideous golden head.

'Save us!' wailed Woodget.

Out from the temple the statue of Scarophion came – into the upper airs he heaved his glittering, gem-encrusted body and, sitting astride his neck, his claws gripped tight about the horns that twisted back from the gleaming skull, was the High Priest. Over the rock the idol slithered, pulling the last of its flexing coils from within the temple, and, to Woodget's increasing horror, the giant serpent writhed its monstrous way down to the water and flowed into the sea.

'I don't understand!' Thomas cried. 'The statue . . . how?'

'When the newly formed worm inside the egg was killed by the hallowed fragment,' Simoon uttered fearfully, 'the Dark One's spirit did not shrivel back into the void as I expected, but took possession of a different raiment.'

'Quick, Tom!' the fieldmouse shouted. 'It's movin' fast!'

Behind them, surging through the waves, its powerful tail propelling it with great speed, the gargantuan golden image came thundering in pursuit of the small rowing-boat.

High into the dim sky, the skilfully fashioned head rose, the pale light of the distant dawn glinting coldly in the myriad facets of its burnished scales. Pouring from the ravening jaws, behind the cruel pinnacles of the diamond-tipped fangs, the rivers of black, oily smoke billowed into the sky and blotted out the faint gleam of the failing stars above. Furiously, in that painstakingly crafted, repellent visage, the ruby eyes were burning with a limitless intelligence and with a sudden clanking of metal, the segmented neck lashed forward.

Towards the tiny vessel the immense head lunged and a torrent of yellow flame went shooting from the great, black throat.

Through the darkness the fiery stream issued,

blasting out a trail of scorching death.

In the boat, Woodget stared up at the blistering rivers of flame and squeaked in fear, spurring Thomas to row faster, and the lethal, terrifying deluge fell only yards behind them – striking the water with a boiling hiss of scalding steam.

From high above, wreathed in the choking fumes that flooded from the apparition's maw, there came the sound of shrieking laughter as the rancorous sable threw back his head and crowed his devilish glee.

In the boat the occupants were swallowed by despair and Woodget turned around to see how far they still had to go before they were clear of the reef, then muttered at his own foolishness – they would never be able to outpace that glittering monster.

That statue was closing on them now; every lash of its tail, every lithe thrust of its superior might, brought it nearer to their fleeing craft and Woodget knew that the next time it spat a rain of fire upon them it could not fail to miss and they would be engulfed in a ball of incinerating flame.

At his side, his fingers on the tiller, Simoon bowed his shoulders and hung his head, but with his arms straining upon the oars, Thomas was determined not to abandon hope and stared defiantly up into the resplendently diabolic face of Scarophion's new form as a desperate and reckless idea took control of him.

'Simoon!' he called eagerly. 'Can you summon a mist – like the one that surrounds the silver ship of Hara, the *Chandi*?'

The jerboa looked at him curiously. 'Such a veil will not defend us,' he said forlornly. 'My powers are useless against the Coiled One. In the past it took all of our order to destroy him, I cannot do it alone. The hope of the Council – the one chance I foresaw – has proven ill.'

'Can you or can't you?' Thomas demanded impatiently.

The prophet nodded.

'Then be quick about it!' the mouse bawled. 'Make it rise up all around us if you can.'

Simoon closed his eyes and set to work at once, murmuring under his breath and, as Thomas heaved on the oars, the surrounding waters began to bubble and wisps of white vapour rose into the air.

Through the last of the steepling, fencing rocks, the little boat swept – then through the meandering channel that split the hidden reef.

Like a storm of splendour, roaring a fanfare of disaster and ruination, the statue came after, ploughing effortlessly through the water and slicing through the layers of mist which now spread across its surface.

'I need more!' Thomas yelled to Simoon. 'A great big bank of it!'

Anxiously, Thomas laboured; his paws were almost raw and great blistering weals scored them. In his arms the muscles ached and screamed with pain but, gritting his teeth, the mouse ignored the tortuous fatigue and out of the murderous reef and on to the open sea the boat shot.

Yet hot in pursuit came Gorscarrigern. Cleaving a path through the mounting fog, his terrible, gilded head came racing and, with his long hair streaming in the wind, the High Priest spurred his sovereign on.

'What vain, childish tricks do they attempt now?'

the sable hooted in derision. 'Do they suppose thine eyes cannot pierce the mist to see them? Is that how they hope to escape you, Most Worshipful Malevolence? Disgorge your withering fires, destroy those who have dared to interfere in thy aggrandisement!'

In the growing light of the morning, the huge jaws shone brightly as they yawned open and into the dense, white fog another river of flame erupted.

This time it missed the boat by the merest fraction. As the fires came thundering down, the waves bucked and the craft pitched and rocked upon them as its timbers charred and the mist was suddenly illuminated by the dazzling flames.

Sitting closest to the blasting inferno, Woodget fell back from the tremendous heats as a fount of steam broiled upwards and at his side Simoon shook his head.

'We cannot weave in and out of this cloud to evade the demon serpent forever,' he told Thomas. 'In a moment he will have us.'

'Not if I can help it!' the mouse shouted at him. 'Now, turn the rudder sharply – we're going back into the reef.'

The jerboa furrowed his brow, but there was no point in contesting with Thomas, no point in anything any more.

In a tight curve they wheeled around and Woodget buried his face in his paws when the leviathan coils of the living statue reared above them and Simoon steered them straight beneath its polished, arching body.

Back into the treacherous reef, Thomas rowed the

little craft and high in the enveloping mist they heard the High Priest's scornful tones mocking them as the idol twisted around and the opulent, ghastly head came bursting through the thick, clinging clouds.

Swiftly it came, yet Simoon pulled hard on the tiller and the boat jerked sideways, following the twisting path of the channel. Through the mist the head of the statue dived, plunging down until it skimmed the water then up again – sweeping agilely through the blanketing fog.

'A few more of those . . .' Thomas mumbled to himself and, hearing him, at last Simoon understood and he grew agitated with excitement.

'Watch out!' Woodget squeaked.

Thomas leaned back when he next pulled on the oars and the bloody glare of the ruby eyes flooded the boat as the marauding, priceless head rioted across its bows.

In a snaking loop the serpent rumbled over the boat and the High Priest trumpeted with mordacious mirth to see the mice and Simoon fall prey to his relentless, vitriolic and revenge-wreaking master.

Up into the fog the statue soared, towering like a fabulous, minted mountain, its loathly head rising high above the topmost swirl of cloud and the warm rays of the rearing sun burned and flared across the golden mirrors of the gorgeously wrought scales that plated the gleaming spectre's neck.

Silhouetted against the rosy beams of the morning, the High Priest tossed his head and the long dark hair whipped about his sharply boned features.

'Now, My Lord!' he screeched. 'Let your supreme magnitude topple down and dash them to death!'

For an instant the perilous jaws clanged shut then they fell open again and with a deafening roar the golden nightmare plunged back through the mist.

In the boat, Thomas threw Simoon a desperate glance.

'Now or never!' he yelled.

The jerboa's briar-like brows trembled but he gave the tiller an almighty wrench and Thomas heaved on the oars for all he was worth.

'A plague upon you, Sarpedon!' the mouse hollered. 'Go back to the emptiness that awaits you!'

Woodget stared at him then looked nervously upwards. Through the fog, falling like a gold-smithied symbol of the sun, hurled from the chariot of a sky god, the head came speeding and flames dripped from the yawning mouth.

Suddenly the keel of the boat scraped against the sharp rocks beneath as they left the safe channel but Thomas still pulled on the oars and in an anguished voice repeated to himself, 'Not yet, not yet.'

Then as the mists parted and the maw came lunging down, the mouse grabbed hold of Woodget and yelled, 'Jump clear – get out!'

Leaping from the boat, they splashed into the surrounding water. But too late Scarophion and the sable who rode upon his neck saw the impending danger.

Directly behind the little craft, rising from the reef and appearing without warning from the swaddling cloud, reared an adamantine crag of solid stone.

A pitiful, air-splitting bellow gusted from the statue's gullet and, with terror in his eyes, the High Priest shrieked shrilly. But there was nothing they could do, the velocity of the glittering god's descent could not be checked and so, into the small rowing-boat the bejewelled, golden head battered and the craft splintered like matchwood. Yet immediately after, the gigantic and awful countenance went slamming into the immovable fist of rock behind.

Thomas clung on to Woodget as the bed of the ocean lifted and quaked with the shuddering violence of the tremendous, impacting blow.

Careering helplessly into the steadfast stone, the gilt head exploded with a thousand, sparkling splinters and projected like precious missiles from its crumpling features flew a horde of spinning, scintillating treasures.

Like flaming meteors, the ruby eyes shot high over the sea and, from the steel fangs, as they bit deep clefts into the rock, the diamonds went skimming over the waves.

Then down crashed the serpent's body and into the sea it thundered – with an almighty, foaming tumult.

For several minutes, as the serpent's head lay crushed and beaten beyond redemption against the rock, the monstrous tail lashed furiously, but the movements quickly subsided and with a final spouting splash, the tail fell into the sea.

At once the ancient spirit which possessed the idol fled the crushed and mangled fabric of the hideous, glittering titan and, like an immense cloud of shadow, drifted up into the fog, to vanish into the ether and return to the void without any further hope of re-entering the living plane.

The woeful terrifying menace of Suruth Scarophion, the Dark Despoiler, was finally at an end. No more would the threat of his return trouble the waking world, or strike fear into his enemies. His malignant tyranny was over at last, no longer would his name be a byword for pain and horror. The banishment was finally complete and eternal, and with a blast of salt air the cloud of his trembling shade was dispersed and his evil might passed into the echoing dark. Beyond the walls of creation he was thrust, and through the vast gates of night to the very mansions of the dead where his foul demonic spirit was doomed to rage – trumpeting its imprisoned fury until the very ends of time.

The fear of his reign was finished and the new day which rose about Thomas and Woodget as they stood up on the rock, surrounded by the twinkling sea, gleamed clean and bright and they breathed deeply giving glad grateful sighs.

Staring incredulously at the buckled, twisted sculpture, the mice found it difficult to believe that only minutes ago it had been animated with horrid, writhing life and threatening them with death.

Tentatively, moving a little closer to the shattered scales and broken sections of its dented body, Woodget peered at the gloom that lay inside, then he looked about him and stared in horror at Thomas.

'Simoon!' he cried. 'Where is he?'

Thomas glanced around for the aged jerboa but of him he could find no trace and his gaze became fixed upon the floating debris of the rowing-boat.

'He did jump when we did – didn't he?' the fieldmouse asked. 'Don't say he was still in that thing when the monster came a-smashin' down on top!'

The mice stared at each other desolately but then

a mumbling groan issued from behind the great, gold-bestrewn rock and with hope surging inside them they clambered over the broken idol and hared through the shallows to where the jerboa lay, groggy and bleeding from a cut in his forehead – but alive.

Deliriously, Woodget crouched beside him and dabbed at the wound with sea water. 'Don't you go a-frettin' now,' he soothed. 'Everything be fine. The snake god's done for and we'll come out of this in one piece yet.'

'Ahhh,' sneered a hissing, rabid voice, 'there you are wrong. The battle is not quite over, not yet.'

Staggering from around the rock, with a broken shard of gold in his claws came the High Priest and he looked upon the mice and Simoon with no other feeling but malice and an unholy craving for vengeance.

But the destruction of the statue and his unwilling involvement in that calamitous disaster had wrought a drastic change in his appearance.

When the gigantic serpent had exploded into the towering stone, its golden scales had gone flying in all directions but, perched directly behind the gruesome, rupturing head, the sable had suffered a hundred razoring cuts.

Through his once sleek hide, the deadly, gleaming treasures had sliced deeply and his flesh hung in bloody rents all over his body. One of the sharp, glinting scales was still embedded in his shoulder and over his hatchet face the fur was sticky and gouted with scarlet.

Yet none of that mattered now; all he yearned for,

all that inflamed his embittered soul was the aching desire to kill and butcher those who had vanquished his master.

Pushing himself forward, he lifted the spike of gold in his claws and aimed it at the jerboa's head.

But Thomas grabbed hold of him and dragged the sable aside – flinging him against the clattering wreck of the statue's ruptured head.

'Watch it, Tom!' Woodget cried, seeing the High Priest come bounding back.

Thomas ducked but the sable was prepared for that and he struck the mouse's temple with his fists before spinning around in an attempt to thrust the shard deep into his side.

Yet, whilst Thomas stumbled under the blow to his head, Woodget had leapt to his feet and sprang on to the High Priest's back – covering the sable's darting, red-rimmed eyes with his paws.

Screeching in fury, the High Priest turned and deliberately fell against the crag, squashing the fieldmouse between him and its sharp stone in an effort to rid himself of that puny annoyance.

Squealing, Woodget let go and fell into the shallow sea water, arching his back and whining pitiously – unable to move.

Above him, the High Priest drew back his thin lips to reveal his needle-like teeth but before he could lunge down, Thomas came crashing into his side and in his paws he held one of the shattered oars.

Brutally the two fought – the golden shard clashing against the splintered wood. Savage were those deadly blows and watching them locked in battle, Woodget was disturbed to see his friend's face take on some of the sable's despising resentment and bitter hatred.

Fiercely the strokes swiped the air. Once Thomas caught the High Priest a glancing blow across the arm, but the creature rallied straight away and flew at him all the more viciously.

Courageously Thomas strove against the wrathful enemy and though the sable was almost twice his height, the pains and afflictions of the night had taken its toll of him and so, for some time, the mouse held him off and at one point almost looked as though he might be victorious.

But in the end, the sable's natural belligerence and pugnacious spirit swelled within his tattered breast and stroke after stroke rained down upon the splintered oar until it was knocked from the mouse's paws, and Thomas was pinned against the rock with the glinting spike pressed at his throat.

'So perish all who come between Sarpedon and his designs,' the High Priest spat.

Thomas shrank against the stone as the sable gloated, and waited for the shard to drive into his neck.

Yet the High Priest continued to leer at him and Thomas suddenly saw a trickle of blood drip from the cruel misshapen mouth.

Down fell the servant of Scarophion and there, revealed behind him, stood Woodget – with a steel fang ripped from the statue's jaws clenched in his little fist and both it and his paw were drenched in the High Priest's blood.

Shivering, the fieldmouse stared down at the lifeless body and great tears welled in his eyes.

'That's fer our friends!' he uttered huskily. 'Mister Mulligan, Captain Chattan and Karim!'

Gently, Thomas put his arm about his friend's shoulders and took the weapon from his paw.

'It's all right, Woodj,' he said, 'the enemy's finished now.'

Woodget shivered and stared at the blood which stained his paws, then hurried to the water's edge where he washed them clean. In all his life he had never harmed anyone, and now he'd committed murder. His noble heart was racked with remorse and he squeezed his eyes shut to keep from weeping.

Watching his anguished face, Thomas understood what was passing through the fieldmouse's mind. The endearing air of innocence which shone in Woodget's face was gone for ever and he tried his best to comfort him.

'You didn't have a choice,' he said. 'The villain would have killed us both. You saved me, Woodj – don't torture yourself over the likes of him, he weren't worth it.'

Woodget sniffed, then looked about them. 'But how does we get off this reef and back to port, Tom?' he asked in a small, faint-hearted voice.

Thomas had been pondering the same question, and he gazed thoughtfully out to sea – to where the morning sunlight was shimmering over the water. To his surprise he saw that, upon the horizon, a great wall of white mist was moving and he shielded his eyes against the sun to peer at it curiously.

'Woodj —' he began.

'Verily,' Simoon's rich tones interrupted and when they turned they saw that he was sitting up in the shallows, wringing out the velvet folds of his robe, his keen eyes seeming to pierce the swirling bank of fog in the distance. 'Yonder is the silver ship of Hara. Come to give whatever assistance she may. Do not forget that within the Black Temple there is still a host of scaly terrors to be dealt with, but I think we might allow the valour of our friends to contend with them.'

Woodget caught his breath. 'But who be aboard her?' he murmured.

'All those in the city who were not slain. Many of the drugged guards were not found or murdered, and there were others. Sobhan Giri, whose name shall always be remembered for saving the children of Hara, stands upon the prow behind the figurehead and even now is sighting us. But the commander of that most blessed ship is a rat named Jophet – a rare and most trustworthy exception to his kind.'

'Jophet!' the fieldmouse declared. 'Why he was on the *Calliope* and tried to put me off mixing with old Mulligan – nearly succeeded too, he did.'

Simoon splashed to his feet. 'Indeed,' he admitted, 'and that was at my behest, for I knew what fate awaited the Irish nomad. The fragments had to go to the Scale; I did not wish for you to become embroiled in the grim business. Yet it is good my wishes were not hearkened to, for if it were not for your stout hearts, I quiver to think what would have ensued.'

'Then Hara will be rebuilt,' Woodget sighed. 'I'm glad.'

'Maybe,' the jerboa said softly, 'but never to its former glory. The magic of the mountain has departed and they shall have to rely on the skill of their bows and blades to keep the lesser dangers at bay.'

'Well I couldn't go back there,' Thomas said, 'there's too many ghosts for me.'

'A pity,' muttered Simoon. 'For some phantoms ought to be confronted.'

Then Woodget smiled up at Thomas and in a small, meek voice asked, 'Is it over, Tom? Is all the horridness ended?'

'Yes, Woodj,' Thomas replied, 'it's over.'

Beside them, Simoon the prophet knitted his bristling, brambly brows but said nothing and together they awaited the silver ship of Hara.

Journey's End

When four days had passed and the celebrations were finally over, the white and silver ship returned to India, but Thomas, Woodget and Simoon did not go with her.

After his many labours, the jerboa was weary and had decided that the time had come for him to retire and fade into the shadows. His part in the theatre of the world had concluded; his role had been to contest the Dark Despoiler and now, without the threat of his infernal return, Simoon began to feel the weight of his many years pressing upon him.

Retrieving such items that Madame Akkikuyu had not stolen from his pack, he hoisted it upon his back one more time and bowed low so that his sprouting beard touched the ground.

It was a bright, sunny morning in Singapore and by

the docks they said their goodbyes.

'Farewell, my friends,' the prophet said solemnly. 'In the great battle against Scarophion you have proved your worth. Yet there are other wars to fight, other enemies to slay, perhaps one day we shall meet again – if fortune smiles upon me.'

'Where will you go?' Thomas asked.

Simoon's dark eyes glittered and he shrugged. 'Where the forgotten track leads me,' he said. 'But now I feel as though I could sleep for an age or more. The wheel has turned and I do not belong in this world. Perhaps when it turns again I shall awaken.'

'Goodbye, Simoon,' the fieldmouse snivelled, wiping his nose on the back of his paw. 'I'll miss 'ee.'

The jerboa placed his mittened fingers upon Woodget's russet-coloured head and smiled sadly before pulling the fringed hood over his brow and turning away.

Thomas and Woodget watched his small figure go shambling through the dockyard until he disappeared.

'Just you an' me again then, Tom,' Woodget said. 'When's that ship due that'll take us straight home?'

Idly, Thomas kicked a pebble. 'It'll be here soon enough.'

'Fancy a walk till then, Master Triton?'

'Alright, Matey, but only if you'll stop calling me that ridiculous name.'

Woodget chuckled and, chatting amiably, they wandered along the dockside and down towards the river bank where the Lotus Parlour stood empty beneath the rickety wooden pier.

With his paws behind his back, Thomas stepped out

on to the old boards and listened to his friend talk about the things he would do when they returned home.

'First off,' the fieldmouse said with a wag of his head, 'I'll tell that Bess Sandibrook exactly what I thinks of her – so that'll be settled. Lor, won't she gape when I tells her of the times we've had. Does you think she'll believe me, Tom? I knows our Cudweed won't.'

'I'll back you up,' Thomas laughed.

'They were a right scurvy lot them scaleys, weren't they? Dunno if I can make 'em sound wicked enough.'

Thomas sighed. They had walked far along the pier and the high tide was sloshing below the boards. 'Mind you,' he said, sitting down and dangling his legs over the edge, 'in this, no sides were blameless.'

Woodget plopped down beside him, but unlike Thomas his feet could not reach the cooling water. 'How'd you mean, Tom?' he asked.

'Well look,' Thomas began, 'that Green Council were willing to sacrifice anything, weren't they? And they did too! Mulligan, the entire city of Hara – not forgetting the other shrines – just so the Scale could get their claws on all nine pieces.'

Woodget considered this then tilted his head to one side and looked at the wobbly light patterns upon the sparkling water. 'But they couldn't just give them to the enemy now could they?' he murmured. 'They'd have been right suspicious.'

'I suppose,' Thomas grunted. 'But it makes me wonder all the same.'

For nearly half an hour the two friends sat there in the delicious sunlight and when they decided it was time to leave, Thomas glanced back along the pier and saw that a large, shabby shape was hobbling towards them.

Thomas thought that it was one of the many beggarly folk that drifted around the shanty town, for it held in its paw a wooden bowl containing a few jingling coins. Yet that was all he could guess for the figure was wreathed and wrapped in countless dirty rags and the face was hidden in the swathes of the binding.

'I bain't got no moneys,' Woodget lamented. 'Poor dear, she looks all in.'

Thomas squinted at the stranger in surprise. Woodget was right, the figure was female – but it was a very lame and a very fat one.

Closer to them the beggar creature came, tirelessly shaking the bowl in supplication.

'Spare a coin, sir,' she said. 'Spare a coin.'

'I'm sorry,' Thomas answered, 'we don't have none.'

'Hang on, Tom,' Woodget piped up. 'She's welcome to the bit o' bread an' cheese we was saving fer our lunch. Us can allus find work on the ship to earn some more.'

And so the fieldmouse began to unfasten his bag and rummage around inside it.

Very softly, a faint uncanny melody drifted upon the air as the shabby-looking creature began to whistle through her teeth a haunting tune that Woodget thought he had heard somewhere before.

'Here y'are,' he cried, lifting the bread and cheese from the bag. There's a couple o' nice biscui—'

Woodget's voice faded, for the beggar was not looking at him, her concentration was bent upon Thomas, and to his consternation, the fieldmouse saw that his friend seemed suddenly pale and drawn.

A blankness had settled across his face and his eyes were glazed and vacant.

''Ere, Tom,' the fieldmouse began. 'You look plain awful. What's the matter?'

Thomas made no reply and continued to stare fixedly ahead.

Woodget touched his friend's forehead and passed his paw over his eyes but still he did not respond.

'I don't like this,' he muttered, turning to the beggar. 'Could you give me a lift with him? He's a lot bigger 'n me an' I reckon he needs to—'

Again his voice trailed into nothingness for at last he recognised the eerie whistling and beneath the swaddling rags he caught a glimpse of the creature's feet.

One was the fleshy claw of a rat, but the other was a splayed deformity covered in warts and scales.

Standing before him was Ma Skillet, she who had escaped from the Black Temple with her frazzling hide, but in her panic she had not managed to save all of it from Simoon's rapacious flames – so forever she was condemned to remain half rat, half creature of the Scale.

'What does you want?' Woodget demanded fiercely as he reached inside the bag again for a small knife that Jophet had given to him. 'There bain't nowt fer the likes of 'ee here no more.'

Ma Skillet said nothing, but stooped over Thomas and, removing the wrapping from her disfigured countenance, blew upon him lightly.

'Stop it!' Woodget cried.

But Mother Lotus waved her claw before her and

mechanically, Thomas turned to face the fieldmouse.

'Listen, Tom!' Woodget shouted. ''Tis me – remember?'

But Thomas did not know him; under the spell of the abhorrent creature he was powerless and when she instructed him to push the fieldmouse into the water he was compelled to obey.

Into the river Woodget splashed and he thrashed his arms feverishly.

'TOM!' he yelled plaintively. 'TOM!'

The automaton that was Thomas heard nothing, only the silken tones of Ma Skillet who told him to keep the struggling fieldmouse from clinging to the pier's struts.

'No!' Woodget cried, his mouth filling with river water. 'TOM – HELP ME! PLEASE! YOU KNOWS I CAN'T SWIM!'

Ma Skillet cackled to herself and watched with satisfaction as the little fieldmouse's head bobbed under the surface, emerging a second later, spluttering and retching until at last he sank below the water and did not return.

Rubbing her claws, Mother Lotus looked at Thomas and imagined the torture he would feel when her arts wore off and, with this malignant thought smouldering in her spiteful mind, she lumbered away and vanished out of memory.

The morning passed and still Thomas sat as still as stone. Then, when the day was over and the evening grew chill, he stirred from the enchantment and stared stupidly about him.

'Woodj?' he called. 'Woodj – where—'

Then he remembered, and in stilted flashes he knew all that he had done.

Frantically he stared over the edge of the pier and saw that upon one of the splintered struts the fieldmouse's blue woollen hat had snagged and there above the low tide it hung.

Snatching it to himself, Thomas leapt into the river and dived for his friend's drowned body. But the tides had taken it and after many hours of relentless searching, the mouse clambered back on to the pier and in a thin, dreadful voice that was filled with anguish and unquenchable remorse – he screamed.

Sadhu

Gwen Triton crept back into the snug candlelit room on board the Cutty Sark and, with a sorry shake of the head, looked around at the mess that was scattered about her husband's sleeping form.

Thomas was slumped over the small desk and, biting her lip, she glanced over his shoulder. But the pages were devoid of any writing as she had suspected they might be and, despairing of the wreck he had made, she sat down upon the bunk and sobbed silently.

Yet far away, in the once great and fabled city of Hara, a mongoose was scaling the thousand steps that ascended the mountain and at her side, clinging to her paw, her young, toddling grandson was treading very carefully with a most solemn and sober expression upon his face.

At last he was climbing the great mountain where the two great eyes were carved above the expanse of shattered rock; it was his first visit to the Holy One and he was extremely excited at the prospect.

'Remember this day, Little Chattan,' his grandmother told him, 'for the sadhu is most holy and devout. You must not ask him any questions.'

'Why, Nanna Sobhan?' the youngster queried. 'Will he punish me?'

His grandmother chortled. 'Of course not,' she said tenderly, 'but his mind is too full of other matters to dwell on the talk of small boys.'

Up they climbed until at last they stood upon a rocky ledge where a small, ash-dusted figure sat hunched upon the bare stone and his eyes were staring into the vast, unseen distance.

Sobhan led Little Chattan around the ledge until they stood before the crouched shape and she bowed respectfully. Looking up at his grandmother, the boy did the same but his eyes could not tear themselves from the Holy One.

'Sadhu?' Sobhan said gently.

The figure breathed deeply then shifted slowly as if rousing from a deep slumber.

'Sobhan!' he declared. 'Forgive me, I was far away. Now let me see – who is this young warrior you have brought before me?'

Little Chattan gurgled with amusement but blushed and looked shyly at his feet.

'It is my grandson, Sadhu,' she announced proudly. 'Little Chattan – one day we hope he will be as brave as his great uncle.'

As she said this, Sobhan watched the Holy One's face, but not a flicker of remembrance showed there.

'I pray for that also,' the sadhu said. 'The tales

of your brother rank amongst the most noble of our histories.'

Sobhan hung her head, then bit her lip as the aching wish to tell him swelled inside her again.

'Sadhu!' she blurted.

'Peace, little daughter,' the Holy One hushed her. 'I know what is written in your mind, it is in mine also. Yet let that part of my life remain unknown to me. Where else would I be but here with you, my people?'

'But there are things you ought to know,' she said desperately.

The Holy One shook his head. 'No, let them sleep. We must obey the will of the Green; he does not wish me to recall such events, so I am content.'

'Do you never have even a hint of a memory?' she murmured. 'Is there nothing you can recall?'

'The songs of Zenna are too strong for that,' he answered mildly. 'When she brought me to this place she had sustained me for many, many days and for that I cannot condemn her.'

'Yet I wish I could speak to you of—'

'You have a fine grandson, Sobhan,' the Holy One said briskly. 'It pleases me to see him. Now, permit me to return to my meditation.'

Sobhan nodded and leading Little Chattan away, began to descend the great stairway.

Holding on to his grandmother's paw, Little Chattan looked back at the curious figure of the sadhu.

'Can we visit him again, Nanna Sobhan?' he asked.

'Yes, Little Chattan, we may.'

The boy smiled, he liked the Holy One and thought he looked very wise and serious – even if he was a fieldmouse.

THE DEPTFORD HISTORIES

Book One: The Alchymist's Cat

Robin Jarvis

It is the winter of 1664 and young Will Godwin, an alchymist's assistant, chances upon a mother cat and her three new-born kittens in a London churchyard.

Taking pity on the freezing family, Will carries them back to his master's apothecary shop. And there, among the bubbling bottles and evil-smelling jars in Dr Spittle's laboratory, unfolds an extraordinary tale of sorcery, villainy and murder . . .

THE DEPTFORD HISTORIES

Book Two: The Oaken Throne

Robin Jarvis

It is a time of magic and a time of darkness. The Starwife, leader of the black squirrels, lies dying, betrayed and poisoned. But as the bat army launches a devastating attack on her realm, she staggers to a window and summons aid . . .

These terrible events are to draw Vesper, the young bat, and Ysabelle, the squirrel maiden, into taking a fearsome journey – in a desperate attempt to save their lands from destruction.

THE DEPTFORD MICE

Book One: The Dark Portal

Runner-up for the Smarties Book Prize

Robin Jarvis

In the sewers of Deptford there lurks a dark presence which fills the tunnels with fear: Jupiter, Lord of All, an evil being who aims to take over the world. Worshipped by the fearsome rats, Jupiter's dreams could well come true.

Until into this twilight realm wanders a small and frightened mouse. Far from family and friends he hurtles the Deptford Mice into a doom-laden world of terror and sorcery.

Can the mice ever survive against such evil? Or have they lost the comfortable world they once knew forever . . .

THE DEPTFORD MICE

Book Two: The Crystal Prison

Robin Jarvis

An innocent young mouse lies murdered in a moonlit field, as the screech of an owl echoes across the ripening corn.

Newly arrived in the countryside from the horrors of Jupiter's lair, the Deptford Mice find themselves once again facing terrifying evil, embroiled in a series of horrible murders.

At first the simple country mice suspect Audrey, one of the Deptford newcomers – but the truth turns out to be far more sinister.

THE DEPTFORD MICE

Book Three: The Final Reckoning

Robin Jarvis

The ghostly spirit of Jupiter has returned, more terrifying than ever before. Bent on revenge, he smothers the world in an eternal winter of snow and ice.

Huddled around their fires, the Deptford Mice are worried: the mystical bats have fled from the attic, and underground a new rat army is gathering strength. With food short, and no sign of spring, the mice know that a desperate struggle confronts them.

Who knows how many will survive . . . and at what cost?